CITY IN
THE DRAGON'S
EYE

ALSO BY JORDAN LOYAL SHORT

CITY IN THE DRAGON'S EYE

DRAGON REICH BOOK ONE

JORDAN LOYAL SHORT

Book Cover by Trif Book Design

Formatting by Luke Tarzian

Edited by Sarah Chorn, Chris Chinchilla, and Nathan Hall

CONTENTS

This book includes:

Smoking, Naughty Language, Recreational Potion Use, Bigotry, Dick Jokes, and Violence.

To my parents…for having sex when it mattered most.

The Continent

Nordheim

Eisdorf

Alfglenn

Grunwald

Cairn Dungregor

Dungregor

Eucharein

Reinwald

Czenuzel

Kumavia

Grunburg

Jarlsbeck

Kandelberg Pass

Saint Jene

Hintreux

Strownka

Spanza

Tesselona

Weissmar

Esselsdorf

Heidelbronn

Wittsburg Castle

Ostaria

Truffel-Lomaire

Iscrana

Jsilano

Rhodenz

Lorentio

Allerain

Lesalle

Dannbridge

Westonshire

Viktor's tumor was born on the day the armistice was signed.

Winter had come, and with it, news that would shake the continent from Jarlsbeck to the Red Coast. The war was over. After three years of bloodshed, boredom, and bad food it was really done.

Viktor was going home.

Maybe he should have stayed vigilant. Maybe he shouldn't have been daydreaming. But Viktor had half a mind to march off now, to leave behind the frozen latrines and lumpy bedrolls. To hell with the army. The second he got back Viktor was going to wolf down a plate of his mama's schnitzel. And he'd finally kiss Karla again. A big wet one. Not to mention drown himself in Herr Fischer's home-made rye beer.

Home! His cheeks hurt from smiling. Maybe Viscount von Holt would chew him out for ditching the rest of the patrol, but with news like this, even the viscount couldn't stop him from telling Schmidt.

Peace.

Viktor could hardly believe it.

He trotted into camp sporting a gap-toothed grin and a woolen great coat over his chainmail. The mountain air was bracing, but the sun was out, the day still full of promise.

Schmidt stood guard duty by the firepit. He frowned at Viktor's approach, his droopy mustache exaggerating the scowl, but Viktor didn't let it bother him. Not on a day like this.

Schmidt was always frowning. It was nothing new. Viktor liked to joke that Schmidt had once seen his own mother naked and his face had just gotten stuck like that. Everyone had a good laugh at that one. Except Schmidt, naturally.

Their camp perched atop a hill overlooking the snowy forest south of Kandelberg Pass. Empty tents dotted the summit, their owners out on patrol. Viktor unshouldered his blunderbuss and leaned the stubby weapon against a fallen log.

"You're match cord has gone out," said Schmidt.

"Oops, sorry." Viktor fumbled with the tinder box tucked in his belt. He picked up his firearm by its trumpet-shaped barrel. Honestly, Viktor hated the damned thing. Everyone acted like guns were so great, like their invention was going to turn the tide of the war.

But it was obviously too late for that.

He wished the dwarves had never invented the awful things. His blunderbuss was loud and clumsy and he'd burned his fingers on it at least a dozen times. Worse, he had a recurring nightmare about the one occasion he'd managed to kill a Rumavian soldier with the contraption. It featured a bear riding a unicycle and a naked dwarf scolding him for not washing his hands. Viktor didn't like to talk about it.

Those dwarves, he wondered sometimes whether all of their marvelous inventions were a good thing. He'd even heard that they had built a flying machine. What would they think of next? Viktor shook his head.

He set his hand on Schmidt's shoulder. "Maybe you should sit down for this."

But instead of listening to the momentous news, Schmidt held up his hand. "Hold on." He craned his neck to look past Viktor out into the surrounding wilderness. His ever-present scowl deepened.

"Pay attention, Schmidt! You won't believe this."

"I thought I saw something out there."

Viktor bounced on the balls of his feet, feeling like he could jump ten feet in the air. The short sword strapped to his hip flapped against his leg. "They've signed an armistice!"

"Bullshit." He finally had Schmidt's full attention.

"It's true. We intercepted a courier. A kid with pimples wearing a stupid-looking hat. The war is over."

"So…we've lost." Schmidt blinked away tears. He sat abruptly, as if he might lose his balance.

"Don't look at it like that, yah?" It's not like it was a shock or anything. Everyone knew they were losing. "Schmidt, we're going home."

"If the damned *runts* hadn't pulled out we could have won this thing."

Viktor swatted Schmidt on the back of the head. "So what if the dwarves went back to Cairn Dunngregor? Don't *you* want to go home, too? No more freezing our wieners off out here in the middle of nowhere fighting Rumavian conscripts and smelly-ass Death Knights. This is great news."

"So help me, Viktor, if this is another of your pranks."

Viktor held up his hand like he was swearing an oath. "I promise, Schmidt, it's true."

Before Viktor could react, Schmidt threw his arms around Viktor's waist and hoisted him off his feet with a grunt.

"Home." Schmidt released him, beaming as he rubbed the pulled muscle in his back. "When?"

Viktor shrugged. "No orders yet. Can't be too long if the war is over, though."

"This calls for celebration. I am going to brew some tea!"

"Forget the tea, Schmidt. I know where the viscount keeps his stash." Viktor did an about-face and marched toward the viscount's tent.

"Where are you going?"

Viktor rolled his eyes as he ducked under the canvas flap. "Relax, Schmidt."

"Viktor, don't you dare."

Viktor was always surprised at how nice the viscount's tent was, even out here in the middle of nowhere. There were bearskin rugs strewn across the floor, and a proper bed. The viscount even had a table with a stack of maps draped over it. Viktor detoured to inspect them, harboring a secret hope that they led to buried treasure. But they were only maps of Kandelberg Pass and the surrounding landscape. "Schmidt, you worry too much," Viktor hollered over his shoulder, dropping to his knees to drag the bottle of brandy out from beneath the bed. "I've got a good jump on them. They won't be here for at least ten minutes. I'm sure the viscount will share when the others get back to camp. We're just getting a little head start."

Viktor emerged from the tent with an elaborate bottle wrapped in silver foil. He popped the cork, threw Schmidt a bob of his eyebrows, and took a swig. Viktor tried to hand the bottle to his friend.

Schmidt stared past him out into the woods.

Viktor turned to look but there was nothing there. "Did you see something?" When Schmidt didn't respond Viktor shoved the bottle into his hand. "He's not going to court-martial you. The war is over."

Schmidt shook his head, almost like he was shaking off an idea he didn't like. He swilled a mouthful, and coughed, handing it back. "Did you ever think you would make it home?" Schmidt asked.

Viktor paused with the bottle almost to his lips. "If you asked my father, I was dead as soon as I touched the Well. But I don't know, I always kind of figured I'd be okay."

Schmidt rubbed his temples as if he were soothing a headache. "Magic. The minute I touched the Well my nerves were shot."

"My grandfather was a tumorling." Viktor slugged the viscount's brandy. "Scales growing like a rash, mad as a broken cuckoo clock, the whole bit. So I always knew there was a chance I could tap the Dragon Well." Viktor handed the drink to his friend and stared down at his boots. "The cancer killed him, eventually. When magic goes wrong, it goes really wrong. I guess we're lucky. We made it through a whole war with none of that shit."

Schmidt wiped the mouth the bottle with the hem of his tunic. Viktor ignored the gesture as Schmidt took a sip and passed the booze back. "I'm sorry." Schmidt was talking about Viktor's grandfather, of course.

"Yah," said Viktor. He concentrated for a moment until he sensed the bright pinpoint in his chest that was his connection to the Dragon Well. Calming himself, he sucked in the Breath, drawing a waft of power through. It was the very first manifestation they had taught him in boot camp. *The Breath of Azzax.* A sharp intake of air that brought with it a faint ember of the Dragon Well's power. Emboldened by the liquor in his belly, he exhaled a little puff of magic into his hands for warmth, tasting a hint of campfire on his own breath.

Schmidt scowled but let it slide with only the slightest shake of his head. Viktor knew it was a bit perverse of him to take a risk like that while he was talking about his tumorling grandfather, but hell, he was cold, and sometimes thinking about it all made him reckless. Sergeant Hoffmann, though, had been very clear about the rules during his training.

In. Never out.

The Breath was about drawing power from the Well, but every recruit could feel the burning temptation to unleash it. Viktor had taught himself this little trick to keep his fingers from freezing while on sentry duty. "Everyone was so proud when I Channeled the first time. Even my father. But tumorlings are another story. No one wants to end up like that."

Schmidt shook his head. "Well, I certainly won't. If the war is over, I'm going home. All this fighting and magic is too much for me. Weaving is a good profession. Good money. My uncle says there's always a job for me. That's enough. And..." Schmidt looked a little abashed and changed the subject. "What will you do when we get home?"

Viktor slapped his thigh. He didn't have to think too hard to rattle off what he wanted. "I'm going to eat ten pounds of Mama's apple strudel. I'll get my job back at the Fischers' restaurant. I'll go dancing. It'll be like the war never happened." Viktor stared off into the trees for a moment. "But what were you going to say, Schmidt? Come on. There's something else you are looking forward to."

Schmidt scratched at his beard, hiding a grin. "My cousin, Drucilla. She's a real stitch. I'm always laughing around her."

"Your cousin? That's a bit weird."

Schmidt scowled. "Well, she's my second cousin."

"Still weird."

"What about you?"

Viktor shrugged. "Karla and I used to write each other every week, but something happened. Her letters haven't been getting through."

"Everyone else's have." Schmidt had the audacity to drop his scowl, offering a sad smile in its place.

Was it really that bad?

"Don't be so gloomy." Viktor ground his teeth. He slugged at the bottle again. "I'm sure there's a perfectly reasonable—"

From the corner of his eye, Viktor spotted movement in the trees. Schmidt turned to look.

Perched on the gnarled branches of a naked willow, two vultures surveyed the wilderness around them.

Schmidt's hand went instinctively to his sword. Viktor sniffed the air, eyes closed to focus on the smell. Amongst the earthy tang of soil and horse dung, almost hidden by the cold, he caught the faintest whiff of rot on the northerly breeze.

"Death Knights," whispered Schmidt. "This close to camp?"

Viktor ignored Schmidt, eyes darting, ears straining for the enemy's location.

A woodpecker tapped somewhere in the forest. Voices carried on the wind. At first Viktor thought it might be the Death Knights, but then he recognized Heinrich Grossman's shrill laugh. It was the viscount and the rest of their troop returning to camp, having a gay time, blissfully unaware that the war could still be lurking nearby. For a few heartbeats, Viktor and Schmidt froze.

Too often had Viktor witnessed the cold butchery of the Death Knights. His dread rooted him to the snowy earth, and he stood there dumbfounded as fate circled his comrades like carrion birds.

Viktor pictured his brothers-in-arms locked in desperate battle. He imagined their faces: the viscount's haughty smirk, Gunter's devil-may-care grin, even Grossman's pouty lip trembling in fear. He couldn't abandon them. He couldn't stand here doing nothing. He couldn't let these Rumavians win.

"Not today." Viktor hiccupped. "You rotten bastards." He scrambled over to snatch up his blunderbuss. Charging out of camp, he shouted, his boots churning the muddy ground. "Ambush! Death Knights!"

The sharp report of a blunderbuss drew his attention to the woods north of the camp. A hundred paces or so down the hillside, the timber grew thick enough to hide the action. There was nothing to it but to run, to follow the shouts and the gunshots until he found the fighting. Viktor pelted over the naked snow, plunging into the forest, wishing as he always did that he'd taken a piss before the battle. He fumbled with a paper cartridge from his kit. Biting the end off, he poured the shot and powder into the flared barrel of his gun, cursing as he spilled some of the black grains onto his hand.

A scream echoed through the forest. Ahead, a fiery flash lit the gloomy wood and a loud bang shook snow loose from the trees overhead. Two figures wrestled on the ground, rolling in a desperate struggle.

A Death Knight, green light spilling from its iron helm, straddled a man who thrashed beneath him. It was Gunter, pinned to the frosty earth, his cocky grin nowhere to be seen. In its place, a snarl that reminded Viktor of the Heidelmann's vicious dog, Fluffy. The Rumavian wore black chainmail trimmed in wolf fur and a forest-green tabard emblazoned with the skull and sickle.

The awful stench of death and gunpowder hit Viktor's nose. He cocked his matchlock and fired. A cloud of smoke billowed forth, but instead of the harsh crack of a proper shot, the firearm emitted an embarrassing toot. In his haste Viktor had forgotten to pack the load and the ball came out with no more force than if Viktor had hurled it at the Death Knight.

Viktor cocked back and swung the weapon, connecting with the Death Knight's helm. The stock splintered and the helmet tumbled from the Rumavian's head, revealing the withered, deathly pale face within. Behind him, Schmidt stopped to prime his weapon but there was no time. Viktor dropped his broken blunderbuss in the snow and drew his sword, swinging at the horrid creature. The blow severed the Death Knight's arm, and the bastard turned to watch it sail through the air with frightening indifference. Still, the distraction was enough for the pinned soldier to buck the knight off him and roll clear.

Viktor seized the moment. With the Breath of Azzax, he drew a wisp of power from the Dragon Well to bolster his backswing, his muscles tensing with the strength of dragon flesh. He grunted, the jolt of magic searing through his arm as he beheaded the Death Knight. The creature's shriveled head toppled to the muddy ground, the green light within sputtering out.

The man who'd been grappling with the Death Knight pushed himself to his knees, his face covered in bloody pine needles.

"Gunter, are you okay?" Viktor reached down and helped his comrade to his feet.

"But…the war is over," Gunter pleaded.

"Tell *them* that," said Viktor, already dashing into the clearing at the heart of the battle.

A half-dozen Death Knights and a score of Rumavian foot soldiers battled what was left of Viktor's contingent. Ten of his comrades fought side by side, wearing their brown woolen great coats emblazoned with the dragon of Reinveldt. They wielded shortswords, those few who had been issued blunderbusses already having discharged them and cast them aside for weapons more suited to the brawl.

Just behind the action, the Zoller brothers lay on their backs in the snow, thrashing in pain. It looked like some twisted game of snow angels. *Saints,* Viktor told himself, *what an awful thought.*

Another gunshot startled Viktor. He *really* had to pee.

Schmidt and Gunter bumped into him from behind, taking in the carnage.

Gunter stepped forward and leveled his blunderbuss at the scrum. "Let's crack some skulls, boys."

It sounded absurd. Forced, certainly, even a little shrill. But just then Viktor was grateful for the bravado. Gunter and Schmidt fired their weapons, downing a pair of Rumavian peasants. Unlike the heavily armored Death Knights, the serfs wore shaggy furs, and carried a hodgepodge of weapons, from scythes to axes to home-made spears. Viktor's compatriots drew their swords and, screaming mismatched war cries, followed him into the enemy's flank. The first hack of Viktor's sword cleaved a Rumavian boy nearly in two. He felt the viscount's brandy creep up his throat as he put his foot on the enemy's chest to wrench his blade free.

A Death Knight clad in black iron turned to inspect the new arrivals. Viktor glimpsed the wasted face within the helm, its hideous eyes aglow. The ugly bastard tipped its head back and shrieked, its inhuman voice twisting Viktor's guts like one too many of Grandma Gerda's cheese curds.

Gunter lunged past Viktor, stabbing forward with his blade, trying to catch the Death Knight with its guard down. His sword slid through a gap in the armpit of the knight's armor and bit deep into its flesh. The Death Knight's eyes flared a sickly green and the rotting stench of the Void Well's magic filled the air. The Death Knight clutched the back of Gunter's head and skewered him with his saber.

"Really?" Gunter sounded more annoyed than anything. For just a tick, Viktor thought maybe the chest wound wasn't as bad as it looked.

Gunter had always been the first to laugh at war's hardships, the first to volunteer for dangerous missions. He was handsome and funny and much smarter than Viktor. And this thing, it had just gutted him and tossed his body aside like an apple core.

One second Gunter was all of those things and the next he was gone.

Could Viktor be snuffed so easily? The thought spurred a sudden itch to spin on his heel and run into the woods. Were it not for the viscount's brandy he might have fled, but the courage in his belly shrugged it off. He stepped forward, his blade sweeping down in an overhead strike which the Death Knight parried. The creature circled him, its toothy grin showing through the split in its helmet.

An all-too-human scream filled the clearing as another of

Viktor's comrades died. From the corner of his eye, he saw Conrad Dunn turn his back on the fight and run for it. Viktor wrestled the urge to follow, the urge to pee as well. Somehow, he had never really expected to die. War was funny like that. Just a bullshit bore until the axe fell.

"Steady, men!" The viscount's words might have been brave, but his voice cracked. His great coat was torn, one lapel dangling like a blood-soaked rabbit's ear.

The Death Knight standing before Viktor swung his saber and Viktor bobbed out of the way. Over the knight's shoulder, more figures approached from the ravine. His hope swelled as Viktor imagined reinforcements coming to their rescue. But then he picked out the green dots of the Death Knight's eyes.

So much for Mama's cooking.

With desperation bordering on panic, Viktor opened himself to the Dragon Well, drawing in the Breath of Azzax. It burned in his chest, seething to escape, its strength searing through his flesh. Viktor swung his sword with the Might of Dryxa, with every drop of his own fear. The Death Knight easily blocked, but the Might cracked the Rumavian's sword in half and Viktor's blade bit through the Death Knight's helm down to its chin, snuffing the foul light in its eyes.

Viktor roared. But even as the power coursed through him, an arrow sailed over his shoulder and Schmidt cried out. Viktor turned to see him stagger, the arrow jutting out the back of his neck. Viktor's moment of triumph withered as he saw the shock in Schmidt's eyes, saw the blood spurt from his wound, saw his friend fall.

"Retreat!" cried the viscount, the normally sophisticated officer looking panicked and disheveled in his blood-drenched coat.

The second Rumavian contingent emerged from the ravine, poised to envelop his already beleaguered comrades. Viktor really was about to die. For a heartbeat, he imagined how Gunter had felt as the sword punched through his chest.

When the last of the Rumavians climbed out of the gully, Viktor spied the scrawny courier they had let go—the one with pimples and a stupid fucking four-cornered hat.

The war was over. This was all for nothing. The viscount had wanted to take the courier prisoner and Viktor had...oh Saints...he had talked him out of it. He was just a boy after all. "Let him go home to his mother," Viktor had said. They had let this little bastard go and this was their thanks?

A puff of smoke escaped Viktor's lips.

The last of the Rumavian reinforcements pressed up behind their line, all clustered together in fighting formation. Viktor sucked in a lungful of air that tasted of woodsmoke and sulfur. The Breath of Azzax crackled in his lungs.

In. Never out.

Viktor spewed fire on the enemy. The Breath scalded his lungs and singed his nose hairs, its bright flames hosing the Rumavians, igniting the contingent like it had been doused in oil. The magic felt like lava in his veins, a river of power rushing from the pinpoint in his chest that bound him to the Dragon Well. It was incredible. He felt ten feet tall. Like he was more than a man. More than everyone around him. He felt like he could knock over the forest with a sweep of his arm, melt all the snow from here to Rumavia with the fire in his lungs. He felt that place inside him where the magic seeped from the Well, and for an instant the pinpoint swelled, spasmed, and dragonfire shot through his veins. The power roiled inside him, a chaotic swirl that coalesced in a twitching knot beneath the skin on his left arm. A lump.

Dizzy, he fell, a drunken smile on his face as the burning figures danced before his eyes.

The viscount shouted orders. Steel rang out against steel and fire drank of flesh. Viktor passed out for a moment, awakened by a gunshot. His arm itched like hell. He scratched at it as the last of his flames dwindled and the viscount commanded the men to dispatch the lingering Rumavian soldiers.

Figures loomed over Viktor, their hands checking him for wounds. Viktor flickered in and out of consciousness.

Someone grabbed his arm and rolled him onto his back.

"Holy Saints!" Startled, the viscount scurried back a step. "What is that?"

"Did you touch it?" someone else asked.

"That's not how it works." The viscount fell silent, regaining his composure. "Bandage that up." He sounded like he was going to cry.

Viktor wasn't sure what all the fuss was over. They had won. Somehow, they were still alive. Why did they still sound so worried?

"I think I peed," said Viktor.

Someone took hold of his wrist, tending to the wound on his forearm. In that moment, before unconsciousness claimed him, before the bandage covered it, Viktor glimpsed the dragon scale, the tumor born on the first day of peace.

D oktor Oberman lifted the tent's canvas flap and ducked inside the field hospital. The air smelled of soap and sawdust and the faintest waft of gangrenous wounds. A fitting metaphor of Reinveldt's shame. The war had ground these boys into dust, and try as one might to tidy up the horrific human mess, the stench of their pain still lingered in the air.

To Oberman's left, a young man coughed incessantly, spitting into a bed pan. The doctor scoped about with clinical detachment, seeing the wasted youth of Reinveldt as he must, as the kindling of a great fire about to catch its spark. Four beds lined opposite sides of the enclosure with a central station stocked with jars of antiseptic, gut sutures, trays of forceps, scalpels and such.

It was too cold in here; though the patients were draped in woolen blankets, he could see the steam from their breaths. All but one, an officer with his leg in traction. Oberman glanced at his companion, and a knowing look passed between them, but there was no time to spare for the dead.

His assistant carried a clipboard, and glancing down at it he tapped his finger on a bed number. "This one, Herr Doktor. In the corner."

Doktor Oberman approached a cot in the back of the tent. It had been a harrowing trip all the way from Wittsburg. His legs ached, unaccustomed as he was to such overland journeys via horse-back. But with the war over, with the nation so in shambles, his compatriots had thrown themselves into action. If they were to save their beloved Reinveldt, time was of the essence. Only the cold incisions of a proper surgeon could excise the infection that had so ravaged the fatherland.

"Shall I watch the door?" his assistant asked.

"I won't be long."

The soldier he had come to visit was one Viktor Spiegel. An enlisted man, but a channeler of the Dragon Well, one whose tale had risen to his attention. Even lying helpless on the cot, Oberman could tell he was quite a specimen. Good Reinish stock: tall with sandy blond hair, a strapping young man, though a bit bruised and scabbed in his present condition.

Doktor Oberman took the patient by the wrist, but opted to leave his leather gloves on rather than take the boy's pulse. None of the other patients seemed to have paid his arrival any mind, but experience had taught him caution, and patience. Better to simply leave his gloves on than risk discovery. When the young man did not stir, Oberman deduced that he was sedated. It was probably for the best, as Herr Spiegel was likely to have a host of questions, questions Oberman could not, or would not answer. The doctor crouched at his bedside. Gently unwrapping the bandage on the patient's forearm, he inspected the tumor, a single bright red dragon scale about the size of a five-mark coin.

Most would look upon this mutation with mingled shame and horror, but Doktor Obermann found himself smiling. "You've done well, Herr Klein."

His assistant blushed. "Thank you, Doktor. Are you..." Klein glanced around at the other patients to be certain no one was eavesdropping and lowered his voice. "Are you going to invite him?"

Doktor Oberman stared down at the wounded soldier. The cancer made him perfect for the doctor's experiments, but more than that, he was a perfect specimen in another sense. Given the right direction, he could become one of them.

At last, Doktor Oberman shook his head. "No, Herr Klein, not yet. Let him first see what the world thinks of a tumorling."

3

The wagon rolled into Grunburg just as the sun was setting. To Viktor, his hometown had never been so beautiful. Rose tinted clouds hung like gauze above the thatched roofs and latticed windows. Dotted by elm and birch trees and crisscrossed by cobblestone streets, the village looked just as he had left it three years ago, save a few snowdrifts piled in the leas of its cottages.

The men in the wagon had been told to expect a celebration when they returned home, but there were no garlands strung across their path, no revelers gathering in the streets.

That suited Viktor just fine. More than anything, he simply wanted to go home, eat his mama's cooking, and see his family. The other men on the benches beside him were excited for the dance, and the more Viktor thought of it, the more he supposed he looked forward to it, too. He hadn't danced with a woman in a few years. *Ha!* His last dance hadn't been with a woman at all. The memory flashed into his head, bringing with it a smile that soon faltered as he was reminded of his partner's fate. When they'd been denied leave last spring, the viscount had bought them a stupendous amount of liquor. He remembered laughing so hard, dancing around the fire with Schmidt. Not a scowl in sight. But Schmidt was in the ground now. Stupid, he thought, to miss a scowl so much.

The wagon lurched to a halt and Dieter chucked him on the shoulder. "Why so glum? We're home."

Viktor nodded. He should be excited to dance with Karla again, but to be honest, the idea twisted his stomach with dread. What would she think of him now? Had her letters really gotten lost or was there another reason she hadn't written? Viktor steered his thoughts toward the safety of his mother's kitchen and a smile sprouted on his face as he pondered what she might make for his homecoming meal. Steaks and baked potatoes dripping with butter, he decided, and apple strudel for dessert.

Dieter offered his hand to help Viktor down from the wagon as if he were some sort of invalid. Viktor swatted it away and hopped out.

"I'll see you at the dance tonight." Without waiting for a reply Viktor set off for his parents' house. On the way home, he passed Otto Zimmerman and waved, but Otto turned away, suddenly intent on inspecting the gutters across the street. It was odd, almost like Otto didn't recognize him. Viktor put his head down and hurried past, blushing.

He did his best to shake off the snub, reminding himself that there was strudel waiting. He pictured it browning in the oven, dusted with crushed almonds, and quickened his step.

His family lived in a two-story house, quaint, the viscount would have dubbed it, though perhaps not. On closer inspection the thatch looked a bit in disrepair, telltale mold smudging the eaves. Though he had left the mountain blizzards far behind, there was still a chill in the air.

His excitement wavered. For the first time he worried that perhaps he would not be welcome. But that was absurd. He climbed the stoop, took a deep breath, and knocked.

The door flew open and his little sister Helga stood gawping at him with her pale blue eyes. She had grown, not truly a girl anymore, though she did look a bit thin. Helga practically tackled him, wrapping her arms around him and peppering Viktor on the cheek with kisses. He had missed her sixteenth birthday. A thing he shouldn't feel guilty for, and yet, he did.

"Viktor!" Helga shouted in his ear. "What are you doing, knocking like a stranger? You're home."

Everyone kept telling him that.

So smile, he chided himself.

He picked Helga up off her feet and spun her around. His brother Eric tottered over, the boy's unruly mop of blond hair flouncing as he wrapped his arms around Viktor's leg. Viktor set Helga down and bent over to hug his little brother, surprised and a bit teary-eyed that Eric remembered him. Papa stood on a stepladder at the far side of the room, digging through a box of typeface with ink-stained fingers. His father managed a smile, but it vanished as his eyes fell to Viktor's arm.

The oven door slammed shut and Mama's head popped up on the far side of the cutting block.

"My baby." She shouldered past his father, almost tipping over the ladder.

Mama wrapped Viktor in her spindly arms, a tiny woman with the strength of a bear. He stooped down to hold her tight. "You're home now," she whispered in his ear, her breath like a warm blanket.

Bent over her, head buried in the yellow kerchief tied over her graying hair, Viktor inhaled the scent of her soap, her sweat. She tutted, stroking his back as his tears leaked into the kerchief.

"I know," she said. "I know."

Viktor's father cleared his throat. At the sound of this rebuke, Viktor straightened, wiping his eyes.

"Hello, Papa."

"Welcome home, son." His father glanced down again at the bandage on his arm. Viktor could only guess what was going through his mind. He barely remembered his grandfather, but his father had never had a kind word for Opa. What must he think now to see his son with the same cancer? "We've heard all about your heroics. As has the rest of the town. Quite a lot of gossip."

Viktor's mother came to his defense. "Let's not get into all of that now. Today is for celebrating."

Viktor noticed that his parents' eyes strayed to his sister, worry creeping over their faces. Helga smiled, but tears glistened in her eyes.

"What's wrong?" Viktor asked.

"It's nothing." She looked away, hands fidgeting; she clasped them behind her back. Something was clearly wrong. Dread settled in his stomach.

His father sighed. "The whole town heard about...about your tumor."

"Heinrich." His mother interposed herself between them, but Viktor and his father locked eyes over the top of her head.

"He'll find out sooner or later. It seems that having not one but *two* tumorlings in our family was too much for a pack of snobs as upstanding as the Kellers. Wolfgang has broken off his engagement with your sister."

"No." Viktor had not been ashamed of his ailment before this news. Terrified, yes. Shocked, too. But now, he could not meet the eyes of his family. He stared down at his worn boots, fighting the urge to retreat, to take out his knife and gouge the tumor from his arm, to drink. Saints, to drink himself into a blackout.

Helga looped her arms around his waist. Tiny, like his mother, she could barely reach all the way around him, but to be fair, he was a bit of an oaf.

"I'm so sorry, Helga." Viktor fought another losing war against crying in front of his father.

"Shh. To hell with Wolfgang. To be honest, I cringed at his laugh. Every time I said something funny it sounded like I'd stepped on a cat's tail. A girl can't go through life like that."

"I love you."

"Everybody loves me. That's how I know I'll find a better man."

Viktor kissed the top of her head.

"Let's eat!" exclaimed his little brother, already seated at the table.

"Yes!" Viktor's mouth watered. "I've been dreaming of your cooking for three years, Mama."

For the first time, his mother looked abashed. "I'm afraid we couldn't afford steak." The admission surprised him; they were not wealthy, but his father was a printer, which had always been a prosperous profession.

Viktor glanced at his father, who took it as an affront.

"Times are tough, Viktor. There is no money for frivolous things like books and newspapers." His father sometimes remarked that sarcasm was lost on Viktor, but even he couldn't miss the bitter twist of his father's lips. "Meat costs ten times what it did before you left. Many have it worse."

The family all nodded at the truth of this.

"I got us a big fat chicken," said Mama. "With rosemary and pepper. And I baked huge potatoes." She used her hands to show how big they were.

"That sounds fucking amazing."

"Language," his parents said in unison.

"And strudel?" Viktor asked.

His mother paled. She shook her head. "I knew that's what you'd want. But there are no apples." She looked at his father, who avoided her eyes. "I set aside a jar just for tonight. But last month…" She turned away, her shoulders trembling. "The cupboards were bare, Viktor. I could hear your brother's tummy growling."

"It's okay, Mama. I'm just glad to be home."

AFTER DINNER one of the other veterans, Dieter, came around to fetch him. They walked through the wintery streets of Grunburg in anxious silence, a light drizzle falling like mist. Dieter stopped under the eaves of Herr Schubert's house to roll a cigarette.

"I wonder what the girls will think of us," said Dieter, striking a match.

"What do you mean?"

"Nothing. Just nervous, I guess."

Viktor cupped his hands and blew into them for warmth. The gesture unsettled him. Thinking of his trick with the Breath of Azzax, he stuffed them in his pockets. "I hope Karla is there."

Dieter almost dropped his cigarette. He brushed ash from his lapel as they headed back into the street. Dieter tried to hand Viktor the cigarette but Viktor shook his head. A pair of ravens settled on the thatched roof of Herr Fischer's restaurant, where Viktor had worked before the war. The lights were off. Strange. It was supper time. "You didn't hear?" Dieter asked.

"Hear what?" A knot formed in Viktor's stomach.

"She's engaged to that guy, Karl Haas."

"Karl and Karla." Viktor covered his hurt with a laugh. In the back of his mind, he had worried that something like this had happened. But to hear it was like a punch in the stomach.

"Pretty stupid. They'll probably name their firstborn Karl Jr."

"And every time someone shouts, 'Karl, you idiot!' they'll all three turn and look." Viktor forced a smile, but it faded as they made their way to the dance. What a fool he was, to expect a girl like that to wait three years for him. Here he was mooning over her as if they were going to get married and she hadn't even bothered to write and tell him it was over. *Fool!* He fought the urge to hit himself. He didn't want to show Dieter how humiliated he felt. Viktor knew that people would be talking about it, laughing at him behind his back. And now he came home a tumorling to boot. He suddenly wanted to skip the dance altogether, but he couldn't let them see how much it hurt. Viktor couldn't help but imagine the gossip if he turned around and went home, if he retreated.

The lodge was decorated with red and gold bunting as well as flags of the now defunct Kingdom of Reinveldt. It was a defiant show of patriotism. The kingdom had officially been disbanded by the Armistice. In the cities, a coalition of their enemies kept the peace, soldiers from Rumavia, Alfglenn, and Westonshire acting as an interim government until a referendum could be held and a new government installed.

Despite the bunting, the beer hall had a dreary feel. The wall-paper peeled in places, the air filled with the faint stink of mildew. Viktor surveyed the faces gathered around the dance floor for Karla, but of course she wasn't there. She was engaged now. To someone else.

A portrait of Saint Jene the Dragon Slayer hung on one of the walls, cobwebs adorning its frame. Viktor had idolized her as a boy, until he began squabbling with his father and his father's esteem for

Saint Jene had dimmed his own. Fires smoldered in hearths on either side of the room, but it was still cold. Viktor's eyes went to the sparse crowd of women milling about the far wall. He was too early. There was no music yet and everyone was still sober. He debated leaving but Dieter passed him a flask.

"It's too quiet."

Dieter agreed.

They milled around for a few minutes, introducing themselves to the girls. And just when Viktor felt the welcome flush of Dieter's booze, he spotted her. Karla.

She wore a blue frock that matched her eyes, with bluebirds embroidered all up one side. Her smile lit the dreary room. Viktor swallowed, his heart pounding. She swept her gaze across the crowd, her eyes landing on Viktor. His breath caught, a new war erupting inside him, hope on one side and humiliation on the other. Her smile twitched and she looked quickly away. Her chest heaved and Viktor was certain she was about to look back at him and smile, but she didn't.

She was talking to another veteran, not Karl Haas.

Why was she here? Where was this fiancé of hers?

One of the miller's daughters struck up the kingdom's anthem. She had a pretty voice, but it was somber rather than stirring. A few people joined in, though it was a halfhearted affair. Viktor tried to make eye contact with Karla but her eyes slid right across him. Afterwards, Bruno Konig took a seat at the harpsichord in the corner and played something a little livelier. More attendees filtered in and the mood perked up a little.

Viktor tried to work up the courage to go over to Karla but she was clearly avoiding him. He wanted to know so badly why she was there. Was there some fleeting hope that they could be together? *Don't be stupid*, he told himself. *She can hardly look at you.*

Grunburg's brewer gifted two kegs to the event and Viktor, having worked at Herr Fischer's restaurant before the war, popped the bungs and tapped them. After exchanging a few puns with Dieter, they got to work on the beer in earnest, trying not to watch Karla dance.

"Just go talk to her, Viktor."

But he couldn't do that, not without a little more courage in his belly.

Once Viktor had polished off another beer he scoped the dance floor, sweat beading on his forehead. Dieter noted his anxiety and gave him a playful shove. "Just ask any of them. It's only a dance."

Dieter was right, of course. He was doing it again. Maybe he had built up things with Karla in his head. Well, he ought to get on with his life. He ought to show her he was getting on with it, anyway. So, Viktor sucked in a lungful of air and puffed out his chest, jutting his chin out. His mother had always said he had a fine, strong jaw. Viktor spotted a blond girl with big dimples and doe-brown eyes. She looked away, clutching her elbows apprehensively as he approached. With a grin he realized it was Margo Weisfeld, all grown up.

"Margo, would you like to dance?"

She glanced up at him, seeming startled, and then looked away, unwilling to meet his eyes. Her gaze roamed the dance floor until she found Dieter hovering nearby. Margo ducked past, saying, "I promised Dieter."

Dieter accepted her outstretched hand and shrugged at Viktor.

A little crestfallen, Viktor searched for another partner and his breath caught as he found himself facing Karla.

Just ask her, he told himself, putting his head down and marching over to the girl.

"Hello," he said, but she still wouldn't look at him.

After a pause that felt as long as the war, she gritted her teeth and made eye contact. "Hello, Viktor." At last, a softness found its way onto her face.

Viktor smiled. "It's good to see you."

She clasped her hands before her.

Sweat beaded in Viktor's armpits and he wondered for a horror-filled moment if he stunk. Maybe that was why no one wanted to dance with him. But he had bathed before the dance. That couldn't be it. Still, he battled for a split second against an idiotic impulse to self-administer a sniff test.

Just ask her, he prodded himself again. "I was wondering if you would like to dance?"

She turned one way and then the other, clearly charting an escape route, and Viktor was certain she would say no, but at last she surrendered. Viktor took her hand as the harpsichord started up, noting her hand was as clammy as his own. He led her onto the dance floor and put his arm around her waist. She winced. He wasn't sure what he'd done wrong. Was that too familiar? It was just where you put your hand when you danced.

"I heard you're engaged." He nearly choked. "Congratulations."

She blinked furiously and shook her head. "Karl...enlisted in autumn." She rested her head on Viktor's chest. He knew she could hear how fast his heart was beating, but he couldn't slow it down. "Didn't even make it a month. His cannon backfired."

"I didn't know," said Viktor. "I'm sorry."

"Why should you be?"

He thought maybe he should say something, but the moment passed. He twirled her, feeling wrong about it, but that was the next step in the waltz. He trod on her foot and apologized but she didn't respond. With every measure the dance felt more and more awkward. He could tell she wanted to say something.

"It's okay if you don't want to dance," he offered.

"It's fine," she said, as stiff as before. "Mother says I need to leave the house more."

Maybe there was still a chance for them.

As soon as the thought crossed his mind he felt guilty. "Like my friend Dieter says, it's just a dance."

"It's not that."

They danced like strangers, a question building inside Viktor until he could no longer contain it. "Why did you stop writing?"

The harpsicord played on, ignorant of the tension. At last, Karla simply whispered Karl's name in his ear.

The hair on Viktor's neck stood up. He nodded, imagining that everyone must be staring at them.

Viktor spun Karla around and when they came back together

her grip rested for a heartbeat over the bandage on his arm. She ripped her hand away like she had touched a hot stove.

The music kept playing but their dance was over. "You know you can't catch it," Viktor said.

Karla backed up a step, her face pinched. "I know that."

She had the decency to look ashamed of herself, but that wasn't much comfort.

He tried to talk and had to stop and clear his throat. He wanted to run, but he'd stood his ground in worse spots. "Thank you for the dance, Karla. I'm very sorry about Karl."

She looked about to cry as she ducked back into the crowd, but Viktor knew her tears were not for him.

4

In the months after Viktor left his hometown he worked at a string of odd jobs. In Esseldorf, he found employment at the Red Swan Brewery, sweeping, scrubbing, and, when no one was looking, sampling their fine ales. But one afternoon these samples made Viktor careless, and when he rolled up his sleeves in the summer heat another employee spotted his tumor.

Viktor was fired before the shift ended.

In Weissbad, he worked in the kitchen of the Schwarz Family Inn. Frau Schwarz doted on him, having lost her own son in the war. But Viktor let a snake oil salesman talk him into buying a cure-all. The ointment itched like the devil, and when Frau Schwarz caught him scratching at his tumor, her matronly affection vanished overnight, unlike his malady, of course.

In town after town it had been the same. He found a job and kept it for a while, always hunting after a cure for his tumor and never finding one. But sooner or later, some nosy neighbor or careless accident would unearth the truth, and he would pack his things and move along.

Viktor's homesickness grew keener, even as the months turned into years. Wherever he went he did his best to keep searching, keep hoping, but as he lay awake at night, feeling the slow spreading ache that radiated from his tumor, it started to seem like there was no hope to be found.

Then one day, his father forwarded him a letter, and he was on the move again.

When Viktor's carriage rounded a bend in the country road, the shattered walls of Wittsburg Castle came into view. The little keep had once been a frontier fort, but during the war it had been sacked by the Rumavian army, its walls breached in two places, the gaps still scorched by mage fire.

As the carriage pulled up to the castle, Viktor leaned out, inspecting what was to be his new home. Wittsburg Sanitarium specialized in the treatment of his condition. Apparently, the physicians here had had great success helping tumorlings. But Viktor despised being treated as an invalid. True, his ailment had gotten worse in the years since the war ended, but it wasn't the physical pain—the damned itching—that was the worst. What hurt most was the way people treated him. He had done nothing wrong. In fact, he had earned his tumor in the line of duty. Still, rumors of madness and superstitions about tumorlings followed him from job to job, and town to town.

He had been invited to the sanitarium by Doktor Oberman. His letter made it sound as if they were on the verge of a cure. For Viktor, it was worth the chance. He quit his job as a grocer's assistant and traveled for six days, crossing half of Reinveldt in hopes of finding a cure. Viktor knew that as soon as his condition was revealed they would have fired him anyway.

As they approached the castle the carriage followed tracks that led not to the main gate, but to one of the breaches in the wall. It seemed the portcullis was inoperative and the inhabitants had adopted this detour to avoid fixing it.

Inside the walls, a group of men in hospital gowns stopped their game of croquet to watch the arrival.

The keep itself had been equally battered by the siege but evidence of repair could be seen in bricked-up patches in the walls and new windows.

Viktor climbed out of the carriage and collected his suitcase. Three old men sitting on the steps of the keep were engaged in a heated discussion. At a loss of what to do, Viktor hovered on the edge of their conversation, eavesdropping.

"Reinveldt is the greatest nation in the world, Franz." The speaker possessed an impressive mustache that danced as he harangued the other two. "How can you say otherwise?"

Franz, the oldest of the men, with a well-oiled white beard, shook his head. "Maybe once, Ernst."

The third man's head swung back and forth between the two as if watching an intense game of badminton. Viktor's father had always spoken derisively of those who held such patriotic views, but in Viktor's days in the army, the notion had gained a bit of ground in his estimation. There was a camaraderie in the army he hadn't experienced since. Every once in a while he felt a wistful nostalgia for those days, as rotten as they often were. The old men's argument was nothing new. He had heard many such conversations over the last few years, and always they left him yearning for the days before the war. Before everything had gone off track.

Ernst hammered his fist into the palm of his hand to emphasize his point. "No! That is the sort of defeatist attitude that lost us the war. Reinveldt is still the greatest nation that has *ever* existed."

"Technically it is not even a nation any longer," said Franz. "The reconstruction."

"Don't try to hide behind that intellectual double-talk, old man." Ernst took a quick step toward the other. "Reinveldt is forever."

This fellow Ernst's fervor was so sudden that Viktor worried he might need to step in to defend the other old man, but Franz only laughed, the shaking of his head redoubled. "Admit it, Ernst. We lost. How can you say otherwise?"

"Another lie! We were betrayed." For the first time, Ernst noticed Viktor's arrival. "Boys like this fought for Reinveldt. For our people. And what did they get? A knife in the back."

"Get ready for a rant, boy."

A dwarf hustled down the main steps to greet the carriage and the conversation fell silent. The dwarf wore a tweed jacket with patched elbows and an argyle hat, an annoyed expression on his clean-shaven face.

Viktor winced. He hadn't expected Doktor Oberman to be a dwarf. He didn't have anything against dwarves, per se, he just hadn't been around them much. His grandma on the other hand had always said to "never trust a runt." And while of course that was a bit old-fashioned, he'd always thought of his Oma as the sweetest old lady he'd ever known. There had to be some good reason for that venom, right?

Viktor glanced at the old men, who turned pointedly away. He knew he was being silly. He had come all this way for help. It was stubborn and stupid to get picky about that help now. With a deep breath he turned to the dwarf. "Hello, sir."

The old men headed off into the courtyard, picking up their argument in hushed tones.

"Good afternoon. You must be Viktor. Welcome to Wittsburg Castle."

"And you must be Doktor Oberman."

The dwarf scoffed. "Hah, not bloody likely. I'm Malcolm Lanigan, but you can call me Doktor Lanigan." He held his hand up for Viktor to shake it.

Viktor hesitated and then accepted Doktor Lanigan's hand. "Are you his assistant?"

"Well." The dwarf bristled at his suggestion. "I suppose so. I'm almost as new here as you are. But I have been studying arcanomorphic tumor genesis for three decades. Just as long as Doktor Oberman."

"Arcano what?"

"Arcanomorphic tumor genesis. The peculiar malignancy triggered by too much magic."

Viktor blinked. "Um…"

"Magic tumors, lad. I was led to believe you've got one of those."

"Oh, yah. Of course." Viktor felt a little stupid and it irritated him. "Are you from Dunngregor?"

Doktor Lanigan shook his head. "That's a common misconcep-

tion. Of course, my family is, originally. But we've lived in Brandover for generations."

"Ah, of course." Viktor folded his hands together, unsure what
to say next.

"Well, I have important things to do, lad. Let's get you settled
in."

Viktor's room turned out to be a drafty, dismal affair. It featured
a lumpy bed covered in a coarse woolen blanket, a small fireplace
that admitted an arctic draft, and a massive portrait of some dour
lord making a strange sign with his left hand. It was all perfectly
creepy in Viktor's opinion, and he began to regret his decision to
pack up and move halfway across the country on the vague promises
offered by a single letter.

After a hearty dinner of roasted pork and mashed potatoes,
served in the dining hall below, Viktor retired to his room and
turned in for the night. The floors creaked and outside a storm
rattled the windows. His bed proved to be a trial, the mattress
stuffed with what he felt certain were bundles of sharpened sticks.
Worse was the itchy, comically thick woolen blanket. Despite the
brutal draft from the fireplace, the blanket was so thick that Viktor
was soon sweating. After tossing and turning for hours, Viktor finally
decided to strip down naked and huddle beneath the smothering
blanket. And yet sleep still proved elusive. Rain pattered against his
window and howling gusts of wind roused him every time he
managed to drowse.

In the wee hours of the morning, Viktor was startled from his
fitful sleep by the creaking of the floor outside his room. Viktor froze
beneath the woolen monstrosity, ears straining, alert to the possibility of an intruder. A door slammed in the hallway and he heard a
muffled voice. An argument followed the sounds of a scuffle, and it
prodded Viktor from his bed. With the ridiculous blanket draped
over his shoulders he went to the door and peeked into the hallway.

"But I'm already awake!" a crazed old man with long, greasy
white hair shouted as two orderlies dragged him along.

"Hey!" said Viktor. "What are you doing?"

"Go back to bed," one of the orderlies commanded.

"What are you doing to him?" Viktor shot back.

The old man tried to break free of the orderlies but they wrestled him under control. As the patient thrashed about, Viktor noticed a patch of green scales growing up his neck like a rash. The biggest of the two sanitarium workers turned back to Viktor with a scowl. "He's a loon. We're transferring him to another ward. And put some clothes on!"

Viktor realized his blanket had parted like the curtain of a burlesque. He covered himself with a gasp and retreated back into his room. He listened as the orderlies manhandled their patient down the staircase and felt vaguely guilty for not helping the old man. But what could he do? He shuddered, not from the cold, but the idea that someday he too might lose his mind. Viktor went back to bed and lay there, trying to quiet his thoughts. The storm passed and still he couldn't sleep. Soon the birds were chirping and light peeked over the horizon. Viktor rolled away from the glare spilling into his room, cursing.

When Viktor at last fell asleep, a knock sounded at the door, startling him awake.

"Just a moment," Viktor grumbled. He dragged himself out of bed and hustled into his clothes, shivering at the chill which lingered in his room. "Come in."

An older man strode in with silver hair and piercing blue eyes behind gold-rimmed spectacles. He wore a fine black suit with red trim and white buttons down the front. In his gloved hand he gripped a dragon-headed cane.

"Good morning. Doktor Oberman?"

"Your intuition does you credit. I am indeed Doktor Emile Oberman, at your service. I hope I haven't disturbed your sleep."

Viktor opened his mouth to unload the story of his "sleep," but thought better of it. "Thank you. I mean, thank you for inviting me here."

"Think nothing of it. I am happy to help a good Reinish boy."

"Uh…yes, thank you."

"I can take one look at your eyes and hair and know you come from one of the old bloodlines. I consider myself a humble servant of our people's destiny."

"Destiny?" Viktor's forehead crinkled as he tried to puzzle out this unexpected start. It reminded him of the horse trader who came through Grunburg every summer. He had a spiel, too. Viktor hoped Doktor Oberman's wasn't a long one. That horse trader really liked to hear himself talk.

"During the first Dragon Reich, our people served the great Wyrms who ruled the continent. The Reinish people have tapped the Dragon Well since ancient times; it's our birthright. You're familiar with the legends of course?"

"About the Dragon Well? A bit. My oma used to talk about that kind of stuff but I didn't really pay attention."

"It's important you understand our history. Our legacy."

Viktor wasn't sure what bearing all this had on treating his tumor, but he knew it would be rude to contradict his host. So, he smiled and nodded, as if the doctor's lecture might cure him. "Go on."

"In olden times, so the story goes, the ancient beings, demons and dragons and so forth, divided the power of creation into what we today call the Wells, or metaphysical reservoirs of energy. Before their extinction at the hands of Saint Jene and the other Dragon Slayers, those so-called 'Saints,' the dragons bequeathed us with their power. But, of course, magic comes at a cost. A tumor can sometimes be the result of calling power from a Well. I consider it my special contribution to our people to shepherd those who have experienced tumor genesis through this difficult experience."

Viktor nodded. "Yah, big thank-you. Does mean that everyone here taps the Dragon Well?"

Doktor Oberman snickered. "No, no." He paused to consider his words. "The nature of the experiments we conduct requires a variety of subjects."

That answer made Viktor a little uncomfortable, but he didn't want to press. He had probably misunderstood what the doctor was driving at. Viktor was no great thinker, he did that sometimes.

"May I see it?" asked Doktor Oberman.

It pained Viktor to bare himself like this, which of course was ridiculous. He was here precisely so the doctor could treat him. Naturally, Oberman would have to inspect the tumor. Still, Viktor had never willingly shown his affliction to anyone. He rolled up his sleeve, exposing a bandaged area on his forearm. He looked at the doctor who gave him an encouraging nod and then began to unwrap the bandage. Beneath it, three red scales sprouted from the skin on the back of his forearm. They clustered together, angry, coin-sized sores which looked almost like scabs at a glance, but upon closer inspection had a certain luster. From the moment he had awoken in the field hospital with a single dragon scale on his forearm, Viktor had hidden the growing tumor like a terrible secret. Now, Doktor Oberman reached out to touch the scales and Viktor shied away from his grasp.

"I can assure you, Viktor, it is perfectly safe to touch them. It's not contagious. And even if it were…" He held up his leather gloved hands and waggled his fingers.

"I know. I just——"

"The old superstitions are sometimes hard to break. But it is precisely by applying our reason and not our fears that we come to understand the true nature of the transformation." He reached out again and this time Viktor allowed him to inspect the scales more closely. The doctor turned Viktor's arm this way and that, even ran his fingers over the scales, noting the slightly raised ridge that divided each scale down the middle. Viktor shivered. He looked up to find a strange smile on the doctor's face.

The physician went on. "Am I to understand that your grandfather was also a tumorling?" Doktor Oberman released his arm and Viktor began to wrap it up again. Viktor's family had always treated this information as a shame not to be spoken of, but he supposed it was medically relevant.

"Yes, that's right."

"A recent tumorling in your bloodline suggests a strong genetic connection to the Dragon Well. It's no surprise that you are able to Channel its magic. What can you tell me about your grandfather's progression? Did it start as yours did? Did he draw too deeply?"

Viktor folded his arms. This subject always made him squirm, but he had come too far not to commit to the process. He sighed. "I was just a baby when Opa's tumor started. But my mother said it began with his eyes. Actually his left eye. He'd been working double shifts at the bottleworks. Opa used the Might to schlep kegs all day. He just woke up one morning and his eye was red, a pupil like a cat's eye appeared."

"More accurately a dragon's, of course." Oberman waved off his own interruption. "I'm sorry. Go on, go on."

"Well, he lost his job at the bottleworks, even though he'd been using his magic in his work. And then he started to drink a lot. My mother said he became violent at home, too, but maybe that was the alcohol. Maybe it was the tumor." Viktor shrugged. "The scales spread from his eye. By the end, he was covered head to toe. They even say he had a wing growing out of his back. Just one, though. And it didn't work very well."

"Fascinating. And how did he die?"

"He was just dead one morning. I was only eight, so I don't remember much. He was sleeping in the barn by that point. Oma said she went out to check on him and he had died in the night."

Doktor Oberman nodded. "Such advanced arcanogenesis is extremely rare. I am pleased to say this makes you a perfect candidate for what we are doing here."

"You think you can cure me?"

Doktor Oberman tapped his cane on the stone floor. "You served in the army, did you not?"

"Yah."

"I am given to understand that you acquired your tumor in the service of our nation. My thanks. I am curious to learn the extent of your abilities. Channelers of the Dragon Well can employ a variety of powers unique to it. Can you tell me which manifestations you achieved?"

"Well, the Eyes of Zed."

"A most useful manifestation and perhaps the most common. What else?"

"All of us were trained to manifest the Might of Dryxa."

"I would be shocked if a strapping young man such as your-self could not. Dryxa was one of the mightiest dragons of the First Reich. You should be proud to call upon his strength, though the metaphysics are a bit unclear. I often wonder if the Great Wyrm now somehow persists in the Well, or if the ability is simply named in his honor. But I digress. Please, go on. Were there others?"

"They tried to teach us a bunch in our training. But the only other I did happened just once."

"Yes, your letter spoke of your final battle. Manifesting the Breath of Azzax, that is to say *expelling* the Breath, is exceedingly rare. Teaching such manifestations is difficult and not particularly effective. The intake is a common means of accessing the Well's power, though not the only one. Of course, as your case demonstrates, the technique is fraught with danger. Most could not expel the Breath even if they tried. I have found in my research that more often the most powerful manifestations are achieved spontaneously. But greatness comes with risk. It is not surprising that it resulted in the genesis of your tumor." Doktor Oberman licked his lips. "I think I can help you."

Viktor felt a chill. "So you *can* cure me?"

Doktor Oberman stepped closer and set his hand on Viktor's shoulder. "I completely understand your concern, Viktor."

"You do?"

"Yes. When I was only nine years old I was afflicted by a rare condition. An infection of sorts in my bone marrow. It was quite painful. Quite debilitating. And worse, the other children were quite cruel. I have seen the way society treats the ill. With taunts, with exclusion, with violence even. The common ilk cannot even imagine your suffering, but I have lived it. A sickly boy on crutches, tormented by the healthy boys, bullied. You begin to see yourself as they see you. But we must not let ourselves be changed by their cruelty. We must seize this pain and make it a catalyst. There is no cure for your affliction, Viktor. But I believe I can guide you safely through this process."

"This process?"

"I know it's frightening, but what we're doing is revolutionary. With my help, you can do this."

"Do what?" Viktor knew what the doctor would say, but part of him still wanted to believe this was all a misunderstanding.

"Viktor," said the doctor. "You are becoming a dragon."

"What? Like my grandfather? No thank you, Doctor. I came here to be cured."

"Ah," said Oberman. "But cured of what? You think of it as an ailment because you have been conditioned that way. You think you are so very different because of the stigma of your tumor. But you are not alone. Everything society has told you about magic is a lie. The newspapers these days are controlled by the wealthy, by dwarves and foreigners."

"I just want to get better."

"Better?" Oberman shook his head, looking at Viktor with pity. "You are not sick. You are a dragon at heart. You have been mistreated. You have been lied to. But across the nation young men like you are opening their eyes. They know in their hearts that none of this is their fault. The Kingdom of Reinveldt has been defeated, humiliated. Because it was betrayed, by dwarves, by the newspapers and intellectuals who convinced our nation to surrender."

"My father runs a newspaper."

"Yes." Oberman nodded, gravely. "And how did he welcome you home? Like the rest of them, he blames you for his own failings. Does he not? He thinks your tumor is a manifestation of his own disappointment. The real disappointment is what has become of our nation. Weak. Muddied. Defeated. But not all of us are defeated. Some of us remember how things were before we allowed ourselves to be corrupted by foreign influences. Don't you remember what it was like before the war?"

Viktor opened his mouth, ready to object, but it was true. He did remember what it was like before the war, and he longed for that time. Everything was so much simpler, so much better. Viktor suffered a pang of nostalgia, reminded of his hometown, of apple strudel and Karla with the sun on her hair, of late nights at the restaurant brewing beer with Herr Fischer. Was there really a way back to times like those? Everything was so much grayer now. Things really had changed. He couldn't argue with that, but it didn't mean he was going to let this nut make him sicker. "What does Doktor Lanigan think of this…treatment?"

Oberman laughed, a sharp, joyless bark. "That dwarf? He was only appointed to his position by the feckless bureaucracy in Jarlsbeck. He won't be a concern much longer."

A night in the Ox Street jail felt rather scandalous. And filthy, of course. It really was quite filthy.

His father must have been absolutely bloody furious.

What fun it would be to see the look on his jowly face at that very moment. Devin sniggered like a schoolyard bully as he imagined the illustrious Lord Thistleby's fit of pique. No doubt, his father's red-faced blustering had achieved the hue of those candied cherries he was always popping in his mouth. But heaven help the maids, with a certainty they had been subjected to the first draft of Devin's dressing down.

Enough was enough, though. Obviously, his father was dawdling, a vain effort to punish Devin for his alleged crimes. Well…not so alleged, he supposed, surveying the cell.

Devin had never spent a night in jail. In fact, his father usually had him out within the hour. A bit of a bother to listen to his lectures, but it was typically over soon enough. Devin had to admit, though, that perhaps this time things had gone a tad too far.

The young nobleman sat on a filthy cot in a cramped cell, trying to ignore the thug glaring at him. The bald criminal wore a torn blue tunic and had an amateur tattoo of a mermaid over his droopy right eye.

Devin was very much trying to imagine himself in one of the Lord Jasper novels. The daring and handsome Lord Torrence Jasper would never be intimidated by a scoundrel like this. He'd have rattled off a quip that would leave this degenerate speechless. Then he'd beckon the guard over and bang his head against the bars—

The scummy fellow pushed off the wall and the motion shattered Devin's daydream. He flinched, then tried to cover up by adjusting his wig. As the thug loomed over him, Devin shoved his hands into his pockets in a last-ditch attempt at nonchalance.

"That's a bloody nice shirt," said the ruffian. "You should give it to me. Now."

Devin had to admit he may have gotten a bit cavalier. Winding up in jail had demonstrated he was not, perhaps, the master Ward Man he imagined himself to be. Perhaps if he told the thug who his father was... Alas, this fellow looked like the sort to shank his mother for a pint of rotgut and unlikely to listen to reason or respect his betters. What would Lord Jasper do?

"Guard!" Devin hollered loud enough to be heard in the precinct room of the city watch, where a single officer dozed, his feet up on the desk.

The thug feinted at Devin. "Fuck you looking at? I said give me your bloody shirt."

Devin shouldn't have been there in the first place. Every day the Goldsmith spent an hour at Madame Churlington's house of ill repute. Every day. The man's pipes ran like clockwork. So why had he come home in the middle of the job?

"Oi. I'm just teasing, Mr. Fancy. I ain't taking your shirt. I want to be friends." This ruffian's rotten-toothed smile was more horrifying than his threats, or perhaps it was the vaguely amorous glint in his eye.

"Guard!"

Devin stood and hurried over to the bars, standing just a few feet away from where the constable was snoring. "Guard!" The guard startled awake, tottering on the back legs of his chair for a moment before tipping back down onto all four. He stretched, rising to his feet and squirming a bit. The disheveled watchman reached behind himself to tug free the underclothes wedged in his backside.

"Quiet, you two."

"I need to be moved to my own cell this instant."

"He thinks I'm unfriendly." The thug and the constable shared a laugh.

"Careful, buster, this one's daddy is in the Quorum." The thug laughed. The constable didn't.

The thought crawled its way through the grimy workings of the criminal's brain. *Ha! Not so tough now, you villain!* Devin delighted to see the rogue's bluster vanish at the mention of his father's seat on Westonshire's ruling council of mages. Actually, the man seemed to be having trouble wrapping his mind around the complexities of their new dynamic.

Devin stood a little straighter, hardly worrying at all whether he was about to be attacked by this ghastly hooligan. No, he could see the man deflate, as he should, given their relative stations. Ridiculous at all that he should be in this place. His father really must be furious to keep him waiting so.

The watchman tucked in for a nap and the thug sat on the cot across from Devin, fidgeting. It took him a moment, but he soon recovered a little of his nerve. He stared at Devin, eyeing the young noble more critically than before.

"Which one is it?" He cocked his head to one side. "Not one of the new bloods. Too much of a dandy. You must be from proper old stock." Ever so slowly the wheels of the felon's mind ground onward. "But you aren't in the Channeler cells are you? No magic yourself. Pity. Would be better if you could get us out of here. So which one is it, then? Percy? Heartsbridge?"

Devin crossed one leg over the other. "You're wrong. I am a new-blood bastard. Black Lung is my mother."

"Horse shit. Black Lung's a mite scary to whelp a little twat like you. That witch's womb would have eaten you alive. Come on, let's have it."

"Fine. Lord Thistleby is my father."

The thug whistled. "Fucking hell. You know I saw his duel with Lord Bailey. Turned him inside out, he did. Fucking horrible."

"Sounds like Father."

"HE'S HERE." The guard tucked in his shirt as he stood, licking his finger and rubbing ineffectually at a stain on his tunic.

Devin put his wig back on and buttoned his jacket. He self-consciously ran his finger over the fuzz growing between his eyes. Spending the night in jail had given him no time to tweeze his unibrow, and now he imagined it had grown in like a mink stole draped over his eyes. He fussed with the cuffs of his hunter-green shirt, an elegant little number that he now regretted. Black and green were Rumavian colors, if one were inclined to fret over such things. He often wore them because Thomas said it made his eyes pop, but also because it irritated his father. Now he lamented the choice, sure that it would stoke his father's ire all the more. Plus, with his brow unplucked, he didn't want to draw any more attention to his unfortunate grooming predicament. Devin rose from his cot and approached the bars of his cell.

Behind him the thug said, "Good luck, you posh little slag."

"Thanks, Phil."

"Don't let him push you around," the criminal advised. "But don't say nothing smart neither."

The guard unlocked the cell. "You'll tell your father you were treated civilly, of course?" A rat scurried by. "I mean, it's true we locked you up. But we treated you well, right? Even Phillip's on his best behavior."

"He won't care one way or the other."

"Fair enough." The guard stepped aside to let Devin out of the cell. "In case he does, though, maybe mention that we were just doing our jobs." He took off his hat and held it in both hands before him in an approximation of parade rest, only pathetic.

"I'll be sure to mention the back rub."

"The…what?" The guardsman panicked.

"It's a joke. Get out of the way, man. You are far beneath my father's notice."

"Thank you, sir."

"An absolute pleasure." Devin headed for the door.

"Master Thistleby?"

He stopped and looked back over his shoulder. "Yes?"

The guard hustled over to his desk and opened the drawer, holding out a small black leather bag. "Your things, sir."

Now *that* was an impressive display of bootlicking. Not even Devin would have expected the return of his thieves' kit. The pistol, on the other hand, he probably should have inquired after. It was terribly expensive. Those dwarves and their *Fabrik*. What contraptions would their tinkers' magic turn out next? Devin took the flint-lock out of the bag and stroked the pearl inlaid handle. A smile found its way to his lips as he tucked it into his belt, feeling rakish and dangerous. Most gentlemen were still wearing rapiers. Devin scoffed at how quaint they seemed. Though of course, since Cairn Dunngregor had sealed its gates, even men of considerable means would balk at the pistol's price.

Devin noted with a coy smile that his coin purse was not included with his other effects. "Consider the rest a tip." The guard blushed as Devin vanished the thieves' kit into his jacket so his father wouldn't see it.

A carriage waited out front, black lacquer and gold filigree yoked to four glorious white horses. It stood in stark contrast to the muddy streets and ramshackle tenements of Gutter Town. From within the carriage, his father had not yet deigned to look at him. The driver, too, stared straight ahead, never so much as glancing at Devin as he approached.

"Father."

Lord Archibald Thistleby III sat inside the coach as if Devin hadn't said a word, fat and stern, and crabby as ever. After a long, awkward pause, Devin reached for the door to climb in, but his father's silver-tipped cane lashed out, whacking his fingertips.

"You are not coming with me." Devin's father was making his disappointed face, an exaggerated frown with a periodic twitch of regret. Saints, Devin was sick of that face. It took a laudable dose of restraint to keep from rolling his eyes. *Oh, Father, let's hear it, your latest sermon.*

Devin waited, but the lecture went unspoken.

He digested Lord's Thistleby's pronouncement about not coming with and judged it a rather lenient punishment, all things considered. Even he had to admit that getting caught in a burglary was a colossal cock-up. Though he had no coin in his pocket, he supposed undergoing the embarrassment of borrowing fare for a carriage of his own was a small price to pay to demonstrate his contrition. He stole a furtive glance at his impoverished surroundings. On second thought, perhaps he would wind up stabbed quite a lot in one of these rubbish strewn ditches. In that case, the punishment seemed rather harsh. Devin briefly considered asking for an advance on his allowance before rejecting the idea.

"Very well," he said. "I'll make my own way home."

"No." Lord Thistleby's chins wobbled.

"No?"

His father finally looked Devin in the eye. "No. You are not coming home."

"You've made your point, Father. I'm exhausted. I'm filthy. I need a bath. I just want to go home. Please don't drag this little exile out another night?"

Lord Thistleby bit his lip until it turned white. "You are a humiliation to this family. You could have been the heir to the lordship, to our piece of the Quorum. Instead, you gamble and drink and squander your allowance on wigs and scarves and overpriced shoes. As if that weren't enough, now you have stooped to common thievery. I gave you everything, Devin. And obviously it's ruined you. Now you're running around like some sort of cat burglar. How utterly facile. Your peers are laughing at you. Worse, they are laughing at me. It's those idiotic novels. I rue the day your mother introduced you to that drivel. If she could see what a wastrel you've become."

The contempt on his father's face turned Devin's stomach. "Father, you're scaring me. It was just a prank. A little escapade. You were young once. Surely—"

"Silence!" The horses flinched. His father's eyes glowed with fiery magic, as if he meant to incinerate his only son on the spot. "You have embarrassed me for the last time. Give me your key."

Devin stammered, his brain fumbling for a way to placate his father. "It won't happen again."

The twin embers of his father's eyes cooled. He held out his hand. "Your key."

Devin bowed his head, not daring to show his father that he was on the verge of tears. He held out his key to the manor and felt his father's soft hand snatch it away. Lord Thistleby rapped his cane on the roof of the carriage and its driver whipped the horses into motion.

Devin watched it round the next corner. He stood fighting to breathe until a passerby hawked phlegm in the gutter. Aghast, he took in the squalor around him. All that shabbiness was sure to hide a stabber or two.

Devin rested one hand on the priceless weapon tucked in his belt and reassured himself that, if it came to it, he could at probably hand over the pistol in exchange for his life.

6

Viktor found a game of Three Saints in the kitchen. The cook and two of the sanitarium's patients sat at a table in back, smoking pipes and playing cards. Viktor heard the clink of coins as he came hunting for a snack and invited himself to join.

His first instinct, after his awkward conversation with Doktor Oberman, was to leave the castle right away, but staring out through the breach in the wall he saw nothing but wilderness. Worse, a downpour opened up while he stood in the courtyard, dark clouds stretching across the horizon. He didn't relish setting off in a storm. So he had instead set about securing some rations and not long after found himself sitting at the table holding a three and four of swords, and a knight of stars. He knocked once, signaling he only wanted one card. The cook beside him added a second coin to his ante and set aside two cards to exchange.

"So," Viktor asked. "What do you three think of Doktor Oberman?"

The table fell silent.

After an awkward pause, the frail patient to his right bet three coppers as if the question had never been asked. Viktor raised his eyebrows. "Sore subject, I guess."

"Oh, don't mind me." A gruff voice behind him said, startling Viktor. Doktor Lanigan shuffled across the kitchen and plucked a sausage from the pantry. As the dwarf left, the cook cleared his

44

throat. It was Viktor's turn. He looked back to the game, but his gut told him to talk to Lanigan. Maybe the dwarf could give Viktor some straight answers. He folded his cards and stood. The cook scowled.

Viktor patted his belly. "Your cooking needs out." He left the kitchen in pursuit of the dwarf, following him down the hallway. Something was off about this place, and if the dwarf was the odd man out, maybe he could see it, too.

Lanigan trundled down the hallway, humming a little ditty and waving the sausage around at the end of each verse.

Viktor called out. "Doktor Lanigan!"

"Goodness," said the dwarf. "You scared me."

"Sorry. I hope you didn't choke on your sausage."

The dwarf snickered. "How are you settling in?"

"It's been an adjustment."

"Aye." Lanigan looked down at the half-eaten sausage in his hand. "It was a wee bit rough for me, too. Don't exactly fit in, as you can see."

Viktor nodded. "Doktor Oberman may have mentioned something to that effect."

"Oh now that's a gentle way of putting it."

"So…you haven't been here long."

The dwarf swallowed. "Hardly. And if I have any say I won't stay long either. Oberman and his lackeys have me filling out paperwork and greeting new arrivals. Not sure the last time I treated a bloody patient."

It got quiet. Not awkward, just quiet, like each was waiting for the other one to say it. Viktor looked up and down the hall to be sure they were alone. "Have you noticed anything odd since you've been here?"

The doctor's demeanor transformed at once. He checked over his shoulder and lowered his voice. "What do you mean?"

"Oberman. He said some pretty weird stuff to me. Does he seem strange to you? He does not like you, by the way. Because you're a dwarf."

"Well you have a keen gift for observation, laddie."

"He said something disturbing," Viktor admitted. "I mean something else. Besides the dwarf stuff."

Lanigan looked like the sausage he was chewing had gone rotten on his tongue. "Well," said the dwarf. "Don't be shy. What *else* did you find disturbing?"

"He said he wanted to help the process. He wants to let the tumor run its course."

Doktor Lanigan flinched as if the notion had slapped him. "No. No, that can't be. That's quite mad."

"He said it and he meant it. He also said that the patients here were part of an experiment."

Lanigan's head snapped up. "The basement."

"What?"

"Something is going on in the basement. I saw folk coming and going from one of the outbuildings. I asked about it and Oberman nearly bit my head off. There's an orderly on duty whose arms look like bloody tree trunks. Maybe not an orderly at all. Maybe he's a guard." The dwarf tapped the side of his nose.

Viktor ought to just hit the road. Whatever was going on here wasn't his problem. But something about it irked him. Viktor had come all this way for help and this asshole Oberman had tricked him. He had never meant to help at all. "Show me."

"Now hold on, lad. That's reaching into a barrel of snakes. Maybe we just have a chat with Oberman and clear this up."

"You just said he was mad."

"Not in those exact words, and don't you go wagging your jaw about it." Lanigan shook a fistful of sausage. "I have my reputation to think of."

Viktor waved him off. "I'm going to the basement. The question is, do you want to see what's down there, too?"

Lanigan popped the sausage in his mouth like it was a cigar and twiddled his little thumbs. "I suppose I do."

"Then lead the way."

Doktor Lanigan escorted Viktor through the east wing of the castle, past the feast hall and the staff rooms, to an isolated courtyard with a small outbuilding in the center. An orderly stood out front, under the eave to stay out of the rain. He wore white scrubs under his coat, but Viktor spotted a truncheon tucked into his belt.

The orderly watched them approach, eyebrows furled in suspicion. "Oberman sent *you* with the new subject?"

Lanigan froze. The guard narrowed his eyes, his suspicion mounting with every beat of Viktor's heart. The silence grew unbearable. Viktor nudged the dwarf. The doctor put one hand to his chest and gestured grandly with the other. "Yes. He did." Lanigan projected his voice as if on stage, a bit player in the village theatre.

"Fine," said the guard, somehow oblivious to the dwarf's disastrous performance. He stood to one side so they could enter the outbuilding. With a glance at Viktor, the dwarf headed inside.

"Doc?" the guard asked.

Lanigan audibly gulped. "Yes?"

"Aren't you forgetting something?" The guard's hand strayed toward the club tucked into his belt. "The password."

Lanigan laughed, shrill as a parrot. His hands came out of his pockets, gesticulating of their own accord. He mopped a bead of sweat from his ample forehead. "No need." He coughed. "Oberman said it's fine?"

The guard frowned. "Was that a question?"

"Oh," said Viktor, "what about the handshake?" He extended his left hand.

The guard quirked an eyebrow, automatically extending the wrong hand. When he realized his mistake, he looked up just in time to catch Viktor's fist right on the jaw. He flopped in the doorway, drool leaking from the corner of his mouth.

"What are you doing, you daft git?" Lanigan sounded panicked.

"He was onto us. Honestly, you were so bad at that. 'Oberman said it's fine?' Get the door."

"I'd like to see you act, you big galoot," Lanigan grumbled under his breath as he opened the door. "You know I was a member of the dramatic society at the University of Jarlsbeck."

"Stagehand?"

"Just grab his bloody ankles, you arse."

47

Viktor dragged the guard inside and relieved him of his club, noticing a strange tattoo on the inside of his right forearm, a symbol he'd never seen before. Viktor rifled through the guard's pockets and came up with a ring of rusty iron keys. At the back of the room a trapdoor led down a spiral staircase into darkness. Viktor took a torch from a wall sconce and held it over the stone stairwell, peering down into the tunnels beneath the castle.

"Nothing to worry about here."

LANIGAN LEANED PAST VIKTOR, squinting into the dancing shadows cast by Viktor's torch. "Do you hear that?" asked the dwarf.

"No."

"It's a voice."

"Hello?" Viktor called.

Lanigan swatted him on the thigh, hissing. "Keep your voice down. Who knows what's down there."

They both squinted into the darkened corridor.

"Come on." The dwarf puffed out his chest and shuffled down the stone hallway to door on the right, jiggling the handle. It was locked, but, as Viktor soon discovered, from the outside. A massive cast iron bolt of crude construction held the little wooden portal in place. They exchanged a look. Lanigan shied back, but Viktor stepped up and pulled it open, cringing as it creaked. "Sorry," he mouthed.

"You already shouted," whispered the dwarf.

The room turned out to be empty save a tidy cot with a tucked-in sheet and a clean nightsoil bucket beside it. They continued down the hall, passing more identical cells until the voice the dwarf had heard sounded again, this time just ahead. It was deep, and raspy. Viktor paused outside one of the cells, listening to the singsong gibberish from within, the hair standing up on the back of his neck. He held his breath and unlocked the bolt.

In the dark, a misshapen, gigantic man squatted in the corner on a pile of hay. Wispy hair hung in its brutish face. It wore a filthy blanket like a robe. Unlike the other rooms, there was no furniture in this cell. It reeked of feces and something musky. The massive prisoner didn't seem to notice their arrival or the light of Viktor's torch. Doktor Lanigan pressed in behind him and yelped as he got a good look at the cell's inhabitant.

"By the Crucible, look at him." The creature would've been at least eight feet tall if could have stood up in this cramped cell. It had a jaw like an anvil and a runny nose.

"Hello?" Viktor said. "Hello there?"

The giant didn't respond.

"Is he a real giant?" Viktor asked.

Lanigan snorted. "My kin wiped out the last of the giants at the end of the Mountain Wars."

The misshapen prisoner looked sharply at Lanigan and all three froze. Lanigan shied back a step. Viktor listened to the giant's wheezing breath. But the moment passed and the hulking creature seemed to lose focus, staring back down at the floor.

"He's no giant," said Lanigan. "This poor soul is a tumorling."

Viktor stared in horror. This thing had once been a man?

And then it had gotten sick. Just like him. Somewhere along the way, this person had touched the Jotun Well, just as Viktor had touched the Dragon Well. This poor thing probably thought it a gift at first, like Viktor had. Yet somehow this wretch had drawn too deeply on the Jotun Well's power and it had sparked this change in its flesh.

The idea horrified him. Would the dragon scale that had sprouted on his own arm slowly spread through his whole body, leaving him a twisted deformity like this?

Viktor tapped his forearm with the truncheon, where the dragon scales grew beneath his sleeve. He ground his teeth. The itching started again, but Viktor dared not scratch it, though it took all of his will to resist.

"What do we do with him?" Viktor asked.

"For now, we leave him. I have a bad feeling we've only scratched the surface of what's going on down here."

They continued down the hall, throwing uneasy glances over

their shoulders, but the giant tumorling never stirred. Along the way they passed several more empty cells. Viktor walked face first into a cobweb, which the dwarf seemed to find a little too funny for their current predicament. Grunting his disapproval, Viktor turned a corner and followed another corridor to a large door at the end of the hall. Unlike the others, which had the creepy feel of an ancient dungeon, this door looked new and modern, cut from fresh pine, with an ordinary doorknob.

They stopped before the door, straining to hear muted voices on the other side. Viktor pressed his ear against it, making out Oberman's raised voice. The doctor was…calling out numbers? Viktor opened the door enough to peek at what lay beyond. Candles lit the next room. He pushed the door open a little further and crept through. Viktor stood at the top of a flight of stone steps that descended into a large open basement. Banners hung from the ceiling, but in the poor light Viktor couldn't tell what was on them. The stone pit was populated by three figures standing around a vat of glowing water.

Oberman rattled off what sounded like a series of measurements. "Twelve percent saturation." He dipped a metal rod into the glowing water. "Fourteen percent. The decoction is complete."

Viktor was even more confused now. What was Oberman up to? A spike of fear stabbed him. What if there was a perfectly reasonable explanation for all of this? And here he was breaking in. Maybe he should have just left after all.

The three men joined hands around the vat and intoned a long, low note.

Never mind, thought Viktor. *That was* definitely *weird*.

He could feel the power reverberating in the sound. It was like standing in the fog after a lightning strike. When the note concluded, Oberman and his assistants let go of each other's hands.

"Lights, please," said the doctor.

One of the assistants walked to a large metal lever and lifted it. Gas lamps sparked to life around the room, revealing a laboratory full of copper and glass tanks and tables full of beakers and books.

Viktor noted the banners overhead, marked with the same

symbol as the orderly's tattoo. It reminded him vaguely of a stick-figure drawing of a dragon, like a cross with diagonal lines slashing from each of the four compass points in a sort of spiral.

"Ah," said Oberman, looking up at Viktor from the far side of the room. "The guest of honor has arrived. Clever of you to have found us so quickly."

Lanigan tugged on Viktor's sleeve. When he looked down, the dwarf pointed to the far side of the room, where a series of riveted copper and glass tanks held figures suspended in water. Each of the victims were hideously deformed. One looked like a goat-man with leathery wings and a series of cancerous mouths along the left side of its body. Another looked withered, skin and bone with a deathly pallor. One seemed entirely human save a large eye blinking on his forehead.

"What the hell is wrong with you people?" Viktor started down the stairs toward Oberman and his lackeys.

"Viktor!" Lanigan hissed. "What are you doing? We have to get out of here."

Oberman glared at the dwarf. "You keep poor company, Herr Spiegel. This place is sacred to our Society. That dwarf profanes it. He is unwelcome."

Viktor licked his lips. He felt a little thrill that shamed him for a heartbeat; it was almost like being back in the war. "You don't want *him* here?" It felt good to be so sure of something for once. And he was sure that whatever was happening in this room, it was wrong. "Well, guess what? We're *both* putting a stop to whatever the hell is going on down here."

"You are welcome, Viktor, because you are deserving. Because your blood holds the strength of a dragon. This runt is a filthy animal, tainted by the Tinker's Well, his precious Crucible. In short," Oberman grinned at his own pun, "he is not one of us."

What Viktor disliked most about this man was how he made him think about his sweet oma…and about himself. Really, he was fine with dwarves, he had just never known one all that well. And his oma would never have supported the sick shit going on in this laboratory.

"I'm not going to let you turn me into some monster. I came here to cure my tumor, not make it worse."

Oberman removed his apron as Viktor reached the bottom of the stairs. "Viktor," he said. "We are more alike than you want to admit." The doctor peeled off his gloves with an air of melodrama, unveiling glossy, red scaled hands that ended in wicked talons. Viktor and Lanigan froze, shocked as Oberman pulled up his sleeves to display the dragon scales which covered his arms.

Viktor's mouth hung open. He had never seen a tumorling with so much...tumor. He had always thought someone would be dead by the time it got that bad. Well, at least they'd be completely mad. Though, looking around that wasn't so far off. Shocked and honestly a little intrigued, Viktor edged down the stairs and crossed the floor toward Oberman and his assistants.

Oberman held out his arms to either side and his cronies bowed. "Viktor, you are not becoming a monster. You are becoming a dragon. A true dragon, like me. Your blood gives you the right, no, the responsibility to be more than just a man. We are above the ordinary. We are greatness made flesh."

Viktor shook his head. "Honestly, you look like you forgot to wear oven mitts." He turned to one of Oberman's assistants and clubbed him over the head. The man crumpled into a boneless heap. Viktor spun on the other, thinking to clout him, too, but the orderly was ready. With superhuman agility he darted out of reach. The man's skin rippled as he began to dragonshape. Scales erupted over his cheeks and forehead and his eyes seethed with red light.

"Behind you!" Lanigan shouted.

Viktor turned as a rag wetted with a caustic smelling chemical clamped over his mouth.

V iktor awoke with a pounding headache. He was strapped to a cot in one of the dungeon cells, the soft murmur of the giant tumorling's gibberish filtering in from the next room.

"Hello?" Viktor called. "Is anyone out there?"

He struggled against the leather belts holding him down but couldn't budge them. He went still, listening to the tumorling babble.

"Lanigan?" Viktor shouted. "Are you there?"

Fear set in. Fear that he would be trapped here. That Oberman would conduct whatever ghoulish experiments had broken the giant's mind on him next. He had come here to escape that fate and now he was doomed to it. Doomed to sprout scales and claws and wings. To go insane and die a sick and confused, like his grandfather. Viktor broke out in a sweat. He fought a wave of panic. It was as though the room was filling with water and he was about to drown.

He had to get out of here. He couldn't end up like that. But, of course, there *was* a way. He could feel the lingering connection to the Dragon Well like the taste of sugar on his lips. It was a paradox. He could open himself to the Dragon's might and break his bonds. The idea set his heart to pounding. Of course, calling the power would only make things worse. It would only speed his tumor's growth.

But a voice inside him scoffed at his worry. After all, what choice did he have? Without the Well he was powerless. He was doomed to torture and experimentation. Doomed to madness. The only sensible thing to do was open himself to the Dragon Well now, to escape, and after that to never call on the power again.

He didn't think about it long. Truth was he was glad to have a reason. Viktor opened himself, let the fire sear its bright path through his veins. And with his newfound strength, he snapped the leather cuffs restraining him. Basking in the glow of his power, Viktor indulged himself, savoring the heady feel of the Dragon's glory. Finally, he cut himself off from the flow.

Viktor shivered, noticing for the first time the chill in the air.

The veins in his left arm still burned, and the flesh around his tumor felt like one of the damned rashes Dieter was always complaining about after leave. He pulled back his sleeve, half expecting to find more dragon scales spreading out from his tumor. But it remained a blotch of three scales, no further hint of the cancerous transformation awaiting him.

Viktor removed the torn cuffs from his wrists and bent forward, unbuckling his ankle restraints. He stood, wincing at the pins and needles he felt in his legs. When he recovered, he realized the door was locked.

"Sweet Saints. I'm cursed."

He banged his shoulder against it, worried one of the guards would hear, but with no other way out, he had to risk it. Unfortunately, the lock held firm. He was trapped.

Well...not exactly. He still had access to the Well. Things were no different than a moment ago. Though he felt a little foolish about his previous resolution to use the Well just the once, he really didn't have much choice. He would use it to break the door open *and then* he would stop. It was better than being trapped in here.

Resolving to touch the Dragon Well one last time, he called its power. The Might of Dryxa surged through him. It felt like he had drunk ten pots of Schmidt's tea. He barged into the door with his shoulder, knocking it off its hinges, and stood panting over its wreckage, savoring the retreating caress of the Dragon Well.

Viktor retrieved the candle from his cell and brought it with him as he began his search for Doktor Lanigan. He crept down the corridor, following the sound of the dwarf's snoring to a cell at the far end of the hall. Knowing Oberman's opinion of dwarves, Viktor was more than a little worried for Lanigan's fate. Sure, the little fellow did nothing but complain and point out Viktor's mistakes, but to be honest, the ornery little bastard was the only one Viktor could really trust. He slid open the iron bolt and entered the cell. Inside, Viktor found Lanigan lying on his back on a straw mattress, snoring. Viktor shook him awake.

The dwarf punched him on the shoulder. "For fuck's sake, lad. Do not startle me like that. You nearly stopped my bleedin' heart."

Viktor offered his hand to help the dwarf up but Lanigan slapped it away. The doctor swung his legs over the side of the bed, but they didn't quite reach the floor.

"Aww," said Viktor.

Lanigan made a rude gesture and hopped down, following him out of the cell. Viktor turned right, headed back toward the surface.

"Wait," said Lanigan. "Let's have a snoop."

"We already did that," said Viktor. "That's how we got caught."

"Before they put me under, I was listening to these idiots wagging their tongues. It was like they didn't think I could hear them." Lanigan tugged at his collar. "Or maybe they just thought it didn't matter cause I'd not have the chance to do much about it."

"And?"

Lanigan balled his fists. "And Oberman is gone. He got some letter and was off like a bee-stung mule. That bugger sounded ready to piss himself he was so worked up."

"Worked up about what?"

"I only know what I overheard. One of his confederates wrote to tell him they'd found something, and next thing you know Oberman was so excited he was rushing out the door."

"All the better for us to sneak off."

"I am telling you, laddie, just the thought of whatever that letter said makes the hairs on my neck quiver. It's trouble with a capital T."

Viktor stood in the hallway, arms folded. His natural reaction was to say no to "a snoop," just to get a rise out of Lanigan. But his good humor vanished at the thought of Oberman. That son of a bitch. He was just another snake oil salesman, promising him a cure and instead making it all worse. Maybe they could find some evidence here and give it to the local sheriff or something. He liked the idea of sticking his finger in the bastard's eye.

"All right," said Viktor, holding up his index finger to note his conditions. "But we've got to make it quick, and after that I'm done. I'm going home."

"Suit yourself." Lanigan rubbed his hands together. "He had a desk in that laboratory down there. Let's have a peek."

They headed back down the dim, underground corridor, and turned the corner to the new door at the end of the hall. Despite the dwarf's confidence, Viktor listened at the threshold for a minute until he was convinced that the lab was abandoned.

He pushed open the door to the laboratory. Viktor turned on the gas lamps and looked around the dungeon to be absolutely certain they were alone.

But they weren't.

Viktor cringed at the hapless deformities suspended in the water tanks. He stood in front of one tank which held a demonic tumorling. With its shriveled wings and twisted horns, it was eerily like how he had always pictured his grandfather. The tumorling stirred and a cascade of bubbles leaked from the apparatus strapped to its face. Viktor flinched.

"Over here," said Lanigan, sifting through the contents of Oberman's desk.

Viktor retreated from the tanks and walked over to join Lanigan as he combed through the stack of papers. They skimmed through the documents in silence until Viktor found an open envelope containing a letter written on expensive paper that smelled faintly of cologne.

"'My dear colleague,'" he read aloud. "'It is with great...ex-ex-exuberance that I write to inform the Society of my discovery. That locale that we have discussed has been unearthed. But the import of its discovery is no mere footnote of arc-arc-uh...'"

Lanigan snatched the letter out of Viktor's hands. "Oh for pity's sake, let me read it. Don't tax that lump of yours."

Viktor's cheeks burned, but before he could voice the zinger on the tip of his tongue the dwarf started reading the letter aloud.

"'But the import of its discovery is no mere footnote of archaeology.'" The dwarf looked up. "That's when scholars dig up old cities and tombs and such."

"I know that," Viktor snapped.

"Mmhmm." Lanigan continued reading. "'I can feel the thrum of Dragon Song within. Dare we dream that the relics inside have the power to assert control over the tumoring process? In my blood, I know this is true. With this discovery, I believe we are close to triggering a mass tumoring event. A New Awakening is at hand. This is the beginning of everything we have worked for, everything we have imagined. The mirror is here. After all of our searching. We only need to find a way in. Come at once, doctor; by the time you arrive the excavation will be nearly complete.'"

"The Awakening. My oma used to tell stories about it when I was a kid. When men grew so wicked that a plague of tumorlings swept across the land."

"Cheery sort, that grandma of yours."

"Is the letter signed?" Viktor asked.

The dwarf shook his head. "Let me see the envelope." Viktor handed it over. "This stamp, I recognize this building. It's the Tower of Tomes. It's at the university in Dannbridge."

"Like, in Westonshire, across the channel?"

"Do you know another Dannbridge?"

"Probably there is." Viktor folded his arms. "What was that about a mirror? The letter made it sound like that could cure me."

"Sounds a bit optimistic."

"Complete control of the tumoring process. If these guys are willing to go through all of this," Viktor gestured around at the tanks full of tumorlings. He shrugged. "I don't know. Maybe there really is a cure."

"Sounds more like they're going to make more tumorlings than fix the ones we've got."

"We're going to find that mirror."

A gust of a wind cut their argument short. They turned to look at the door and saw the torches in the hallway guttering.

"Someone's coming," said Viktor. "We should get out of here. We have to find that mirror."

"Don't get ahead of yourself, lunkhead." Lanigan eyed the exit. "Uh, after you."

Viktor was getting a little tired of Lanigan's barbs. "How very brave of you. I'm not your bodyguard, you know."

The dwarf put his hands on his hips and sighed. "No, it's probably better for you to think of yourself as a particularly dense skull."

"What?" Viktor cocked his head. "Oh, you're the brains. Then we are royally—"

"Just go."

8

Devin pressed a silver coin into the bouncer's calloused hand and headed backstage. He passed through a hallway decorated by mounted rapiers and the painted masks of former champions. Brass sconces with lit candles alternated with these displays, though several of the candles had gone out, lending an ominous mood to the passage. At the end, Devin found a door marked #3. He wiped his sweaty palms on his pantaloons, knocked, and entered.

Inside, a shirtless man with his face painted like a tiger was doing the splits.

The sight triggered some faint waft of déjà vu, but Devin pushed aside the orgies of yesteryear to focus on today.

Despite the clandestine nature of his visit Devin took a moment to marvel at Neville's flexibility. Alas, he could only admire the duelist's physique for a single fluttery heartbeat before his nerves kicked in, his sour stomach threatening a return to the arena's disgusting commode. "Neville, my good man. You look positively fabulous!"

The fighter looked up from his stretch, his anxiety comically childlike behind the tiger stripes painted on his cheeks. "Shut the door, Thistleby. Did anyone see you come in?"

It was just like *The Three Jewels of Camford*, Devin told himself. Lord Jasper would know what to say. "Relax, Neville." Devin closed the door behind him and donned his most confident smile. "I'm hardly a stranger around here. Nothing out of the ordinary."

Neville stood up and made his way over to a mannequin wearing a tiger-striped tunic. He stripped the costume off the dummy and pulled it on over his head, careful not smudge his painted face. Sulking over to a full-length mirror in the corner, the fighter stared at his reflection. "I'm not sure this is a good idea."

"It was your idea, Neville. Don't go getting cold feet now." Devin whisked up beside him and made eye contact in the mirror.

Neville turned away and brooded on his answer. "I've never done something like this."

"Neither have I. And that's why it will work. No one will suspect that Neville the Needle and the son of a Quorumite conspired to fix a fight. They'll never see it coming."

Neville stared back, his handsome face twisting in cowardly contortions. "It's a bad idea, Devin. The more I think about it, the more it ends tragically. Maybe a lord's son can get away with this sort of thing, but I don't want to get caught between Oscar Red Sleeves and your father. It's not too late for us to pretend this never happened."

Three Saints! The man was a chicken-shit. Hardly the tiger he affected for the crowds. "Father has nothing to do with this, and Oscar Red Sleeves will never know. And *it is* too late, Neville. I've already placed my bet." This was not, strictly speaking, true, but there was no reason Neville would know.

The duelist looked stricken, sullen resignation casting an exaggerated frown on his face. "Do you have any idea what the Red Sleeves will do to us if they find out?"

"Neville, they won't. And you know I have connections." Devin smiled, a little worried it might look as fragile as it felt. He pulled a coin purse off his belt and tossed the bribe to Neville. If this didn't work, he'd be flat broke. Or near enough. Not *broke* broke, but of course he needed to visit the tailor, and renting a decent flat wouldn't be cheap. It was embarrassing having to sleep in Thomas' guest house. *Saints*, he thought, *imagine being* broke *broke*.

Devin shivered.

It was fine. In an hour, he'd have enough coin to bankroll a damned mansion on the Gilded Shelf. As long as this sniveler didn't go flaccid the minute he took out his sword. "Neville, you came to me in a bad way. You. Came. To me. That mistress of yours is getting expensive, right?"

"What? No, mother needs surgery."

"Right, I knew it was something like that. Well, you can't chicken out now."

"Between the Red Sleeves and the Thistlebys, if something goes wrong…I just don't want to do this anymore. Maybe you aren't acquainted with the Red Sleeves as well as you think. They're right vicious bastards. I've even heard rumors they're in bed with that tumorling witch, Black Lung. You might be used to enemies like that, Thistleby, but I'm not."

"Neville, old chum, it's too late for quibbling. Your plan is going to work. Just don't lose your nerve." When Neville didn't relent, Devin held out his hand and motioned for his coin purse. "Fine, give me my money back; that mistress of yours will just have to live without the finer things."

"It's for my mother!"

"That's the spirit, Neville. For your mother! Good." Devin nodded once. "We're in agreement. Neville the Needle loses in the second round. Tough break. This is just the deposit, Neville. When I win, I'll triple that." Neville paled. "You all right? You look like you're about to puke. Neville, look at me. *Do not* use the public commode, it's ghastly. And of course, you can't back out now, old boy. They'll kill me if I lose…or rather, if you win."

Neville nodded. "Fine. Down in the second. I've got it."

Devin fetched the duelist's rapier and helped Neville clip on the tiger ears. The final outfit wasn't the best he'd seen in the arena, but better than some. The ears looked a mite silly, or maybe it was Neville's pouty expression. But Devin judged it a good time for a white lie. "You look fierce, Neville. Like a real tiger. Are you ready?"

"Yes. Just let me be alone. I have to psych myself up for the fight."

Devin looked at the tiger costume one last time, suppressing a smirk. "Okay, I'm leaving. Next time I see you you'll be so rich you'll have to psych yourself up to count all the money I bring with."

Neville turned away to finish applying the tiger makeup. Devin clucked; he could at least have *acknowledged* Devin's joke. In the third Lord Jasper novel the dwarven guild master never laughed at Jasper's one-liners. And everyone knew how *that* ended.

Devin let himself out.

The arena colonnade bustled with spectators. Sunlight shone through the pillars, casting shadows over the crowd. Men in frayed waistcoats and knee-length britches and women in petticoats queued for entry to the general seats. Banners hung from pillars, celebrating the animal spirits and ancient heroes represented in the fighters' costumes. Hawkers plied the crowd, selling skewered meats, candied nuts, and tankards of ale. An urchin missing a leg sat in the middle of the thoroughfare holding out his hat for alms.

"There you are!" Devin's friend Thomas approached, toting a wooden mug in each hand. He wore an immaculate suit with an embroidered vest and ruffled shirt. His easy smile instantly settled Devin's nerves. Thomas' emerald eyes lit up in faux outrage, but of course he was having the time of his life slumming with Devin. "This is an absolute travesty. I had to pay an entire farthing for this wine and it came in mugs. Mugs! I understand that it's Tyrant Fall but honestly, at those prices, I'd expect a sommelier. At least a bloody goblet."

Devin held out a hand to accept a mug. "You're filthy rich, Thomas. Think of it as a patrician's largesse. That filthy wine hawker probably has a hut full of waifs to feed."

Thomas smiled, his white teeth gleaming under his whisper-thin mustache. He pulled back the proffered wine as Devin reached for it. "No, sir. These are both for me."

"Come off it. I need a drink. And now I'm penniless. I can't afford these festival prices, even to support the wine merchant's hungry brood."

Thomas' smile dropped. "You did it, didn't you?"

"Halfway there."

"Devin, I want you to understand that I love you despite what an utter fucking imbecile you are. So when I tell you that you're going to get yourself killed, know that I'm doing it out of love."

"Oh my." Devin covered his mouth in mock scandal. "You're in a dramatic mood today."

"Look, Devin, I know you're accustomed to your father tidying up your messes."

"Ouch."

"But even if you weren't on the outs with him, this would be going too far. These people are savages. They'll slit your throat if they find out. And that is no exaggeration. They will hold you down and drag some filthy knife that probably just cleaned a fish across your neck. I mean it, Devin. I have a bad feeling about this."

Devin waved away Thomas' tedious fussing. "You and your feelings. They won't find out. You, me, and Neville are the only ones who know. It's fine."

"You're awfully cavalier about this."

"I'm cavalier about everything, my boy." Devin quirked his eyebrow, not letting on that he was suddenly self-conscious about his as yet unplucked brow.

"Quite so. And that's the problem."

"I'll call it all off if you give me that wine."

Thomas scoffed but held out the mug.

Devin sipped the wine, frowning. "Hmm, no, I take it back. Tastes like someone dropped a bit of cheese in it."

"I know."

"Do you think it's poison? In one of the Lord Jasper novels, the son of a cheesemonger tries to poison Lord Jasper because he tumbled the milkmaid and the cheesemonger was jealous. Can you imagine a cheesemonger making love?"

"I'm afraid you've lost me. You know I don't read those dreadful novels."

"We'll have to renegotiate the price of this wine. Give me a coin. I really am broke." Devin squeezed Thomas' knee. "It's for a good cause."

Looking skeptical but entertained, Thomas dug into his purse for a silver coin. With it, Devin bought a skewer of what was purportedly goat, though with these people one could never tell. Best case scenario, Devin thought, goat. He walked over and offered the meat to the urchin begging nearby. "Fortune look not unkindly today," he whispered.

The urchin scowled at him. "Fuck does that mean? I'll not be sucking your cock."

Devin recoiled. "As if I'd let a filthy little wretch like you near Sir Baldwin."

"Wow," said Thomas, cringing by way of apology to the beggar. "That was such a touching gesture, Devin. Let's take our seats before he finishes the goat and comes at you with the skewer."

"Honestly, you try to be nice to these people." Devin's rueful smile vanished. "There's one more thing I have to do first. Go get us a spot and I'll catch up."

Thomas frowned but kept his mouth shut. He'd always liked that about Thomas. He was the rational one in their…friendship. The voice of reason. But he didn't try to control Devin. When he was set on something, Thomas just shook his head and sat back to watch the show.

Devin trotted down a flight of stone steps to where the Red Sleeves bookie operated. It was a private area, almost a cantina, with sun-bleached wooden tables set up overlooking the arena floor. At the back corner, a muscular man with red tattoos and a shaved head held court. Devin ducked past and made for a table on the far side of the patio where an oily-looking fellow with similar tattoos smiled at his approach. "Well, if it ain't his fancy lordship, Devin Thistleby."

"Oran, my good man, just the chap I wanted to see." Devin pulled out a chair.

"I was beginning to wonder if you were still in jail after the guild job went bad. Oscar isn't happy with you, you know."

"Oh, that?" Devin waved it off. "A bit of bad luck. But I've got just the inside scoop to make it up to him. Might sway the odds. Maybe that will cheer the ornery bastard up."

"Careful," said Oran, picking at a stubborn bit of food between his front teeth. "Let's hear it."

"First, my wager." Devin grinned, trying not to show how much he needed it.

"Coin?"

"Credit. But you know I'm good for it."

The bookie finally got a shred of meat out from between his teeth. He admired it for a moment before flicking it away. "Fine, credit it is."

"And I want to double my usual bet."

Oran cocked his head. "Must be some good dirt."

"Are we agreed?"

Oran craned his neck to see if Oscar Red Sleeves was looking his way, then shrugged. "I suppose we can arrange that."

"Good. That's two thousand on Gabriella Iovani in the last bout."

"I thought you were friends with Neville. Betting against your friends now, are you?"

The truth was a touch complicated. "I got him stupendously drunk last night. I just saw him throw up in his dressing room."

"Is that a fact?"

Neville's prefight ritual was always the same. He stayed home with his mother and she fried him a whole chicken, so he knew for a fact that Neville hadn't gone out in public.

"He had never tried a Continental Creme before. My good friend Thomas is something of a cocktail afficionado. The drinks got wilder and wilder as the night went on. I saw him drinking wine with hot sauce and lemon zest by the end; he called it a Bloodfire Tipple. Smelled awful."

Oran shrugged. "I'd try it."

"Absolute dog piss, but this morning there is no denying the hangover. He was shouting at the birds to shut the fuck up. The birds!"

"All right, Devin. Thanks for the tip."

Devin turned to leave, nearly running face first into the muscled chest of Oscar Red Sleeves. The gangster's head was shaved to hide his balding, but the stubble was growing back. Three sets of gold earrings studded his lobes, and red tattoos were scrawled thick on his hands and arms, creeping up his neck. He smiled, revealing decidedly shabby teeth.

"A shame about the guild job." Oscar laced his fingers together in a threatening display of patience. "Your arrest seems to have gotten you in quite a pickle with Daddy. How did you cock it up?"

A pair of Oscar's hired muscle waited just out of ear shot. One a squat, short man wearing a long leather coat and the other an eye-catching woman. She wore a black jacket with gold buttons that might have been fashionable last spring. It accented her blond hair but those buttons were dreadfully out of date. She watched Devin from across the room. He supposed she was pretty, and more than a little dangerous. No doubt she would be driving Devin to distraction, if that was his cup of tea.

Devin bit back a little sass and took a deep breath before speaking. "Well, the information you gave…I mean…our information was wrong. There were extra guards suddenly. I'm not sure what happened but—"

"Let me stop you there, Mr. Thistleby." Oscar leaned closer, until a waft of his wine breath hit Devin's nose. "I like you. I do. But you messed up. As a professional…" Oscar slapped his chest with both hands. "…If I don't hold you accountable, every scumbag in the city will try to take advantage of me. I have to do what I have to do. You messed up. Plain and simple. You took an easy job and you cocked it up. Now you owe me."

Devin managed to keep his mouth shut. He wanted to tell this thug to take his horrible breath and go sit with the other plebs, but that bravado might have gotten Devin's fingers stomped on. So, he decided for once, that silence might be the wiser course. Oscar probably didn't have the balls to kill a Quorumite's son, disinherited or not, but he might do the bit with the fingers. The little blond tart behind him took a loud bite of her apple.

"Good," said Oscar. "I think we're on the same page. This little tip on the fight is a nice gesture, might make a few extra coins shaving the odds, but it's just a gesture, mind you. We'll need something a little more concrete. We'll talk more after the fight."

Oscar headed back toward his table in the corner and his goons followed from their lookout positions. The woman pushed off the wall and sauntered past. She tossed the rest of her apple to Devin as she strutted by. "Well, ain't you neck deep in shit, your lordship."

He looked down at the apple he'd caught and gagged. "What year does she think it is?" Devin clucked to himself. "Bless her heart...but gold buttons?"

He threw the apple in a rubbish bin and set off in search of where Thomas was saving his seat.

9

Viktor and Lanigan slept one fitful night in the forest, huddled together as the chorus of birdsong announced the approach of morning. Viktor wasn't sure which was worse, the scything wind, the damp ground, or Lanigan's constant carping and warnings not to get "fresh."

A downpour began before the veiled sun peeked its head over the horizon. It hadn't awakened them per se, as the nearest to sleep they had achieved was a miserable doze, but the rain had certainly added to their woebegone mood. They trudged south, toward the town of Dunnkettle, skirting the only road that led away from the sanitarium.

Viktor wished he had never come to this place. His hopes had gotten the better of him again. It was foolish to believe that some doctor could make everything right. All he had to do was set aside everything in his life and move to a ruined fortress in the wilderness. Not that the life he'd left behind was anything to crow about.

It had been over three years since the war ended, and ever since this damn tumor appeared, his life had just felt wrong. In a way, he was stuck. He couldn't go back and he couldn't go forward. It felt like he was trapped in someone else's life. In *his* life he would have gone home after the war to a hero's welcome. It would have been a good life, laughing with friends in the beer hall, meeting pretty girls, not sleeping in the woods with a dwarf, not being looked at by everyone like some kind of deviant, like trash. He would have found a wife, maybe not Karla, but a beauty in her own right, a good mother, funny, and she would have learned his mother's strudel recipe. Maybe he'd have opened his own restaurant someday.

Anything was better than a life spent staring in horror at the scales creeping up his arm.

The dwarf's incessant stream of complaints weren't helping his mood, either. He would have thought dwarves were made of sterner stuff, but Doktor Lanigan whined about the rain, about his sore feet, about how fast Viktor was walking. It was exhausting.

"Enough!" Viktor finally interrupted his tirade about the mud. "I get it. You'd think you'd never been in the rain before."

"For two days straight? I have not."

"Do you want me to carry you?"

The proposal quieted the dwarf, though it appeared not to have improved his mood.

"Look." Viktor pointed skyward where a column of chimney smoke rose through a break in the tree line.

"At last," said Lanigan. "Civilization."

"I'm going straight to the pub. I'm going to order a bowl of stew as big as your head. Come on, I'll buy you a pint."

"Are you quite mad, son? We can't just go waltzing in there. We've got to be careful. Some of Oberman's goons could be waiting for us."

The dwarf's observation deflated Viktor. "But I'm starving."

"Let's just watch our backsides for a bit longer, eh?"

Viktor wanted to argue. He was hungry. And sore. And soaking wet. But Lanigan was right.

"Okay, you wait here. I'll scout the village. A dwarf will stick out more than if I just go alone."

Doktor Lanigan sighed, nodding his agreement. "I know it goes against your nature but try not to do anything stupid."

"Ha, ha."

"I'll circle around and wait for you in that copse of trees on the far hill."

"Fine." Viktor's stomach growled.

Lanigan waggled his finger. "Don't do anything stupid."

"You already said that."

"I thought you might have forgotten by now."

"Careful, I might leave you alone out here."

"Don't threaten me with a good time, laddie."

"I've had it up to here with you." Viktor held his hand about waist high. Lanigan snorted and Viktor took it as a win.

There wasn't much to the village. A few outlying fields and farmhouses before the town proper. A score of houses all cut from rough lumber and painted with whitewash lined a single muddy street. At the center of town a few larger wooden structures surrounded a village green.

Viktor pulled his hood down over his face. As miserable as the rainstorm was, it provided a good reason to cover up, and he was grudgingly grateful for it now.

Viktor chose a route through the outer homes, pausing here and there to stop and survey his surroundings. A smattering of villagers scurried about their business, but they were too intent on getting out of the rain to pay him any mind. Viktor made his way to the main street.

A covered boardwalk ran along the storefronts on the west side of the road, so he crossed the street to get out of the rain. He left his hood up, wary of unwanted attention. Ahead, a sign hung above the door to a tavern, painted with the likeness of a mermaid holding a tankard of ale in each hand. He very much wanted to stop in, especially considering the smell of fried pork wafting from the doorway. His stomach protested, but the dwarf was right: reconnaissance first.

Viktor forced himself past the tavern. Continuing along the boardwalk, he reached the constabulary. He wondered what the likelihood of getting help would be. Between himself and Doktor Lanigan, surely the constable would have to listen to their story. Maybe. Or maybe Oberman had bribed him, or worse, maybe the constable was one of Oberman's fanatics.

You're getting paranoid, Viktor, he told himself. The constable was there to stop crimes like Oberman was committing. It was his duty. Viktor weighed his options, instinct screaming at him to not go inside, while another part of him whispered that the constable could put an end to this whole nightmare and arrest Oberman. It was then that Viktor noticed the "wanted" poster hanging beside the door. It had pretty good sketches of both of them, though the artist had exaggerated the squareness of Viktor's jaw.

"Wanted for Murder," it read.

Well, shit.

That decided that. The dwindling possibility of stew was the saddest part of the whole thing. What now? They needed to get far away from there. That much was certain.

The boardwalk creaked as a heavyset man stumbled out of the tavern behind him. Viktor turned away and headed down the block.

"Martin," the drunk bellowed. "Is that you? You owe me a silver mark, you cheap asshole."

Viktor kept moving, hoping the guy would give up.

"Hey! I'm talking to you, you cheap bastard."

Afraid the drunk would draw undue attention, Viktor turned so the man could see him. "Wrong guy."

The drunkard squinted at him. He toddled forward a few steps and set his hand against the door of the constabulary for balance. "I don't know you."

"Nope." Viktor turned away, hoping that was the end of the conversation.

"I know everyone in Dunnkettle." Suspicion darkened his tone. Viktor cringed as the drunk pieced it together. "You're one of them loonies from the sanitarium. The murderer. A god damn tumor-ling." He spat into the mud.

"Here's that mark I owe you." Viktor tossed him a coin and noted the man's confusion as his eyes struggled to trace its path through the air. He went to catch it and missed.

Viktor crow-hopped forward and landed a haymaker on the drunk's stubbled chin. The coin clattered across the boardwalk and rolled through a crack in the planks as Viktor caught the drunk from falling. He scoped around, unsure of what to do with the uncon-scious man. Well, he was a drunk after all. Viktor shrugged, pleased with his reasoning. He lowered the sot to the ground and dumped him in a heap.

At the far end of the street he discovered a stable, but the groom was nowhere to be found. Viktor stuffed a handful of oats from a feed bag in his mouth. Dry and slightly moldy as it was, his belly rejoiced.

Things were looking up, he told himself as he saddled a horse. But Dannbridge was far away, and a horse wouldn't carry him across the channel. No, Viktor couldn't let his worry take root, he just had to follow the letter, follow Oberman. How some magic mirror could cure his tumor Viktor couldn't even imagine. Let the dwarf piss and moan. Viktor on the other hand…had…had…had lost his train of thought.

"Saints, I need a nap." Viktor ate another musty mouthful of oats and led his stolen horse out of the stable. "And you need a name, big fella." He patted the horse's rump. "How about Lanigan."

10

I zola looked over her shoulder to make sure no one was watching.

Perched atop a sliding ladder in the library, she pushed off, riding down the rail to the end of the aisle with a little squeak of delight.

She couldn't help herself, and really why would she want to? This was the only library on campus with sliding ladders. It was basically designed for this. Izola fancied it was plain wrong to let them languish in disuse. Maybe she should be more serious, act like a proper professor, even if she wasn't one quite yet. Seers knew, she was up against it. The thesis review for her tenure application took place in three days.

It was a sobering thought. Three days until her ex-husband humiliated her. Three days until she lost her teaching position. Three days until she was evicted.

The idea that Logan had somehow connived his way onto her thesis review board wiped the grin from her face. She could almost smell his overpowering cologne and see the smirk on his face. It was an absurd conflict of interest. She wondered idly if she hadn't changed her name back to Scrivani, would this have still happened? But, of course, it wasn't an oversight. It was petty revenge.

Izola pushed her spectacles up the bridge of her button nose and inspected the leather-bound spines on the top shelf with grim focus. She needed something ironclad to defend her theories or her ex-husband would gleefully trash her thesis before the other professors.

What an absurd predicament.

Not for the first time, Izola chided herself for falling for the dubious charms of Logan Blythe. She had been a teenager of course, a stupid, starry-eyed girl, manipulated by a dashing young professor. They had met in the shadow of the Tower of Tomes, and she had let the romantic air conjure a man from the stories in her head. True, he was handsome and intelligent, but she had ignored the nagging voice in the back of her mind. She had turned a blind eye to his flirtations, his intellectual laziness. She'd wanted to see the best in him and so she had. For all of her gifts, she had not foreseen the outcome, which was so obvious in retrospect. She'd given up her career in academia to raise their child, and in return he'd fucked one younger, skinnier undergraduate after another until Izola could no longer pretend that it wasn't happening.

But with Page off to school in Jarlsbeck, everything had changed. She was trying not to worry about her daughter, trying not to fret that Page would make the same mistakes she had. Izola was trying to focus on living her own life for a change. And it wasn't all bad. She almost wished she could hand Logan the divorce papers again just to see his smugness collapse into utter shock. He just couldn't believe she'd left him.

And now he was exacting his revenge.

Well, not if she could help it.

Izola went back over the titles one more time to be certain that the book she sought wasn't there. Maybe a little magic was in order. After all, what good was seerdom if you never put it to work? Izola climbed off the ladder and opened her leather satchel. She pulled out her hex book. Dipping her quill in her inkpot, she opened her book and turned to a blank page.

The tome she sought had been referenced in so many other books; she knew that if she could just find the original source, it would hold revelations about the Tyrant, prove her thesis, and wipe that smug look off Logan's face once and for all.

Maybe. Probably.

Closing her eyes, Izola opened herself to the Libram. She inhaled the scent of musty books and smiled. The Well flowed into her, bringing the detached precision she always felt when she touched the source of her magic. When her heart settled back into a steady rhythm, Izola scratched the name of the book she was after onto the empty page.

An Exhaustive History of the Early Quorum.

Izola felt a little tug on her quill, but it was just the once, and so faint that the book clearly wasn't on this shelf. She closed her hex book and huffed. Why was everything so difficult? Sometimes it seemed like there was someone out there actively working against her. Someone besides Logan, of course. He was definitely out to get her. With his charm and his dimples, he'd have half the thesis committee eating out of his hand, making snide comments about her before she even presented her evidence.

Izola stuffed her things back into her satchel and marched through the library toward the front desk, the hardwood floors creaking beneath her feet.

The University of Dannbridge had a number of libraries on campus, this one focusing on more esoteric matters and rarer volumes. Students weren't allowed to check books out from here. As a professorial candidate, she didn't, strictly speaking, have privileges in this library. But that was only a bit of bureaucratic red tape, nothing to worry about. Now, if only she could find what she was looking for.

Izola strode up to the counter, a grizzled slab of varnished oak emblazoned with hand-carved initials and ribald slogans. It looked the sort of surface she would expect to find in a pub, except that upon closer inspection its crude taunts were directed at philosophers and novelists instead of lovers and rival patrons. One such message gouged into the wood read "For a good time read *The Lady of Three Loves*." Izola grinned; it was a rather saucy tale.

A sour-mouthed old woman perched atop a stool on the other side of the desk. She had yet to look up from her work. A kerosene lamp with a green shade burned on the counter beside her. Behind the librarian a giant bank of cubbies was overstuffed with an abundance of scrolls. The antique scent of wood treated with vinegar filled the air.

Seconds ticked by without the librarian acknowledging her arrival. Eventually it passed into a delay that Izola considered rude. She cleared her throat.

The older woman took her time marking her place and finally looked up at Izola, then removed her glasses and tucked them into her breast pocket. "Was that you playing on the ladders in the history section?"

"Isn't that awful?" Izola kept her voice to a respectful whisper. "I find that so childish. This is a library, for heaven's sake."

The librarian looked decidedly skeptical at her cheeky evasion. "How can I help you, Professor?"

Perhaps they had begun on the wrong foot, but the librarian had also made a helpful assumption based on Izola's age. She was not yet a full professor, but Izola saw no reason to correct the woman by pointing out her mistake. "I am looking for a particular volume, and it isn't in its place on the shelf."

The librarian stabbed a knife into the scarred surface of the desk. Rage flashed across her face. She pulled out her spectacles again, leaving the blade quivering in the desktop. Had she been holding a knife this whole time? Where had it come from? "What is the name of the book?" the librarian demanded.

"*An…*" Izola coughed, eyes still locked on the quivering dagger. "*An Exhaustive History of the Early Quorum.*" A few questions came to mind about the sudden appearance of the knife, the stabbing part, too, of course, but the knife tidily curtailed Izola's inclination to ask them. Funny that.

The librarian turned to consult the card file behind her. She scanned the drawers, selecting one on the right, at eye level. She mounted a step stool and pulled the drawer open, fingers deftly flicking through it until she found the appropriate card. "It should be on the shelf. It was returned two weeks ago and hasn't been checked out since."

"It wasn't there."

"So you said. Most likely someone browsed it and put it back in the wrong section. Every shelf is checked once every three weeks. It'll turn up."

"What if it was stolen?"

"Unlikely. We have wards. It's here somewhere, but someone put it back on the wrong shelf."

"Assholes."

"Yes. You know the sort, always playing on the ladders and so forth."

Izola acknowledged the librarian's witticism with a tip of her head. "Which sections have been checked since then? If it's here, it should be in an unchecked section, right?"

The librarian removed her glasses again and waved them toward the right half of the library. "Sound logic. Let's see...since then, sections 8 through 27 have been sorted, but that leaves over a third of the shelves. Does that really help?"

"No," Izola admitted.

In response to Izola's silence, the librarian went back to reading her book. Izola felt a little jolt of confusion upon noting that the dagger had disappeared back into the librarian's possession. It proved a good stopping point for their conversation, so she drifted back from the desk, not wanting to turn her back on the librarian for some reason.

Izola wandered around for a while, running her hand along the book spines. Sometimes the contents of a book would jump out at her, a little flash of insight, a touch of the old Scrivani magic, but no such luck this time.

She climbed the stairs to the second floor and looked over the shelves below. She needed to find this book. Everything she had worked for was in jeopardy. To an unbiased review board, her theories about the Tyrant were well out of the mainstream, but she had rigorously supported her conclusions. Mainstream theories about Dannbridge's legendary ruler were vague at best. It was almost like no one wanted a closer look at the reign of Westonshire's most notorious historical figure. If Logan hadn't weaseled his way onto the committee, she would have felt confident that her thesis had enough scholarly merit for her to attain her tenure. But she knew Logan would not-so-subtly point to her theories about dragons and secret societies as fanciful speculation.

An idea began to nibble at her. It was a bad idea, to be sure, but it wouldn't go away.

She could practically hear her grandmother's nasal voice admonishing her not to do anything foolish, but desperate times and all that. The Scrivani women had access to the Libram in a way few others could muster. Her grandmother had told stories about tugging the strands of fate. Or more properly, Vinatelli's Web, as the manifestation was known. It was powerful magic. The sort of stuff she would have wanted Izola to use only in the direst of circumstances, but Izola knew gran would want to wipe that pompous look off Logan's face, too. And if she didn't secure her tenure, what would she do with herself? She could lose her teaching position. She could lose her housing. The more she thought about it, the more it seemed reasonable to take a risk like this.

It was a spell Izola had never tried before, and not once had her gran failed to mention the possibility of dangerous repercussions. Then again, losing your job and your home and having your smug prick of an ex-husband laugh about it was a pretty nasty repercussion, too.

It was definitely a bad idea, she decided. She ought to accept the likelihood that Logan would poke holes in her thesis. That was the wise thing to do, the mature thing, to let Logan win, not to risk something worse. But she could already see him gloating, and to wipe the look off his face, she would tempt fate. And damn the consequences.

Izola opened her hex book to a blank page and meditated on the chain of events leading from her finding the book she was after to the look of defeat she wanted to see in Logan's face. In her hex book she wrote the phrase her grandmother had taught her. "Fate is woven from the threads of will."

She sniffed, detecting the first hint of biblichor, that delicious, musty vanilla scent of old books that foretold the working of the Libram's magic. From right to left, she wrote the phrase backwards as if she were looking at it in a mirror. She let her mind drift as she wrote the phrase front to back and back to front, again and again, her quill snaking its path down to the bottom of the page. When she reached the end a sharp cramp seized her hand, twisting it into a claw. The quill fell from her grasp.

Vivid pictures raced through her mind. An overwhelming barrage of imagery flashed faster and faster, fire and death, books and symbols, faces, some strange, some familiar. All tangled in the threads of fate, each vision vanishing from her memory as soon as it was gone, until finally, the chain of events slowed and she witnessed an exhausted young man in a cheap waistcoat thumbing through an ornate volume. He tucked it on a shelf and went on to the next book in his stack.

The magic felt like pins and needles in her fingers, her lips. It made her dizzy. Izola tasted acid in her throat and coughed. The things she had seen evaporating like a fading dream. For a brief, bizarre moment, she felt as if she were caught in a spider's web, the strands clinging to her as she struggled free of the strange sensation.

Is that how the manifestation had gotten its name? Vinatelli's Web. For but a heartbeat, she could see the gossamer threads going every which way. But one was brighter than the rest.

Izola speed walked through the aisles, ignoring the librarian's scowl as she followed the strand. It faded with every step until she had to squint to make it out. The thread led Izola over to the shelves at the edge of the philosophy section. She bent down, victoriously discovering the misplaced copy of *An Exhaustive History of the Early Quorum*.

This was it! Izola sat cross-legged in the aisle and immediately began to pore over the tome. It contained concise biographies of the seven original Quorumites, the pupils of the Tyrant who had overthrown the dictator and shattered his crown into seven Shards, passing on its potent remains as emblems of rulership. But this was nothing new to her; many sources included such histories. There were a number of entries detailing specific Dragon Marks. One showed the mystic symbol for Heritage, one for Unmaking, each with detailed notes written in the Dragon Tongue. She paused on the Unmaking Mark, captivated by its destructive potential. Not that she could do anything with it, of course. Most scholars would find the inclusion of such arcanum terribly out of place in this history.

The thought only spurred her on. Izola flipped to the appendix, where she found what she was really searching for. Her heart thudded as she looked at the hand-drawn representations of the pieces of the Q. Her eyes leapt to the measurements, detailed in the description. Only a few of the Shards of the Tyrant's crown had been cataloged this way, but Izola held her breath, doing the math on her fingers.

"It's too big," she whispered. An irrepressible smile invaded her face. She cried out, "I have it!"

The librarian's shush hissed through the stacks like a gust of wind and Izola clamped down on her joy, picturing another sudden appearance of the librarian's dagger.

11

evin and Thomas perched at the rail, their seats twenty feet above the sands of the arena. Thomas held out another mug of dubious vintage for him and Devin slugged the dregs of his last round to make way for its replacement. The afternoon sun had warmed the stone bench they sat on, and the glare was now behind them, casting the stadium in glorious golden hues.

Around them, the merchants who could afford these seats hobnobbed with one another. They placed side wagers and, Devin assumed, gossiped about their sad little lives as the lower classes often did. He and Thomas stuck out like pearls in the mud, but at least they weren't the only ones complaining about the wine.

Thomas leaned in and lowered his voice. "So what's the story with your father? How did he react to your…incarceration?"

"React?" Devin shook his head. "The illustrious Archibald Thistleby doesn't react. He calculates. And it would appear that the scales have finally tipped against me. If I was a political liability before, I'll be a pariah after it gets out that I was arrested for burglary."

"Surely you're exaggerating, Devin. You don't give him enough credit. He's not an unfeeling monster." Devin stared at Thomas until he amended his evaluation. "All right, he's not an *entirely* unfeeling monster. Let the dust settle and then you can approach him again. Even if he's more concerned about politics than about you, he still cares. He'll come around. Give him time."

"He's had my whole life, Thomas. My parents aren't like yours. When you grow up with money and power, like my father did, you expect everyone to do everything you want. New rich don't understand." Thomas looked briefly miffed, but Devin ignored it. "Things don't go exactly as my father plans and he's outraged by it. Father always has to have his way."

"You grew up with money and power."

"And look how I turned out."

"*That*," said Thomas, "is an excellent point."

Trumpets blared and the crowd surged to its feet, cheering as the gate to the arena floor opened and the master of ceremonies strutted onto the sand. He wore a fool's motley: a patchwork of gold fringe, and vibrant patterns. Upon his head he sported a conical cap, the sort in which mages of olden times were often depicted. When he reached the center of the stadium, he stopped, and a hush stole over the crowd.

"Citizens of fair Dannbridge!" His voice resounded in the amphitheater. "On this beautiful day, let us put to rest all of our cares. Let us drink liberally of the cup of sport. Let us cast fortune's die. For today, we shall witness the gods clash upon the sands of this arena. Spill your coins upon this sacred ground as libations to the lords of battle.

"Behold! In our first bout, the cupbearers of the Void and Divine Wells shall clash. Let those whose skill and magic attest their virtue score the final touch!" With a mock thrust of an imaginary sword he bowed, and upon righting himself he bellowed, "To arms!"

The spectators cheered once again as the combatants took the field. The first duelist to enter was clad in black armor draped in ornamental chains. He had his face painted like a skull and pulled his blunted rapier out to salute the crowd. The master of ceremonies heralded his arrival by calling out, "Hail Ivan Vladislav, the Duelist of Death, the Vanguard of the Void!"

Thomas clapped for the fighter and shouted in Devin's ear over the booing crowd. "He must have some of that Rumavian blood of yours."

"Har har." Normally Devin could get a bit touchy about his mother's ancestry, but he allowed Thomas more latitude than most. He tipped his head to acknowledge the jibe. Devin sighed, feeling wistful, and perhaps a bit conflicted about his mother. She probably could have smoothed over this mess he'd gotten in if she hadn't gone back to her homeland. He could hardly blame her, though; Devin had lost count of his father's affairs. No use moping, he supposed. Devin dredged himself up from the doldrums and threw Thomas a cheeky grin. "I should have known you'd cheer for the foreigner. You nouveau riche are all such contrarians."

Thomas chuckled into his wine as the next fighter arrived. The woman hardly wore a stitch of clothing, just a thin woolen shift that covered a scandalously small stretch of her alabaster thighs. On her head, she wore a faux golden crown adorned with wings.

"I'm rooting for this one." Devin bobbed his eyebrow to needle Thomas.

"Lady Azaria the Undefeated, Avatar of the Sacred Well, Herald of the Divine!" shouted the fool.

As she drew her rapier, the master of ceremonies trotted off the arena floor and the trumpets' fanfare sounded. The combatants took positions opposite each other and the crowd, at least in the civilized sections where Devin and Thomas watched, took their seats.

A bell sounded and the duelists began to circle. The fighter dressed as the death avatar lunged forward, his sword darting at the woman. She parried the thrust handily and scored an easy touch by jabbing her blunted rapier into his belly. It all looked a bit sloppy to Devin. A chorus of boos echoed from the cheap seats as the crowd voiced its disapproval for the early end to the round. The woman held her sword aloft and turned to regard the mob. She spun in a circle, saluting them before she settled back into her guard stance to await the next bell.

Devin faced Thomas and rolled his eyes. "Might be a quick match."

"Maybe the death guy can talk the emcee into best of five."

"No one even cast a spell. At this rate it'll be Neville's fight before I finish my wine."

"Nervous?" Thomas asked.

"Perhaps a bit."

"I suppose it's too late to get out of it now."

Devin set his mug at his feet and wiped his sweaty hands on his pantlegs. "What else was I supposed to do? I don't have a coin to my name. I don't even have anywhere to sleep tonight. Your father is going to wonder if I keep staying over."

"You can crash at my flat in Wildflower. Though, I think the housekeeper is on holiday."

The bell signaled the start of the second round. Lady Azaria lunged forward, her rapier crackling with electricity, hoping a quick spell might end the fight immediately. But Vladislav didn't take the bait. Instead of blocking the electrified sword, he dodged out of the way and retreated until she could no longer maintain her manifestation.

The crowd cheered, anticipating more of a show than the end of the first round had promised. But Lady Azaria pressed her advantage, following up her spell for the round with a flurry of ripostes, her rapier stabbing in quick successions at her adversary's face and then body and then face again. But to his credit, this Vanguard of the Void parried with sufficient skill to prolong the fight. When his opponent relented her assault, Vladislav held his spell hand in the air, concentrating on a manifestation of his own. His fist glowed green with arcane power, but before he could get his spell off, Lady Azaria stepped forward smartly and landed another easy touch to his midsection. The bell chimed thrice to signal her victory and the crowd erupted in jeers, the cheap seats tossing rotten fruit and dumping their sour ale upon the sands.

Devin went in search of more wine as the first intermission started. It embarrassed him to have to beg a few coins off Thomas to get it, but he tried to make a joke about his predicament and Thomas was nice enough not to mention the indignity. When Devin returned to his seat, the second fight was already underway.

Devin found it difficult to focus on the duel. He kept looking over his shoulder as if he'd find Oscar Red Sleeves standing behind him with a cleaver. He tried in vain to concentrate on the arena floor and keep his mind off everything that could go wrong. But he needed money. Badly.

He wanted to be independent of his father. What a laugh. His botched burglary had managed that, if not precisely in the way he'd intended. But now he was on his own. He was broke and indebted to a thug. The only thing that perked him up was imagining that little dash of justice he'd get using Oscar's own money to placate him.

But every time Devin managed a little smugness, he pictured what his father would say if he got wind of this scheme. As if his condemnation weren't bad enough, his hypocrisy would be unbearable. After all, his father was a Quorumite. His cabal of wizards ruled the city. They didn't give a shit about laws. They were bigger crooks than Devin could ever be. They got to pretend that every bribe, every shady law they enacted was all for the greater good, instead of lining their own pockets and ensuring it was impossible for anyone else to challenge them.

Devin drifted into a hypothetical argument with his father in which he made some excellent and quite cutting points that he had failed to think of in the heat of their last quarrel. Of course, his merciless brain kept replaying the argument, supplying his father with new ammunition for his counter arguments. By the time three bells again signaled the end of the bout, Devin had worked himself into a tizzy.

Like the cock on a spinning weathervane, Thomas had clearly sensed a shift in the wind. He was always so sensitive to Devin's moods. Thomas scooted closer to Devin, but Devin was too annoyed to be comforted.

"I wouldn't have to do all of this if my father hadn't disinherited me. You know that if I could tap the Dragon Well, none of this would matter. I would be like my sister, his precious heir."

Thomas emitted a note of disgust. "Here we go again." He scooted a few inches away. "Devin, I swear on the Tyrant's broken crown, if you launch into another of your tirades, I'm going to leave. Yes, it's a shame that you haven't your father's aptitude. But he knew the risks when he married a Rumavian. Maybe someday you'll tap the Void Well."

"Saints alive, he would absolutely shit himself."

"It's simply awful he chose to pass you over. But to be fair, you haven't done the sort of things your sister has to prepare himself to rule. Can you imagine Devin Thistleby joining the army? And honestly…" Thomas grabbed Devin's forearm to emphasize his point. "Honestly, I'm so sick of your whining about it. Even if he passed you over for heir, you were still such a rich little shit you could have done just about anything. Go down to the Sink sometime and look at the beggars living down there and see if your problems don't sound ridiculous. I mean—"

Devin pulled his arm free and swilled his wine. "It was never about money, Thomas."

Thomas shook his head and turned to the fight. He muttered something but Devin couldn't hear what he said.

Neville the Needle emerged into the arena as trumpets sang and the crowd stomped its feet.

The spectators chanted. "Ne-ville! Ne-ville! Ne-ville!"

Coin rained upon the sand as the duelist slashed his rapier through the air in an impressive display of swordsmanship. He wore his complete costume, a skinned tiger's face covering the top of his head, its mangled pelt draped over his back, and tiger stripes painted on his muscular chest and his face. He wore bracers covered in tiger skin, and a necklace of teeth, presumably from a tiger, Devin reasoned, proud of his logic and then feeling instantly dumber for his pride.

He wanted to poke fun, maybe make a joke to dispel the tension, but it was too loud for Thomas to hear him, and to be fair, Neville's costume looked a little fiercer with the whole getup.

Devin's palms were sweating again. He glanced at Thomas, who gave him a sympathetic smile and then turned his attention back to the arena. The fighter stared up at him and Devin's mouth ran dry as he hoped for some subtle sign of reassurance. But the duelist's attention was torn away by the sound of trumpets announcing his opponent. A woman in green and turquoise entered the colosseum; an elaborate, oversized peacock tail fanned out behind her.

Devin and Thomas shared a look. Thomas sometimes liked to tease him by calling him "Peacock," in reference to his obvious panache. Just as he sometimes called Devin's unibrow "Jerome." A term of endearment that Devin pretended to hate. But Devin's smile was understandably a bit tense, all things considered, and his smile faded with his next breath. He turned back to the fight.

Known for the efficacy of her spells more than her bladework, Gabriella Iovani was an up-and-coming duelist looking to make the big leap to the High Games. She strutted around the sand to the adulation of the crowd, unhooked the tail, and tossed it to the ground. An attendant scurried out and carried the prop from the arena.

The master of ceremonies entered from the gate again and held up his hands for silence.

"Connoisseurs of carnage! Believers in the blade! We come now to the pinnacle of the day's entertainment. These hallowed grounds have never been graced by two finer competitors. I welcome first, the Demon of the Sands, the Rakshasa of the Arena. Heaped in glory and wading through the blood of lesser duelists, he is our reigning champion. Scream like the souls of the Abyss for Neville the Needle!"

The crowd went wild, stomping their feet and clapping their hands. They screamed and chanted his name as he stabbed his rapier into an imaginary opponent. The emcee held up his hand for silence and the cheers died.

"Now witness the glorious rise of the Seeress of Swordplay, the Oracle of Ostentation, the Peacock of Rhodenz, Gabriella Iovani!"

If the crowd had been boisterous before, its outcry swelled to a fever pitch. Men hooted and performed rude gestures as Iovani twirled, her footwork precise even as she strutted.

Trumpets sounded and the master of ceremonies backpedaled through the gate. Neville advanced and Gabriella Iovani settled into a guard position. As he closed within a blade's length, Neville lunged. Gabriella side-stepped his attack and pivoted toward his flank. She stabbed at his ribs but he deftly dodged out of the way.

They circled one another, probing with half-hearted feints. Gabriella made a show of darting in and out, of adding ornamental flourishes to the ends of her attacks. She danced around the arena, putting on a show, and Neville joined her, his rapier blurring through a flurry of attacks that brought the crowd to its feet. Their slashes and parries were almost too fast for the eye to follow. Until with a dazzling feint, Gabriella sidestepped the Needle's assault, and as he shifted his weight, unveiled her true ploy.

She began her manifestation as he teetered off balance, an indigo light shining from her eyes. It was impeccably timed, the sort of split-second diversion that separated the good duelists from the great, but Neville improvised, kicking sand in her face as he sorted out his footing. She flinched back, retreating as she blinked away the grit.

Neville never hesitated. He hustled forward as she fell back, his rapier moving with perfection to set her up for a feint that drew off her defenses and landed a simple touch to her belly. It almost looked easy.

Devin clutched his stomach, fighting a sudden urge to run to the toilet. It was only one point, he assured himself. Just to make it look good. He turned to Thomas, whose eyebrows leapt toward the sky. "It's fine," Devin said. "It's for show."

Thomas offered Devin the rest of his wine. Devin looked around and realized that he had already finished his own. "I probably shouldn't," said Devin, accepting the mug.

Neville paraded around the arena floor, slashing his foil through the air and egging the crowd on as they began to chant his name. Devin glared at the fencer, silently willing Neville to look him in the eye. But as much as Neville played to the crowd, he pointedly avoided Devin's gaze. The twisting of Devin's intestines intensified. He had once eaten a curry that felt like this.

Devin looked around, searching for the nearest lavatory, only to catch sight of one of Oscar Red Sleeves' goons leaning against a pillar near the main concourse, watching him. Devin swore.

The blare of trumpets sounded the beginning of the next round. It was Gabriella Iovani's turn to go on the offensive. But Neville's bladework proved as exemplary as his reputation. The duelists exchanged a furious salvo of attacks and parries, but the Needle demonstrated his legendary skill and footwork. At the culmination of the exchange, Neville bounced onto the balls of his feet, leaning slightly forward. But Gabriella was no fool; she took a step back from the feint, and sprung forward again.

Neville was not known for his manifestations. It was his blade that had won him fame and propelled him to the elite level of champion. But he could manage a spell or two. Yet it seemed that Iovani had not considered this possibility in the heat of their exchange. As she transferred her weight onto her back foot, Neville buried the point of his blade in the ground and a black tendril writhed forth like a snake beneath the sand. It slithered forward in a rush and ensnared her foot in a mesh of little black roots. The shock of it loosened her grip on her foil and froze her in her tracks for but a heartbeat. In that moment Neville swung his blade, swatting Gabriella's foil from her hand.

"No!" Devin shot to his feet.

Defeated, Gabriella Iovani held her arms out to either side, inviting the winning touch. With no great hurry, Neville, dipped his head, acknowledging her sportsmanship, and reached out to gently tap the tip of his rapier against her belly.

"No!" Devin leaned over the rail, cursing down at the victor. "Neville, you slug! You cheat!" But his accusations drowned in the thunderous applause.

Thomas tugged at Devin's sleeve and hissed in his ear. "We should go."

Devin tore free of his friend's grasp. "Neville! Do you hear me?" But the crowd was on its feet, cheering, and Neville was looking anywhere but at Devin.

"Devin!"

"What?" With cheeks burning, Devin swung to face his friend. Thomas merely pointed at the thug standing by the nearest exit to the concourse. Behind the ruffian, Devin spied Oscar himself approaching, the blond woman at his side. "Shit. Oh, shit. Thomas can I borrow a small fortune?"

"Absolutely not."

"Then run!" Devin shoved past a heavy-set man at the end of their row. The unfortunate spectator spilled wine down his shirt. He threw his now empty mug at Devin, which bounced off the back of his head. Devin cursed, rubbing the welt, but he didn't dare slow down.

The general exodus of the crowd created a confusion that gave them a chance to escape, but looking back over his shoulder, Devin spied Oscar's thugs closing in. They elbowed their way through the crowd, jostling against the flow until, after a barked command from Oscar, they drew their blades and a path "magically" opened up before them.

"This way!" Devin ran up to a railing and hopped over. Thomas jumped it as one of Oscar's thugs made a grab for him. The Red Sleeve got hold of the hem of Thomas' coat and hauled him up short. Devin skidded to a halt and pivoted. He slapped Thomas' attacker in the face. The thug looked so shocked he let go of Thomas' coattail.

"Oh my god, you hit him!" Thomas squealed with delight as they ran off.

The pair pushed their way through the crowded concourse, past the grand colonnade and down the front steps of the colosseum. Oscar and the woman ran after them, red-faced and shouting.

"This way!" Devin turned down an alley teeming with flies and piles of rubbish.

Devin looked back to find Oscar and the blonde enter the alley behind them. He darted past a wino who reached drunkenly toward him. "Benny," cried the bum. "Give us a kiss!"

Giddy with adrenaline, Devin blew him one, almost losing his wig in the process. He stumbled out of the alley onto a nearby street lined with kiosks and street vendors. At the end of the block, a small crowd in drab clothing had gathered around an orator standing on the steps leading up to a brick building. Gargoyles glared down from the gabled roof. Devin and Thomas charged through the group, but the blonde had nearly closed the distance, her knife swishing through the air behind them.

"The divine are vessels of infinite mercy——" Devin plowed through the dour congregation, interrupting the orator's speech. "Hey! Watch it, cocksucker!"

With the blonde hot on his heels, Thomas grabbed hold of a turnip cart and tipped it over in her path. The gangster stepped on one of the turnips and her ankle gave out. She tumbled to the ground and cursed in pain as she sprawled over a bed of rolling vegetables.

"Nice one!"

Just as Devin thought they had escaped the Red Sleeves, Oscar and the third thug appeared at the far end of the block, having circled around. Her cursing growing louder and frankly more personal, the blonde pushed herself to her feet. She collected her knife and made a lewd gesture with it.

Devin pulled up short as Oscar and his goon fanned out to hem them in. He turned to the woman and smiled. "Sorry about that. Still friends?"

She pantomimed sliding the knife across her throat and winked at him.

"Fair enough."

Thomas tapped him on the shoulder and pointedly looked past Devin to another alley.

They made a break for it. The three Red Sleeves converged, a dozen paces behind them now. Devin and Thomas sped through the alley, tipping over crates of garbage until they reached the edge of a canal.

Devin looked right and left, searching for a way to cross, but the buildings were so close to the water they couldn't even run along the shoreline. A gondolier smoking a long-stemmed pipe sat atop a set of stone steps that descended into the water. Devin dashed across the bank of the canal to where his gondola was beached. He jumped in, Thomas right behind him as the gondolier leapt to his feet and cried out. "Oi! That's my boat."

Devin bent to the hull to pick up the gondolier's pole. He shoved off, moving deeper into the water as the gangsters emerged from the alley.

Devin and Thomas shared a look, sweaty, their hearts thumping. Devin smiled. "I haven't had a workout like that since the last time your cousin was in town."

Thomas shook his head, trying to repress a smile. "You'll wish that goon had gotten a hold of you when I'm done with you."

Oscar Red Sleeves cupped his hands to his mouth and shouted. "Devin Thistleby! You're a dead man!"

Again, Devin and Thomas looked to one another, and this time, neither was smiling.

12

Viktor could smell the sea, still miles away. It reminded him of a holiday his family had taken in Weissmar. He pictured the idyllic bungalows dotting the shore. The girls in their bathing gowns. The gulls wheeling overhead, swooping down to snatch spitz cakes and wursts from the hands of unwary children. The wave of nostalgia swept over him and brought an unexpected smile to his face. A parade of images marched through his head, better times, the days his father had doted on him, before his troubles at school had dimmed that paternal affection. His brother hadn't been born yet and his sister was a precocious toddler. Like every teenager, he had wanted nothing to do with his family. Now he wished he could go back. Viktor remembered a puppet show they had watched on the boardwalk, a caramel apple dripping onto his sister's pudgy fingers.

"Why are you just standing there, you oaf?" the dwarf groused.

The sound of Doktor Lanigan's voice was enough to start Viktor grinding his teeth again. They'd sold their stolen horse in the last village for coin to pay for passage across the channel. Lanigan had complained about riding it and now he was complaining about walking, too. Viktor said, "For such a little fellow, you have a giant mouth."

"I'm sorry to point out that you are standing in the middle of the road like a simpleton. If I hadn't said something you'd be drooling by now."

"No one asked you to follow me around."

The dwarf gasped.

Well, it was true. And still, the faintest twinge of guilt kept Viktor from saying something harsher. The dwarf had told him at least ten times that his idea was stupid. "Honestly, I don't know why you are coming. You think this is such a bad idea. Why are you even here?"

Doktor Lanigan puffed up. "You're my patient."

"Oh, please."

Lanigan's mask of certainty slipped. "Where else could I go? My people are in Brandover, and anyway, I wouldn't want to drag them into this mess."

Viktor folded his arms. "Admit it. You're as lost as I am. More."

"Fine!" The dwarf stomped his foot. "Are you happy? You've made us into criminals and now I don't know what to do."

"Me?"

"Yes you. We could have had a quick peek around the basement and snuck off, but you had to go cracking heads. Violence isn't the answer to every situation, you know?"

That stung. Viktor didn't think of himself as violent. At least, he didn't like to. But if he let his guard down, the war crept in, and memories like that were hard to shake. "That's not fair. It's not my fault Oberman had a bunch of deformed freaks locked in his dungeon." He didn't like that word, freaks. He wished he hadn't said it. He felt guilty he had just left them there, but they were too far gone to let loose and he hadn't had the heart to kill them. It made him so angry. "I'm not the one that did that to them. And I'm not going to end up like them. You can keep acting like we don't know what to do, but I know where I'm going…more or less. That mirror in Dannbridge might be a cure and it might not, but it's the only chance I have left. So will you please stop this complaining and let's get a move on, yah?"

Lanigan cleared his throat and pointed south. The ocean stretched across the horizon, the gray, overcast sky like a reflection of its dark waters. He harrumphed, a sort of half-apology which Viktor accepted. Malcolm Lanigan might have been a stubborn little bastard, but like it or not, they were neck deep in the same shit.

Their quarreling lapsed as they trekked through the outskirts of the town, arguing only briefly about what might be the most plausible cover story. In the end, the dwarf's simple explanation that they had been offered a job in Dannbridge won the day, mostly because Viktor had exhausted his supply of more colorful alternatives.

The streets of Heidelbronn had none of the charm of a holiday town like Weissmar. This was no seaside retreat; it was a fishing town. Populated by stern house fraus, tattooed sailors, and a biting wind that cut through every layer of his clothing as easily as the dwarf's barbs could nettle him.

They stopped at a pub for fried fish and beer before heading to the docks. Despite the fact that it wasn't very good, it was the best meal he'd ever eaten. The pair spent the better part of the day going from ship to ship until they found one bound for Dannbridge on the evening tide.

It wasn't exactly as luxurious as the dwarves' newest marvel, the zeppelin, which made daily flights across the channel. But it would get them from one side of the water to the other.

The *Alba Marie* was a good-sized barque carrying tools made in Jarlsbeck to the capital of Westonshire. The horse hadn't garnered enough coin to book their passage, but to his surprise Lanigan produced a modest stash sufficient to secure them a berth on the overnight journey.

Their cabin was the size and smell of a water closet, with two bunk beds on the outer wall.

"You can have the top bunk if you'd like," said Viktor, biting down on a smile.

Lanigan narrowed his eyes. "I suppose that was passing clever… for a man who can't spell clever."

"'For a man who can't spell clever.'" Viktor mimicked Lanigan's Dunngregor accent.

"I've always wanted a parrot. Now I'm not so sure."

"A what?"

Lanigan snorted as he claimed the lower bunk.

Before they were under way, the subtle motion of the vessel caused a twinge of seasickness, but Viktor did his best to soldier on. It wasn't so bad after all, a bit like a hangover, and he'd had plenty of those over the past few years.

"I've never been on a boat before," Viktor admitted.

"By all the gods, take me now. I'll never do this again," Viktor vowed. "Never."

Above deck, thunder raged and rain pelted the ship. The *Alba Marie* pitched one way and then the other, the merciless motion turning their insides out.

Lanigan's skin had taken on the greenish pallor of his upchuck. He sounded like he was in shock. "I couldn't even drink an ale right now."

The air in their tiny room smelled like Lanigan's feet. Every roll of the deck twisted Viktor's tortured stomach. On the plus side, his stomach was empty, having already made three trips topside to spill his guts into the channel. The problem was that he still felt the need to purge himself, and now even that relief was gone. He was glad he had made it to the rail; as bad as Lanigan's feet stunk, it was, he supposed, marginally better than the stench of vomit.

"Please, put your shoes back on."

"I should have gone to the mountains. Anywhere but here. How did I let you talk me into this?"

"Me? I specifically told you to piss off."

"Yes," said Lanigan, "but you obviously didn't mean it. I knew you were afraid to ask me to accompany you. Someone has to keep an eye on you. You're like a child."

"Oh, that's rich. If you shaved that stubble you'd be a dead ringer for my little cousin, Dolph."

"How does anyone live like this? It's unnatural." The dwarf held up a finger as he gagged.

"Not in here!"

"I'm fine." Lanigan's puckered face said otherwise.

Outside their cabin, footfalls tore down the hallway as a sailor raced by.

"Go up there and puke," Viktor said. "You're being stubborn. It smells bad enough down here without you spilling your lunch all over."

"Smells like your onion breath, you mean. That's the only reason I feel ill. The sea is nothing. All this tossing and turning is like a pony ride next to that breath of yours."

"You're saying I'm the one who stinks? You stink! Smells like a goat farted inside a pumpkin. Put your damn shoes back on."

"It helps me relax. Feels good to have the wood against my bare feet."

"I hope you get a splinter."

"Oh, that's just lovely. Here I am, sick as a dog, far from home on account of you and you—"

"On account of me?"

"Ach, you big goon. I could have gone about my life just fine if you hadn't shown up causing trouble, beating folks up."

"Folks? Folks? Don't make it sound like it was a nice family from Esseldorf. You know damn well those heads needed cracking. And do you think they would have us let us go? Plus, it was you who said we should go down in the dungeon."

"Well, yes, but—"

A wave canted the ship sharply to port. Lanigan and Viktor tumbled out of their bunks and ended up tangled in a pile against the inner wall. When they got their feet under them, Lanigan dry-heaved, his fists clenched as he struggled mightily to keep from barfing on Viktor's feet.

"Come on," said Viktor. "We've got to get you on deck before you make a mess."

Viktor steered the dwarf toward the door.

"Get your paws off me. I'm go—" Lanigan clamped down to keep from hurling.

For all his tough talk, the dwarf's knees buckled. Despite Lanigan's curses, Viktor tucked him under one arm like a sack of potatoes and lumbered out the door, down the hall and up the stairs. Thunder rumbled in the distance and somewhere in the hold horses brayed in terror. Before Viktor crested the steps, Lanigan's stream of invectives was drowned by the roar of rain pummeling the deck. It soaked them both as Viktor emerged from the hatch. The doctor's fist pounded against his side and Viktor looked down in time to see the dwarf vomit on his boot. Viktor dropped him, briefly thankful for the downpour.

Lanigan shouted. "You must be the—shit! Oh shit!"

Viktor spun, off balance, as the deck tilted. A wave surged from the gloom towering over the mast. Lightning flashed, etching a moment of panic in the night. Sailors pointed, they scurried, they prayed.

The ship climbed the wave, the angle of the deck tipping almost vertical. A scream ripped through the air as a sailor plummeted past him, tangled in the rigging. Water broke over the bow and Lanigan and Viktor slid across the slimy planks, swept toward the aft end of the ship. A pulley swung from the mast, clipping Viktor in the side of the head.

All sounds were strangely muted. From a distance, Viktor felt himself roll across the deck, the hot gush of blood pleasantly warm on his face. He saw the railing flash by and then waves doused him. He felt bad that Lanigan was probably going to die out here. Maybe he'd been a tad harsh on the little guy. Nodding to himself as he dangled, half submerged over the edge, Viktor resolved to let himself fall. Better that than drag Lanigan with him. After all, he was a tumorling. What did he have to look forward to?

"Don't you dare!" Lanigan shouted, his words somehow finding Viktor's ear in the maelstrom.

Hanging from the side of the storm-tossed ship, Viktor took Lanigan's outstretched hand. The dwarf strained to haul him aboard as Viktor clawed uselessly against the side of the ship.

"Whenever you're ready, you wee lamb! Pull yourself up!"

The barque crested another wave, rain and sea froth blinding. Viktor's feet slipped on the slick hull, scrabbling for purchase. "I'm trying!"

"The one thing you're good for is lifting things. Lift your bloody self!"

A flash of lightning lit the sky, silhouetting two figures behind Doktor Lanigan. Their appearance startled Viktor even as it kindled hope that they could help the dwarf pull him over the rail. Viktor caught a whiff of smoke tinged with sulfur, like a forest fire burning despite the torrential rain. It was a familiar scent: the scent of someone using the Dragon Well. The ember of hope their appearance kindled was snuffed out as one of them brandished a knife.

Viktor shouted a warning to Lanigan but it was lost in a peel of thunder. The assassin stole up behind the dwarf. Viktor scrambled to get up the side of the ship, his panic mounting, reaching out with his free hand to try to grasp the rail.

The shadowy figure grabbed a fistful of Lanigan's hair and jerked his head back. "The Thule Society sends its regards, runt!"

The assassin's blade sliced a deep gash into the dwarf's throat. Viktor felt Lanigan's grip go slack. Hot blood gushed over their clasped hands. In the faint light of the moon Viktor glimpsed the fear in the dwarf's eyes. Guilt washed over Viktor like a wave breaking over the bow and he threw open the door to the Dragon Well, hoping to quench his shame in a surge of fiery power.

Malcolm Lanigan's body toppled past him, swallowed by the sea. Nerve pain radiated from Viktor's tumor, arcing up his forearm, into his shoulder. A burning sensation sheathed his skin, and scales blistered across his flesh as Viktor instinctively dragonshaped. The bones in his fingertips tore out of his flesh, forming razor-sharp black talons that dug into the wooden hull. It hurt like hell but he shrugged off the pain and levered himself aboard with a surge of Dryxa's Might.

Landing on the deck beside the assassin, he heard Lanigan's murderer curse over the din of the storm.

The pain in Viktor's arm pressed in toward his heart, a searing ache that he feared could spread his tumor's malignant power through his whole body. Terrified by the prospect, he slammed the connection closed. The sudden absence of magic staggered Viktor, he flopped against the rail. The scales his magic had conjured evaporated like ash wafting from a fire, and Viktor almost wept, the sudden fear that he could not change back almost overwhelming.

Malcolm's assassin did not hesitate. He lunged forward, blade thrusting out to stab Viktor, but Viktor stumbled sideways, swatting at the knife. It raked a path along his bottom rib on the right side, the new pain another shock to his already beleaguered system.

Viktor drew on his army training. He shoved the man back a step, his eyes catching a flicker in the moonlight as the second assassin moved around to flank him. Before the new assailant struck, Viktor let the Dragons' power in again, this time in a measured trickle as they'd taught him in the war.

The two assassins came at him together, one slashing high and the other low. Viktor scrambled backward from the assault but the rail of the ship was behind him. There was nowhere to go. He had to kill these men or be killed by them.

With a sharp intake, Viktor drew in the Breath. His spine snapped straight and his lungs filled with air that crackled as if on the edge of ignition. In. Never out. A lesson hard learned.

The world slowed. Rain pelted him and the deck tilted as the ship rose up the ramp of another wave. He felt the wet planks beneath his bare feet, just realizing he had lost his boots to the sea. Lanigan was right, it felt good. As the vessel crested the wave and the assassins shifted their balance to compensate, Viktor struck. Backstepping, he pushed off the rail, feinting toward the attacker on his right. The assassin to his left seized the apparent opportunity and closed in behind him, but Viktor spun around. His fist lashed out, the backs of his knuckles catching the man on the temple. The assassin's knees wobbled and Viktor pounced, grabbing him by the scruff of the neck and tossing him over the side. Before the killer had hit the water, his conspirator's blade slashed at Viktor's back. Viktor rolled to his left, sloshing across the deck and colliding with a mounted dinghy. The ship tilted hard to port, and both Viktor and the assassin took a moment to regain their balance. Sailors cupped their hands to their mouths, vainly screaming into the howling wind. Loose rigging whipped through the air as the ship rose up the side of another wave, her nose drifting away from the crest, threatening to capsize.

At the wave's peak, the assassin tried Viktor's trick, darting forward as the ship began its plunge down the other side. But the crack of timber and a sudden lurch of the deck arrested his maneuver. Viktor flung up his hand in defense, catching hold of the killer's wrist. He wrestled the blade from his hand as water swamped the deck and craggy rocks surged from the darkness to shatter the *Alba Marie*.

Viktor plunged into the frigid water. With one last surge of draconic power he stabbed the confiscated blade at his attacker, but he only struck a piece of the fractured hull.

A current sucked Viktor under the water and he kicked against the unyielding power of the sea. But the sea would not be denied. It pulled him down, the pressure fit to burst his eardrums. It spun him again and again, dragging him down until he didn't know which way was up.

When the tidal pull released its iron grip, the buoyancy of the flotsam he had stabbed pulled him to the surface.

Gasping in the bitter air, the taste of salt water and blood in his mouth, he clung to the section of the hull. Waves as high as the oldest trees lifted him to glimpse the distant lights of Dannbridge before he sunk once again beneath their brutal plummet.

Professor Izola Scrivani awoke to the stomping of her upstairs neighbor…again. "Not today of all days, you drunken old letch." She snatched the broom she kept by her nightstand and pounded on the ceiling. "Professor Wimbley! Keep it down!" To herself she muttered, "You could at least wait 'til the sun was up to get sauced, you fusty old twat."

Izola needed her beauty sleep. After all, today she'd have to defend her dissertation. And of course, the instant that that terrifying thought entered her head, Izola knew she wouldn't get another wink.

What time was it anyway? Wait…the sun *was* up.

"No need to panic," she told herself.

A messenger would be there at seven to wake her. She'd arranged it just in case, prone as she was to oversleeping. Naturally, Logan knew she was a night owl and had scheduled her defense at an ungodly hour just to be an ass. But if he thought that was going to knock her off her game he had another think coming.

Bells rang out in the distance. Obnoxious bloody things. The Tower of Tomes was halfway across campus and still the noise set off a headache. It was probably best she drank some water. Izola supposed she shouldn't have been drinking last night, but how could she have slept otherwise?

The bell tolled eight bloody times. Eight. It was like eight nails driven into her head. Wait… It was eight o'clock in the morning. *Bugger!* She'd missed her wake up call. Oh, no.

No, no, no, no, no, no, no, no.

She was already late.

Izola shot from her bed, spewing filthy language as she stubbed her toe. She scampered to the outfit she had laid out the night before and pulled the dress on over her night clothes. There was no time to bathe, no time to comb her hair. She tore her bookbag from the dining nook and jumped over a pile of laundry on her way out.

Not bothering to lock the door behind her, Izola sprinted across the commons. Saints, her head felt like an overstuffed meat pie.

She'd be lucky to get across campus without tossing up last night's dinner. Lucky to get there before the council adjourned. What a disaster! Maybe Moira could keep them from rejecting her tenure, but if she missed her dissertation defense, even her mentor would be hard pressed to save her rapidly crumbling credibility.

Izola hustled past the ivy-draped bricks of the dormitories, past the columned facade of Westbastion Hall and the ducks swimming round Gullheller Fountain. She raced across half of Dannbridge University, the worst scenarios echoing through her pounding head.

At last she reached the oversized flagstones of White Square and shoved her way through the crowd of milling students to the massive open doors of Milner's Hall. Already a sweaty, disheveled mess, she pelted upstairs and barged through the third door on the left.

"I'm here!" she gasped. Izola doubled over, hands on her knees. For a terrifying moment Izola thought she might vomit red wine all over the tiled floor.

Wouldn't that just be the proverbial feather in her cap?

Logan's smarmy voice jarred her from her misery. "You're late. I hope it wasn't too much of an inconvenience to make it to your own thesis defense."

Izola looked up to see her ex-husband seated on the other side of a long conference table beside four other professors. His cologne filled the room.

"Professor Blythe." She managed by dint of colossal effort to keep her tone civil as she addressed her ex-husband.

Izola felt a little flash of victory as Logan glanced at the hourglass on the table, the last grains still flowing, and saw the irritation on his face. She might be late, but she hadn't missed the ten-minute grace period. Of course, that paltry triumph fell flat on its face as she realized that Moira wasn't there.

"Where is Professor Duncannon?"

Logan smiled. "Professor Duncannon was called away on urgent university business. As the next most senior professor on the committee, I will be chairing this meeting."

Un-bloody-believable. Not only had he swindled his way onto the committee, but he was now the chair? Utterly ridiculous. Could there be a more obvious conflict of interest?

Logan turned to a man beside him, someone she'd never seen before. He wore leather gloves and wire-rimmed spectacles that accentuated his piercing blue eyes. "This is visiting Professor Emeritus Doktor Emile Oberman. In Moira's absence, I've asked him to fill in."

"Perhaps we should reschedule?"

Logan tutted. "You've already kept this committee waiting long enough. Perhaps in the future you should arrange for a campus page to wake you up." He turned to Doktor Oberman and winked. No one else saw it, but she did. The infuriating toad. Had he really sabotaged her wake-up call? Logan flipped over the hourglass. "You may begin."

The gloating little weasel. What had she ever seen in him?

"She seems a bit befuddled, Professor Blythe." This snide remark came from the visiting professor. His accent sounded like he was from Jarlsbeck. "Perhaps we should cancel this meeting. Let the girl try again later."

Girl? Who the hell was this prick?

"Forgive me, Doktor Oberman." Izola cleared her throat. "I thought that I was acquainted with all of the notable scholars of art history in the Kingdom of Reinveldt."

"The kingdom is no more, my dear. Perhaps it is that inattention to detail that is really troubling you."

She could probably get a spell off before they tackled her. Curse this Jarlsbecker and her smirking ex. Of course, if she hexed them in the middle of her thesis defense she could kiss tenure goodbye. So, she smiled daggers at him, even as she imagined breaking the hourglass over the Jarlsbecker's head. He must be one of Logan's buddies. He would vote against her and of course, Logan would, too. That meant she would need all three of the other votes.

Right, time to get at it.

"I'm not troubled at all, Doktor Oberman. I was merely attempting to ascertain the depth of your expertise on the subject. I'll do my best to help you keep up."

He winced at the retort, his eyes going flat. A vicious smile spread across his face. "I am a physician by training, *Associate* Professor Scrivani. But I am also a student of history. I found your thesis quite fascinating, if perhaps a bit fanciful."

Beside him, Professor Goodfield leaned forward and picked up his quill. The old man pushed his comically oversized spectacles up the bridge of his nose and pointedly eyed the hourglass.

Of course, get to it, Izola. She suspected Goodfield would support her, he was a curious and openminded sort, and perhaps as important, one of Moira's closest friends. Foxglove was a good bet, too; the only elf on the panel, she was equally openminded, and perhaps more important, she hated Logan Blythe. As any self-respecting woman would.

Logan nodded at Goodfield's implication. "Miss Scrivani, you may summarize your thesis for the panel."

What she really wanted to do was point out that this Jarlsbecker was unqualified to participate in the proceedings, but with Logan as chair, it was as pointless as teats on a bull.

Izola opened her bag and dumped out a stack of papers, an inkwell, and a quill. She fished out a book which she had specially prepared for her presentation, set it on top of the pile and looked up, addressing Goodfield, Dillberry, and Foxglove.

"As we all know, premodern Dannbridge was ruled by the

Tyrant, a figure at once infamous and mysterious." Izola opened the book she had created for this presentation and turned to the first page. She'd spent hours writing this passage and preparing the accompanying illusion spell. Moira had cautioned that the manifestation was all a little flashy, but Izola knew that not even the esteemed professors of Dannbridge University were immune to a bit of showmanship. And Aldonto's Illumination was certainly that. As Izola laid out the basis of her essay the ink on the pages flowed, floating out of the book to form the indistinct apparition of a man, the crown on his head vivid in her illusion, the rest of him indistinct. Foxglove leaned forward, visibly savoring the earthy scent of old books, dry leather, hints of vanilla and mildew, the scent of her magic.

"When the original Quorum overthrew him and shattered his crown, all references to the Tyrant's personage were obliterated from local art and local records. The particulars of this individual were blotted from the pages of history. Even magical means were employed to banish all traces of the Tyrant's identity from memory."

Professor Foxglove's pointed ears perked up and she murmured appreciatively, but Oberman scoffed, muttering, "Parlor tricks."

Izola ignored him, pressing on. "Now, what do we know about the Tyrant? First, he was male. The accounts of his downfall at the hands of his apprentices assign him a masculine pronoun. Second, he was a mage of the highest order." With a flourish, the illusion hovering over her open book waved its arms and fire flared around the figure. Oberman snorted in derision, but Izola ignored him. "The cabal which unseated him was comprised of his students in the magical arts, each a practitioner of stupendous arcane achievement.

"Third, he was not human."

"Preposterous." Logan shook his head. "As if an elf or dwarf could have ruled Westonshire."

Professor Foxglove turned to Logan, her ponytail flouncing over her shoulder and her mouth pinched in a hard line.

It was typically lazy of Logan to throw out this blanket assertion.

Recent scholarship, in fact, suggested the possibility of Elvish culture in the southwest during the pre-Tyrannical period. But that was neither here nor there. He was relishing his power as head of the committee, a sad little knock-off of the Tyrant's dominion. Izola raised her voice to be heard over Logan's snigger.

"I did not say that. I said he was not human. Over the years, various sources detailed in Appendix A have catalogued the Shards of the Tyrant's crown as they have changed hands from one Quorumite to another. They've been sighted in public for various reasons and have been the subject of rare but detailed written accounts. Of the seven Shards, five have been described in sufficient detail to extrapolate the size of the crown. In total, the circumference would measure 58 inches, more than twice the average size of a human head. Even accounting for his ego, that is beyond a reasonable range."

No one laughed at her joke. It was fine, she told herself. She would try it on Moira later.

"Fourth, something about the Tyrant's identity was dangerous. After all, why else go to such lengths to obscure it?"

"Spite," said Doktor Oberman. "The Quorum were jealous of his legacy."

This earned an odd look from Professor Foxglove.

"Spite?" Izola cringed as Foxglove jotted down a note. "Alice Thistleby, one of the original Quorumites, sacrificed her life to work the spell that hid the Tyrant's identity. Spite is a powerful motivation, but would you give up your life for it? I wouldn't."

Foxglove crossed out her note. Izola couldn't help but bob her eyebrows at Oberman.

"All of this," she continued, "points to the first element of my thesis." Izola read the next line of her book, unlocking its magic. The indistinct figure with the shattered crown solidified, grew wings and red scales. "The Tyrant was a dragon."

"Yet another ludicrous assertion."

"Doktor Oberman, you have yet to hear my arguments. If you listen, I will present plausible evidence that not only was the Tyrant a dragon, but also that a cult of dragon worship persists, both here in Westonshire and on the continent."

Doktor Oberman swallowed something he was about to say, and fixed her with an odd look. He gathered himself to reply, but before he could speak Logan set his hand on Doktor Oberman's gloved forearm.

"I concur with our esteemed guest," said her ex-husband. "This presentation smacks of frivolity, it has been one conspiracy theory after another. Frankly, I expected better of you than to waste this council's time with these wild and unsubstantiated assertions." Logan donned a look of mock sympathy. "As much as it pains me, I move to hold a vote now. I think we've all heard enough."

Izola sat there, dumbfounded, as Oberman nodded.

"I second the motion," the Jarlsbecker said.

"Very well." Logan didn't meet her eyes. "Those in favor of awarding tenure?"

Professors Foxglove and Goodfield raised their hands tentatively. She'd known that Logan and Oberman would not, but she was gutted when Dillberry shook his head.

"Those opposed?"

It had all gone to pot. The professors filed out. Logan said something condescending, but she didn't hear the words, she could only tell by his tone. It all felt strangely far away, as if it were happening to someone else. Was this a bloody joke? First, she was late because her messenger didn't wake her, then her mentor was called away, replaced by this visiting professor who wasn't even an historian. It all smacked of a conspiracy, a cruel jape executed by her no-good, bloody ex. Logan Blythe was a low-down shit, no doubt. But she had never thought he was this spiteful. Or maybe she had, and she just never thought him this capable.

But he had certainly done a number on her. What would even happen now? This possibility had never occurred to her. She was undone. This fucking day.

Early as it was, Izola resolved to go home and open a bottle of the good wine.

"**G**ood heavens, what is that bartender doing?" Devin wrapped his knuckles on the grizzled tabletop, trying to get the man's attention. "Honestly. It's like he's ignoring us on purpose."

Thomas squinted across the dim tavern as the barkeep scurried back and forth trying to keep up with the festival crowd. "Maybe he is." Thomas smoothed his wig. "We look a little out of place."

Devin rolled his eyes. "When did the help get so touchy? So we're slumming. He should be grateful we're gracing this dump with our presence. I think we lend the establishment an air of sophistication."

Thomas eyed the prostitute picking her nose at the next table. "That's a very rosy way of looking at it."

Devin pressed his hands together as if praying. "Don't tell me you've gotten touchy, too."

"No, no. I whipped a servant this morning."

"Yourself?"

"Well, no, I had another servant do it. In any case, abusing the staff will only get spit in our wine."

"Might make you feel better about whipping that servant."

Thomas slapped Devin on the shoulder. "I do feel bad. I don't know why, though. Marcus is such an idiot. How hard is it to launder a suit properly?"

"I wouldn't know."

"Well," Thomas admitted, "I wouldn't either. Hmph, now I feel worse."

"You're just thirsty."

"Very. And you're in a mood."

Devin adjusted his cravat. "Is it that obvious?"

Thomas pinched the bridge of his nose. "Oscar Red Sleeves is a low-down, murderous thug. You tried to steal from him. A man like that...who knows? I don't think it matters who you are. I'm not sure if it's dawned on you yet how much trouble you're in. And it should. The man is simply an animal. You have to understand that a crook like that lives on his reputation. He can't have some uptown dandy stepping on his toes."

"Dandy? Do you really think?"

"It's all relative, Peacock."

Devin made an annoyed face. "You know, there is a scene in *The Man From Alfglenn*—"

"Oh." Thomas closed his eyes and tipped his head back. "Here we go."

"What?"

"You're not in a Lord Jasper novel, Devin. This is serious. Oscar Red Sleeves is not some mustache twirling bravo. I dare say that if Lord Jasper ran up against his sort he'd wind up floating face down in the harbor."

"Ludicrous!"

"Who's ludicrous? You're ludicrous."

An older man with white burn scars running up his neck bumped into Devin's chair as he was passing by.

Devin voiced his offense. "Pardon me, good sir."

"Pardon me, good sir." The drunk mocked Devin's posh accent to the great amusement of nearby patrons. The prostitute who had been picking her nose clapped. "You like that one, Giselle?"

She nodded.

"The clientele here is ghastly," Devin said.

"Pardon me, your lordship." The scarred drunk sketched a formal bow, his voice still imitating Devin. "Please, accept this humble gift by way of apology."

Devin and Thomas watched him go, confused. "Well," said Devin. "At least he wasn't a ruffian."

"Yes, but what was the gift?"

"I was wondering myself—ack!" The smell hit Devin's nostrils like a bucket full of nightsoil. "I think we should try our luck at the bar."

"Oh! Heavens! It's like a rat passing a deviled egg."

"Come, Thomas." Devin pulled his ruffled shirt over his nose. "The poors have won this round."

They scurried to their feet and elbowed their way through the crowd. A loud cheer went up and Devin looked back to the rear of the tavern where a rough group had strung up a scarecrow decorated with an elaborate crown. Devin casually removed his wig and tucked it in the pocket of his coat. He patted the pistol tucked in his belt to reassure himself.

When they reached the bar, Devin jostled his way to the front of the line and Thomas followed, keeping an apologetic distance. Devin stood at the counter and called for the barkeep: a rough-looking fellow with tattoos you could barely see on his dark skin. But as many times as Devin called for service, the man moved right past him, his eyes sliding over Devin as if he were invisible.

Finally, Devin set a gold sovereign on the bar and it drew the bartender like a lodestone. When the fellow came over to collect it, Devin leaned in and yelled over the crowd.

"Do you know how to make a Continental Creme?"

The man looked at him as if he'd just peed in his own hat and put it back on. "We got gin and we got beer, mate."

"A bottle of gin, then. Have you any chocolate?"

The bartender reached beneath the counter and produced a bottle full of murky liquid. He set it on the counter, the corner of his mouth ticking like he might erupt in hysterical giggles. "You want chocolate, you can fish it out of the loo."

Devin cringed. He was about to lambast the cretin when he realized that the tavern had gone quiet. The bartender looked over his shoulder, eyes widening as he stepped back. He collected the coin from bar and retreated to a safer distance.

A lump of dread formed in Devin's belly. He turned to find Oscar Red Sleeves, flanked by thugs.

"Everybody out," Oscar commanded.

A chorus of whispers was quickly followed by the scuff of barstools as the patrons scrambled to make themselves scarce.

Devin put his head down and sidled up to a group on his its way out. An old rummy stumbled from the pack and Devin took him by the arm to steady the drunkard. *Genius, old boy. You're a master of disguise.*

"Not you." Oscar pointed a grubby finger at Devin.

Bollocks, Devin Thought, foisting the rummy on the nearest patron.

Oscar swung toward the door where Thomas, having blended into a gaggle of his own, was almost to the exit. "And not your little friend."

Thomas stopped, his shoulders sagging.

"Oscar." Devin smiled. He thought for a tick that maybe this was the moment to whip out his little pistol, but Oscar hadn't come alone, so even if he shot the oaf Devin would still have to deal with his henchmen. "Silly for me to take it this far. I know." Devin held his hands palms up, confessing his blunder. "But I know just how to make it up to you."

"Shut your bloody mouth, unless you want to watch me feed your chum his own balls."

It seemed like a good time for Devin to hold his tongue. Obviously, he could fix this. With his father's money, or perhaps his father's influence. He just needed to stay calm and dangle the carrot at just the right moment.

Oscar looked over his shoulder as the last patron was leaving. "Digby." He turned to one of his goons. "Go out there and make sure no one is eavesdropping."

A long, pants-shitting silence ensued. Digby's footfalls echoed as he went outside on his errand.

Oscar turned back to Devin. "You really are an arrogant little swish, aren't you?"

Devin assumed the question was rhetorical, but Oscar seemed to be waiting for an answer.

Hoping to inject a little levity into the atmosphere, Devin pantomimed Thomas eating his own balls. Oscar grinned, revealing a gold tooth. Devin realized then that he had never seen the man smile. Not surprising, he supposed. And given the malice in that look, not particularly encouraging, either.

"Good," Oscar said. "You're listening. Keep listening. Your life and your friend's life depend on it. You stole from me. Or at least you tried. And not only did you steal money, you stole a bit of the fear I instill. Sure, you're the son of a lord. Normally, I'd agree that makes you untouchable. But if I let you walk around Dannbridge with your balls still attached, it makes me look weak."

This fellow certainly had a weird thing with balls.

"Are you smirking at me?"

Devin shook his head, emphatically.

"You're lucky I am a businessman at heart. And your stupid decision to muck about with me coincides with a business opportunity. You are going to steal something for me. You fancy yourself a Ward Man, right?"

"I'm quite good at—"

"Shut your bloody mouth." Oscar waited to emphasize the silence. "You are going to steal your father's Shard of the Quorum."

Devin spit out a laugh. "You expect me to steal a brutally powerful magical artifact from one of the most powerful mages in the city? An artifact that will grant its possessor a seat on the council that rules Dannbridge? Are you joking? Tell me you're joking." But Oscar looked deadly serious. "It's impossible."

"Not for you."

"For me, too. Not only is it warded beyond belief, it's...I mean, have you ever seen a piece of the Q in real life?"

Oscar shook his head.

"It's like looking at the sun. If I tried to touch it, it would probably cook me from the inside out. That is not an exaggeration. Only an archmage can safely handle something like that, and only briefly. Why do you think the pieces are all locked up in vaults and towers? Why do you think the lords don't carry their Shards with them? It's like keeping a lit fire in your pocket. I just can't do it. I'm not capable."

"Find a way."

"I don't think I will. It's suicide to try and handle that thing. Not that I would ever make it that far. My father is no fool. His wards will be second to none. Dizzyingly complicated and deadly. I am not an archmage."

"Think of it as a challenge, mate."

"As I said, it's tantamount to suicide."

"Too bad for your friend then."

Dread. Devin squeaked. It took him a minute to speak. "What?" he finally said.

At a nod from Oscar, one of the other Red Sleeves grabbed Thomas by the arms and held him in place as he struggled.

"Hold on now," Devin pleaded.

Oscar slid a knife from his belt. "Think of this as a ticking clock."

"Wait!" Thomas cried.

Oscar stepped forward and jabbed the blade into Thomas' belly.

Devin's friend yelped. He doubled over in pain, but the thug holding his arms kept him on his feet.

"Peacock?" Thomas looked to Devin for help, but he was helpless. "Oh, fuck. I'm going to die."

"Shut up, you little twat." Oscar turned to Devin, holding up his bloody dagger for inspection. "My knife work is precise. A gut wound like that takes three days to bleed out. Awful, screaming days, true, but... There will be three of them. Like I said, clockwork. Get me that piece of the Quorum, Devin Thistleby. I don't care what you have to do. And if you think about telling dear old Daddy about this, think again. Look me in the eyes. I will kill your friend before I die. I will take him with me no matter what. So no tattling. You fancy yourself a Ward Man. Prove it." Oscar motioned for his thug to follow and he dragged Thomas, moaning as he laid a trail of blood out the door.

Devin stood in the empty pub staring at the red trail. He set his hand on the butt of his pistol, wishing he'd had the courage to use the damned thing. But he hadn't. Coward that he was, just like his father always said, a man of no account. He had let them hurt Thomas. He had let them take him. And he hadn't done a thing to stop them.

The bartender poked his head in, and seeing only Devin remaining, he started back toward the bar until he slipped in Thomas' blood.

"Mate," said the barkeep. "Looks like we both stepped in it."

15

Viktor woke up to a crab pinching his earlobe. "Ow."

He swatted it away, but the sudden movement churned his insides. He puked seawater onto the rocky shore, the taste of saltwater and bile unforgettably foul. A group of fishermen stood nearby, laughing. He overheard them speculating about the events of the previous night, all of which sounded a great deal more fun than what had actually happened.

A vicious wind set him shivering.

Dawn spilled over the horizon, painting the city of Dannbridge with golden highlights. Viktor pushed himself to his knees, taking in his surroundings. He seemed to have washed ashore on the outskirts of the city, where fishing shacks and cottages dotted the coastline.

Viktor looked up and down the shore both hoping and dreading to find the dwarf's body nearby, but the sea had taken him once and for all. Malcolm Lanigan was gone. And that was Viktor's fault. If he hadn't latched onto this stupid notion that this trinket Oberman was after could cure him, maybe Lanigan would still be alive, still carping about the weather and taking little chip shots at Viktor's intelligence.

It didn't sound so bad now.

He just wished that he could have said thank you. After all, Lanigan had been hauling him back aboard when the assassins struck. He died saving Viktor. And something about that hit harder than the rock which had shattered the hull of the *Alba Marie*. It made Viktor want to lay down and bury himself in the sand.

He was so stupid. He just wanted to go home, to have his mama cook him something hot, to just go back to the way things were before this mess, before the war, before his tumor.

Viktor turned back to the sea and squinted over its sun-dappled waters toward Grunburg. But he couldn't go home. Not yet. Not until he found Oberman, found a cure. It all sounded childish now, a pipe dream. Just hop on a ship and chase down some madman and it would make everything better. Stupid. Just like him.

He could have cried just then, but somehow he felt he didn't deserve it. So he mashed those feelings down, like a ramrod packing a load of gunpowder into his blunderbuss. If he started crying now, how would he ever stop? And besides, these fishermen would make fun of him.

A sea breeze stole the fleeting warmth of sunrise. Viktor shivered, hugging himself as he looked up the beach to where a slum-covered hill obscured much of his view of Dannbridge. Rooftops peeked over its crest, buildings of wood and brick crowned with soot-darkened chimneys and cedar shingles. In the distance, more elegant architecture of gothic stonework jutted here and there from an oppressive fog.

Shattered pieces of the *Alba Marie*'s hull and torn shreds of her sails littered the beach. Viktor stood up, feeling the bitter chill in the briny air. His bare feet were blue; his fingertips, he discovered, were blue, too. Worried about what else might be blue, Viktor snuck a peek, to the uproarious amusement of the watching fishermen.

Scowling at them, he turned to find the fragment of the ship to which he had clung, the assassin's dagger still lodged in the hull. Hands shaking, Viktor bent over and wrenched it free. He inspected the knife. It had a long blade, made from Nordheim steel with a lacquered oak handle and a mark inscribed on it. A mark identical to the one he had seen tattooed on the guard in Oberman's dungeon.

A stick figure almost like a dragon. Like a cross with slanted lines at the four cardinal points, angled in a spiral like a head, wings, and tail. He tucked the dagger in his belt.

Viktor made his way up the shore to where a path led off the beach into the outskirts of Dannbridge. It was early, but already the bustle of city life crowded the streets. A few of the city folk gawked at him, barefoot, sopping wet, and pale as a ghost, but most ignored Viktor completely.

Light rain drizzled over the streets, but the smells of fish and sour wine still cloyed his nose. The neighborhood through which he entered Dannbridge was full of three- and four-story tenements, empty laundry lines strung between them. Among these buildings the stink of sewage overpowered all others. Viktor pulled his shirt up over his nose, but the city folk looked at him like he was a bandit, so he pulled it back down. Before long he could mostly ignore the stench.

Even at this hour, revelers gathered. A group of young men lay on one sidewalk, singing a song about the Tyrant, and occasionally, without success, trying to stand up. Viktor inquired of one of the celebrants and discovered that it was a festival week. Tyrant Fall, the besotted teenager called it. The name tripped vague memories of his boyhood schoolhouse, but he couldn't recall much beyond the fact that the Tyrant had once ruled Westonshire.

The sun came out and burned away the fog, drying up the drizzle. He finally stopped shivering, noting that his hands and feet had lost their bluish pallor.

Viktor wandered a while longer, through what the locals called Gutter Town, taking in the festival atmosphere and squalor. He traipsed aimlessly until he came to a street where the crowd flowed around an open area on the sidewalk, giving someone a wide berth. The bystanders had formed a bubble around a woman who sat cross-legged in the gutter. Beside her, propped against a lamp pole, she had a wooden sign with the words "Fortunes Told" crudely painted in blue letters. She wore a disheveled, old-fashioned robe the color of a stormy sea. Viktor couldn't tell what all the fuss was about, she just looked like an old beggar, but the crowd was at once fascinated and wary. A brave girl edged from the circle into the clearing and dropped a copper coin into the fortuneteller's cup. The child shrank back, looking ready to bolt.

Viktor still couldn't see what was so interesting until the old woman looked up at the girl…and a third eye opened on her forehead. A collective gasp sounded from the crowd and as one they edged away from the tumorling.

Was this what Viktor had to look forward to? A life begging in the streets, living off the scant pity and the morbid curiosity of strangers?

The old tumorling's eyes bore into the brave girl, who trembled under her scrutiny. The crowd held its breath.

The fortune teller clapped her hands together, startling the onlookers and the little girl most of all. The third eye on her forehead flicked to Viktor for an unsettling moment, then returned to the child.

"Sweet girl," croaked the tumorling. "When the fires of night burn as bright as day, you must awaken. When the sleepers walk you must run. To the sea like the sun rising. To the shore where breaks the dawn. Remember, girl, to the sea."

The little girl looked around as if she had been expecting more and then retreated to her father, who waited at the edge of the circle. Viktor stepped forward, conflicted about the pity he felt, but still compelled to toss a coin into the beggar's cup. It was the only money he had left; not much he could do with it, anyway, he supposed. It would hardly buy a hunk of bread.

He turned to leave, not interested in having his fortune told, but the crone's raspy voice froze him in his tracks. "Kindred."

Viktor turned to face her, his backside puckering like it was about to kiss itself goodbye.

The tumorling had closed her third eye and the other two studied him kindly. A smile formed on her withered lips. "Thank you," she said.

Relief flooded over him and he returned the smile. Turning to leave, his stomach growled.

He wandered the streets of Dannbridge, unsure of what to do with himself, vaguely thinking of Oberman, of the cure which the letter had hinted at, and the dire prospect of a New Awakening. He wondered about Oberman's "Society" and what sort of people belonged to it. But mostly he thought about all the food he could see people eating.

He found himself staring at a young woman wolfing down a sandwich. Rather, it was the sandwich that caught his attention. It looked to be ham on rye with thick slices of red onion. He couldn't see it, but he imagined that perhaps it had a bit of stone-ground mustard as well. Yes, there it was, when she bit down, he could see it bulge from its hiding spot beneath the bread.

Seated at a wooden table outside a tavern, she looked up at him, talking with her mouth full. "See something you like?"

Viktor blushed. His stomach growled once again, louder this time. "Sorry," he said.

"Are you one of those creeps?"

"What is *creeps?*" Viktor asked.

"One of those blokes with a baby cock. So he's cheesed off at the whole world. Like that bloke there." She pointed at a fat, middle-aged man with a greasy beard at the far end of the picnic table she occupied. Caught staring, the man averted his gaze and busied himself eating a chicken leg.

"No, no," said Viktor. "I am attracted to your sandwich."

She swallowed, leering, her head swaying back and forth. "Ish okay. I mean. It's okay. You're not so bad yourself." She tried to stand up from the picnic table, caught her foot on the bench, and promptly toppled over onto her face. The remains of her poor sandwich sprawled on the sawdust sprinkled out front of the tavern. "Shit," she said, laughing.

Viktor helped her to her feet.

"Bugger!" A note of sadness crossed her face. "I think I was in love with that sandwich."

Still holding her by the elbow, Viktor bent over and reassembled the sandwich, picking off some of the sawdust. "I'll eat it."

She plopped back down on bench. "You look handsome. Handsome. Handsome." She tested the word, as if it were suddenly foreign. "But you talk funny."

"Yah, I'm from Reinveldt." Viktor took a bite of the sandwich, his soul rejoicing. He closed his eyes to savor it. "Are you drinking alone?"

She seemed to notice for the first time that she had lost her friends. She said her name was Trina and she insisted that her friends were here somewhere. Everything was a little fuzzy, though.

Viktor chowed happily on the sandwich and chatted with the girl while she sobered up. Several times during the meal, she propositioned him, but grateful as he was for the food, he was still a tad queasy from seasickness and in no mood for what she had in mind. Besides, the water had been very cold. Very. Cold.

She was pretty enough, if perhaps a little thin for his tastes. When he told her of the shipwreck, and of Malcolm Lanigan, she softened a bit, her attention taking on a more motherly tone. If, of course, your mother happened to be a drunk who lightly implied every few minutes that her flat was nearby. He asked Trina where he might find some shoes and a mischievous glint shone in her eyes.

"Follow me," she said, taking his hand.

It would be too generous to say that she was now steady on her feet, but her swaying, stumbling gait took on a rhythm that felt less catastrophic.

His new friend guided him through the streets, ignoring the catcalls of her newly located friends as she departed in the stranger's company.

Trina led Viktor through a number of alleys, passing a surprising amount of people asleep on the ground. He wasn't sure if these were vagrants or regular folk who had taken a night of celebration one cup too far. It seemed like too many people to fall into either camp. With his bare feet he had to be careful; there seemed to be a shocking amount of broken glass littering the streets.

Viktor and Trina emerged from an alley at the edge of a sinkhole whose size shocked him. He froze, staring in awe at the massive pit hundreds of yards across and full of garbage and collapsed buildings that had once stood at its edges. As they approached, the number of people sleeping off their hangovers grew to the point of absurdity. All around the pit, passed out drunks lay sprawled, snoring, tossing and turning. It smelled like piss.

"Yah, that's crazy." He stood at the edge, looking into the giant hole. The hair on the back of his neck stood on end. He almost felt like he could hear breathing, the rise and fall of some gigantic beast snoring louder than all the drunks put together, and yet silent. It was there and it wasn't. Viktor sprouted goosebumps.

"I know." Trina let go of his hand and spread her arms out grandly. "Welcome to the Sink. My uncle Burt always said this is where the cabal took down the Tyrant. You should hear his stories. Have you in stitches, right quick. Handsy bugger, though. Uncle Burt always said the Tyrant's buried somewhere under all that. The Tyrant Fall parties here are crackers, but this year was wild. I mean...blimey."

"What is blimey?" Viktor was still distracted by the sound of breathing, looking around for its source. "I don't understand."

She shrugged. "What's to understand? We're on holiday." An amorous spark lit her eyes. She edged closer to him. "Sure you don't want to pop over to my flat?"

It had been a long time since he'd been with a woman, and honestly, just flopping into a bed sounded amazing, but he remembered his tumor and Viktor was convinced she would be disgusted by it.

Slyly, he turned away from her as if surveying the edges of the Sink and pushed up his sleeve, discovering that the original scales had spread into a cluster of cancerous dragon flesh now the size of his hand.

He couldn't breathe.

All thoughts of trysting with Trina vanished. His heart raced and tears threatened his eyes. An ache set in, throbbing in the bones of his forearm, but Viktor couldn't tell if his worries or his tumor had brought it on. He couldn't think about it or he would panic. All he could do was tamp it down, crush it into the dark place within himself. "You thought I could find some shoes here?"

She gestured around them at all the drunks, some just beginning to stir as the sun cleared the horizon, cutting through the last of the morning fog. "Take your pick."

Viktor was no thief.

The idea scandalized him at first. He had never stolen a thing in his life. Except that horse in Dunnkettle. And a chocolate once from Oma's pantry. But he felt very bad about those things.

He really needed shoes, though. Maybe he could pick someone dressed a little nicer. Here and there he spotted revelers garbed in fine silk shirts and embroidered coats. Surely, these rich people could afford new shoes. Still, the idea bothered him. He looked at his feet, pleased to discover that they were nice and pink.

Trina saw the warring impulses and bewilderment on his face and took pity on him. "All right, you great big arse. You don't have to steal them."

"I don't?"

Trina blinked, unsteady on her feet. "I can see it bothers you. But that means you'll have to do it the hard way."

She took him by the hand and guided him back into one of the alleys.

"I don't understand. The hard way?" Viktor looked around the alley, searching for a reason she had brought him here.

With a smile, she pointed up.

Viktor lifted his gaze to the laundry lines strung between the tenements, discovering several pairs of shoes tied together by the laces and flung over the lines.

"It's a tradition," said Trina.

I zola walked home in a daze. The early revelers were already out, sitting on blankets in the sun, sipping, and in some cases guzzling wine. It was the first day of Tyrant Fall, but Izola was in no mood for a party. The shock of losing her tenure had set in, lending a surreal air to the campus festivities.

Despite the spring sun, she felt a chill as reality settled in. Her life revolved around Dannbridge University. Her daughter had moved overseas, her friends were her colleagues, her hobby was work. Without her position at the university she had nothing.

There had to be a way to fix this. Some way she could prove her theory, shove it in Logan's smirking face. She could appeal. There had to be a way to appeal.

A bottle shattered behind her. Izola started, spinning around to find a naked redhead with a blanket draped over his shoulders and a paper crown adorning his head.

His smile revealed wine-stained teeth. "Today," he declared, "I shall rewrite history."

Izola blushed, averting her eyes. Back along the path from which he'd come, a drunker voice called out. "We're coming for you, Tyrant!"

The naked ginger giggled, stepped unsteadily around the broken glass of his wine bottle, and capered off toward the arts building.

Izola let herself smile. There was some way through this mess, she just had to keep going.

Calmer now, she resumed her journey home, to the faculty housing along the western edge of campus. Beyond the brick and pillar architecture of the university, the cliffside of the Gilded Shelf marked the northern edge of the school grounds. Perched atop the rise, the palatial estates of the city's gentry overlooked Dannbridge.

Izola turned onto the cobblestone path that led to her apartment, making way for a small group of students who wished her happy Tyrant Fall. She managed to smile in return but keeping the smile on her face was a chore she soon abandoned.

When Izola emerged onto the lane where her townhouse was located, she was startled to find her front door ajar. Before she could react, two men carried her sofa out onto the lawn.

"What the hell?"

Ignoring her outrage, the men, dressed in filthy coveralls, loaded her couch into a wagon parked at the edge of the cobblestone street.

"Here we go." One of the movers, a middle-aged man with a hairy mole on his chin, folded his arms and turned to her.

"What are you doing?" she demanded.

He pointed. "Read the notice."

With a glare, Izola stormed up the walkway to where a handbill was nailed to her front door.

"Notice of Eviction," it read.

"Logan, you snake."

The second mover had the decency to look ashamed. "You can get whatever stuff you can carry."

"What are you doing with everything else?"

"Read the notice," said Hairy Mole.

Izola stared him down until he folded.

"Your stuff goes in storage," he finally confessed.

"What about me?" He started to say something but Izola cut him off. "If you say 'read the notice' again I will curse your little pecker to fall off."

"Oi, ma'am! I'm just doing my job."

The second mover intervened. "Go to Bartleworth Hall and they'll find you temporary housing in the dorms."

"The…dorms?" Horror. Absolute bloody horror. Was she really

supposed to go back to the dorms? The tremble in Izola's voice so shamed the men that they went back inside for another load.

For the second time in the last few days, she felt for a moment as if she were tangled in a spiderweb. She could feel the threads of fate clinging to her, tugging her toward something. Izola cursed under her breath. She fought the awful notion that all of this was her fault, that she had meddled in the magic of fate and now she was snared by it, like something had a hold of her. But for all of the spine-tingling dread, she still had no idea where to go from here. If she was doomed to some misfortune, at least the universe or whatever could spell it out for her.

At a loss of what else to do Izola followed them back inside to gather up some books and a bottle of wine.

17

Viktor lost his friend Trina in a park. A surge of new arrivals to the festivities flooded the grounds, resulting in a great deal of cursing, shouting, shoving, and, Viktor suspected, more than one person trampled beneath the surging crowd.

He wandered for another hour, grateful for his new shoes, which were quite fancy, with shiny black leather and gold eyelets for the laces, but also a little worried about his new friend. He hoped she could find her way home all right, this festival was a bit crazy. But as much as Viktor worried, it accomplished nothing. So he explored the city a while, finding himself in the neighborhood of Dannbridge's harbor, what the locals called Colossus Bay. If he squinted, Viktor could just make out the hand of an enormous statue jutting from the water, but it was so crusted in coral and bird shit that it looked more like a pale claw reaching out of the harbor. Viktor stared out at the sea.

Somewhere out there, Doktor Lanigan's corpse was being picked clean by squabbling seagulls. Murdered by dragon fanatics. And worse, Oberman's goons had done it for a reason. More than just simple revenge for knocking a few heads together at the sanitarium. This...Thule Society...or whatever they called themselves, were up to something, and they were afraid Viktor and Lanigan would get in the way.

Viktor rubbed his aching forearm. That letter from Oberman's colleague. All of its talk about unearthing something secret, something powerful. The lines about mastering the tumoring process, about triggering a mass tumoring…had to be real. You didn't kill to protect a theory.

Viktor wondered if perhaps this mirror they sought could really reverse his tumor. After all, the letter had said they'd have complete control of the process. He had noted that line; he'd hung his hopes on it. Viktor unrolled his sleeve to look at the patch of scales on his forearm again. It was like staring at someone who had been trampled by a horse, disturbing and yet he could not look away. Viktor jerked his sleeve back down to cover the tumor.

Trying to piece everything together made his head spin. He was certain that if the dwarf had lived, Lanigan would have figured it all out by now. But Viktor was a dolt. He'd always had trouble in school and trouble at the print shop, too. He could clearly picture the look of frustration and disappointment on his father's face every time he accidentally swapped a letter or two. And it seemed his stupidity now might cost him his life. His tumor was going to eat him alive.

How could Viktor possibly puzzle out what was happening? As much as he wanted to tear down everything Oberman had planned, Viktor had no idea where to start.

A bell tolled further inland, and looking off in the direction of the sound, he, for a moment, felt a tug. It was as if—and he knew this sounded ridiculous—but as if a strand of hair or something pulled him that way, like a rope was tied around him and someone was pulling on it. But just a wisp, it wasn't really there. It was just for a second and then it was gone.

Weird.

Lacking any other direction, Viktor set off toward the bell. He asked a stranger where the bell was and discovered that it was in the Tower of Tomes at the University of Dannbridge.

Viktor almost did a little hop, and trying to rein himself in at the last second, he stumbled. The stamp. Of course, it was the same place as the stamp on Oberman's letter. Oberman's colleague might be there. Oberman was a "doctor" after all; why wouldn't he have ties to a university? Quickening his step, Viktor soon found himself on the grounds of the illustrious center of learning.

A long avenue lined with flowering magnolia trees approached the heart of the campus. Everywhere he looked were manicured gardens lined with elegant trees and stately architecture. He had never liked school, but he *loved* this place.

The only thing he didn't love about it were the people. First of all, it was crowded. He didn't mind being around people. In fact, he liked it, but this was a little much. And second, everyone was very drunk. Very. Drunk. Viktor loved a good party, but holy shit.

"Excuse me, miss. I am looking for a Doktor Oberman."

The girl he questioned wore a crown of dandelions braided into her hair. "It's Tyrant Fall, guv." She spun away from him, dancing to the cadence of a distant drum circle.

It was after the fifth such rebuttal that Viktor literally stumbled over a pair of students sitting cross-legged on a blanket, passing a pipe back and forth between them.

"I say." The bespectacled young man wearing a paper crown looked up at him. He turned to his friend and giggled. "But what do I say?"

"What?" His friend laughed, too. "I don't get it." He accepted the pipe, but looking up at Viktor, held it out to him instead. "Do you wish to partake?"

"No, thank you." Viktor had in fact partaken a time or two. But he could hear his mother's gasp in the back of his head, the one she'd used when Auntie Gertrude had caught him doing it. Anyway, he really shouldn't. He had important things to do.

"Maybe just a little, yah."

"My guy." The crowned smoker passed him the pipe. "You're a Jarlsbecker, like that prick Oberman."

Viktor coughed. "You know Oberman?"

"Yeah, that chap is scary."

"Do you know where he is?"

The smokers looked at one another and shrugged. The one with the pipe coughed, holding up his finger to indicate he had something to say when he was done coughing. "He was with Professor Blythe."

"Ugh, that guy." The student shook his head.

"Such a phony."

"His wife is all right, though."

"No, they've divorced. That was nigh on a year ago. I told you that."

"I feel like perhaps you did. That makes perfect sense."

"Hey!" Viktor interjected. He felt a sudden urge to do jumping jacks. Although he wasn't certain it was entirely because of the news. "Where can I find Oberman?"

"We said we don't know, chap. They did his ex's tenure thing and she did not look happy."

"Are you still what's-her-name's teaching assistant?"

"No, but I was there to see what's-her-name."

"Please," Viktor asked, smiling. For a moment he became very self-conscious about the smiling. Was he…smiling wrong? That was silly. And so he laughed. And then became self-conscious about that, too. "What was in that stuff?"

"The finest herbs and spices." The student scratched the tangled hair beneath his crown.

"I'm sure it will be fine," said Viktor. "What about these people who know Oberman? How can I find them? What about this woman? Would she know where to find him?"

The student in the paper crown puffed his pipe contemplatively. "No idea, chap."

"Well, where is she?" Viktor wanted to run there, or maybe not run, but he certainly felt antsy. Maybe he should try on one of those paper hats.

Between the two of them, the smokers managed to give Viktor directions to faculty housing where this ex-wife of Oberman's colleague lived. Izola Sibola, or something like that. It felt like a thin lead, but he hadn't had much luck otherwise.

The crowned smoker pulled the pipe out of his mouth as Viktor left. "Be sure to congratulate her on her tenure!" They laughed again and his mate chucked him on the arm.

Viktor strolled across the campus, admiring the landscaping and architecture. This place was beautiful. Fascinating. An irrepressible smile worked its way onto his face. Where before he'd been annoyed by the revelers, he now found himself chuckling at their antics. It really wasn't like him to be such a killjoy. He'd been so angry since he'd gotten his tumor. All of this misadventure had only made things worse. He couldn't shake the feeling that he was going about this all wrong. He had already made so many stupid mistakes. He just wished he had never gotten his tumor, never gone to the sanitarium, never gotten Lanigan killed, never wound up here, on the far side of the channel trying to figure out what to do next.

Relax, he told himself.

It all seemed a little absurd. A little funny, even. Maybe he was the wrong guy to figure all of this out and stop Oberman's insanity, but he was the guy doing it. Viktor thought that was kind of great. Really great. Really, really, great.

The brick path led through some hedges to an open green with townhouses at the far end. Viktor pulled up short, taking a moment to register what he was seeing. Hundreds of half-naked students ran about the field, screaming and playing what looked to be an elaborate game of tag. On the far side of the field, in front of the townhouses, two men were packing up a wagon while a woman harangued them.

Again, Viktor felt that strange sensation, like he was tangled in a bunch of hair. But probably it was just the herbs he'd smoked.

Viktor started across the field toward the woman, judging her to be this professor...Scrinaldi...the smokers had described. Crossing the field proved more hectic than he had first expected. Dodging drunken students left and right, he managed to get halfway across. After ducking past an unshaven drunk who nearly collided with him, Viktor glanced up and got a good look at the professor.

He accidentally inhaled some saliva and started coughing. Even though his eyes watered he couldn't take them off of this Professor Scribonia. She was older than him, her hair pinned up in a bun, hints of grey at the temples. In one hand, she clutched a bottle of wine, and in the other, a leather book bag. Her glasses magnified her brown eyes. He felt a flicker of guilt as he admired her pleasantly plump figure. She was…beautiful.

Viktor cleared his throat and quelled his coughing fit. He smoothed his rumpled clothing, trying to make himself presentable, before a young man running by snatched the crown off his own head and planted it on Viktor's. He had only a split second to be baffled before another, much larger drunk wearing a toga made from a bedsheet tackled him.

"I'm the tyrant now, cunt," the man screamed in his ear, drool dangling from his lips. He snatched the crown off Viktor's head and jumped up, running off toward the other side of the field whooping and doing half-assed cartwheels that displayed every inch of his under carriage.

Viktor fought the strange impression that this wasn't real, that it was too weird. Maybe he shouldn't have smoked after all. That stuff was…uh…he'd lost the thought there.

Viktor looked up to see if the professor had noticed him. Of course she had. She looked away as soon as their eyes met and Viktor felt a flush as his face turned red.

He pushed himself to his feet and hurried over to her.

"Professor Scrumbolini, I presume."

Her smile twisted into a confused frown. "It's Scrivani."

"Sorry, Scravini."

"No. Scrivani. Scri-va-ni. Izola Scrivani."

Viktor had already butchered this. He knew he was turning red. *Stop*, he told himself. *This is about finding Oberman. Focus.* "I am looking for Doktor Oberman."

Her eyes narrowed.

This was going badly. As usual Viktor had all the charm of an ogre. A twinge of paranoia spiked his heart rate. Did she know he had been smoking the weed? He should say something nice to throw her off the scent. "Yah, congratulations on your ten year."

"My tenure?" Izola's nose twitched. It was really cute but also Viktor suspected she was mad at him. He should have listened to his mother; she hated the smokers, called them bungheads. Was he a bunghead?

A drunk ran past them, shrieking. Viktor watched him dart toward the edge of the field where another man caught his eye. This one didn't look like a student at all. He was a little older, his head shaved, red tattoos covering his arms, and one on the back of his head that looked suspiciously like the insignia on the assassin's dagger which he had confiscated.

"How do you know Doktor Oberman?"

Viktor's head whipped back around toward Professor Scrivani. She looked mad as hell. "I was Doktor Oberman's..." What was the Westonshire word for patient? "I was his pupil." Viktor spared a glance for the tattooed goon who was strutting out of view, past the fountain at the far end of the field.

"Oh, great," said the professor. "Another Jarlsbecker here to make my life miserable. Well, let me tell you something." She jabbed a finger into his chest. "I am sick to death of everything and everyone. I don't know what you think gives you the right to show up at my home, which isn't even my home anymore, and start harassing me. I'm sure you and Logan and your buddy Oberman will all have a good laugh about how you mucked about with my life, but I think it's sick and cruel of you showing up here. This is taking it too far!"

Viktor backed away, holding up his hands in surrender. She was talking so fast that he didn't understand some of it. "Whoa! Whoa! I didn't do anything."

"Don't play dumb with me."

Viktor felt there was a quip there, but it sort of fell apart.

Two girls tackled a heavyset man painted head to toe in purple makeup at the professor's feet. She scrambled back to keep from getting tangled up in the pile of laughing students. Izola looked up at Viktor, furious, and shouted, "That's it!" She spun away from him on her heel and stormed off the field.

Viktor looked from Izola to the tattooed thug, each headed in opposite directions. He sighed, taking a lingering look at the retreating figure of the professor, and turned to follow the goon with the Dragon Mark tattooed on the back of his head.

18

Izola had run out of patience *and* wine by the time she left Bartleworth Hall. The admin assigning her temporary housing looked down her nose at Izola, who was drinking from the bottle, but it was afternoon by then, and it was Tyrant Fall. What did she expect? It was quite judgmental, Izola decided. This officious little git had no clue what she'd been through today.

The laborious process was full of mind-numbing minutiae, form after form, endless waiting, pointless questions; a procedure designed to erode her into accepting the dungeon cell which inevitably awaited. Apparently, they were understaffed because of the holiday, making it all the slower, all the more soul crushing.

Seer's Eyes, she'd been evicted. She hadn't seen that one coming.

A gallows smile found its way to her lips.

But all the waiting gave Izola time to think. Perhaps it was the wine, but she decided that she needed to do something really awful to Logan. Not kill him; it would hurt Page if her father died, obviously...but something truly nasty. A curse? One of the books she had gathered was blank, just in case. A little of the old Scrivani magic just might be in order. It would serve the prat right.

There in the waiting room of the housing office Izola opened the book and stared at the blank pages, feeling the storm of pain and potential inside her. She wrote the words "I loved you and you humiliated me." Her pen was poised to write more, but she couldn't.

Sighing, she put the cap back on and closed the book. It was a good start. At least it was true. She needed to vomit a torrent of words onto the page if she really wanted to curse him, but something in her felt blocked.

Izola had never cursed anyone before. It surprised her that she didn't feel guilty at all about it. Of course, if Page knew she was trying to curse her father it would only make things worse between them. The Seers knew there was already enough tension between Izola and her daughter. If she killed Logan, at least Page would see how much the letch had wronged her.

Perhaps there was a little guilt, but her curse book was far from finished.

When the admin finally handed her a sheet of paper and a key to her new room, Izola left in a bit of a fog, half drunk and wholly distracted by an overwhelming urge to hit back at her ex-husband. She headed in the direction of the dormitories, passing through the grand colonnade lined by cherry trees to the statue garden outside the Daimler Building. Izola descended the Asterion Steps to the plaza in front of student housing.

At the base of the stairs, a boy with a sweet falsetto strummed a mandolin to the polite attention of his peers. Naked men wearing crowns of dubious quality dotted the square, the throng of students absorbed in drinking games and lively chatter.

Someone lost a game of dice in dramatic fashion and a cluster of the party goers erupted in gay laughter. Izola spotted an unattended bottle of wine beside a stone bench. A little sotted by the first bottle, she brushed aside the question of its ownership. With a shrug, she picked it up, walking a little faster.

"Hey!" A young woman with the symbol of the Quorum painted on her forehead sat up on a nearby blanket. "That's our wine."

Izola looked her dead in the eye. "I saw my ex-husband smile today."

"Geez, lady, take it."

Izola pointed at the young man beside her. "Don't trust that little prick."

"All right, lady. Enjoy the wine."

Izola made a flourish, nearly dropping her book bag in the process. "I'm sure he's neat. It's his penis you should worry about."

With that she spun toward the dorms and redoubled her pace. The Thistleby Building looked like something from one of her nightmares. Broken glass and vomit garnished the steps to the entrance. Revelers sat in the open windows smoking pipes, and somewhere inside some miscreant was playing a pan flute, quite badly. Shuddering in anticipation of sleepless nights and rowdy neighbors, Izola entered her new home. Fruit flies scattered at her approach as she waded through spilled ale and the smell of unwashed laundry. Down the hall, a girl's shrill laughter grated on Izola's sole surviving nerve.

It will be fine, she lied to herself. *This is only temporary.* Izola checked the sheet of paper the admin had given her and for the first time realized her room, B013, was in the basement.

"A literal dungeon."

Izola descended the musty staircase to the basement. A long hallway lit by a single lantern waited at the bottom. If she were murdered, Izola would have to decide whether to haunt her assailant or her ex. She waded into the gloom, letting her eyes adjust, squinting at the dusty numbers painted on the doors until at the end of the hall she discovered B013. A voice muttered on the other side of the door.

No! Seer's Eyes, no. A roommate.

It was too unfair. She held up the sheet of paper looking for the bad news but it was too dark to read.

Should she knock?

She did have a key after all. No, Izola decided to knock. The muttering fell silent.

"Who is that?" a man's thickly accented voice called from the other side.

"Professor Izola Scrivani. I...I've been assigned here. I suppose we are roommates." Izola dropped her voice. "Kill me now."

Bolts slid unlocked and a man with a caramel complexion and a wispy combover opened the door. He wore an old-fashioned suit, the sort she hadn't seen in years. "Your papers?" he asked.

Izola handed him her room assignment. The man produced a monocle hanging from a chain around his neck and studied the document with a comical air. There was something familiar about him, but she couldn't place it right away. It nagged at her, you didn't meet someone from the Afaran Coast every day. Let alone someone so…interesting. How did she know him?

"Forgive me, *Associate* Professor Scrivani. It has been quite some time since I shared my quarters. I suppose if everything is in order… Please, forgive the mess."

He opened the door, backing away with oddly careful steps. A bitter smell and bright lamplight spilled out. Inside was a two-person dormitory as she might have imagined, a tiny box with which to share the worst day of her life. And it bristled with weird devices, books, and bottles of dubious ointments.

Great. Her new home looked like the inside of a lunatic's brain.

She studied her roommate once again. His fingers were stained black and his fancy old suit was frayed at the cuffs. He bobbed his head a little too fast and giggled as his eyes fell to the floor, not to avoid eye contact, but to admit the extremity of the disorder in the room. His careful steps had picked their way through the narrow path navigating the eclectic groups of bottles on the floor.

Why did he look so familiar?

"A moment." He held up an ink-stained finger. Her new roommate stooped and began to move the bottles on the floor to one side of the room. He pointed at one of them. "Be very careful with this one," he said, continuing to make room for Izola. When he had cleared a path, he winced, his smile looking as if it pained him.

Hesitantly, Izola followed him into their dorm room. Even before she entered, the caustic stench of chemicals assailed her. The bedroom had been converted into a laboratory of sorts. One cot remained neatly made up, while the other had a slab of wood laid over it which was in turn covered by shelves full of jars and beakers. In the middle of the makeshift workbench, a small cast-iron vat bubbled with no discernible heat source under it, emitting tendrils of green vapor. Stacks of books lined the walls in chaotic fashion and a few racks of vials had been mounted above them.

"Home sweet home," Izola said, breathless.

"Forgive the mess, my dear. I have been speaking with the Uber Toads for days now."

"The…what?"

"Terrifying extradimensional beings. It seems someone in Dannbridge has attracted their attention." The alchemist plucked a vial from one of the racks on the wall and held it up to the lantern mounted above it. Satisfied at having confirmed its contents, he held it out to her. "I have developed this concoction, if you'd like to hear them, too."

"If I drink this, I will hear…the Uber Toads?"

"Correct."

"That's very thoughtful, but no, thank you."

"Probably wise. They are quite terrifying." As he replaced the vial, Izola noticed that one of his eyes was green and the other purple. *Professor Wormwood!* "Forgive me." He put one hand to his chest and sketched a formal bow. "I am Doktor Jabar Wormwood."

Izola shook her head in disbelief. He looked exactly the same as the last time she saw him, once she got past his disheveled appearance; he hadn't aged a day. "Izola Scrivani. Do you remember me?"

"Ah." Jabar held up a finger. "I once purchased quite a unique book from an itinerant merchant. Bertolo Scrivani."

Izola cocked her head. "What? My great-grandfather? That's impossible."

"He was missing one of his canine teeth. A very funny man. This was some years ago in a suburb of Saint Jene. Have you been to Ostaria?"

"No. You are telling me that you purchased a book from my great-grandfather who has been dead for forty years?"

"Has it been that long?" Wormwood began clearing the contents of his workbench, stacking them haphazardly around the room to free up her cot.

"How old are you?" she asked.

"Unfortunately, I have spent a great deal of time in astral projection. Would you like to try it?"

"What? No."

"I suppose by simplistic chronological perspective I will be 174 years old on Saturday."

The warm and fuzzies she'd been feeling at reuniting with her old teacher dried up a little. Still, Izola remembered him fondly enough. But...174?

"I'm sorry, you are telling me that you're nearly two hundred years old?"

"My time in the Other makes me feel much older."

"But...how?"

Wormwood surveyed the messy room, teeming with burbling experiments and ancient books.

"Science."

"Just...science."

"That's right, my dear, the science of magic. The art of the arcane. The power of the potion."

Izola nodded, biting her lip. "All right, let's table that for now. Do you remember me, Professor Wormwood?"

"Please, Doktor Wormwood. I haven't taught in years. Too much politics these days. Archibald Thistleby and Black Lung have a veritable proxy war in the admissions office. I prefer to float above the fray, like the proverbial cloud." His gaze drifted, as if the idea were carrying him away.

Izola was forced to concede that particular point. After all, university politics had landed her in this mess. "You were my Natural Alchemy professor ages back. Before I left the uni to have my daughter, Page."

He donned a pair of blue tinted spectacles and squinted at her. "I don't remember you."

Flattering. "Well, I remember you. You were always so animated. So different from the other professors."

"What a charming recollection," he cut her off cheerily, still clearing out her side of the room. "You must have been very young. I haven't taught in quite some time."

"I was sixteen. Early admittance. I only took your class for a month or so. I had to withdraw quite suddenly."

"Happens to the best of us, my dear." For a moment Izola thought he was choking, but soon discovered it to be a laugh, of sorts. He cleared his throat. "What brings you to the basement of the Thistleby Building?"

"Exile." Izola set her books down at the foot of the bed and started hunting through Wormwood's alchemical tools for a corkscrew. She sat on the edge of a wooden chair stacked with books. "I presented my thesis today. Only my ex-husband maneuvered himself into chairing the review committee."

"Dreadful."

"Yeah, it was. Long story short, my thesis was rejected and I lost my tenure. Oh yeah, and I was evicted of course."

"So sorry. What was your thesis?"

For the first time, she felt a tad ashamed to say it out loud, as if it were suddenly ludicrous. But it wasn't, and she'd be damned if she'd let Logan win that easily. "I proved that the Tyrant was a dragon, and that a Dragon Cult persists in Dannbridge to this very day. They didn't even let me finish."

"That's really a shame. Especially since it's so obviously true."

Izola found a corkscrew. "Wait, really? You think so?" Her warm and fuzzies bubbled back to the surface.

"Oh, of course. For a while it was quite fashionable. About a century ago, clubs like the Fraternal Order of the Scale and the Thule Society were all the rage."

"You know about the Thule Society?"

"A century ago it was quite out in the open."

"Yes, it's gone to ground. But that's quite different from the Order of the Scale. It's just a fraternity. My husband's fraternity, in fact."

Wormwood reached out and patted her knee. "Oh, now that's *really* suspicious. Maybe it is just a fraternity nowadays, but eighty or ninety years ago, there was a fad. You know, these days some of those old ideas are not so popular. But back then they were normal. A lot of young men obsessed with their heritage, it was quite a cloak-and-dagger affair. But then some of those rich sons started breaking out in tumors. These days people treat tumorlings like pariahs, but back then, they were monsters. Too much embarrassment for proper families. But since Black Lung's rise to power, I suppose things have changed a bit. She's the first tumorling to join the Quorum…well…ever. I'm not normally one to put much stock in rumors, but the rumors about her are more than a little frightening. All these Dragonists, that's what I call them, they all seem to idolize her. It makes me wonder why your husband and his colleague went to the trouble of scuttling your thesis review. Maybe your ex-husband's fraternity is a bit more sinister than you suspect."

Izola popped the cork on her pilfered wine. "That little weasel." Was it possible his motives weren't purely personal? She was getting paranoid. "Do you think they could be *plotting* something?"

"By god, I hope so." His grin looked a touch manic.

"It's Tyrant Fall." Izola took a pull off the wine bottle. "They'll be celebrating at their clubhouse. I mean, it's probably better to just poke in and have a peek than sit around fretting about it."

"Say no more," said Wormwood, reaching for a vial from one of his racks. "Just let me change."

19

Viktor followed the thug with the red tattoos into the campus cafeteria. A sparse crowd of holiday diners sat at long wooden tables eating stew from wooden bowls. The soft shuffle of feet and murmured voices lent the place a sleepy atmosphere. Overhead, cobwebs hung from the rafters.

The enforcer barged into the hall with all the subtlety of a thunderstorm, turning every head in the building. He marched over to one of the lunch ladies, growling threats until she opened her cash box and doled out a gold coin. Just as the thug was about to grab it, the lunch lady closed her fist around the coin, her hairy lip trembling. She whispered something that made the gangster go pale.

"Nice," Viktor whispered.

The goon's head swung around to discover who had said that. Viktor ducked behind one of the tables pretending to tie his shoe. He waited out the thug, imagining a few good one-liners the lunch lady might have said. Beside him, a women slurping broth looked down at him with a total lack of curiosity. The door exiting the cafeteria slammed and Viktor shot to his feet, scrambling after the extortionist.

It turned out that he was easy to follow, stopping as often as he did, hassling the shopkeepers of every kiosk and corner shop on campus.

Part of Viktor wanted to intervene, but he kept telling himself he needed to follow the brute until he led him to the rest of his gang. Plus he was still quite stoned and figured it best to let the smoke mellow a bit before he really got into it with these guys. Even as the intoxicating effects started to subside, Viktor kicked himself for getting distracted when he had important things to do. It had seemed like something the old Viktor would have done. At the time, it seemed like a way to get back a little of what he'd lost. But now he felt foolish and wished he would just sober up already.

The gangster continued on his rounds, leaving the beautifully maintained campus, and heading back toward the seedier areas closer to the water. He went from peddler to peddler, rounding up coin. At one point, Viktor watched the thug argue with a shirtless tattooist. The two squared off, bickering. The brute grabbed the tattooist by the neck, spitting threats in his face until the street artist finally decided it was better hand over payment than to take a beating.

Before heading off the thug surveyed his surroundings. As his eyes swept over him, Viktor snatched a dress off a street vendor's rack and held it up to himself, trying to blend in.

"Oh," said the shopkeeper, an old woman wearing a comical amount of rouge. "I like that on you. It would really show off your calves."

"I'll think about it," said Viktor.

The enforcer moved on and Viktor smiled at the old woman, putting the dress back. After a moment of indecision, he decided to talk to the tattooist instead of pressing his luck following the thug.

Viktor approached the spot on the sidewalk where the artist, covered head to toe in faded tattoos, hunched over another shirtless man. His client lay face-down on a small wooden table with a dingy quilt thrown over it.

"Ow!" said the face-down man.

"Stop sniveling." The tattooist bent to his work again, jabbing a needle into the customer's back. When Viktor's shadow fell over the tattooist, the artisan squinted up at him. "Almost done, boy-oh. You can have a go next."

"Yah, I have a question."

"I can draw a broken crown. I can make letters. Whatever you want, old Martin will fix you right up. Drop your ass on that chair."

"It's not about that. That man you were just arguing with, you gave him a tattoo like this, yah?" Viktor held out the assassin's knife.

The artist squinted at the mark, his face twisting in fear. "Put that away," he hissed.

"So you did?"

Martin inspected his work on the other fellow's back. He wiped away blood with a filthy rag and shrugged. "All done. Come on, boy-oh. Up you go." He patted his canvas on the ass.

The customer rolled over. "Already? Wasn't so bad." He tried to look over his shoulder at the tattoo and turned in a circle like a dog chasing its tail. When it proved impossible to get a better angle he gave up and showed his back to Viktor. "What do you think, mate? I ain't paying if it's a whiff."

Through the raw patch of skin Viktor glimpsed the outline of a crown with a crack running down the middle. "Wonderful." Viktor gave it two thumbs up. Obviously suspicious, the man nevertheless handed Martin a couple of coins.

The tattooist saluted him as he walked away before turning back to Viktor. "You ought to forget you ever saw that symbol."

Viktor shook his head. "It's important."

Martin studied him up and down. "Even a big bloke like you is only going to get hurt chasing after the likes of them."

"Them?"

Martin shook his head in resignation. "Red Sleeves."

"What?"

"You don't sound like you're from around here." Martin tilted his head back and faintly nodded at the gravity of his own warning. "Around here, everyone knows the Red Sleeves. A nasty pack of cutthroats. You'd be better off steering well clear of them."

"Tell me about them."

"You sure? It won't be no beating if you cause trouble. Stick you full of holes and dump you in the gutter without thinking twice, they will. That bloke Oscar Red Sleeves is sick. A right killer."

"I was in the war. I'm no lamb."

"Suit yourself, mate. You might want to head up to the uni and try to visit Drachen House. Something's up there. A bunch of the lads have been down for tattoos like that this week."

"What's Drachen Haus?"

"Boy-oh, you ain't gonna like it."

20

Devin stepped in a pile of dog shit outside his mansion.

"Oh, honestly." He scowled down the moonlit lane toward the Fulminster Estate where the offending lapdog originated. *Horrid little beast.* Devin leaned against the wrought-iron gate to wipe his foot on the lawn. With a careful inspection of his new Isilano loafers, he cursed under his breath and scoped around once more to make certain there were no witnesses to this indignity.

His father may have taken his key to the mansion, but Devin had been sneaking in and out of Thistleby Manor since he was a teenager. With one last glance over his shoulder, Devin planted his foot in the bottom fold of an ornamental crest with a winged rose and vaulted himself over the fence. His leggings snagged on the pinnacle as he came down, tearing a run in them.

In a fit of pique, Devin tore off his wig and spiked it on the ground. "Vex my life!" he hissed. Then, filled with sudden remorse, he plucked his wig off the ground and apologized to it.

Dogs barked near the manor house.

Devin facepalmed. "Barnabas! Agatha!" He hissed. "It's me."

Two canine shadows trotted forward, growling faintly until they were near enough to catch his scent. The hounds nuzzled him as he addressed the pair. "Yes all right. Love you, too. But this is a new suit." To be fair, he realized glumly that his attire was already a bit unkempt after the day he had had. An image of Thomas' face as the blade bit into his stomach flashed through Devin's mind and he pushed it away. His stomach soured, acid creeping up his throat.

Barnabas whined, cocking his head at his master, but Devin was stuck. His heart pounded, palms sweaty. This wasn't some Torrence Jasper novel. This was real, and he was no storybook Ward Man. He was a fuck-up. A fuck-up who might just get Thomas killed.

Barnabas barked.

Bless him, really. The good old boy had broken the spell.

The dog barked again. "Yes, all right, Barnabas. Enough."

A light went on in the servants' house and Devin scurried for cover behind a manicured hedge. As the door creaked open, Danby appeared with a lantern in one hand. The old butler wore his sleeping robe and a tasseled wool cap. "Is someone there?"

Shit! This was all a cock-up now.

Barnabas looked from Danby to where Devin hid behind the bush, wagging his tail.

The butler squinted and Devin knew he had been spotted. He stepped into the light before the servant could sound the alarm.

"Danby," Devin whispered at the top of his lungs. "Danby, it's me."

"Master Devin?"

"Yes." He closed the distance between them, realizing that he was tiptoeing. "Keep your voice down." Devin looked over the butler's shoulder into the servants' house but saw no one else stirring.

"Master Devin, you're not supposed to be here. I have *very* explicit instructions on the matter."

As shameful and demeaning as it felt, there was no other way. He simply had to do it. Devin gritted his teeth, bracing for it.

At last he managed to say, "Please."

Danby gasped. "Master Devin?"

"Please, Danby."

The butler looked as awkward as Devin felt. "Well...I...I..."

"And something else, Danby."

"Oh?"

"Thank you," said Devin.

"Master." Danby blushed. "Whatever for?"

"Oh, you know. All the fine butlering you do."

Danby stiffened, a tear threatening to streak from the corner of his eye. "Thank you, sir." He sounded quite out of breath.

Devin hadn't counted on Danby gushing so. That part was as awkward as he'd feared, but in a way, it was sort of nice that he had so affected the old man. Devin fancied himself a good egg, really. His breeding, no doubt.

"In any case," Devin whispered. "I've just got to pop in and pop out. I know father's on the warpath, but it would be kind of you to go back to bed. I'll let myself in." He considered adding a threat but felt it would be a tad gauche.

"Right," Danby whispered. He pantomimed locking his lips and tossing the key over his shoulder. "You were never here." The butler backed inside the servants' house with exaggerated care and slowly pressed the door closed.

Barnabas and Agatha loped up the rise toward the manor house, to the kitchen window where Devin came and went after hours. The front door was a noisy affair and he was in the habit of avoiding it when the clamor threatened to rouse his father and the litany of disappointed advice sure to follow. Devin arrived a moment later at the bay window bulging from the kitchen wall. The central pane was cut from stained glass in the figure of the Thistleby Crest, dragon wings set behind a thorny rose. The other two panes were ordinary windows that could slide up and down. Father didn't know it, but the cook, Mrs. Blair, smoked her pipe over the sink and she opened the windows to air out the kitchen a few times a day. When he was thirteen, Devin had taught Mrs. Blair a simple trick to disarm the wards from the inside. Now every time she smoked, she left him a way in.

Devin ran his hand over the symbols painted on the windowsill. He felt a warm pulse of magic emanating from them and cursed. He had to wonder if Mrs. Blair had suddenly quit smoking her pipe, or had his father perhaps been wise to his ploy all along?

Well, Devin would show him. Maybe his father knew this trick, but it was by no means Devin's only way in.

He set out at a brisk pace around the side of the house to where the masonry featured an ornate facade of oversized, thorny roses creeping up the wall like a sculptor's trellis.

With a resigned inspection of his favorite suit, he began his climb up the wall. The intricate stonework afforded excellent hand-holds as he ascended. Up he went to the third story, not looking down. Lord Jasper wouldn't look down.

Devin got all the way to the top where a ledge of a single brick's width wrapped all the way around to the second window. It was his sister's old room. She was away on campaign of course, so she would not be inside. If his father had barred him from entry through the kitchen, his own bedroom window surely sported fresh wards and a lock that cost more than his now-soiled suit. But his father, for all of his cunning, didn't think like a Ward Man, he thought like a wizard. He wasn't likely to have fortified Ariana's room.

Devin made his way along the ledge, still not looking down. Not thinking about falling, or failing, or getting Thomas killed, or proving his father right.

Instead, he thought, *Careful, careful, careful, fuck!*

Devin had looked down and saw the huge gap between himself and the ground. He pictured himself with perfect clarity toppling from the ledge and rotating three quarters of a turn to strike his head on the cobblestones below. His wig felt unbearably sweaty and he struggled with the urge to fling it away like an attacking bird.

Steady.

If he could picture Devin Thistleby falling to his death he could picture Lord Torrence Jasper, cool as an iceberg, edging toward Ariana's window. Finally, Devin was pleased to find himself in posi-tion before the window. They could scoff at his love of the Lord Jasper novels all they wanted, they simply didn't understand.

Devin held his hand over the wards and smiled to feel the peri-odic pulse of the bypass he had counter-warded into the symbols. At the precise rhythm, he spiked the wards with a little jolt of resistance to break the spell. He winced as a bit of the magic sent a barb of pain up his arm. The wards would take another ten minutes or so to collect enough ambient power to trigger again. Devin needed to hurry to be sure he was in and out before they did.

He slid the window open and crawled through, rolling onto the mountainous pile of ruffled pillows atop his sister's bed. He crept to the door and waited for his heart to slow, listening in the darkness, a swath of moonlight cutting through the room to spill onto a dressing couch by the toilet door.

When no evidence of discovery surfaced, he made his way into the hall. Devin stopped in front of his own bedroom and considered freshening up. But no, he chided himself. He needed to get in and out before his father realized it. He knew he wasn't much of a friend, dragging Thomas into his affairs the way he had, but Devin would be damned if he cocked all this up over a clean suit. To their peers, Thomas was nouveau riche. Most of them looked down their noses at him, but really, Thomas was the only friend he had. All the others might come to his parties and make small talk, but deep down, Devin knew they looked askance at him, too. It was like everyone could see that he was a screw-up. Not a serious person. He wasn't destined to hold the Q. He wasn't Quorum material. They all thought he was a joke. Well, if they could only see him now. Let them try to make fun of Lord Jasper, of Devin being a Ward Man, after he actually stole his father's piece of the Q.

It had never been done before. He'd be a fucking legend.

Devin passed his room and kept on until he came to the door of his father's study. The door jamb was wrought from obsidian with silver inlay, very out of place in the wood and tapestry style of the rest of the mansion. He could feel the magic radiating from the protective symbols, but it was no surprise that a treasure of this magnitude would have such formidable security. Normally, wards like this were well above Devin's ability to circumvent. As much as he loved pretending to be Lord Jasper, he was not a dashing, elite Ward Man. Perhaps he was more than a novice, with a bit of obsession and some natural talent, but he was no master burglar. And he was obviously not as cool under pressure. And yet, these ironclad wards had presented their puzzle many years ago and he had long since devised their solution. The only trouble was he had yet to work up the nerve to try his theory.

Devin wondered what his father might do if he caught him. He wouldn't kill him, probably. But his fury would be apoplectic. Devin pictured himself doused in dragonfire and reflected that it would simply not do to be caught in the act.

Licking his thumb and forefinger, he rubbed the tips together until metastatic energy crackled between them. Devin touched one finger to the symbol at the center of the threshold of the study to discharge the buildup. Then he stood and traced a new symbol in the interval between the two inlaid in silver. The symbol he drew glowed with arcane light, freezing the wards' effect in stasis. Holding his breath, Devin turned the doorknob and entered his father's study, half cringing at the prospect of a hidden ward slagging him on the spot.

But Devin survived his entry and found himself in the rather sleek library of Lord Archibald Thistleby III, member of the Quorum, father of the fucking year. And as Devin stared past the leather sofas and immaculate bookshelves, he beheld the soft light of the Shard ensconced on a simple plaque on the wall. The elegant furnishings held the piece of the Quorum as their focal point, framing the shattered relic of the Tyrant's crown.

It was about six inches long in Devin's estimation, curved slightly to the left. It made him miss Thomas all the more.

The golden Shard shone with an internal light. It was sharp on one end and a little bulbous on the other, as if the metal had started to melt. Had that happened when the Quorumites defeated the Tyrant? Such history. Such power.

Devin passed the antique desk to stand before the glowing fragment of metal mounted on the wall. Though he could see no wards in evidence, he could feel them, masking the artifact's power like a lace curtain drawn closed to shut out the sun. He held up his hands a little more than a foot from the Shard and closed his eyes, sensing the dimensions of the wards' power, and the relentless energy of the relic they contained. With concentration, he could almost see the hidden wards drawn in a circle around the mounted artifact.

It was laughable that he might have inherited this one day if not for his unerring ability to make a mess of, well, everything. Devin sighed. This stupid thing. He wondered what his life might have been like without it, but the Q was too much entwined in his family history to imagine things otherwise. Could stealing it repair all the damage it had done to their family? No, not likely. It would probably make it worse. Fucking thing. Devin wished he could snatch the Q from its display and dash it on the floor. But Devin knew his flesh was far more fragile than this Shard of the Tyrant's crown.

The matrix of wards shrouding it was powerful, but the design made perfect sense to him. He could see the logic of it and knew just where to apply a little bit of misdirection to open the wards. That wasn't the problem, though. It had been years since he had been so close to the Q. He'd forgotten the overwhelming nature of its power. He knew, of course, that it was dangerous to hold. He supposed he had never given much thought to taking it–it always felt more of a curse than a blessing—but he realized now that it was too much for him to contain. Even from behind the wards he could feel the power it radiated stinging his skin. Without their protection, he wouldn't get halfway down the lane carrying that bloody thing. It would fry him.

Well, shit, he thought. *Now what?*

He couldn't just grab it and run. He'd have to find a portable solution to contain its power.

A creak from the hallway plucked a note of fear on his spine. Or was it just the house settling? He needed to get out of here. He'd have to come back when he could find a way to safely handle the Q. This plan was as buggered as the village strumpet on payday, and honestly, Devin was in dreadful need of a good sherry.

I zola had nightmares about parties like this.

Far better, in her estimation, to spend an evening curled up with a good book than to spend it packed shoulder to shoulder with a thousand cross-eyed mouth breathers.

Izola and Wormwood stood outside of Drachen Haus in shock. Students had trampled the lawn into mud. A circle had been cleared to form a chicken fighting arena where two boys with girls on their shoulders faced off against each other. The pairs circled one another to the uproarious cheers of their classmates.

"Well," said Wormwood, lacing his fingers together and twiddling his thumbs, "this is much stranger than I anticipated."

"How the devil do we get through this crowd?" Izola adjusted her book bag on her shoulder. "I don't think I like this."

"Ah, perhaps I can be of service." Wormwood opened his coat, revealing several vials tucked into custom-made pockets. "We have options."

"Let's hold off on all that until it's necessary…whatever *that* is."

Izola led the way as they pushed through the outer fringes of the milling crowd, passing a young man holding his girlfriend's hair as she heaved her guts out.

Izola felt a twinge of misgiving. Maybe she was grasping when she imagined that Logan's old fraternity was part of a conspiracy to silence her thesis. More likely it was just Logan being a horse's ass. But Wormwood claimed the Order of the Scale had once had open ties to the Dragon Well and to the Thule Society. Izola worried she might be getting desperate to put so much stock in Wormwood's eccentric theories.

She wondered for a moment if that was how everyone else saw her, a bit of a nutter, but Izola shoved the uncomfortable thought away as a trio of bare-chested young men with letters painted on them whistled at her. She was almost thankful for the distraction. Almost.

One of them asked, "Why'd you bring your grandpa?"

Wormwood reached inside his coat but Izola stopped him, wondering what chaos those vials in his jacket might contain. She took his hand and led Wormwood toward Drachen House, away from the catcalls of Drachen Haus' finest.

As she wove through the crowd, Izola felt a strange sensation, like a spiderweb brushing over her face. The feeling was accompanied by a sense of déjà vu, but she couldn't say why.

And then she saw him.

"Oh shit," said Izola.

"What is it?"

Not ten feet away, Izola spied the young Jarlsbecker who had accosted her outside her townhouse. She suddenly felt a little warm as if she'd been running, and her heart was racing. He surely wasn't hard to look at: standing a head taller than the students around him, with a barrel chest and a thick head of artfully unkempt hair. She pushed all of that nonsense away, though. He was too young for her, for one thing, and probably one of Oberman's cronies to boot. That she'd even thought it flustered Izola.

"Hold on to my shirt, dear," she said to Wormwood, steering away from Viktor as she pressed into the throng surrounding the fraternity.

Izola could hardly believe it, but it was worse inside. The air held the suspended funk of a thousand armpits mixed with the tang of sour wine and the lingering waft of shameless farts. She clutched her leather book bag tight, afraid someone might try to snatch it. Young men shouted over the din, alcohol lending their jubilation the exuberance of a fistfight. Two grand staircases wrapped around the edges of the giant foyer to meet on a landing overhead, from which two naked boys were being dangled by their ankles. Below, more fraternity members tossed olives and dates up to the suspended pledges, who tried to catch the morsels in their mouths.

Izola and Wormwood elbowed through to the room at the back where tipsy girls in flower crowns danced inside a drum circle. The bitter scent of herbal smoke lingered in the air. Wormwood and Izola shoved on to the next room where they came to a hallway with a door at the end. Before it stood a decidedly out-of-place thug with red tattoos on his hands and arms, his head shaved. Clearly, he was standing guard, and just as clearly, judging by the empty hallway, he was very persuasive.

To demonstrate this, he bellowed at them, "Fuck off, cunts."

Without missing a beat Wormwood spun on his heel. But to Izola's surprise, he used the motion to conceal a little sleight of hand. Reaching inside his coat for a vial, Wormwood sucked the contents into his mouth. Izola gawped, fascinated by the skillful misdirection. Wormwood held up a finger as if something had just occurred to him. He spun sloppily back toward the thug and closed the distance between them with a feigned stagger. Just as the thug cocked back to slug Wormwood, the alchemist spit his potion in the man's face. The guard crumpled to the floor like a marionette whose handler had been poisoned to death by an eccentric alchemist. With a giggle, Wormwood turned around and sketched a theatrical bow.

"Is he?"

"This goon now embarks on the Journey of Carthusian into the astral realms of the fell Spider Prince."

"So…dead?"

"He will return changed…or not at all."

"…Right."

Izola stepped over the goon and pressed her ear to the door.

There was too much noise coming from the party to hear what transpired within the room, so she looked back at Wormwood and shrugged. "Should we…I don't know…make a plan?"

Wormwood smiled, his teeth still tinted blue from the potion he had spit in the guard's face. The alchemist opened his coat and pointed at the various vials as he explained.

"This one makes me pretty, but I don't want to use it here. This one makes me ugly, and mean, but it's dangerous. This one is for my erectile dysfunction. This one is quite flammable." He skipped over an empty slot. "That's where the poison was. Oh...this one causes very realistic hallucinations of the demon clowns."

"Yeesh. I'll leave it up to you. Probably not the one for your knob, though." She reached for the doorknob, cringing momentarily at an intrusive thought, before she gave the knob a twist. It was unlocked. "Shall we?"

They stepped over the threshold into what proved to be another stairwell down.

Cringing as the first step creaked, Wormwood seized Izola by the shoulder. "Wait," he hissed, pointing in the air beside her head. "What is that?"

"What is what?"

"It's like a diaphanous string or something." His finger traced the path of this figment back down the hallway they had come from to discover a figure standing at the far end. "Fascinating. A bit of Fate magic?"

"You," said Viktor.

"He's one of Oberman's cronies," she whispered.

"Hey! I heard that. I'm not a crony. I am very angry with this Oberman." He punched the palm of his hand to demonstrate his intentions.

"Ssshhh. Keep your voice down." Izola looked at Wormwood, who shrugged. They crept back into the hallway away from the stairs. Viktor, sensing their wariness, tiptoed toward them. Izola furrowed her brow. "So, you aren't a friend of Oberman?"

"I tried to tell you this earlier but you wouldn't listen."

"Well, you were hardly forthcoming about it. As I recall, you ran off."

He pointed at her. "Nein, that's not fair. You...well...you..."

She put her hands on her hips. "I'm waiting."

Wormwood interjected. "If I may, perhaps this is not a good time." He turned to Viktor. "Oberman has wronged you?"

"Yah."

"Just as he has wronged Izola. And you believe he is up to something?"

"Yah."

"As do we. I suggest we pool our efforts and investigate this shady character together."

Izola looked at Viktor; he was grinning a little too widely. She narrowed her eyes, but honestly, she was repressing a smile of her own. Why? The Seers only knew.

"Fine," she said. "Wait here and guard the hall."

"What? I'm going down there. It could be dangerous."

She grabbed him by the shirt and pulled him down to her level. For a split second she lost her train of thought. "Ugh, it's not like we are going to go down there to brawl. We're sneaking." She let go of him and he resumed his full height. Her eyes travelled across his frame. "And something tells me sneaking isn't your strong suit."

Viktor opened his mouth to respond but Wormwood set his hand on Viktor's chest to stay the rebuttal. "Please," Wormwood whispered. "Are we not on the same side? Be a good lad and watch our backs."

Viktor looked at Wormwood and then Izola, grinding his teeth. "Fine."

With one last look at her sentry, Izola returned to the staircase and started her descent, even as they could hear voices below. When she and Wormwood had passed under the level of the previous floor, they paused, crouching in the shadows, peering through the banister. A fire burned on the far side of a large room where a strange assortment of men stood about listening to a figure seated by the hearth. Some of the men were students, some thugs like the guard they left insensible above, and others were well-dressed men of quality.

She couldn't see his face from her hiding spot, but as the seated figure held court, Izola recognized his voice: Doktor Oberman.

"Yes, my thanks to Professor Blythe for the use of his office. I've been working on behalf of our patron at the excavation site for days and what we have uncovered is truly fascinating. Gentlemen, we stand at the threshold of a new age. The blood of dragons sings. The power of the Well calls to us, bids us to take our rightful place, unearth our true legacy, and reclaim what has been lost to the weakness and confusion of the modern era. The birth of a new Reich is at hand."

The hair on Izola's neck stood on end as she ducked down in the stairwell. Fear churned her bowels like a belly full of week-old left-overs. She turned to head back up the steps out of earshot from the group in the basement, only to see the door up top open and Viktor back toward them.

"What are you doing?" she hissed.

"I tried to get your attention but you weren't listening."

A trio of men, clad in black suits with red shirts, brandished long knives.

"You three." One of them pointed his knife at her. "The game's up. Stop right there!"

Below, the men in the basement gathered at the foot of the stairs to investigate the commotion. "What are you doing here?" a clean-cut young man shouted up at her.

Izola stood wringing her hands. "We...we were at the party and we were just looking for a bathroom."

One of the well-dressed men above called out. "Look at her little rat face. She doesn't belong here."

"Hey!" Viktor barked at him, but the man waved the knife and it was enough to silence Viktor.

"The guard is lying in the hall. This big bloke must have knocked him out."

Men pooled at the foot of the stairs, glaring up with hungry eyes.

"Now, gentlemen." Izola shied back up the steps and bumped into Viktor. She looked over her shoulder and their eyes met. Despite their predicament, seeing him was a relief.

Beside her, Wormwood produced a vial from inside his jacket.

"Which one is that?" Izola asked.

"I apologize in advance."

He uncorked the vial and a searing astringent smell filled the stairwell as he splashed its contents toward the two groups of men hemming them in.

Viktor plugged his nose. "It smells like that awful gin you all drink."

Wormwood tossed the vial down the stairs.

"Look out!" The men below shrank back as if it might explode, but when nothing happened they overcame their fear, inching up the stairs.

Viktor cracked his knuckles. "I don't want to do this, but you've given me no choice," he declared.

"This is just a misunderstanding," Izola bluffed, but with slow steps, they continued their ascent, the trio up top inching down to enclose them in a pincer attack.

"What the bloody hell?" Another thug making his way up the stairs froze. "Did you hear that?"

The handsome student beside him paused. A puzzled look crossed his pretty face. "Who is that laughing?"

Izola turned to Wormwood, realizing which potion he had used. "No."

He winced. "Take my hand, my dear. We mustn't get separated. Just remember, it isn't real." Wormwood bobbed his head from shoulder to shoulder. "Well, not in the classical sense."

Downstairs, a man shrieked. "Mother, no!"

A scuffle broke out below and Izola turned to flee, only to catch sight of a clown scuttling across the ceiling to perch above the exit at the top of the stairs. Its head rotated 360 degrees to reveal a face painted white, its eyes missing, a curly green wig emanating a sickly miasma. The thing bore down like it was passing a stubborn turd and another set of arms sprouted from its torso. The newborn arms juggled a pair of nicked-up cleavers.

"Guess my name and you get a gumdrop." Its voice reminded Izola of a little boy shouting.

Viktor stepped backwards away from the horrid thing and his

feet came down on the edge of one of the steps. He lost his balance and toppled past her into the crowd below.

The clown smiled, its teeth broad and stained. Then it clacked them together and licked its lips, its voice suddenly deep. "Bubba's gonna show you all his tricks."

Izola screamed.

Below her, pandemonium erupted. Demonic laughter drowned the screams of men. Viktor flailed about, wrestling with the crowd at the bottom.

Izola looked from the open door to the clown perched above it.

Its giggle cracked. "Come to Bubba, honey."

22

Viktor struggled to no avail with the men pinning him down. Where were Izola and her friend? Had they really run off and left him here?

"Open those windows!" Oberman commanded.

The cloying stench of Wormwood's potion still filled the basement parlor.

At the foot of the stairs a short fellow wearing a tuxedo with a red bowtie screeched. "Why did Mummy say those horrible things?"

A tattooed woman shoved the hysterical man aside and parted the onlookers ringing Viktor. He did a double take, chagrined to find her attractive, strikingly so. Pinned as he was, the woman kneeled on Viktor's chest. He was so startled by the blonde's appearance that he gave up his struggle. For a moment, his face flushed to have her straddling him, but then he glimpsed the horrible clown coming down the stairs and panicked, trying to buck her off.

"Now, now," she purred.

"Eva, don't torment him," Oberman said. He raised his voice for everyone to hear. "All of you, open yourselves to the Well and you will see it is a trick." The panicked fellow in the tuxedo flinched and his eyes glinted with red light. After a moment, he relaxed, laughing uncomfortably.

The clown shouldered past him, scuttling closer on spider legs. It had the face of a monkey and wore a little red hat, its face caked with rouge and eye shadow. "Trixie wants the big boy," she muttered. Trixie crept to the edge of the circle of men holding Viktor down. Oberman stood beside it, both of them grinning at Viktor.

"My, my, Viktor. I must say I am surprised to find you here. I thought you'd be languishing in my lab." Oberman looked around. "Do you still see it? It's only in your mind, Viktor. Open your connection to the Dragon Well and it will banish this illusion."

The blonde atop him, gently turned his head until Viktor faced her. "It's all right," she said. "Open the Well and it will go away."

Viktor couldn't help himself. He knew he was being goaded, but the clown reared up on its spider legs and Viktor sucked in the Breath.

The demon clown exploded in a cloud of dust. Viktor felt the rush of connection to the Well. His skin itched. He tensed, and then grew still, sated.

"That's a good boy," said the blonde.

Viktor squirmed. She was really distracting. And he was horrified to note that he was stirring beneath her. He wanted to scream curse words. This woman was beautiful, but she was also one of Oberman's goons.

"Good," said Doktor Oberman. "Doesn't that feel better?" When Viktor didn't answer, he went on. "I must assume that you have followed me here, and I must say, I am impressed by your initiative."

"I came to stop you," said Viktor.

"Oh? That's unfortunate. Stop me from doing what, exactly?"

"Lanigan and I found your letter, about Dannbridge, and whatever you have found here."

"Lanigan? Oh, that troublesome dwarf. And where, may I ask, is he now?"

"You bastard. Your assassins killed him."

"My friend, I assure you, I did no such thing. Perhaps my associates in the Society deemed it necessary. They are quite determined to keep our little order a secret, for now."

"I know what you're going to do. You're going to infect the city with tumors."

Oberman tipped his head back. "That is a simple way of looking at it." He gestured at the others gathered in the basement of Drachen House. "Only our bloodline will be awakened. The mongrel Wells can rot in their stagnant ways. But the Dragon Folk will accept their grand destiny or perish. Yourself included."

The blonde wiggled atop him suggestively, and Viktor blushed, his blood pumping. "Don't you want to be with us?" she asked.

Viktor looked away from her, embarrassed at his body's reaction. "I don't want this tumor getting worse." He addressed the doctor. "The letter made it sound like you could cure me."

"The Mirror can do that. But when the time comes, I don't think that's what you'll choose."

"Oh really?"

"Let him up, Eva." Oberman tapped the blonde on the shoulder. "Yah, let him up. It's okay. Scoot. Scoot."

Reluctantly, the tattooed woman got off of him, but not before running her hand over his stomach in a familiar way. The other men released their holds and backed off, almost as embarrassed as Viktor was.

The short guy in the tuxedo pointed at Viktor's predicament. "Nice one, chap."

Oberman looked down at him. "It seems our offer is more alluring than you've let on." The men around him laughed. Oberman held out his hand to help Viktor up but Viktor ignored it. "Don't be childish," Oberman said. "Clearly you are unhappy with the way things have turned out for you. Don't you want to restore Reinveldt to its glory days?"

"I just want to go home."

"I see your struggle, Viktor. It was my struggle. All you want is for things to be put aright. You gave everything to your country and you were betrayed. We were all betrayed. You can't go back home because they look at you as if you are filth. That tumor of yours is a blot to them. As long as we live in a society that treats our power as if it were a disease, things will never be right, they will never be like they used to."

A lump formed in Viktor's throat. Was it so much to ask just to be able to go home and live in peace? Why did everyone have to treat him so badly, just because he was sick? Oberman might be mad as a cat in the sticker bushes but he was right about that. It was wrong.

Viktor self-consciously rubbed his forearm, where beneath his shirt, cancerous dragon scales sprouted. He could feel an ache in the bone beneath them and, a new dread swelling in his mind, he wondered if this were the next symptom of his tumor, the next stage of its unstoppable march through his body.

Oberman nodded. "You can see the truth of it, Viktor. These scribblers and dwarves have taken our birthright. They try to rob us of our power by calling it a sickness. But we can be great once more. Join us, Viktor. Membership in the Thule Society is not offered lightly."

Maybe Viktor was dense, but that didn't quite track. It wasn't dwarves giving him the stink eye when he came back from the war. It was his neighbors. No, Oberman was trying to wind him up. Fucking snake oil salesman.

"Leave me alone! I don't want to be some monster man. I don't want to be sick. I just want to be better. I just want to go home!"

"You're a child, Viktor. And it's time to grow up. Think on this: amongst us you can belong. We see what is growing inside of you and we celebrate it. Don't you want to belong? To be a part of something greater than yourself? No." Oberman raised his hand to forestall Viktor's angry retort. "Just think on it, Viktor. We extend our hands in friendship and you spurn us. And still, we are merciful. Because you are one of us, Viktor. What could be more important?"

Viktor was all mixed up now, his arousal withering, replaced by angst and loneliness and guilt. Part of him wanted to cry and part of him still wanted to slug this asshole. The truth was that he did want to belong. He did want to be accepted, to be special even. But in his very flesh, he could feel how wrong his tumor was. He rolled up his sleeve, the dragon scales on his forearm itching, the bone beneath filled with a hollow ache. "This is poison!" Viktor climbed to his feet, glaring down at Oberman. "And you murdered my friend."

"Another dead dwarf is so much the better. You understand that it is because of them we lost the war?"

The blonde smiled at the doctor's statement, and Viktor glimpsed her ugliness, like watching a cruel girl pull the legs off a cricket.

Viktor had heard it all before. Maybe some of it was even true. At the height of the war, Dunngregor had withdrawn into their mountains, leaving the Kingdom of Reinveldt to fight the Rumavians and their allies alone. It didn't matter. Lanigan was his friend, even if he was a stubborn little bastard. And these people had murdered him. No matter what excuses Oberman gave.

"I'll never be like you."

"I can see the war inside you, as I have felt the war inside myself. You are stifling your connection to the Well out of fear. But I can feel your power. You are already one of us. Your potential is astounding. You should be proud. I see a strong scion of the Dragon Folk. Don't fight it. The real sickness is not your tumor. It is that you have been tricked into believing your power is wrong, is tainted. Another lie that dwarves and scribblers dreamt up to keep us from fulfilling our destiny. In the end, though, you will choose yourself. What other choice could you make?"

"No." Viktor shied toward the stairs. "I'm not like you. I'm not going to let you turn me into a monster. Fix me!"

Oberman shook his head. "I cannot do that. You feel the Well aching to flood your soul. Let it in. Join us."

Viktor could feel the temptation of opening himself to the Dragon Well. He glanced at Eva and she bit her lip, eyes full of promise. But her allure was tarnished; it was given cheaply, a ploy, the bait in a trap.

Viktor shook his head.

Oberman sighed. "You will reconsider. You know you can't close yourself off from the Well forever. That tumor, as you call it, will never stop growing. When you are ready, find me. But make your choice soon. You don't want to refuse the Dragon Song when it calls. A reckoning is at hand."

Viktor moved toward the stairs and the blonde moved to intercept him.

"No," said Oberman. "Let him go."

Viktor brushed past her, catching a hint of her perfume.

She leaned in. "Next time we meet, it might not be so friendly. Consider what the doctor offers. I can feel the dragon in you. Don't waste it."

Viktor ignored her, turning back to Oberman with one foot on the stairs. "This isn't over. I'll find you again."

The doctor folded his hands behind his back, looking pleased with himself. "Of that, I have no doubt."

23

"What do you mean it's checked out?" Devin needed this bloody book before he took another stab at stealing the Q. And this unhelpful shrew had stomped upon his every nerve.

"Well, sir, this is a library. 'Checked out' means that someone came in and borrowed the book. Can I make that simpler for you? Did you understand all the words I just said?"

Devin scoffed. "Don't take that tone with me. I need it, today."

The condescending old woman put her hands on her hips. "Well, I don't know what to tell you. It's checked out, and further-more, it's a restricted book; only faculty members would be allowed to check it out."

"Surely there is something you can do. Do you know who I am?"

She inclined her head to peer over the rim of her spectacles. "I am guessing you are not a member of the faculty."

Fine, Devin thought, *if you force my hand.* "I'd like to speak to your superior."

A look of unfettered joy dawned on the librarian's face. "I am the *senior* librarian."

"I see. Smashing." Perhaps a tactical retreat was in order. "Do you have another book on the subject?"

She folded her arms. "There are very few of those. May I ask why you would need such a book?"

He wasn't about to give this old prune the satisfaction of telling her he wanted to steal a priceless relic but needed a way to hold the bloody thing without melting his fingers off. "Research, *obviously*."

"I'm afraid all such books will be restricted."

"Madam, I am Devin Thistleby." He did a little twirl and regretted it instantly. "Yes, that's right. Those Thistlebys, and I am here at my father's behest. Now kindly assist me and fetch another book or I will be forced to fetch the dean. He's a dear friend of the family, you know."

She chewed her lip so fiercely that Devin half expected blood to pour from her mouth. "Very well," she said, her smile returning, now as frosty as a winter morning. "But locating the appropriate volume could take some time. I hope…" She paused for dramatic effect. "…you are patient."

Devin smiled tightly. "I will wait while you go and…*fetch it*."

They stared at one another like blood-soaked enemies, the silence of the library fueling the palpable tension. The librarian reached one hand up the opposite sleeve like she might produce a hidden weapon, but after a moment's hesitation, she broke eye contact and departed, ostensibly in search of a book, but Devin suspected off to waste more of his time. No doubt she would regale the other servants, or faculty, or whatever they called themselves, with her harrowing tale of an encounter with a real-life Thistleby.

As soon as she shoved off around the corner of the nearest bookshelf, Devin spun the ledger she had referenced toward him. He ran his finger down the column of titles until he came to *Godwin's Wards Volume III*. Beside it was printed the name of Professor Logan Blythe in the librarian's excellent penmanship.

He spun the book back around and departed with all haste, finding the notion of a second encounter with the librarian some-what disconcerting.

A few brief interrogations of various party-crazed students even-tually led Devin to Tenor Hall, a three-story brownstone building with hummingbirds feasting on the rhododendron bushes out front. Devin was scandalized to discover two students making whoopy on a blanket behind the bushes. Worse, it seemed the chap was faster than the hummingbirds. He rolled off and looked right at Devin.

Embarrassed, the young man covered himself and asked, "What are you looking at?"

"The conception of a peasant, I suppose."

With that Devin spun on his heel and entered Tenor Hall. Not wanting to attract undue attention to himself, Devin didn't ask for Blythe by name. Rather, he asked a chap in the hall for the faculty offices and was directed to the third floor.

Devin skulked about until he found an open door with a placard beside it labeled Professor Blythe, Department of History. Glancing in as he passed, Devin noted two men standing in front of a desk looking down at something. He walked past and stopped just out of sight, cocking his ear to listen.

"What if we key the first piece here and siphon off the flow before this group is triggered?"

"Perhaps." The second voice had a thick accent. "I've got a hole in my belly, yes. Let us have lunch and we can revisit the problem."

"I suppose I could eat," said the local man.

Devin hurried away from the door and ducked into an empty office down the hall. He listened as the voices faded in the other direction before he poked his head out to make sure the coast was clear.

Devin slunk down the abandoned hallway to Professor Blythe's office and found it locked. There were no wards, noted Devin, almost disappointed. He fished in his coin purse for his lock picks and opened the door. With one last look, he broke in.

The office was decorated much as he had expected. Framed degrees and awards adorned the walls along with an antique map of the continent. He made his way to the varnished desk embellished with little carvings of flowers. Sunlight streamed through an open window, illuminating the various papers and books stacked on it. Laying on top, Devin discovered a hand-drawn schematic for a set of elaborate wards.

"Hello there." Devin studied the diagram, momentarily distracted by the rather impressive wards it represented. "Don't you look fit," he whispered, admiring the formidable elegance of their design. "Stay focused," he told himself, searching the desktop for the book he was after. Finding the copy of *Godwin's Wards Volume III*, Devin gave a snide chuckle as he pictured the librarian who had sought to thwart his quest. He almost wanted to go back and show her. Probably unwise, though. Devin claimed his prize and turned to go, only to hear approaching footfalls.

"Shit."

He ducked behind the desk, his mental invective mounting as the footsteps entered Professor Blythe's office. Devin crawled into the gap where the chair could be pushed in and held his breath.

"Good, he's not here," said a woman in hushed tones.

"I love this office," said a man with a breathy voice and an Afaran accent.

Devin cringed as the interlopers approached the desk and began to rifle its contents.

A pair of slippers and old-fashioned stockings appeared under the desk. *Go away*, he thought at them. Devin cringed, curling into a ball in hopes of making himself invisible. The man pulled out the chair from the desk and went to sit, stubbing his toe on Devin's clenched buttocks.

"Well, that is equally fascinating." A dusky face appeared, an older man with blue-tinted spectacles and a vintage velvet suit, the sort that might come back in style any day. "Salutations."

The woman gasped. "Is someone else here?" she whispered.

"Yes," said the man too loudly.

"Hush," Devin pleaded, climbing out from beneath the desk. He knew he was caught but then he saw the woman's face. She was perhaps in her thirties, quite pretty, and fashionable in her scholar's robes with book patterns embroidered on the sleeves. She looked as guilty as he felt.

"You're not supposed to be here," he ventured.

"You were hiding under the desk," she countered.

They stood there a tick, each glancing from one face to the other and back in a cycle of perplexed chagrin.

"What are you doing here?" Devin asked.

"I could ask you the same thing."

He clutched the volume of *Godwin's Wards* tighter. "Just fetching a book Professor Blythe borrowed. You?"

"Also looking for something Logan borrowed."

He could tell by the way she said his name that she hated the man. She had floated her disgust like an invitation. It was foolish, he knew, engaged as he was in such a clandestine affair, one of such importance, no less, but the prospect of an ally in his dire straits proved too strong of an enticement.

"I think," he began, pausing to consider the precipice before he plunged. "I think this Logan fellow is caught up in some bad business."

She nodded at her compatriot, who smiled broadly, and jutted her chin toward Devin. "His hands are trembling."

Devin sneered, tucking the book along with his treacherous hands into his armpits. "Well, you two are obviously sneaking about, too."

She also had a book in her hand, and as he looked at it, she mirrored his posture.

Devin soldiered on. "Let us postulate that whatever this Logan fellow is mixed up in perhaps affects us both. Agreed?"

She nodded. "Agreed."

"I really am here for this book. You?"

"It's a long story. He mentioned something about an excavation, or rather his co-conspirator Doktor Oberman did."

"There was a Jarlsbecker here earlier. They were discussing these wards." Devin pointed at the parchment on the desk containing the schematic.

The woman studied the diagram, indicating some writing in an archaic hand at the top. "This!" she shouted, instantly clapping her hand over her mouth to quiet her exclamation.

"Yes?"

"That's a Dragon Mark right there. Interment, or something like that. Strange to see more of these. And the script is Dragon Tongue. This says the 'Tyrant's Tomb.'"

The strange man accompanying the woman jostled Devin aside. "Now *that* is interesting. These wards must guard it." He turned to the woman. "Izola, this is the excavation. This is why Logan scuttled your tenure. He is protecting this, along with that Oberman character. That fellow is the real snake. He is in league with those Red Sleeve thugs we saw at the party."

"Did you say Red Sleeves?" Devin cocked his head.

"You know them?" Izola asked.

"My dear," said Devin, "I'm beginning to think this whole disaster is all of a piece. Through no fault of my own, Oscar Red Sleeves has a bit of leverage on me. He hurt a very good friend of mine, you see, and now in order to save my friend, Oscar has asked me to steal something."

"Steal what?"

Devin considered walking out the door without answering. It wasn't too late to keep this pair from getting in his way. If he divulged what he was after, who knew what they might do? On the other hand, it was just so overwhelming to go this alone. How could he manage to steal the Q, and even if he did, what guarantee did he have that a brute like Oscar Red Sleeves would keep up his end of the bargain?

"He wants me to steal my father's Shard of the Quorum."

The other two stared at him.

The man in blue-tinted spectacles reached into his coat.

"Wormwood, no!"

S hooting pains lanced up his arm. Viktor rubbed his tumor, trying not to worry about the new symptom as he wandered around Dannbridge. He had finally found Oberman...for all the good it had done him. He still had no clue where this mirror might be buried and no idea of what to do next.

Viktor stole a peek at his tumor, a patch of scales spreading over his arm. In the light of a street lantern, he could swear the surrounding flesh had gone a tinge green. It must be a trick of the light, he concluded, picking up his pace, even though he had nowhere to go.

He couldn't help but feel a little conflicted by it all. He hated that slimy bastard Oberman, but now that he had tracked him down and things hadn't gone quite as Viktor had expected, he was at a loss. What now?

Tonight it seemed the crazed festival had dug its talons into every corner of the city. He saw fistfights and vandalism and no end of men and women pissing in the streets. Song and laughter filled the air, along with the sound of breaking glass and the smell of smoke.

Viktor roamed the crowded, boisterous streets all night, worry prodding him along until, lost in thought, he nearly collided with two men scuffling.

"Hey, leave him alone," Viktor demanded.

Two drunks dressed in fancy clothes laughed at Viktor. One of them held a fruit monger in a headlock while the other split his time between trying to pants the merchant and trying to keep his own wobbly feet under him.

The pantser looked up at Viktor. "Oh piss off. It's just a little fun. Have an apple." The bully plucked one from the peddler's cart and tossed it to Viktor, but the errant throw sailed wide left.

"You had your fun," said Viktor. "Enough."

"Piss off, chap," said the pantser. He went for another apple but tripped, sprawling in the gutter. He laughed, wiping muck from his silk shirt.

Viktor closed the distance and loomed over him. He was sick of all these bullies. It seemed like everyone in this city was either some kind of dragon fanatic or just a jerk. What he really ought to do was box this guy on the ear, it might teach him some manners. It was tempting. So very tempting.

An ache had set in at the root of his tumor and it didn't seem to be going away. Viktor was trying to keep it from putting him in a mood, but he could feel the worry building like the headwaters of a dam. He knew that he could dull that pain by taking the Breath, and it was tempting, and it made him mad that it was so tempting.

He could feel a trace of the Dragon Well's power calling out to him, whispering, *Take the Breath*. But it would just make everything worse, and bashing these idiots' heads together wouldn't fix it. Besides, his mother had always been so disappointed in him when he fought. He pictured her with her hands on her hips, a frown on her face after he had beaten up Milo Gutenberg. Milo was always such an ass, but Mama hadn't cared. "You're a bigger boy than that." She'd dug her finger into the side of his head. "Use your noodle for once instead of your fists." With a pang of homesickness, Viktor held out his hand and helped the drunk to his feet. "All right now." Viktor turned to the one holding the merchant in a headlock and his tone grew stern. "Stop."

The bully released his grip on the fruit monger and held his hands up. "Just a joke, you prat. It's Tyrant Fall. We're only having a laugh."

The peddler brushed himself free, bristling, but silent.

Viktor folded his arms and watched as the drunks headed down the street toward a little knot of revelers gathered around an old man playing the accordion by candlelight.

"My thanks," said the merchant. "Want an apple?"

Viktor accepted the gift with abrupt hunger, biting it nearly in half. "Thank you," he said with his mouth full.

"You fancy another one?"

Viktor nodded.

"It must take a lot of apples to feed a big bloke like you." He plucked a few more from the pile, seemingly at random. "Here. These won't last another day. Save me the trouble of chucking them."

Viktor made a basket out of his shirt to hold them. "Hey," he said, pulling out the assassin's knife.

The peddler jumped.

"Oh no, wait. That's not what I meant. Do you know of a club that has red tattoos like this?" Viktor held out the knife handle first. Maybe he'd found Oberman, but he hadn't exactly figured out what he was up to. It wasn't too late to stick his thumb in that prick's eye. "Red Sleeves they're calling themselves."

"Oh, a club you say? That's a proper lot of gangsters right there. Why, just last night they pulled the son of a lord out of a pub down the way and carted him off like a side of beef. Ain't no club. The likes of you don't mean fuck-all to them. Best steer clear."

"Which pub?"

The merchant plucked an apple off the street and gave it a polish before setting it back on his display. "Thanks for scaring off them hooligans. Pub's just up yonder. The Pig & Plenty. Can't miss it. It'll be a madhouse tonight."

"Is this festival always like this?"

"Well, no. In fact, I was complaining about it to my missus this morning, and now this." He snapped his fingers. "You know the bloke who mends my cart said they beat up his son on account of he was a foreigner. It's getting a bit wild this year."

Viktor nodded and thanked the man again before heading off in search of the Pig & Plenty.

As it turned out the pub was indeed impossible to miss. A pack of drunks had gathered around a fistfight in the muddy street out front. Viktor jostled his way through the ring of spectators to get a look and discovered a man pretending to be a chicken as he got his ass unceremoniously kicked. But his devotion to the bit never wavered, even as he was knocked to the ground and booted in the ribs he squawked and clucked at the attacker to gales of laughter from his audience.

Shaking his head, Viktor went inside the pub, which looked more like a warehouse dotted with a haphazard selection of tables and benches. In the center of the room, a dark-skinned bartender scrambled about, a sweaty wreck, barely managing to keep up with the stream of patrons lining up at the bar.

Viktor waited in the queue, annoyed by, but choosing to ignore the pair of sailors who cut in front of him. When he got to the bar, the flustered bartender scooped a few mugs off the counter and stacked them beside him in a sink piled with dirty dishes.

"Hurry up, mate," said the bartender. Viktor expected him to have an exotic accent but he sounded like a local. Viktor blushed, that was the second time that had happened. The bartender wore his curly hair oiled back and had a nose that looked like it had been broken once or twice. "What will it be? Ale or gin? We're out of wine."

"Actually, I have a question."

"Are you bleeding kidding?" He pointed around the pub. "Ale or gin? There's a hundred people here and just me keeping the thirsties away. I've no time for questions."

Despite the bartender's rising tone it was clear he wasn't angry, just desperate. Viktor stepped out of line and walked around the bar to the hinged passthrough in the counter.

"Here goes nothing," he told himself. Maybe this was a long shot, but it had worked with the fruit monger.

The bartender whirled around to face him, flourishing a billy club. "The hell are you doing?"

Viktor pointed to the dishes. "I thought maybe I could help."

The bartender cocked his head, looking at Viktor like he was speaking a foreign language. His eyes narrowed. "And what do you want in return?"

"Just some answers. Maybe something to eat."

The tavernkeep took stock of the swelling ranks on the opposite side of the bar, even now growing surly at the delay.

"Start with the glasses," he said. "And when they're all washed go around and gather up the empties."

Viktor nodded. He had spent a brief stint on the precise, measured work of typesetting, but his inattention to detail had only earned him a cuff from his father. On the other hand, he had spent many afternoons behind the counter of Herr Fischer's restaurant. This work suited him. He set his sights on something simple and he got it done at a pace few could match for long. Frau Fischer had always said he had "hustle." He hadn't gotten many compliments from adults, so he had taken it to heart and always worked hard for the couple. He had also made sure to lift the kegs when the waitress was around to notice, hoping for a compliment from her. The memory brought a smile to his face, but it vanished as he instinctively went to roll up his sleeves. Realizing he had almost exposed his tumor, Viktor resigned himself to a wet sleeve. With a sigh he dunked mugs full of beer suds in the soapy water, then dunked them in the clean water to rinse. By the time he looked up from the dishes his worry had gone and the crowd was even thicker.

Some kind of knife-throwing contest along the far wall seemed to be getting quite rowdy, but the bartender paid no mind. Viktor made his way around collecting dishes, broke up a fight, and changed a pair of kegs. At one point, he was singing an old Jarls-becker waltz his sister liked, and a rummy had taken up the tune, though the words were in two different languages. They sang louder and louder to try to outdo each other until a nearby table had started singing the rummy's version and suddenly the whole bar was singing along.

Time passed in a blur of elbow grease, but Viktor found himself grateful for the distraction. Toward the end of the night it dawned on him that he hadn't had a moment to fret about Oberman, or his tumor. He realized with a smile that he hadn't noticed the ache, until, of course…*that* moment. But he redoubled his hustle and soon his worries were lost in the rhythm of his labor.

Sometime in the early hours of the morning the bartender, who had introduced himself as Clete, cupped his hands to his mouth and bellowed, "We're all out of booze! Fuck off, the lot of you!" The process of getting the drunken patrons out the door wasn't easy. It took time. And shouting. Some demanded more drinks, some to be allowed to stay and sleep it off. One would-be thief tried to vault the counter and make off with the coin box tucked under her arm but she misjudged the leap and ended up sprawled right in front of Clete. Needless to say, Clete's billy club made another appearance, but the drunken woman abandoned her scheme—and one of her shoes—and was out the door on the double.

After Clete slid home the rusty bolt which locked the Pig & Plenty, he slumped into the nearest chair. "Sweet holy Saints, these poor old dogs." He tore off his shoes and dug his thumbs into the sole of his right foot, groaning.

Viktor mopped the sweat from the back of his neck with a bar rag. Clete pointed behind the bar. "Sheena made me an egg sandwich. You can have half. It's in the food bin. Pour us a lord's dram of gin while you're at it."

Viktor fetched the sandwich at Clete's behest and poured them a couple glasses of gin. They sat amidst the daunting mess, sharing Clete's sandwich.

"Never been half so busy in here before," Clete finally said, quaffing his drink. "I'm glad you came along. I'll tell you whatever you want, and a couple of coppers to boot. You saved my bacon."

"Thanks." Viktor downed his gin. "Ack!" He spat on the floor. "What is that? It's horrible. It tastes like a tree."

"It's bloody gin, mate. You never had it?"

Viktor shook his head.

"Well, I'm sure in your neighborhood they serve some foul Jarlsbecker shit and call it honey." Clete sipped his gin. "So what's your story? What's got you all the way from t'other side of the channel?"

Viktor sniffed the glass and set it down. "I suppose I should ask my question."

"Aye, you've earned it."

"Well, it's kind of a long story. I heard that the Red Sleeves were here the other night."

Clete sat forward, taking his bare feet off the chair. "You're not one of that lot, are you?"

"No."

"Oh, good. The ornery bastards. They come in here now and then pushing me around. They make me pay them not to wreck the place. Bunch of filthy highwaymen. You shouldn't get mixed up with that sort. A nice boy like you, don't you have a family to get back to? You got kids?"

Viktor bit his lip and shook his head. "No. I didn't want to be a dad. Not right away anyhow. Someday sure. I would have liked that. Maybe even a bunch of kids." Viktor bobbed his eyebrows and Clete laughed. A shadow fell over Viktor's face. "I guess that won't happen now. Can't imagine who'd want to marry a tumorling."

Clete went rigid. It took a minute, but the fear left his face. In its wake, Clete looked sad.

"I think I would have been good at it," said Viktor. "Being a dad, I mean."

"Just wanting to be one would make you a fair sight better than most." Clete looked like he was about to say something else, but he took a bite of his sandwich instead. The sound of Clete chewing filled the ensuing silence.

"You ever seen this symbol?" Viktor handed over the assassin's knife.

Clete swallowed the last of his sandwich and coughed. "Sure, they got tattoos like this."

"Ever seen it anywhere else?"

"Can't say as I have."

Clete didn't seem too bothered that Viktor was a tumorling anymore, just a bit of a shock at first, but Viktor knew the sorts of things people said about them, so he tucked the knife away to put the bartender at ease. "What happened the other night with the lord's son?"

"They took him off, didn't they? A lord of the Quorum's own son. That Oscar Red Sleeves has balls the size of wagon wheels."

"I think these Red Sleeves are up to something really bad. Maybe this lordling is part of it."

"Maybe." Clete shrugged. "You don't kidnap no lord's son on a whim. Of course, I heard he's back, so maybe it's nothing."

"Who's back? The son?"

"That's right. Ain't no ransom then. Devin Thistleby. Bit of a stuck-up little poof if you ask me. Ain't afraid to spend money, though."

"Where can I find him?"

"His family owns a mansion up on the Gilded Shelf. Huge place. Practically a castle on Mulberry Lane."

"Thanks, Clete. Can you let me out?"

"One last thing, Viktor, though I already owe you. It'd be greatly appreciated."

"What's that?"

"There's an old fella asleep under that table. Could you toss him right quick?"

E va Red Sleeves squeezed a slice of lemon into her gin as Oscar paced back and forth across the office.

"Sit, Oscar. You're going to have a heart attack."

"Fuck right off, love. You don't know the likes of this one. A right dragon is what. Make a tart like you a snack. Down the fucking hatch. Heart attack'd be the lucky way to go."

Eva sipped her cocktail. She hunted around behind the bar until she found the bitters and spiced up her drink. She wanted to rub salt in Oscar's wounds, to stoke his anxiety, but she was too smart for that. Eva wanted him to see nothing but a faithful lieutenant. As much as the Red Sleeves had thrived under his leadership, she knew they could do better.

She could do better.

So best not to show him she realized that. He wasn't shy about stamping out disloyalty. And more than that, she had her eye on membership into the Thule Society, and she doubted there was room for two Red Sleeves in it.

Georgie poked his head into Oscar's study. "She's here, boss."

"Well, don't just stand there like a useless twat. Let her in."

Georgie turned back to admit their guest only to find her standing directly behind him.

Georgie yelped, jumping out of her way.

"Black Lung."

"Oscar." Black Lung wore a severe haircut and a man's suit,

gray with a white ruffled shirt and red accents. The world's most infamous tumorling coughed into a rag, the oily discharge of her lungs staining her smile. She could have been fifty or a hundred and fifty, who could tell with someone like that? "I trust you have made the arrangements we discussed."

Oscar nodded toward Eva. "You can talk around her. Georgie, fuck off."

Without a word, Georgie slipped out the door like an eel. Black Lung glanced at Eva and back to Oscar. Something in her look set Oscar to scowling and Eva felt the sudden urge to follow Georgie out.

"Thistleby remains in possession of his Q."

Oscar cleared his throat. "Well, yes. But everything is on schedule. His son is on board. He'll make the grab tonight, during the assembly."

"Good. I'll be thinking about it while Lord Thistleby is pontificating. But remember, Oscar, I have no patience for mistakes." She coughed, a little waft of smoke escaping her mouth. "Leave the son alive. He might prove useful in the aftermath of his father's ruin."

"If you like."

"I do. Get me that Shard, Oscar Red Sleeves. I won't tolerate failure. I'm sure if you can't handle a task of this delicacy, I can find someone who can." Black Lung turned pointedly to Eva.

Oscar ground his teeth.

And just like that, this bitch had made Oscar open his eyes and see Eva as a rival.

26

"Over here." Izola led her co-conspirators to a little nook on the back porch of Meade Hall where she sometimes liked to read. She sat on one of the stone benches overlooking the lawn south of Gulheller Fountain.

Somewhere nearby a drunken woman was yelling at her boyfriend for "studying" with another girl, her tones climbing an octave with every incredulous repetition of the question, "Studying?"

"I think we need to tell someone in the city watch about this," Izola said.

"Rubbish," Devin replied. "They're young. Let them work it out themselves."

"Not that, you twit."

"Oh really? Not that?" Devin rolled his eyes. "Oscar Red Sleeves was very clear. If we tell a soul about all of this, he'll kill Thomas."

"Who is Thomas?"

"My…friend. My only friend, really." Devin plopped down onto the stone bench beside her. "They already stabbed him and right now he is somewhere, bleeding to death. He needs help. And I am not letting him get killed because of me. Or you, for that matter."

Wormwood fished inside his jacket and pulled out a vial. He uncorked it and swilled the saffron potion.

183

Devin and Izola flinched.

"What was that?" she asked.

"Vitamins," said Wormwood.

"Just vitamins?"

"Well." Wormwood used his fingertip to brush his teeth. "Vitamins and a few more festive ingredients. It is a holiday, my dear."

Taking a deep breath, Izola turned back to Devin. "If you really steal a piece of the Quorum for those thugs, who knows how many innocent people will be killed? No offense, but this is serious business. Are you sure you're up to this?"

Devin bristled. "You'll see. Oscar Red Sleeves will rue the day he underestimated Devin Thistleby."

"You sound awfully sure of yourself."

"If there's one thing I *am* certain of, it's that someone else is behind this. Oscar isn't smart enough. He's ambitious and street smart. But stealing a Shard of the Quorum? He's a thug. He's got to be working for someone more powerful."

"Perhaps it's that Jarlsbecker that was with Logan," she said.

"Perhaps. Whoever is behind all this, they want it for something, something big. You don't go after a Quorumite without a good reason. If they fail at this, my father will turn them into bloody cinders."

"Well, you're right about that," Izola said. "It's all the more reason not to go through with it. You're playing right into their hands."

"Oh," said Wormwood, petting the hair on the backs of his knuckles. "That feels good."

Devin ignored him. "I have to. I saw the wards on that schematic back in your ex's office. They need something powerful to break through. I'm not certain a Shard of the Q is powerful enough, but they'll need it to have a chance. That'll give me leverage. I'll find a way to clean up all this. I have to save Thomas."

Izola took his hand. "I'm begging you, don't go along with this. There's no telling what sort of shitstorm you might unleash."

Devin took her hand and kissed it, sketching a rakish bow. "My dear, I was born to danger. Raised in wealth perhaps, but I have danger in my blood. In my very soul."

"Did you just quote something?"

"No." He stiffened. "I made that up on the spot."

"I've definitely read that somewhere before."

"I'm off," said Devin. "With luck, we'll meet again."

D evin tiptoed over the ancient hardwood floors, his feet
treading a windy path to avoid the squeaky bits. At the
sound of a woman humming to herself, he ducked into an
alcove with a tapestry hanging over it and hid while she dusted the
suits of armor along the opposite wall.

He felt surprisingly calm. In fact, Devin fancied he might have
gotten the hang of this burglary business.

When the maid had gone, he resumed his course toward his
father's study.

Slinking along, he congratulated himself on his steely nerves,
until the creak of a door startled him. Instead of darting for cover,
Devin yelped, one hand leaping to cover his heart. He spun around
to scold the maid only to find himself face-to-face with the lord of
the manor.

"Father, you startled me."

Archibald Thistleby wore a star-themed dressing gown and a
pointy hat. "Tyrant's balls, Devin, how did you get in here?"

Not wanting to admit to his burglary, Devin lied. "Danby let
me in."

"I'll have him tossed out on his ear for this."

"Wait," said Devin, suffering a strange pang of conscience.
"That was a lie." He sighed. "I broke in. Your wards are in disrepair,
Father."

"I should have known. More of your skullduggery. I curse the day your mother handed you one of those asinine novels. I haven't time for this. Black Lung's put forth a motion to the Quorum that could cost me a fortune in new taxes. The devious bitch. I have a thousand things to do at the moment. And coddling you for another instant has been scratched from my list. Out with it, Devin. I haven't got all day."

Heat flashed red on Devin's cheeks and a tear threatened his eye. "I don't want to stay, Father. I only came for a change of clothes and a wig or two."

Lord Thistleby's eyes rose to Devin's, and a sneer settled over his jowls. "Of course. I should have known it would be something farcical."

Part of Devin wanted to tell his father that the reason for his visit was of the gravest concern, that he was here to steal the very source of his father's power. But of course, that would be foolish. And he was done playing the fool.

"You know, just because I haven't your talent for magery doesn't mean everything I do is meaningless."

"But it does, Devin. It does. Do you want to know why I passed you over and chose your sister as my heir?"

The question landed in his stomach like a ruffian's fist. "Why?"

"Because she paid attention. You always had your head in the clouds, always obsessed with something meaningless, something trivial. The latest fashion, your ridiculous novels, those embarrassing wigs."

Devin cleared his throat. "They're quite fashionable, actually." Devin pointed at a portrait of his great-grandfather, Gaylord Thistleby, hanging at the end of the hall. "You practically worship him and he's wearing a wig."

"That was a hundred years ago."

"Fashion is cyclical, Father."

Lord Thistleby waved off the comment, looking exhausted. "Your sister put in the work. And you, well, I suppose I spoiled you."

"I am not spoiled!"

Lord Thistleby had a good long laugh. "Devin. You can't even see how ridiculous you've become."

Now Devin really wanted to tell his father why he was there, but for once he held his tongue. Perhaps after the deed was done he'd see that Devin could accomplish serious things.

The house settled.

Devin groped for a scathing retort, but the moment had passed. "You know, Father, perhaps I'm not the sort that should ever get my hands on the Q, but fate is a fickle thing. You shouldn't discard me. I'm your only son."

"The Q would eat you alive."

"Perhaps it would, but perhaps I'd surprise you." Despite his father's cruelty, Devin worried that he might be right. Maybe he just kept digging himself a deeper and deeper hole. Maybe if he came clean now his father could help him extricate himself. A thug like Oscar Red Sleeves was nothing compared to a wizard like Archibald Thistleby III.

But then, of course, his father opened his mouth. "I'm afraid that every time you surprise me, boy, it is with yet another disappointment. I'm only glad your mother isn't around to hear the other ladies cast aspersions on you. The gossip on that subject is most unkind."

Devin found his confession quite blocked by the lump forming in his throat. Stupid, perhaps, to hold back. Foolish certainly, but he simply couldn't bring himself to ask for help. Devin comforted himself with the rationalization that telling his father would put Thomas' life at greater risk, but in the back of his mind he knew that he simply couldn't bear more of his father's scorn.

"Well," Devin said. "You've made your feelings quite clear. Just let me gather a few things and you'll never have to see me again."

His father looked as if he were about to say something, and a fleeting hope sparked in Devin that he would offer some measure of reconciliation, that then Devin could confess the true purpose of his visit and this whole mess could be resolved. That they could find a way out together. Find a way to save Thomas.

But then his father nodded, content to part ways. Devin imagined his father's vitriol if he were to come clean and he couldn't manage it. He couldn't utter another word.

With a derisive snort, his father waddled down the hallway. Devin stood motionless, rooted in place, until his father slammed a door behind him and the noise jostled Devin from his reverie.

"Right," he said, turning back in the direction of his father's study.

The wards on the door were easy to bypass the second time around. For years his heart would race at the idea of burgling his father's study, but now, standing in the great man's office, he felt numb. Perhaps a bit melancholy. As he surveyed the bookshelves and the arcane trophies and the fine paintings on the wall, he felt none of the fears he had expected in this moment. His father's wrath seemed far away, and rather ineffectual. All he could detect was the faintest twinge of guilt, or maybe it was pity, for what would become of his father when he was no longer a Quorumite.

Devin turned to face the relic, glowing from its mount on the far wall.

This thing defined his father. Without it, what was he? A blustering bully? An overweight old man, lost without the authority it granted. Yes, Devin supposed. It was a twinge of pity, all swirled up with guilt. And perhaps a little anger.

But he couldn't let any of that stop him. He was doing this for Thomas, and whatever the consequences, he would just have to deal with them once Thomas was safe.

With a dramatic sigh, Devin approached the Q.

He slapped his hands together and rubbed them feverishly to build a little metastatic energy, then held up his charged hand. The feedback loop it created caused the wards around the mounted Q to glow visibly.

"This is it, old boy."

Devin closed his eyes, sensing the eldritch current which flowed through the wards. Licking his finger, he drew a counter ward to siphon off power and then he let himself slip into the rhythm of the circuit, until it was just the right moment.

Devin gathered his will and sent a spike of countercurrent into the wards. Theoretically, the opposing energies should have smoothly rebounded against one another, diverting the power harmlessly into the ward Devin had added to the circuit.

In reality, Devin regained consciousness slumped against the far wall. When the dizziness abated, he discovered that the Shard of the Quorum had fallen from its mount. It lay on the floor of his father's study, glaring like a chip of the sun.

Something cold and bulky was stuffed down his pantleg. In his disorientation it took Devin a moment to realize it was his pistol, which had come untucked from his belt in the commotion. Devin took a moment to fish it out of his trousers and re-situate the firearm, reflecting at the same time that it was fortunate that the wards had not caused the weapon to discharge.

He sat against the bookshelves along the wall, the room still spinning a bit, and thought about what might have happened, and whether he should invest in some sort of scabbard for the weapon, to keep it from pointing directly at his precious genitals.

Devin got his feet under him and stumbled over to the Q. He knelt beside it, squinting into its harsh light. *Godwin's Wards Volume III* had an extensive commentary on the wards he was about to use to transport the Shard, most of which amounted to "Don't." But given the extremity of his circumstances, Devin would simply have to ignore such warnings. In the end, despite all of Godwin's caveats, he sounded confident in his ward work.

Devin had brought a dagger along for the purpose of pricking his finger. He did so, pouting a little before he worked up the nerve, but eventually drawing a perfect bead of blood which he used to draw four wards around the fallen Shard.

"Go on then," he told himself. "Pick it up."

Devin made it to the end of the lane before he threw up.

"This is bad," he told himself for the umpteenth time, barely noticing that he had scuffed his new Isilano loafers.

The Q glowed through the leather sack which held it. If anyone were about at this wretched hour it would be hard to miss him staggering through the streets, cursing and vomiting and clutching his radiant prize.

Perhaps his hurried study of the diagrams in *Godwin's Wards* had missed some vital clue. Perhaps he had underestimated the raw power necessary to contain the relic's arcane radiation.

The stinging sensation in his stomach ceased when he dropped the sack. Sweat dripped into his eyes. Devin doffed his wig and used it to mop his brow. He combed his hair from his forehead, looking down in horror as a tuft came free. He stared down at the lock of hair, letting slip a little squeal.

"This is bad."

Devin whipped out his copy of *Godwin's Wards Volume III* and flipped to the appropriate page, his fingers stabbing at the sequence.

"I did it all. It was all correct. Godwin, you idiot."

Perhaps, he mused, the author had had access to a less potent Shard of the Tyrant's crown. Could it be that simple? Cursing under his breath, Devin opened the sack, squinting into the relic's glare.

He ought to drop the bloody thing in a ditch and never look back. What would Thomas think if he saw him now, pale as milk and his hair falling out in clumps? How could Thomas love such a ghastly sight?

And that was really the rub, wasn't it?

Thomas wasn't the sort to turn up his nose over something like that. He'd be the one soothing Devin's tantrums and helping him pick out new wigs.

Here he was worrying about his hair when the gods only knew what had become of Thomas. Devin collapsed onto his ass, burying his face in his hands.

What an utter buffoon he was. And what a gentle soul he'd delivered into the clutches of that horrid brute Oscar Red Sleeves. That pig. No fucking way was he going to let that bastard have his Thomas.

28

Wormwood froze, clutching Izola by the forearm. "Look at this," he said. "Marvelous."

A man stood atop a sagging roof at the edge of the sinkhole. He waved his arms about like a conductor, directing the crowd of drunkards on the street below as they belched out the chorus of "The Man with the Little Hat."

Izola scowled at the group of young men. "It's very weird." She pointed. "That one isn't wearing pants."

Wormwood's eyebrows bobbed. "I know."

Izola stood on her tiptoes to see past the belchers at the crowd of revelers surrounding the Sink. Somehow the landmark had become a focal point for this year's Tyrant Fall celebrations. Enterprising partygoers had set up makeshift taverns, packing in kegs and stringing up paper lanterns. There was more music coming from somewhere, a different song altogether, discordant, off-key. Nearer at hand two women screamed at each other, impugning one another's chastity with remarkable specificity.

"Doesn't it seem like this is quite a bit more rambunctious than usual?"

"How so?" Wormwood leaned in closer to hear her over the belchers' crescendo.

"Look how many people are about. It's never like this. This is bloody mental!"

A sudden silence made her voice carry through the crowd,

drawing a number of dirty looks.

Shaking off the interruption, the belcher with no pants stepped forward and launched into his solo.

Izola and Wormwood paused their discussion to admire the performance. The soloist's penis waggled with every rising note. Somehow that tiny detail softened Izola's distaste. And to be fair, he had perfect pitch.

The performance concluded to thunderous applause from the onlookers. Izola slung her bag over her shoulder to free her hands to clap along. She linked arms with Wormwood and guided him through the revelers to the edge of the Sink. Some saint among these animals had taken the time to string up a rope cordon where the cobblestones had collapsed. Izola and Wormwood stood at the edge looking over the pit; a hundred yards across, steep but not vertical, littered with the detritus of collapsed buildings and rubbish. The floor of the sinkhole was another hundred yards down, where the rubble piled in the center like an inverted nipple.

"Look at that woman's dress, isn't it smashing?" Wormwood gaped at a reveler dancing in a sheer silken gown. "I want to ask her who made it."

"We haven't the time for that."

"This party is so different from the one at Drachen House. Can't you feel that?"

"Feel what?"

"I want to drink." Wormwood scoped around for a handy beverage. "Let's have a drink."

"What? No, we need to get down there and investigate if this is really the dig site Logan and Oberman were talking about."

"It's intoxicating. Feel the vibration that permeates the atmosphere. Remarkable."

"Wormwood, have you taken another one of your potions?"

He beamed. "Just the one. I mean just the one since lunch. But this feeling is something else. That's quite likely bad, eh?"

Izola studied the people ringing the sinkhole. Some of the partiers on the opposite side had made a game of sliding down the embankment on a door they had torn from its hinges. The onlookers pumped their fists and whooped like banshees. Most of them were dancing, or rather, swaying on their feet.

What if all of this madness was more than just a party getting out of hand? For the first time she noticed how many broken windows surrounded her, how many of the revelers were barefoot. There was blood on the ground. Were they walking on broken glass?

"Sorry for this," she told Wormwood.

"Sorry for what?"

Izola cocked back and slapped him as hard as she could.

A nearby couple cackled at Wormwood's assault. The lady applauded. "Now fuck him," she said, her teeth stained with wine.

Ignoring their audience, Wormwood put his hand to his cheek and worked his jaw until it popped. "What was that?"

"You were acting strangely."

He raised an eyebrow.

"More strangely."

"I think that did the trick. It did feel a bit odd. Even now I can detect that vibration. It's almost like one of the Uber Toads is breathing down my neck. Do you know what I mean?"

"Sure." Izola took off her glasses and pinched the bridge of her nose.

It was Wormwood's turn to scan the crowd. "These people may be in a spot of trouble."

"Indeed."

"Well…" Wormwood jutted his chin toward the sinkhole. "Into the abyss?"

"Let's."

They pushed their way to the edge and found something like a trail descending the rubble-strewn slope of the sinkhole. Izola led the way, sliding down, scraping the palms of her hands and her backside as she skidded to a stop on a lip of stone protruding from the dirt. Wormwood scrambled to a halt beside her.

"Look." Izola pointed at the lip of stone. "It's like rock strata, one era built upon another."

Wormwood peered down at the next leg of the descent, a steeper drop this time. "Shall we?"

"After you."

Wormwood slid down to the next strata and Izola scooted after him. When she reached the lip of cobblestones beside the alchemist, Izola nearly toppled ass over tea kettle, but Wormwood grabbed hold of her to keep her from falling.

"That was a close one," she said.

A few bits of crumbled stone rolled past.

The ledge they stood upon sagged, giving the pair just enough time to share a look that said, "Oh bollocks, we probably should have leapt to safety instead of settling for this meaningful eye contact." But by then they were falling. The ground flowed beneath their feet, a river of stone and mud that washed them down the side of the pit.

Izola banged her head on a rock, stars erupting in her eyes. She was still falling when her vision cleared, half relieved the plunge was nearly over and half terrified she would dash her brains out at the end. But every little bit of her was surprised when the dirt and rock at the base of the bowl swirled like the drain of a commode and sucked her in.

This is it, she thought. Would Page ever even know what had happened to her?

But the pang of regret for her daughter's misery vanished as she and Wormwood spilled out into an underground thoroughfare. The mud flow deposited them into a high-ceilinged tunnel, lined on either side by intricately carved pillars.

She lay in the mud, stunned, until beside her Wormwood shook a vial that glowed with bioluminescence. The strap on her book bag had broken during her fall and she busied herself jury-rigging it. Wormwood patted himself to see if any of his potions had shattered. "Now there's a bit of luck," he said, holding up the light to survey their surroundings.

Izola shook off the cobwebs and pushed herself to her feet. She took in the ancient masonry, pointing out a section on the nearest wall. "That is a Veneman Cartouche. See the stalks of wheat carved to look like fangs? It's a decorative motif of the Late Tyrannical Era. I think I know where we are."

29

A raindrop kissed Viktor on the back of the neck and he cursed the weather. It had been a fine spring day but tonight he felt a Westonshire chill in the air. And he had been crouching in a ditch for an hour. Undeterred by his threats, the clouds opened up and soon he was quite soaked as the trench began to fill with rainwater.

Viktor waited across the lane from the Thistleby mansion, following old Clete's tip about the kidnapped lordling. And Viktor was fairly certain that it had been this Devin Thistleby he'd witnessed sneaking into the manor house.

Now he just needed to wait. In the rain. Viktor sighed, his arm aching and his stomach rumbling from eating one too many apples.

He considered relocating to another hiding place, but as he scoped around for a new location he noticed Devin Thistleby climb back over the iron gate while clutching a glowing sack.

Now what could that be, Viktor wondered? He followed the lordling, staying down the lane at a safe distance, watching as Devin stopped and opened the sack. The lordling pulled an object out, glare shining between his fingers. His hands flourished for a moment before stuffing it back in the sack.

Viktor stalked Thistleby down the lane to where it intersected another posh street. The rain let up a little. Revelers sat on blankets in a park, attended by servants pouring wine and holding umbrellas over their patrons.

Devin cut through the midnight soiree in the park and Viktor followed at a discreet distance. The weather had cleared up, and even the breeze had stilled. It was a warm spring night in the City of Dannbridge. Viktor hoped his clothes would dry out soon. Passing through the gas-lit streets of the Gilded Shelf they arrived at one of the city's famous lifts. The contraptions hoisted the citizens of Dannbridge up and down the enormous cliff that separated the affluent neighborhoods up here from the squalor below. A stoop-backed old man sat beside an enormous winch watching the donkey that powered the lift take a shit.

Viktor spied the lordling hand the operator a coin and step into the lift. Viktor wavered for a moment, unsure what to do. If he let the lordling go down without him, he would surely lose him, but joining him in the lift would make it obvious that he was following him, wouldn't it?

He decided it was better to take that chance than lose this opportunity. Obviously, this Herr Thistleby was up to something. It must have to do with whatever Oberman and his accomplices were planning.

Don't mess this up, Viktor.

He scrambled across the street and boarded the lift before its operator could close the gate. The operator took in Viktor's shabby clothes and his mouth pinched into a frown. Nevertheless, he held out his grubby hand for payment.

But Viktor had discovered on his way up that it was technically free to ride the lift. The operator wanted a gratuity, but Viktor was broke, so he took the man's outstretched hand and shook it. The lordling shrank to the back of the cage, clutching his glowing sack, and Viktor did his best to pretend he didn't notice. Up close, Viktor studied Thistleby from the corner of his eye, noting his unwashed clothes and budding unibrow.

The operator grumbled under his breath and locked the gate in place. He stepped away from the cage and stomped back to the mechanism on the cliffside. The old man cranked a large wooden lever which elicited a stupendous clank from the machine. The suspended enclosure lurched an inch and Viktor's heart skipped a beat, certain that the old hunchback had decided to murder him for not tipping. Broke as he was, he couldn't help but feel a little guilty. And, of course, terrified. Viktor spread his feet for balance and grabbed one of the bars of the cage. He wanted to breathe, but it was proving harder than usual. His armpits leaked cold sweat down his ribs.

The lordling couldn't hide his amusement. "First time?"

Viktor loosened his grip on the bars and stood a little straighter. He got his first good look at the other man in the cage. The lordling seemed sick or something, his face pale, his wig askew. He had a beauty mark penciled onto his upper lip and his eyebrow was a little out of control. "First time going down," Viktor admitted. It helped a bit, somehow, noticing the dandy's disarray. "Are you all right? You don't look so great yourself."

"What business is it of yours?" Devin snapped.

Viktor shrugged, trying to act cool as they hung over a deadly drop down the side of a cliff.

The hairs on the back of Viktor's neck stood on end under scrutiny…and over the plummet. He was sure that at any second the lordling would grow suspicious and cry out for help and the city watch would be waiting at the bottom. Or that the strange contraption would fail and they would tumble down the embankment to a grisly death. At last, the cage started its descent and the latter fear took over.

He reclaimed his grip on the bars and clenched his teeth, not daring to look down.

"It's quite safe," said Devin.

"It's unnatural."

"I suppose it is. Of course, so are boots and knives and saddles and everything else that makes men's lives better."

Viktor peeled one eye open. He wanted to be comforted by this idea, but then he made the mistake of looking out over the city. His stomach somersaulted.

Devin tsked. "Looks like there is quite a fire over in Gutter Town. Tyrant Fall has gotten positively wild this year."

"Yah."

"Is that why you are here?"

The question jolted him again. What should he say? Viktor panicked. "No, I live here." Why did he say that?

"Oh, terribly sorry. I assumed from your accent that you were visiting."

Please don't ask me where I live, thought Viktor.

Devin coughed. "So," he said, for some ungodly reason hellbent on chit-chat. "Where do you live?"

Not knowing the city very well, Viktor opened his eyes and pointed off in the distance. "Over there."

The lordling scrutinized him. "In the Goldflower Hills?" He pointedly eyed Viktor's shabby clothing.

Shit, Viktor thought. *I hope he doesn't realize I am lying.*

"You're lying." Suspicion contorted the lordling's unibrow. "Why?"

A wave of claustrophobia sent Viktor back against the bars of the cage. It really wasn't fair that all of this was happening at once. Fine, he thought. If this misadventure was a game of Three Saints the lordling had called his bluff. Time to put his cards on the table and cross his fingers. "All right, I'm not from here. I'm following you because someone told me you're in trouble with the Red Sleeves and I think maybe I am, too. At the very least they know who killed my friend and I really have to do something about this, yah?"

"Oh, thank heavens. I thought you were going to rob me. I mean, honestly, you look a bit rough, except those shoes, they are marvelous. Isilano leather?"

"What?"

"Never mind."

"Yah. What is this glowy thing?"

"Better not to get mixed up in it, chap."

Viktor clasped his hands together. "Maybe we could help each other." He felt a flicker of annoyance that Professor Izola had run off and left him. He couldn't help but think that he would rather team up with her.

"More likely we can get each other killed."

"No offense, your…a…highness, but it did seem like you just

broke into your own house to steal this thing. Probably not a sign that things are going well, yah?"

"Listen here, you oversized urchin, what I do is none of your concern. Frankly, it is disturbing and possibly criminal for you to follow me around like this."

"We're up to our necks in the same mess. I can feel it."

"How could you possibly know what I'm caught up in?"

"Same bad guys, yah."

Devin opened his mouth, a saucy rejoinder on the tip of his tongue, it seemed, but Viktor's point sunk in. The lordling bit his lip. "Hmph," he said. "Perhaps."

"For certain." Viktor braced for impact as the cage set down at the foot of the Gilded Shelf.

Devin opened the cage door, wiping his sweaty face. He coughed again and when he had recovered he looked at Viktor, annoyed. "You coming?"

30

Columns lined the room into which Izola and Wormwood had fallen. The ivory pillars towered to left and right, a shadowy door waiting at the far end of the ruined chamber. Behind the pillars, other doors led out of the room, but each was blocked by an outflow of earth and stone. Upon closer inspection, Izola found that someone had excavated the door at the far end. By the light of Wormwood's glowing potion, he and Izola ducked into a tunnel buttressed by freshly cut wooden supports.

The walls were carved from the same white marble. The columns in the tunnel, more properly caryatids of the late premodern era, were carved in the likeness of knights in stylized plate armor. Izola stopped to admire one of the pillars, brushing her fingertips over the sculpture.

Had someone really excavated all this? Despite the dirt and debris accumulated in certain corners and flooding in through the cracks in the walls, much of the structure had been unearthed. But to clear out a space like this with a brush and chisel was a project of tremendous scope. Was it possible this complex had remained intact all this time?

"Coming, professor?" Wormwood asked.

"This site is fascinating. I want to drop everything and study it, but I suppose we have more pressing matters. All of this marble, though. Can you imagine what it would have taken to import this much of it?"

Imported marble. Beneath the city.

Izola gasped.

"What?"

She rested her hand on the column for balance. "It's true, then."

"What's that, my dear? Are you going to share?"

Izola traced her fingers over an engraving on the pillar. "It's the Winter Palace."

"Is that supposed to mean something to me?"

"When the Tyrant's madness was in full swing, the legends say that he built an underground palace at outlandish expense. The things that happened down here are part of what spurred the original cabal to act. The excess…the insanity they witnessed is what caused the Tyrant's pupils to rebel."

"Oh my. What do you think that ex of yours is up to?"

"There isn't much historical documentation to support it, but there are later stories that claim the Tyrant is buried down here with a trove of riches and powerful magical artifacts."

"Well, let's hope it's nothing more than a treasure hunt."

They continued on, traversing an area where the ceiling had cracked and a number of wooden beams were propping it up. Dust sprinkled from overhead as they passed through, ducking under an area where a larger section had caved in and a makeshift arch had been set up to support the earth above.

Wormwood led them down a cobweb-choked corridor until they came to a passage with burning torches ensconced along the wall. Around the next corner voices carried through the excavation. Izola and Wormwood crept to the edge of a three-way intersection and strained to eavesdrop on the voices ahead.

"…second door isn't at all the same. Stop talking and let me think."

"That's Logan's voice," Izola whispered.

After another pause, her ex continued. "I may have something. Let's go back and have a look."

"Very well," said Doktor Oberman, sounding displeased.

Izola dared to peek around the corner and caught a glimpse of Logan and Oberman heading through an enormous silver gate, deeper into the Winter Palace. The intersection formed a Y, with another tunnel leading off into darkness.

When they were gone, Wormwood and Izola came out of hiding to study the gigantic portal. The open doors stretched twenty feet high, almost to the ceiling, and were constructed of pure silver, engraved with intricate patterns and studded with onyx gems.

"Wow," Wormwood whispered. "Wow."

"The silver alone must be worth a small fortune."

"Not so small." Wormwood swapped out his spectacles for a pair with red lenses and leaned in for a closer inspection. "There is a heavy thaumaturgical residue on them."

"These engravings." Izola pointed. "They represent the three pillars of rule. Might, Order, and Heritage. These are the core elements of the Tyrant's ethos, or propaganda message depending on your perspective."

"Each one is part of a mechanism." Wormwood approached the door. "Look. There are tracks where you could move the plates."

"It must have been some sort of lock. A puzzle?"

"Or a seal," Wormwood ventured.

They stared through the open door at the darkness beyond. "Let's hope not. Logan said there was another door, maybe he's stuck."

"We should go," said Wormwood.

"So soon?" Oberman's voice startled them.

Logan Blythe strode into view from the third leg of the Y, shaking his head. "You just couldn't help yourself, Iz. Could you?"

She backed away. "I think you're right, Wormwood. Let's be on our way."

"Not so fast, love." A gruff voice echoed down the other tunnel. A rough pair covered in red tattoos and shaved heads appeared in the hallway. The shorter of the two waggled his finger. "You're not going anywhere."

Wormwood darted a glance at Izola and shouted, "Run!"

It was almost comical how fast the old man set off. Like he'd been waiting for a flag to signal the outset of a foot race, he sprinted back the way they had come as if the Uber Toads themselves were hot on his heels. Izola followed, doing her best to keep up with the old man. He must have taken that potion for his virility. Everyone scrambled after them, as surprised as Izola at Jabar Wormwood's fleetness of foot.

Wormwood shouldered one of the sagging support beams in an attempt to cut off their pursuit but the cascade of earth and stone that pummeled him in the wake of the collapse clearly proved more than he had anticipated. A rock struck him in the side of the head and knocked him down. Izola tried to follow, but the avalanche blocked her path. When the dust settled a pile of debris obstructed the tunnel, leaving a small void near the ceiling which joined the two sides of the collapse.

One of the Red Sleeves reached after her and got hold of her bag. The strap came undone and she ran on without it. Cursing her loss, she kept running toward the cave-in.

Izola scrambled up the ramp of debris to look through the hole after Wormwood. He reached to grab her hand and pull her through but as their fingers touched, a calloused hand clamped down on her ankle.

31

At the bottom of the lift, Viktor followed Devin through the streets of Dannbridge. A hint of smoke filled the air and it seemed that every person in the city was out tonight. For who would want to miss the culmination of the Tyrant Fall festivities?

"So if you don't hand over that glowing thing they're going to kill your friend?" asked Viktor, eyeing the pale lordling.

"They'll do it, too." Devin coughed into a handkerchief.

"How do you know they won't do it anyway?"

"That's the problem; I don't."

"These Red Sleeves are working for a man named Oberman. Back in Reinveldt he did horrible experiments on people. Yah, nightmare stuff. He was making letters with someone from Dannbridge about something buried under the city. It sounded like…well, it sounded like they wanted to turn everyone in the city into tumorlings."

"That's mad."

Viktor nodded. "Yah. But that's what the letter said. That's what they're up to. You can't give them that glowy thing."

"It's a piece of the Q, man. I have said it several times."

"Okay, you can't give them the Q. They are very bad people. They want to do something bad with it."

"Yes, obviously. But I need to help my friend. It's my fault he's in this predicament."

205

"You can't do it."

"I must."

Viktor balled his fists and puffed out his chest. "I can't let you do that."

Devin stepped back.

They locked eyes.

"Is that so? Are you going to take it from me? Are you a common brigand? Perhaps I've misjudged you." He held up the sack, the Q's light bleeding through.

Viktor ground his teeth. He should. He could. This fancy little man couldn't stop him. But it felt wrong. He didn't really know this Devin Thistleby, but they had started off on friendly terms, and he was only trying to help his friend, after all. If Devin's friend were killed, it would kind of be Viktor's fault. He didn't like that idea.

Devin's chin went up as he sensed Viktor's uncertainty. "That's a good chap. Besides, I have a plan."

"Oh?"

"I know where they'll be holding him. I'll go in and make the exchange. They'll have the windows open on a night like this. You can watch from the alley. When I give the signal, you create a diversion. I'll make a run for it with Thomas and the Q. Keep it simple."

"Yah, I don't know if that's a good plan."

"It's all we've got. Do you have a better idea?"

Viktor reconsidered socking Devin in the stomach and taking the Q, but it just felt mean at this point. Was it better to be mean or stupid? He had no idea. In any case, he didn't have a better plan, so at last, he shrugged.

"Okay," he said. "We'll do it your way."

Devin looked a little misty-eyed. He clapped Viktor on the shoulder. "Thanks, old chap."

They kept on through the streets of Dannbridge. Smoke filled the air now, thick as morning mist. Soon they came upon a band of revelers hooting and chucking bottles at a blazing building. Viktor and Devin gave the spectacle a wide berth, pushing on toward the edge of what Devin called Gutter Town.

Devin led him into an alley in the ramshackle neighborhood.

The nickname seemed right enough to Viktor. The unsettling celebration had left scores of drunks littering their path. Some lay in gutters while others reclined against walls, eyes blurry as they squeezed the last drops from their wineskins.

The Tin Penny was a dump. Viktor could smell the rank odor of dirty cooking oil, cheap beer, and misery from outside the tavern. The alley teemed with flies, the tile roof of the single-story pub clotted in moss and muck and missing tiles. A rat the size of a lapdog stared backed at Viktor and Devin, fearlessly glaring at the intruders. The sign hanging over the façade of the Tin Penny had rusted into illegibility. And someone had worked up the courage to scrawl the word "wankers" on the wall. It was the kind of place where people disappeared, the kind of place little lordlings got themselves stabbed.

"Are you sure about this?" Viktor asked.

"Hardly." Devin turned to head inside the Red Sleeves' headquarters and Viktor called out.

"Wait! What's the signal?"

"If I smooth Jerome like this." The dandy licked his finger and ran it across his eyebrow.

"What? Who is Jerome?"

Devin pointed at his unibrow and then at Viktor, making introductions. "Jerome, Viktor. Viktor, Jerome."

"No, no. That's too subtle. You have to say something. What if I'm ducking?"

"All right, if I say the word 'Bollocks.'"

"What is bollocks?"

Devin held out his hand to cup an imaginary pair of testicles. "Well, literally it means balls. But in this case, it means, 'Oh, shit. Everything has gone to piss. I need help.' Got it?"

"OK, bollocks. Got it." Viktor also cupped an imaginary nutsack and nodded his understanding. He watched Devin head toward the front of the Tin Penny. Viktor took up a spot behind some empty crates and dared to peek inside. The beautiful blond woman from the basement of Drachen House sat with her feet up on a desk while two men in chairs played cards over an end table.

Viktor forced himself not to stare at her, instead continuing his inspection of the room. At the far end, a man in a finely-tailored but blood-soaked suit lay on his side, the rug around him stained red.

From Devin's story, his friend had been stabbed more than a day ago. A pretty awful way to go. It made Viktor angry to think they would just leave him on the floor like that. These people really were animals.

Viktor ducked back down, waiting for Devin to make his entrance, but before he did, the back door of the Tin Penny swung open. Viktor cringed. A thug waltzed over to him, standing on the other side of the crates. Viktor held his breath, certain he was caught, until the sound of the man's stream of urine hit the wooden slats.

Viktor waited, a little frightened at first, but his fear soon gave way to amusement. It was kind of funny, honestly. He was so scared and the guy was just taking a piss. That was when he heard voices from inside the room. From his current hiding spot, he couldn't hear what they were saying over the pisser.

The smell of the man's pee hit Viktor's nose and he almost gagged. Had the thug been eating asparagus? His mother had always said that smell would happen to him if he fooled around with the village hussies. Maybe the dubious charms of the Tin Penny had done a number on the Red Sleeves' plumbing. At long last, the fellow zipped up his pants and hawked a loogie before heading back inside. As soon as the door closed, Viktor rubbed his nose as if it could get the smell out and poked his head back up to eavesdrop.

Devin stood in the Tin Penny's office, holding the glowing bag. The two card players mucked their hands and advanced on him. One of them snatched the sack from Devin and promptly crumpled to the floor with a yelp.

"You're going to need me to handle it. The wards are quite specific."

The pretty woman took her feet off the desk and stood up. "I'm sure we can find a way. Oscar has bet rather heavily on your cooper-ation. Black Lung and Oberman will be very disappointed if it doesn't work out. It might even cost him his head." The blonde laughed and her remaining henchman joined in. Devin shrank back towards the door. That's when he noticed the man lying on the floor. "Thomas!"

Viktor spied through the window as Devin rushed to his friend, but the remaining goon held Devin back.

A cat meowed at Viktor's feet, tearing his attention from the scene. He ducked out of the window, trying to shoo the cat away. It meowed again.

"Go away," Viktor hissed. "Go on."

The cat rubbed against his shin, arching its back. It kept meowing, louder this time. Viktor's heart raced, fearing it would draw attention from inside the pub. In an effort to quiet the cat, he petted it and it started to purr. But as soon as he took his hand away it meowed yet again.

"All right!" Viktor whispered at the damned thing. He picked it up and cradled it in the crook of his arm. Looking back in the window, he discovered the arrival of a blunt-faced killer tattooed all in red.

This must be the notorious Oscar Red Sleeves, he thought. The ugly bald bastard had a brief stare-down with the blonde before he jerked his chin toward the door. "Out, Eva."

The woman stared back at him for a moment before she left, her compatriot dragging the fallen thug out in her wake.

The cat meowed.

Inside, Oscar's henchman, a goon with a milky eye, looked out the window. Viktor ducked out of the way and heard the thug complain. "That damn cat is out there again!"

"Leave it, Milky. For fuck's sake, do you want to kill every cat in the city?"

"If I could."

"Shut up, Milky. You've got another bloody eye. It's a stupid grudge."

Viktor peeped over the windowsill.

Devin stuck up his nose at the strange quarrel and addressed this Oscar Red Sleeves. "Thomas needs a doctor, at once."

"You don't tell me what to do, you dandy little shite."

Devin turned to the window and locked eyes with Viktor. "Oh, bollocks! Do you hear me? Bollocks!"

Oh, that was the cue. Viktor dropped the cat and got one foot up on a crate, trying to vault through the window when a sharp pain exploded in his back.

The cat yowled, retreating into the shadows.

Viktor toppled over, writhing in the filthy alley, clutching at his wound. The pain was followed by an intense, teeth chattering cold. He rolled onto his back and opened his eyes to discover what looked like a blond angel holding a bloody knife.

"It's too bad, love." She smiled down at him. "I'm gutted we won't get that shag before you go."

From the window he heard Devin's panic. "Bollocks! Bollocks!"

"You shouldn't have tried to trick me, Devin." Oscar wiped sweat from his bald head.

"What?" Devin did his best to look shocked. "I don't even know that chap."

Oscar looked out the window where Viktor had been spying. "Well, he's gone now. You're alone. Even your friend is dead." Oscar pointed where Thomas lay curled up on the floor.

"What do you mean?" Terror made his voice shrill. "He's not dead."

Oscar drew a knife. "I'm afraid he is, guv. You done it to him. You really shouldn't've tried to muck about with me."

"I didn't!"

"Pick him up, Milky."

"No!" Devin pulled the flintlock pistol from his belt and levelled it at Oscar. "You stay away from him. You leave him alone!"

"What's this then?" Oscar looked from Devin to the pistol and back.

"It's a pistol, you barbarian."

"Like…for the bedroom?"

"No, you idiot. It's a weapon."

Oscar smirked. He looked at Milky and pointed at Devin. "This dunce thinks he's got a cannon, then?" He turned back to Devin, his smile vanishing. "All right. Fire away."

Devin cocked the hammer. "I will."

"What's that little thing even going to do?"

"You don't want to find out."

Oscar folded his arms. "I think I do."

"I mean it. I'll shoot."

"So fucking do it already, mate. I don't have time to faff around with you. Black Lung is on her way and I need to get to the Sink before she gets here. This little charade is wasting everyone's time." Oscar shook his head. "Milky, take that blasted thing away from the little lord."

Devin pulled the trigger. The hammer clicked but nothing happened.

Oscar and Milky shrugged at one another. Devin looked down the barrel of the pistol and cursed. Oscar stepped forward and swatted the gun out of his hand. "Milky, pick up that posh little twat over there."

The rheumy-eyed thug hooked Thomas by the elbows and dragged him to his feet. He stirred but Milky had to hold him up. The front of Thomas' frilly shirt was soaked in blood.

"Devin?" Thomas managed.

"Thomas!" Devin dashed over to help but Oscar shoved him back. Devin shouted, "Leave him alone!"

Oscar shook his head, sadly. "Wish I could. Wish I could. But a fancy chap like you is too used to getting things his own bloody way. Mark my words, that's about to change. We're sick of shits like you doing anything you damn well please. This'll knock you down a peg."

Thomas saw it coming, but his struggle was too feeble to do anything but break Devin's heart.

In no great hurry, Oscar crossed the room and pushed the knife into Thomas' chest with sickening ease, like he was checking the temperature on a ham. The thug smiled, baring a gold tooth as he twisted the blade. Thomas coughed blood over Oscar's shoulder. His eyes swung to Devin, a single heartbeat of terror and pain, and then he went slack in the brute's unloving embrace.

Devin squawked, a wounded, mortal sound. He shrunk back a step, as if he could run from the moment. He clawed at his own eyes, ill, wanting only to unsee this horror, to undo it. What had he done?

Milky dropped Thomas' body onto the carpet, wiping the blood off his shoes with a curse.

"No!" Devin screamed, rushing forward.

Oscar backhanded him with casual brutality and Devin found himself on the floor, blinking back stars.

He lay on the carpet, insensible for a moment until he felt the warm, damp kiss of Thomas' blood upon his cheek.

I zola stood before yet another silver gate trying not to swoon.
This was it, the fucking Deepwyrm Door! Even her admittedly
outlandish hopes of unearthing the truth about the Tyrant had
never placed her here, at the third and final portal, the fabled
entrance to the Tyrant's Tomb. She needed a bit of a lie down. But
scratch that, there was no chance she'd miss a second of this, especially if…well, if her time was running out.

She ignored the rather unpleasant company around her and
focused on the towering edifice. The gate stood twice her height, the
silver gleaming like a team of servants had just polished it. Mystic
patterns were etched into the Deepwyrm Door, and black gems the
size of her fists studded the warded portal, glowing ominously.

Logan stood beside her admiring the relic, making annoying
little noises as if he were coming to deep revelations about the
nature of the gate. Two Red Sleeves waited at the rear of the room,
smoking corncob pipes and swapping dick jokes.

"I'm not sure why you think I can help," said Izola. "Who
opened the first one?"

Logan puffed up. "I did, of course."

Izola suspected it was a lie. One of Logan's more embarrassing
traits. His vanity.

"Well, then why don't you open this one?"

"This one is different than the first." He pointed at the marble
panels framing the door, each carved into miniature scenes of men

and dragons and sheaves of wheat and similar such representations, probably symbolic figures. "There must be a clue in these. Come on, Iz. This is your area of expertise, my dear. Aren't you curious?"

She was. Intensely so. "Don't call me 'my dear.' And don't call me 'Iz.' You've long since lost the right."

"Don't be cross, Izola. Did you ever imagine you'd make such a find? You should be thanking me."

"Thanking you?" She was absolutely not going to acknowledge that, in a small way, a very small way, she agreed with him.

"Don't look so offended. After all, without our discovery, you would never have been able to prove your theory."

"That all went to pot when you ruined my thesis defense."

"Don't be so small minded, Iz. It doesn't matter what a few stuffy professors think of your work. You have the opportunity to know firsthand, beyond a shadow of a doubt, the truth of the Tyrant. It's all on the other side of this door. Don't you want to know?"

Of course she bloody did. But she didn't want to give him the satisfaction. "So you ruined my career, my reputation, got me kicked out of my home, and now you want me to help because I was right all along?"

"Of course you were, darling. You *are* terribly bright."

"Typical. Stop trying to flatter me, you weasel."

"It's not flattery, Iz. Simply the truth."

"And stop calling me Iz."

"All right, Professor Scrivani." Logan folded his arms. "What do you make of the panels?"

"You won't get a peep out of me."

"That's a shame. Page will be so disappointed."

At the mention of her daughter's name, Izola's stomach dropped. "What does Page have to do with any of this?"

"She is thriving across the channel. Have no fear. The University of Jarlsbeck suits her. She's made quite a lot of new friends there. And, as it happens, she mentioned your work. In a way, you're working together. It was Page who put this whole thing in motion. Wouldn't it be lovely if you two accomplished this together?"

"You're lying."

"No, not at all."

What sort of people had Page gotten mixed up with? Izola had always fretted about Logan's influence over Page, but she had thought her daughter had more sense than to make friends with people like this. Izola felt a sudden, nearly irresistible urge to cross the channel and go to Page at once. Of course, she was a prisoner, she supposed. But how could she help extricate her daughter from this conspiracy?

"I won't help," she said.

Logan glanced over his shoulder to make sure the Red Sleeves couldn't hear him. "Izola, this is dangerous. Not just for you, but for me, too. We don't want to disappoint these men. It could even spell trouble for Page."

Izola felt sick. "What do you mean?"

"I mean, her new friends. Some of them are quite formidable. Not to be trifled with, Iz. And they have invested far too much in this adventure to be denied. If you refuse, I'm just worried they might use her to coerce your cooperation."

"You wouldn't." She should claw his dodgy blue eyes out.

Logan's hand covered his heart, as if mortally wounded by the implication. "Not me, Iz. I would never hurt our daughter. But...well, some of these people are powerful. Even a bit frightening, I'll admit." He leaned closer and dropped his voice. "And they have wagered everything on this."

A clammy hand cradled the back of Viktor's head.

"Drink this," a man said.

Pain lanced up from the wound in Viktor's side as he was pulled to a sitting position, and a potion pressed to his lips. Too weak to question his benefactor, Viktor swallowed the bitter draft. He clenched up, pain shooting from the wound like threads of fire stitched through his veins. His muscles tensed, locked for a moment as if he were going to have a seizure, and then went slack.

The alley stank of garbage and smoke. Above his head he glimpsed the stars. The weird old man he'd met at Drachen Haus with Izola cradled him, tucking the empty vial back in his coat.

A warm flush washed over Viktor and he broke out in a sweat as the potion went to work. A new pain swelled from his stab wound, a ruthless pressure, followed by intense itching in its wake. Viktor squirmed out of the alchemist's grasp, his discomfort unbearable for a few sickening, disoriented seconds, until a bubbling sensation in his flesh drew his eye down. The open wound cinched shut like a pinched mouth, scabbing over in the span of a few heartbeats.

Viktor patted the old man's knee in gratitude, but he couldn't catch his breath to give thanks.

"Rest for a moment," said the alchemist. "The potion is taxing in other ways."

Viktor nodded. He wiped sweat from his face and sucked in a

deep breath. "You're the man from Drachen Haus. You were with Izola."

"Doctor Jabar Wormwood, at your service."

"Where did you come from?"

"Originally from the Afaran Coast, but I've lived in Dannbridge for years."

"No, I mean how did you find me here in the alley?"

"Oh, I followed one of Izola's pretty threads. Actually I followed a couple of those thugs. And then the pretty thread."

"Pretty what?"

"You're all tangled in them."

"I think I missed something."

The old man nodded. "Probably many things. But I'm talking about Fate magic. It's dangerous stuff. Hard to control. It seems Izola cast a spell and now you are tangled in it. Her, too."

"Great." Viktor didn't like the idea that some invisible thread was leading him around. There was something about Izola that pulled him in, that drew him to her, and he hated to think that maybe it was just some spell tugging on him. Were his feelings just someone else's magic? It made his head spin.

Wormwood grinned. "This might be the potions talking, but yeah, it's pretty great. Have you ever eaten spidercap mushrooms?"

"Can't say as I have."

"It's like that, but the webs are way brighter."

"Ok." Viktor sat up. Maybe all this talk of magic was just Wormwood being...colorful. "The professor, where is she?"

"Beneath the Sink."

"The sinkhole. I was there. Is she okay?"

"No, she needs our help. I was going to spy on them to see what they were up to when I found you. A bit of good luck for both of us, I imagine."

"Oh no, Devin." Viktor tried to stand, yelping in pain and collapsing back onto the greasy cobblestones of the alley. A rat skittered by. Once his dizzy spell passed, Viktor felt a strange sensation in his forearm, a tingling that spread from his tumor.

"Don't try to get up yet, the potion is still at work. Give it time."

With a knot building in his stomach, Viktor pulled up his sleeve and found the back of his forearm entirely covered by dragon scales. He jerked his sleeve down, but Wormwood had seen.

"That is an arcanogenic tumor."

"Yes," said Viktor. "I know."

"I'm sorry." Wormwood bobbed his head from side to side. "Kind of neat, though."

Viktor stiffened. "You can have it." But of course there was no way to part with the thing. His shoulders sagged. "What happened to Devin?"

Wormwood craned his neck to squint off into the haze at the end of the alley. "I suppose that was the posh fellow they dragged along. I think I met him once."

"They left?"

"In a great hurry, dragging him kicking and screaming."

"How long ago?"

"Oh, maybe ten minutes."

Viktor tried to rise again and winced. "We have to follow them. You don't understand."

Wormwood laid a hand on Viktor's shoulder to keep him from rising. "Just a little patience, young man. The potion should nearly be finished. I'd be quite cross if you wasted it. You can't imagine the devil of a time I had boiling that much urine. And anyhow, I'm quite sure I know where they are headed. There's no chance of losing them."

Viktor wiped his tongue on his sleeve. "Where are they going?"

"To the Sink, or rather, to the ruins beneath it."

"And that's where Professor Izola is?"

Wormwood nodded.

"Why are they going there?"

"I gather that's what all this is about. Something buried in the ruins."

Viktor ground his teeth. "I think I know what they are up to. One of Oberman's letters mentioned a mirror. It said that it could trigger an eruption of tumorlings. They're obsessed with becoming dragons. The insane assholes. They think they can control it."

"Good heavens, that's delightfully mad."

"We have to stop them. Will you help me?"

"As it so happens," said Wormwood, "I am already invested in this misadventure. I would be quite happy to stick the proverbial monkey dick in their plans."

"The what?"

"How are you feeling? Has the dizziness passed?"

"Yah, I feel better."

"Good." Wormwood stood up and helped Viktor to his feet. "I'll admit I'm a little high right now, but it seems as if most of the city is on fire."

"Oh shit." Viktor emerged from the mouth of the alley and looked up and down the boulevard to see fires blazing in every direction. The streets were filled with bleary-eyed revelers, drinking and singing as if the burning of Dannbridge were a festival bonfire. They streamed westward, moving out of Gutter Town, fights breaking out at random, wildly intoxicated citizens shouting deranged poetry. They even witnessed a pair of young men set fire to a tenement, breaking oil lamps against the walls and putting it to the torch as cheers erupted from the drunks parading through the streets.

Viktor and Wormwood watched the madness with a detached shock.

"What do you think is wrong with them?" Viktor asked.

"Oh, I can feel it, too. I want to dance." Wormwood wiggled his hips to demonstrate. "But I know I shouldn't."

"Where are they all going?"

"Why," said Wormwood, "the same place we are."

34

A pair of Red Sleeves thugs led their procession through the ancient marble corridors of the Winter Palace. Waving their torches in front of them, they cleared a path through the cobwebs blocking the tunnels. Izola followed behind Logan, with Oberman and Oscar behind her.

Ahead, two dragon statues loomed over the door at the far end of the hall.

Izola wished they hadn't taken her books. A place like this should be catalogued, recorded for posterity. It was a crime to part her from her books, and she was feeling a little anxious about it.

The thug out front hesitated, turning back to his boss. "Something different here, Oscar. I don't know, maybe we should find another way around." He held out his torch to examine the incredibly lifelike dragon statues framing the doorway.

As the procession halted, Oscar barked, "For fuck's sake, Georgie, keep moving."

Georgie flinched at Oscar's outburst and turned toward the statues again. "Right. Just a couple of statues. Ain't like they're real Dragons, eh?"

Georgie stepped forward, the weight of his foot depressing a marble tile which emitted a loud click.

Twin gouts of flame spewed from the dragons' mouths, meeting where poor Georgie stood. The other thug, Milky, flung himself out of the way, suffering only minor burns.

Drenched in flaming oil, Georgie waved his arms, screeching, frantic to swat away the fire devouring his flesh. He staggered back and stepped off the tile, the stream of fire winking out. The thug took another step and collapsed there in a burning heap. The rest of the party froze, staring aghast at Georgie's smoldering corpse.

It was quiet other than the sound of crackling fat and dwindling flame.

Milky stood over the smoking body and proclaimed, "Must have been a trap."

A look of profound disgust settled over Oberman's expression. Izola couldn't be certain whether it was a result of Milky's stupid comment or the stench of cooking bowels now filling the corridor.

Logan scoffed. "*Obviously*, it was a trap, you dolt."

"Watch your tone with me, pretty boy. I'll toss you in the fire no sweat."

"Gentlemen," Oberman interrupted. "This is only a setback, and one of many we shall face. Our work is too important to fall to bickering so soon." He turned to Izola and she flinched, even though he had made no move to harm her. "We have our expert on the subject. No doubt she will prove useful. And if she is still reluctant to aid us, perhaps putting her in harm's way will sweep away her reluctance."

Logan cleared his throat. "Well, of course we should get her help, but maybe that's a tad extreme. It would be a shame to lose that...resource."

Oberman grinned like a skull. "There is no better motivation than survival, Professor Blythe. I wonder if you are completely committed to the work we are undertaking here."

Logan stammered. "Of course I am." He looked at Izola, his eyes flicking away in shame. "The work comes first, naturally. I just think it would be unnecessary to put her in harm's way. Someone more expendable should go first."

Milky scoffed. "Up your ass, mate."

Oscar laughed. "Maybe you should go first, Blythe. We could get by with one less blowhard."

Again, Logan glanced at her and then looked away, unable to

hold Izola's gaze. "Fine," he said, turning to address her without making eye contact. "I'm sure you can figure it out, Iz. This is your cup of tea."

Izola held out her hand. "Give me my books back."

"Is that wise?" Oberman asked. "She is a book witch, after all."

"We needn't fear anything overt," said Logan. "The Libram's gifts are quite different from the Dragon Well."

"Why do you need the books?" Oberman asked.

"Notes and references, obviously."

Oberman cocked an eyebrow at Logan, who handed over her bag. Not wanting to draw too much attention to them, she fixed the strap and slung it over her shoulder. Izola picked Georgie's torch up off the ground. She held it aloft, careful not to stand on the marble tile that would trigger the trap.

"Well," she said, holding up the torch to study the doorway. "The tile is too big to jump over. Perhaps we could go to the side and climb over the dragon statue to the door and get our feet on either side of the door jamb without touching the ground."

"After you, love," said Oscar.

Izola shook her head. "Of course that would be quite an acrobatic feat." She scratched her chin, scrutinizing the tableau. "Wait, there's writing above the door."

They held their torches toward the doorway. Logan squinted in the gloom. "It's too dim to read it."

"Allow me." Oberman handed his torch to Oscar and peeled off one leather glove to reveal a shockingly reptilian hand covered in red scales and talons at the fingertips. He held it out palm-up and clenched his eyes shut in concentration. A ball of ruddy light blazed in the air above it, illuminating the passage in a harsh, red glare.

Izola stared at Oberman, coming to grips with the fact that not only was he a tumorling, but one in such an advanced state of arcanogenic malignancy. When she tore her eyes from his scaly hand, the writing chiseled in the lintel above the door was visible.

"It looks like the Dragon Tongue," said Logan, "but I don't recognize a few of the characters."

Izola put her glasses on and studied the inscription. "That's because it's from the Primeval Era. Those aren't characters, they're Dragon Marks. They denote the seven passions. Those three are Domination, Adoration, and...there's no good translation for the last one. Heritage is most often used by scholars, but it's more complicated than that. Xenophobia might be more accurate."

Oberman extinguished the light above his clawed hand and put his glove back on. "Marvelous. We truly stand on the threshold of history. What does it say, my dear?"

Izola plucked *An Exhaustive History of the Early Quorum* from her bag and thumbed through the section with the Dragon Marks as she gathered her thoughts. "Well, it doesn't translate directly, but basically like...these three triumphs proved the Tyrant's greatness."

Logan looked disappointed. "How does that help us?"

"I'm not sure," Izola said. "Look around, maybe there's another clue. But be careful of traps."

"How exactly?" Logan put his hands on his hips.

"I don't know, Logan," said Izola. "Just don't get yourself killed."

They split up to examine the passageway in greater detail. There was a hair-raising moment when a chunk of fractured marble crunched under Oscar's boot and they all froze, fearing another trap. But it was nothing, and before long, Oscar tore a veil of cobwebs from one of the walls running perpendicular to the dragon-guarded door.

"Better have a look at this, witch."

Izola and the others gathered around, holding up their torches. Marble tiles, each about a foot square, covered the wall from about knee height up to Logan's eye level. Each one featured a unique engraving, inscribed with figures and symbols and decorative motifs.

"What are they?" Logan asked.

Izola pointed to a tile etched with a dragon devouring another dragon. "Look at this one. In one of the books I read, probably apocryphal, but then again maybe not. It said that the Tyrant slew his sole heir for plotting against him." She took a step back to see a wall covered in tiles engraved with the Tyrant's tale. "It's a biography."

"What?" Logan asked.

"Each tile commemorates an important event in the Tyrant's life."

"Again, how does that help us?" Logan sounded annoyed. "Honestly."

She shot him a look. Every minute he got worse. It was like he actually believed all the rubbish that came flying out of his mouth. She'd like to punch him in his pretty, smirking face. But she had a better idea. Izola pulled her hex book from her bag and pretended she was looking at some notes. *Here's what the Libram can do, you cocky bastard.* She traced her finger over the text, feeling it all, all over again.

I loved you. And you humiliated me.

Izola slid her finger down the edge of the page, wincing as it gave her a paper cut. A whiff of vanilla and leather wafted from her curse book. She popped her finger into her mouth to suck on the paper cut.

"Hello, Izola, have we lost you?"

She shoved the book back in her bag and spun toward him. "Domination. Adoration. Xenophobia," she said. "Do try to keep up. I'd wager that three of these tiles correspond to those Dragon Marks. Probably just push the tiles in and it disarms the trap."

Oscar squinted at the tile she had singled out. "And what happens if we get the wrong one?"

She looked at Georgie's corpse and didn't need to say a thing. Izola started at one end and studied each of the tiles while the others, Logan in particular, made a show of studying them as well, offering a few unhelpful comments along the way.

"This one." Izola nodded at a tile featuring a dragon perched atop a book and a skull. "In the pre-Tyrannical period, two minor kingdoms vied with the Tyrant for control of the island. The Kingdom of Hartford was ruled by a line of queens who tapped the Libram Well for their magic." Logan gave her a funny look, almost as if he didn't believe her. Izola soldiered on. "The other was a collection of necromantic fiefs ruled by those who tapped the Void

Well. I think this tile commemorates the Tyrant's victory over the other kingdoms of Westonshire."

"Domination," said Oberman.

"That's right."

"Go on then, my dear, push it."

The men stepped back from her as Izola took a deep breath and pressed in on the tile. Another click filled the silence. Her stomach lurched, but nothing happened.

Izola smiled. Despite herself, despite everything, she felt a flush of giddy excitement. She went on looking, unable to keep a smirk of her own from her face, until she found the next tile. "This one here, with a man placing a crown on the Dragon's head."

"Adoration," Logan guessed.

She nodded, pushing in the tile. It clicked, recessing ever so slightly into the wall. She turned to see Oberman's rictus grin.

"I have found the last one," he said.

She came over and inspected the indicated tile. It featured taller figures prodding smaller ones at spearpoint.

"The exile of the dwarven clans," she said.

"Indeed." Oberman looked angry. "Only the Tyrant was too short-sighted. He exiled them from Westonshire only to foist them onto the continent. A mistake which we will not repeat."

The comment dashed her elation. Izola shivered. She looked at Logan and, again, he could not meet her eyes. Had he really changed this much? Or had she always been blind to the kind of man he was? A letch—certainly—arrogant, selfish. But this Oberman was something else entirely. A maniac.

She looked up to see the mad glint in Oberman's eyes as he pushed on the tile. It clicked into place and the floor tile in front of the dragon door clicked even louder, receding half an inch or so into the floor.

"Marvelous, my dear." Oberman gestured grandly at the door between the dragon statues. "Shall we?"

35

A naked man leapt from the third-story roof to gales of laughter from the crowd below. They shrank back as he landed, a curse piercing the night, followed by a woman's heartbroken wail.

"Nathan!" she shrieked. "Nathan!"

This party wasn't fun anymore.

Viktor wanted to stop and console her, but the intensity of the festival left no room for doubt. Whatever was causing all this must end—and fast. He was frustrated by Wormwood's pace; the old man simply couldn't keep up. He kept saying he was "coming down a bit."

Everywhere Viktor turned he saw wine-stained teeth and bleeding wounds. He'd even seen a middle-aged woman with a brutal gash across her face, feeling around on the ground for her eye. It was clear now that whatever was happening had gone far beyond the bounds of revelry. The city was in the grips of utter insanity. The party had become a nightmare.

Then, of course, there were the fires. A pall of smoke hung in the air, scratching at their throats, prickling their eyes. Arsonists egged one another on, occasionally challenged by neighbors and homeowners, but for the most part, they ran amok, setting the city ablaze. Then there were the fights. All sense had fled from Dannbridge. Viktor didn't usually worry much about anything really, but as he and Wormwood made their way toward the Sink, every bizarre spectacle they witnessed filled him with horror.

The revelers surrounding the Sink packed shoulder to shoulder for blocks in every direction, a sea of sweaty, dancing fools. There was no discernible source of music and yet the crowd swayed and stomped to the same hypnotic rhythm.

"How do we get through this?" Viktor shouted in Wormwood's ear.

"Do you hear that?"

"What?"

"Can't you hear it?" Wormwood hollered back, a distant smile on his face. He swayed, in step with the mob.

Viktor cocked his head. He did hear it. Almost. It was like...like...the slow steady breath of some great beast. He felt his feet shuffle of their own accord as his lungs fell in sync, inhaling and exhaling in time with the unseen colossus.

Shocked at how easily he had fallen in with the crowd, Viktor forced himself to stop dancing, forced his breathing into its own arhythmic tempo. "What is that?"

Wormwood wore a crooked smile. "Terrifying, isn't it?"

It was. He had never felt anything like it. It was intoxicating. Even now he could feel the lure of it. He had tasted how sweet it was to be caught in it, to lose himself.

"You're dancing," Viktor said.

"I know. I can't help myself."

"Stop." Viktor grabbed Wormwood by the shoulders, but the alchemist shrugged free.

"I don't want to." Wormwood closed his eyes and tipped his head back in rapture. "I've never felt like this. If I could bottle it..."

"Wormwood, stop!"

The alchemist opened his mouth to say something and then shook his head. He jerked his arm free of Viktor's grasp and shouldered his way into the crowd.

"Wormwood, wait!" Viktor tried to grab hold of the alchemist's jacket but a tide of revelers surged forward, wrenching Viktor in the opposite direction. Viktor caught one last glimpse of Wormwood's face, bliss written on his lidded eyes before he was swallowed up by the crowd.

A man with his face painted red shoved Viktor from behind. People surged past him, frantic to push through the throng. The piercing, ululating cry of a woman was taken up by those around him. Viktor struggled to breathe, the density of the multitude now alarming, suffocating, squeezing him like a petulant child making a fist around a tormented pet.

The human tide drove Viktor toward the Sink. He wrestled, not to fight the surge, for that was impossible, but just to keep his feet, to save himself from being trampled under the irresistible stampede of the mob. He felt the inaudible cadence of the beast tugging at him, lulling him to lose himself in its mad dance.

Beside him, a woman flailed in circles, her feverish pirouettes opening a little space around her for a few seconds before a swell pushed in from the north end of the clearing around the sinkhole. She screamed as the slam of bodies blindsided her. The dancer went down in a tangle with another woman and Viktor stepped on one of them as the host shifted, grinding them under foot.

Viktor struggled toward the epicenter of the revel, drenched in the sweat of a thousand strangers, the funk of stale wine, body odor, and smoke clogging the air.

A piercing light shone from his left and the crowd shrank from it. As everyone shied away, Viktor pressed forward, toward the beacon, until he could see that the throng had parted to allow passage to a small group. At the front, a severe-looking woman in a man's suit held a glowing staff aloft. Behind her, Viktor spotted Devin, and his eyes watered, just a little, in relief.

Viktor shouted, "Bollocks!" over the din, but there was no chance Devin could have heard him.

The pilgrimage passed through the parting host to the edge of the Sink where they descended the side of the drop, given a wide berth by the sea of lunatics.

Viktor forced his way into their wake, where the crowd was thinner but he still had to shove his way through. He pushed forward, fighting the crowd and the claustrophobia. But by the time he reached the edge of the Sink, both the light and the group he was following were gone.

Viktor stood atop the lip of the bowl, looking down into the enormous sinkhole. Hundreds of paces deep and twice as many across. But there had to be another path at the bottom. Devin and the coughing woman, and presumably the blonde, had to have gone somewhere.

Viktor stood at the edge, fighting a strange pressure. The slopes of the sinkhole were conspicuously free of revelers, despite the density of the crowd surrounding the place. Viktor could almost feel a bubble around it, subtly keeping him back. He focused his frustration, his desperation, his anger, and leveled it at the barrier, pushing against it with all of his willpower until he punctured the bubble. The pressure suddenly gone, Viktor tumbled over the edge. He banged his shoulder on an old barrel half uncovered and slid down to a lip at the verge of a steeper drop. Below he could make out what looked to be the facade of some old ruin chiseled from the sagging earth.

His heart hammering in his ear, the smell of garbage overwhelmed the stink of the crowd. Just as Viktor was about to slide down to the bottom, he noticed the quiet. With a sense of dread, he looked up to the rim of the bowl to find a sea of faces staring down at him.

As one, the crowd voiced a hysterical roar, and a thousand maniacs poured themselves into the Sink.

36

Eva Red Sleeves shoved Devin forward. He turned back to scowl at her and looked into the glare from Black Lung's staff. The light stung his eyes, leaving an after image in his vision. He turned away, his head throbbing. Yet far worse than the glare from her staff was the power of the other shard. It bled through the sack in which he carried it, making him queasy, making his hands shake.

And yet Eva and Black Lung didn't seem as affected.

Devin paused, a theory forming. What if it didn't bother them so much because they were attuned to the Dragon Well? Devin knew his mother's Rumavian blood had muddled his connection to it. He had never been able to channel it, much to his father's chagrin. Maybe he was more connected to—

"Keep moving." Eva shoved him again.

"I think I'm going to throw up," he said.

"Silence, you buffoon." Black Lung cracked the butt of her staff on the marble tile and the sound sent a spike of pain through Devin's head. "Both of you stop talking. I'm trying to concentrate."

Devin wiped a bead of sweat from his face and trudged on. He briefly considered the option of simply dropping the sack which contained the Q. The longer he held it, the worse he felt, and he suspected that if he tried to hold it much longer the damage to his health would be permanent, perhaps even deadly. Black Lung seemed much better at it, although he could see some signs of strain in her, too. Her cough was already noisy and disgusting, but puffs of black smoke now emerged from the Quorumite's lips as she hacked. He would drop the Q, but he knew that the instant he was no longer useful, they would kill him. He had to bide his time. He had to survive long enough to pay them all back for what they had done to Thomas.

Sweet Thomas. Devin could feel a terrible cold inside himself. To think of Thomas, to think of his own blame in his friend's death… It didn't stoke a furnace inside him, but rather a brutal, bitter chill.

"What's the point of all this?" he asked Black Lung. "If you want me to keep carrying this bloody thing, tell me why. Is this a coup?"

She spat inky phlegm on the ground at his feet. "A coup? Perhaps it is, in a sense." Black Lung coughed into her rag. "The old order is already gone."

"Already gone?" Devin's pace faltered. "My father, is he still alive?"

"Still alive, but cowering in his home. All of his incessant politicking collapsed the instant you stole his piece of the Quorum."

The news was both a relief and another blow to his guilty conscience. Although his father was alive, Devin may as well have stabbed him in the back. He knew that if whatever Black Lung was planning succeeded, his father would never survive the aftermath.

"You make it sound as if that were a side effect and not the actual bloody point of this conspiracy."

Black Lung dabbed a bead of black snot from under her nose. "Indeed. The squabbling of the other Quorumites will matter little after tonight. Soon, I will become a true dragon."

Devin caught a snide look on Eva's face, but she hid it at once.

"And I will not ascend alone. In the depths waits the Tyrant's Mirror. A relic of the Primal Age. I will transform myself. Then, with its power, I can transform everyone whose blood is true. The Dragon Folk will erupt from the weak mortal flesh they now inhabit. We will become as the gods."

Devin opened his eyes extra wide, as if to say "check out this nutter" to Eva, but found his audience unamused. "Without a doubt you are in desperate need of a makeover. I mean, that hair. But do you really need to take everyone else with you?"

"Not everyone." Her stained smile chilled him.

"What happens to my father and me?"

In the light of her staff, her chin smeared with soot and bile, Black Lung looked a nightmare. "If you are able to survive this you can be of service to me. I'll need a figurehead of the old guard to ease the transition to my rule. Perhaps you can convince your father to be amenable to that position. If not, you will suffice. Would you like that, a chance to be a man of consequence in the new world?"

The allure of holding a Shard of the Quorum had fizzled the instant his hair had started falling out. Strangely, he was quite pleased to discover this offer held no temptation for him. Devin grunted vaguely.

"You, girl." Black Lung turned her gaze towards Eva. "Who waits below?"

The blonde with red tattoos stiffened. "Oberman and Blythe. The professor, Scrivani. And probably Oscar and a couple of others."

"Is this Oberman's first visit to the site?"

"I don't know. Why does it matter?"

Black Lung weighed her words. "Tell me, Eva Red Sleeves, is leadership of the Red Sleeves truly the summit of your ambition? There is another group. We, who have engineered everything that has led to this. We are visionaries. Men and women of purpose and action."

Eva tipped her head to the side, fighting a smile. "The Thule Society."

Black Lung spit. "Admission is a very special honor. Only those of the utmost loyalty, utmost capability, would even be considered."

Eva bowed, hiding a smile, but Devin saw it. And he suspected Black Lung saw it, too. "I am at your service, Black Lung."

The tumorling chewed her lip, eyes narrowed at the beautiful woman who was lying to her.

"Stay here and guard this tunnel."

"What?" Eva flinched. "I'm not staying here. I'm going down with you."

Black Lung's eyes flared with Dragon Light and her voice roared like a mighty beast. "Kneel, harlot!"

Eva dropped to her knees so fast that Devin mused she'd been practicing. He giggled, a little uncomfortable at the exchange, but grateful for the opportunity to set down his sack for a moment.

H e emerged into a long, torchlit hallway. At the far end, Eva Red Sleeves sat on the foot of a broken statue

As he neared, she stood, brandishing a knife. "Stop right there."

Viktor kept running. "We have to move!"

"Viktor? Don't come any closer. Stop!"

Viktor skidded to a halt, out of breath. "There's no time. They're coming!"

Eva looked past him and squinted into the shadows. She raised her knife and took a playful little swipe at him. "I'm not sure how you survived, but you can't trick me."

"It's no trick." He tried to edge around her and she took another half-hearted swipe at him. "We need to run."

"You didn't have to lie to come visit me. I know we have a little unfinished business to work out." She wiggled her hips.

"You stabbed me!" Viktor looked back at the entrance to the hall, ears straining for the first signs of the mad pursuit.

She made a pouty face. "I know, love. But I rather hated it. You should be one of us."

A cackle echoed down the corridor. Eva craned her neck to look past him but there was still nothing to see.

"I mean it," said Viktor. "We have to go."

Eva eyed the bandage on his arm. "Why are you fighting it? You're like us. You're a dragon."

"Don't you get it? Oberman is insane. He wants to turn the whole city into tumorlings. He'll kill us all."

"Kill us? Hardly. He's going to make us great. I'm not afraid of becoming a dragon. Don't you have any imagination? We'll be like gods. We'll do whatever we want."

"Look, lady, we don't have time for this."

A white-haired woman, barefoot and screeching slid through the door, waving her arms to keep her balance. She spotted Viktor and Eva and turned back in the direction she'd come. "They're in here!" she screamed.

The woman charged them, a shard of broken glass clutched in her right hand, the torn skirt wrapped around her waist fluttering. Eva and Viktor backed away.

"More are coming," Viktor shouted. "We need to go!"

Another partier spilled through the door, a shirtless man wielding a brick in one hand. Eva turned on her heel and ran in the opposite direction. Viktor darted after her. Behind him, the mad woman shrieked obscenities.

Viktor dashed through the next doorway, emerging onto a landing at the top of a gigantic, torch-lit spiral staircase. The corkscrew steps spun down into the darkness, hugging the outer edge. A vast emptiness hung in the center, far enough across that Viktor could barely hit the other side if he threw a rock at it. Ensconced torches burned along the wall, but they were few and far enough between to create areas lost in shadow.

The madwoman behind him unleashed a murderous cry and Viktor spun just in time to block her slash at his face. He shoved her aside and she slipped on her bleeding feet, crashing into the railing. The ancient stone cracked under the impact, and she toppled over the side, falling into the immense void through the center of the spiral staircase. A peel of laughter echoed up from her as she fell, cut brutally short as she hit the ground.

Viktor stared down into the shadowy recesses of the staircase in shock. Beside him Eva stepped over an intact section of the railing. She grabbed hold of a rope, saluted him, and said, "You had your chance, love."

With that she repelled down to the next ring of the spiral staircase, but as she hopped down to the next tier the banister where the rope was anchored fractured. Eva cursed, scrambling to get a handhold.

Viktor leaned out over the edge to look down at where she clung to the next circuit of the spiral stair, but there was no time to worry about Eva. Behind him, gibberish screams echoed from the hallway he had just left. Viktor turned to see dozens of maniacs already filling the hall, more pouring in every second from the far end.

"Ooooh, shitty shit."

He turned and sped down the staircase, running half a turn around the arc of the stairwell until he was opposite the first landing. Already, the crowd from above streamed through the doorway, wildly screaming and fighting amongst themselves. One madman, in his haste, failed to make the turn onto the staircase and ran right through the gap in the broken railing, plunging into the darkness below, screeching naughty language.

Viktor turned his attention back to the descent and picked up his pace. One of the steps cracked under his weight and a chunk of stone broke free. He stumbled toward the outer edge, regaining his balance just before careening through a missing section of the rail. Fighting a wave of vertigo, Viktor swerved to the inside of the spiral stair, as far away from the drop in the center as he could get.

As Viktor wrapped back under the first landing, he ran into a stretch of shadows the torch light didn't reach. Looming from the darkness he spied a missing section of the staircase as wide as a wagon wheel. Viktor leapt over the gap, his momentum too great to slow down and think better of it.

He landed on the far side, his feet slipping out from under him as he skidded across the gravel-strewn steps. He fell on his ass, bruising his tailbone on the staircase, and rolling a few times before crashing into the banister. Viktor started to push himself to his feet when a rough hand grasped the collar of his shirt and yanked him up.

A toothless old rummy with a kitchen knife loomed over him. The torchlight caught a mad gleam in his eye as the bearded old drunk croaked the first line of the waltz they had sung together in Clete's bar.

"From far away land they came over sea."

The drunk thrust down with the knife just as Viktor kicked him in the balls. The old man doubled over so hard he hit his head on the railing and knocked himself out.

Viktor pushed himself to his feet, pleased with the tidy result. But the mob giving chase allowed him no time to hesitate. He set off at a run again, the crowd above shouting lewd taunts that echoed through the stairwell. Amidst the caterwauling, a voice caught his ear. It was closer, not so mad in pitch, but one still full of fear.

"Help me!"

Viktor realized that he had completed a second rotation of the spiral. He had come to the place where Eva hung from the railing, one hand holding on for dear life as the other scrambled for purchase.

Viktor stopped.

"Help me, Viktor. Please."

He felt no inclination to help; it would be smarter to peel her fingers off the rail, or just leave her to the maniacs chasing him. He knelt above her, Eva's big blue eyes pleading up at him. Viktor knew in his heart that as pretty as she was, beneath the skin, she was ugly, cruel to the bone. He'd seen it in her smile. But now she wasn't smiling. She was afraid. And it felt wrong to send her over the edge. In a way, it would make him like her: cruel.

He reached out and took her hand. Her smile returned. "I knew it. I knew you were real Dragon Folk. You *are* one of us."

Reaching through the banister, his handhold was too awkward to hoist her over the rail. "What? No. I don't want to be one of you. Just swing until you can get your hand up on the rail. Okay?"

Viktor started a rocking motion to swing her up onto the ledge.

Eva swayed back and forth, reaching out at the end of each arc, trying to grab hold. On the third go she grasped a broken spindle jutting up. "So you really won't join us?"

She was almost there. Almost to safety. Annoyed that she was talking instead of trying to save herself, Viktor said, "No. Never."

He looked over his shoulder to discover that a group of their pursuers had rounded the bend.

"Pity," she said.

Eva sucked in the Breath and the hand holding his erupted with scales. Her grip tightened like a vice. Viktor looked into her eyes, startled to find the Eyes of Zed staring back. Her hand jerked hard, pulling him forward to smack his head against the railing. Stars burst in his vision. Viktor rolled on his back, dazed.

She landed beside him in a crouch. The nearest reveler charged down the stairs and she effortlessly backhanded him, his unconscious body sailing over the banister to his death.

"I quite hoped you'd join us. You are fit to look at, if a bit dim."

Viktor rolled over to face her. He pushed himself to his feet, feeling dizzy, as if he'd sneaked a swig of Oma's schnapps.

Viktor shied away, backing up the steps as Eva's metamorphosis tore talons through her fingertips and covered the exposed flesh on her face and arms with scales. A pair of horns sprouted on her brow, a trickle of blood streaking down her forehead where one of them broke the skin.

A bout of cursing and a loud crack echoed from above. Viktor and Eva looked up in time to see the stairs give way. The block of marble hung suspended for an instant before crashing down and shattering the stairs between Viktor and Eva. The massive chunk of stone tore a hole through the stairwell, caromed off the circuit below and then tumbled over the edge, hitting the ground with a crack a few seconds later.

Eva glanced at the gap between them in the stairs and then looked back over his shoulder. Behind him, a deluge of crazed revelers scrambled down the steps toward him. He turned back to Eva.

"I guess I'll leave you to them." She shrugged and headed down the stairs into the shadows.

Viktor took a few steps back for a running start and bolted forward. A thunderous crack reverberated through the staircase, the stone trembled, dust shaken loose from the mortar above. It startled him from his rhythm.

A column tumbled past, falling through the open air in the center of the stairwell. In its wake, scores of revelers rained down, screaming as they fell. Viktor sprung over the gap and came down in stride, the ominous sound of cracking stone above growing louder. His feet pelted on the marble, the rumble of collapsing stone louder than his pounding heart. Down he ran, one circuit, then two. He could hear the raving lunatics behind him, but he dared not turn for fear of losing his footing on the darkened steps.

Another turn around the spiral brought the foot of the stairs into view. Eva waited by the door leading from the stairwell. She watched him approach, her face marred by scales and horns. He picked up his pace, building momentum for a charge. She squared off with him, crouching, anticipating his attack.

Viktor, sure that a host of the insane followed at his heels, threw his shoulder at her just as he descended the last step. She rolled nimbly out of his way and spun to face him. Viktor tripped over a piece of broken marble and rolled to the ground, coming up head-on with her.

He watched the tide of revelers sweep down the stairs behind Eva.

"I gave you every chance. But I can't let a traitor live." She splayed out her claws, poised to attack.

What was she thinking? Didn't she see the mob flooding down the stairs?

Behind her, the rumbling of fissured stone snapped with a loud report as the upper floors crashed down, a cascade of broken marble. One crack led to another, the structure of the stairwell buckling as each circuit collapsed under the rubble of the ones above.

Eva flinched, instinctively crouching from the falling debris. As the wave of descending revelers came around the last bend, an avalanche of falling marble struck from overhead. The impact thundered over the screams.

A cloud of dust swept through the door where Viktor crouched.

He blinked the grit from his eyes and listened as the moans of the dying filled the room. Beholding the carnage, Viktor spied guttering torches, backlighting Eva's comely figure. She stood in silhouette, the Eyes of Zed blazing from her countenance, untouched by the rubble, like a sculptor's masterwork amid the chaos of a filthy workshop. Eva laughed at her luck, surveying the debris and pulverized bodies that surrounded her.

She looked down at Viktor with deadly intensity. "It seems I'll have to take care of you myself, blood traitor."

Viktor pushed himself to his feet. "I was never one of you."

He patted his belt, realizing for the first time that he had lost the assassin's dagger.

She sneered at him, her scaly nose turned up in pride and disgust. "You fool. Don't you see? We are better, stronger, smarter. It's the Dragon Folk's destiny to rule. To stamp out all the other filth. We—"

Her tirade was cut short by a strident crash somewhere overhead. A final chunk of stone plummeted from the darkness, a section of the staircase as big as a boulder. Eva looked up before it struck, just in time to glimpse her fate. "Wait," she gasped, as if she could convince the stone to spare her, to listen for one more instant to the venom she spewed.

38

His suit was ruined, and just as bad, Devin was beginning to worry he might not survive this fiasco. The city had gone mad, the Q was eating him alive, and he was quite firmly in the clutches of his father's greatest rival, a woman as terrifying and powerful as any of the legends of the original Quorum.

Someone had preceded them, lighting torches and disarming traps to clear their path. Black Lung had said little to him directly, but maintained a near-constant monologue, demonstrating her alternating pleasure and disappointment with her subordinates' progress.

After the titanic stairwell, they had entered a long corridor lined with dragon statues towering overhead in stately repose. The marble figures were interspersed with torch sconces, casting the solemn Dragons in sinister shadows.

"We are almost there," said Black Lung.

It took a moment for Devin to realize the Quorumite was addressing him. He turned to the woman, squinting into the Q's glare atop her staff.

"Almost where?"

"The final door. The others will be waiting there."

"How do you know?"

Black Lung held the tip of her staff toward Devin, enjoying his discomfort as he squirmed away from her Shard of the Quorum. "The final door will require the might of two Shards."

Did she really expect him to use this thing? Honestly, what a demanding wench, with her horrible hair and disgusting cough. She didn't even bother to cover it half the time.

Though it was sealed away in a leather sack, holding the Q was like holding a hot coal. He couldn't imagine what would happen if he opened himself to its power. He wasn't strong enough to control it. And more than that, it felt wrong in his hands.

"How do you know what waits ahead?" Devin asked.

Black Lung stopped, smiling with her soot-stained teeth. "The Tyrant's rebellious apprentices were not the only ones who served him. Though the apprentices betrayed their master, *my* forebearers remained true. They could not stand against the combined might of the cabal, but they knew enough to bide their time. They passed the secrets of the Tyrant's fall from generation to generation so our bloodline might rise up again."

Devin gave her a polite clap. "I feel like perhaps you've rehearsed that one in front of a mirror."

She spit greasy phlegm in his face.

"Agh." He wiped his eyes. "What the fuck, you harpy? Disgusting." Devin sniffed, catching a whiff of something burning. "Do you smell that?"

Pain spiked from his eyes through the back of his head and down his spine. Of its own accord, and to Devin's horror, his hand dug the Shard of the Quorum out of its pouch. Devin warred against the compulsion, but Black Lung thrust her staff forward, its energy radiating toward him. The ichor she had spit in his eyes burned away his resolve, melted his will to resist her domination. The wildfire stench of dragon magic seared his sinuses.

Unable to fight the compulsion, he held the Shard aloft, cringing at its deadly power. Sweat glistened on his upper lip as if he had eaten one of Thomas' culinary attempts. His stomach burbled.

Black Lung grinned evilly. "You will do precisely as I command. Choice is an illusion."

Blood ran from his nostril. "Your...haircut...a bad...choice." Black Lung waved her staff closer and he relented. "Enough, I'm sorry. I yield. Please, no more."

Black Lung relented her control and Devin shoved his father's Shard of the Q back into its sack. He tried not to think of it, but he had definitely tinkled a little. And that was it for his suit, Danby would never get it clean again.

Gasping, he asked, "What do you want from me?"

"It's simple. When the original Quorum sealed this place, they required two Shards of the Tyrant's crown to open it in order to ensure no rogue Quorumite would try to use the relics within to wield power over the city."

"Is that what you're after? All of this for some magical bauble?"

"You're a small man with a small mind. I am but a spark to set the world aflame, and those of us who endure, yes, we shall rule. But what you don't grasp—"

A boom echoed from the tunnel behind them.

They froze, listening to the distant shouts followed by another, louder crack, and finally a thunderous peal that sent a gust of gritty wind through the tunnel in which they stood.

Black Lung turned to him, one eyebrow raised. "Friends of yours?"

"Acquaintances, really."

Izola gaped at the wondrous hall.

Pillars of white marble lined the approach, carved with the intricate poetry of the Dragon Tongue. Giant braziers towered fifty feet high, blazing to either side of the silver gate. Their crackling flames illuminated the likeness of a crowned dragon etched on the doors. In the shadows beyond the white pillars, piles of earth lay heaped where the excavators had cleared debris from the room outside this final door.

And beyond the silver gate, the inner sanctum. The Tyrant's tomb.

Beside her, Oberman exulted in his victory. "Breathtaking, isn't it?"

"It's beautiful," Izola admitted.

Logan walked up beside them and chimed in, not to be left out. "Imagine the power it took to construct a place like this. Not just the magic, but the power over others. How many souls toiled here to construct this palace on a whim?"

"Don't forget," said Izola. "This mad whim became his tomb."

Oberman's elation soured. "We are quite cognizant of this fact, my dear. But we have not come to study the history, we have come to write the future. And I'm afraid that the future has no more need of the likes of you."

Izola retreated a step. "What does that mean?"

"Come now, my dear, you must have realized your fate by now. I respect your scholarly achievements, but their usefulness is at an end. We've passed the traps and we've heard your commentary; all that remains is to open the final seal. And for that, I'm afraid, you will not be the one to assist in our efforts. And so..." Oberman began to remove his glove, exposing his draconic hand.

Oscar and Milky Red Sleeves folded their arms, blocking the way back.

"Doktor Oberman," Logan interjected. "I-I see no need for that. You never said anything about killing her."

Oberman wheeled on him. "You fool! What did you think would happen to our enemies, to the filth who draw upon the lesser wells? They are a blight, and as such, they will be uprooted."

"Don't be hasty," a woman's iron-hard voice echoed from the entrance to the grand hall.

Everyone turned to watch the approach of a suited figure bearing a staff, her unfortunate haircut silhouetted by its glare. Beside her, Devin stumbled forward, looking a leper on the rough side of a three-day bender.

As the newcomers approached, Oberman bristled. "It is no time for mercy, Black Lung. She has served her purpose, better to be rid of her. One less complication to worry about later."

Izola cringed. So this was the notorious Black Lung. She was one of the city's rulers, a Quorumite. Hardly the savior for which she had hoped. In the Quorumite's wake, Devin shot Izola a pathetic look, his wig askew, face pale and sweaty.

Black Lung stopped opposite Oberman. "No," she said. "Who knows precisely what awaits us on the other side of this door? Even when all this is done, it might be useful to have someone with her... skillset around."

Oberman looked shocked. "You don't mean to say that you would have a filthy scribbler whispering in your ear."

"Relax, Doktor Oberman. In the end, we'll take care of them, just like the dwarves, but in the meantime I'll make use of her, as you have."

Oberman's cheeks colored. "Only because it was absolutely necessary."

Black Lung struck the butt of her staff on the ground like a thunderclap. "Enough." She waited until Oberman lowered his gaze. "Good, don't forget your place."

When the Quorumite turned her eyes up to study the gate, Oberman dared a look full of malice. "I won't forget," he said.

Devin dropped the sack he'd been holding. "I need to." His hand went low on his belly. "I need to be alone. The Q, it's causing quite severe dyspepsia. I dare say I have—oh, how do you small folk say it—the splats. The trots? Anyway, I should hurry."

Black Lung looked from Oberman to Oscar and back. "Send one of your men with him."

Izola dared to hope that Devin had formulated some clever ruse to extricate them from their predicament, but the acoustics in the hall left no doubt that he was indeed ill, and as they returned the look of disgust on Oscar's face buried the last of her hope.

Devin looked up from his misery to find all eyes on him. He sneered at Oscar. "It seems your company disagrees with me."

Black Lung turned to Izola. "Scrivani, earn your keep. What can you tell us about this door?"

Logan gave her a sheepish nod of encouragement.

She gazed up at the giant dragon emblazoned on the gate. "Well," she said, pointing to smaller etchings beneath it. "As you can see here and here, a dragon and a throne, along with these pictograms that represent the scepter of dominion, a symbolic representation of temporal power, I presume that on the other side we'll find what was once the throne room."

Black Lung coughed into her handkerchief. "And?"

Izola could tell by the tone of the Quorumite's voice that she was being tested.

"Two things," said Izola. "Look at the sheen of the silver. After all these years, not a speck of dust or tarnish on the gate. It must be magic. Furthermore, everything on the right is a reflection of the left, down to the writing in Dragon Script, which I'm sure you know is backward on this half. It's all in reference to the Tyrant's greatest treasure, though most scholars believe its existence is apocryphal. Not just the Tyrant's tomb on the other side, but his mirror. Variously known as Ludwig's looking glass, in some texts called the mirror of Asha-Zun,"

Oberman licked his lips. "What do you know of the looking glass?"

"Not much, really." Izola knew a little more than she was letting on. She knew that the Tyrant scraped Dragon Marks onto its surface to work his most potent magic, but unsure if they had any idea how to use it, she offered another detail instead. "It's said that it is a window into the Dragon Well itself, whatever that means. Metaphysics is not my area of specialty."

"It's time," said Black Lung, turning to Devin. "You understand the wards?"

"Well," he said, "they're quite brilliant. Something I might have come up with. Do you see these ward trios in the corners? They form an overlapping, multi-directional ward circuit. Really it is a genius design. I can see how it works, but I'd never be able to circumvent it."

"And yet?" Black Lung prompted, spitting on the tiles at her feet.

"And yet there is a bypass mechanism tuned to a very specific thaumaturgical frequency."

Oberman stepped forward. "What does that mean?"

"Don't you see?" asked Devin. "The Shards of the Q are like keys. One here and one here and she'll open right up."

Izola tried not to be annoyed by how excited Devin sounded. Did he not realize what would happen if they let these lunatics inside?

"Good," said Black Lung. "Take out the Q."

Devin's excitement vanished. He looked from the Quorumite to Izola as if she could save him.

"Don't do it," she said.

Black Lung's laugh turned into a coughing fit. When she was finished, she held her staff aloft and walked to the ward Devin had indicated, an inverted T cupped at the bottom by an upward facing half-moon. The lordling didn't move. He stared down at the faintly luminous sack on the ground which held his father's stolen piece of the Q.

His shoulders sagged.

"Pick it up. You know what will happen if you don't."

Devin stooped over and snatched the bag. He held it out at arm's length, looking queasy once again.

Black Lung clapped her staff on the marble and he jumped. "Take it out, Thistleby."

"In your dreams, hag."

"What?" Black Lung looked to her compatriots to make sense of this comment, but they all shrugged, hiding their grins.

Muttering under his breath, Devin obeyed, turning to shield his eyes from the relic's harsh light.

Izola squinted and edged away. Now, she thought, while they're distracted. Izola backed up another step, hoping to slink from the chamber, only to bump into Oscar Red Sleeves.

"Going somewhere?"

She whispered, "Do you really want to let this happen?"

"Love, I'm getting paid." He smiled, his gold tooth on display. "All this dragon shit ain't nothing to me." She looked at his tattoos and frowned. He held up his hands. "Just a bit of presentation, love." He leaned in conspiratorially. "My gran went for all this Dragon Folk stuff. Me? I could never tap the Well. I just crack heads and count my coin."

"You're not one of them?" asked Izola, raising an eyebrow. "If you're not, you're an outsider. How long until they realize it? How long until they don't need you anymore, until you aren't good enough?"

"Shut your little scribbler mouth." He shoved her forward toward where Devin and Black Lung worked on opening the door.

Apparently, it had not been as simple as he'd made it sound. Devin was crying— blubbering, really—as he held out the incandescent relic toward the ward on the massive silver gate.

Even Black Lung looked to be in distress, coughing sparks and dark smoke as she held out her staff, engaged in some unseen feat of willpower.

Devin dropped to his knees, tears streaking through the powder on his cheeks. His hands trembled as he struggled to hold the Q. He sagged, slowly tipping forward, until he finally passed out.

"PICK IT UP, THISTLEBY." Black Lung pointed at the glowing Shard of the Tyrant's crown.

Devin took off his wig and clutched it as if observing a moment of silence for himself.

Growing impatient, Black Lung focused her will on him. Without his permission, his hand reached out and grasped the relic. Sweat streamed down his face and he wiped it on his frilly sleeve. He could feel the artifact's power burn away Black Lung's compulsion. And yet, what else could he do? Devin knew that this would kill him, but he also knew that if he didn't do it, Black Lung would kill him instead. Maybe, just maybe, he could tap the power for just an instant before he died and use it against these swine. It was a long shot, but if he could punish these bastards for what they had done to him, for what they'd done to Thomas, maybe it was worth it.

Devin let down the wards that had been shielding him, however fruitlessly, from the Q's power. A jolt shot up his arm and he dropped the relic. A brutal cold welled inside him and the heat from the Q reacted to it.

"You see," said Oscar. "He *is* a useless little twat. He can't do it." The thug looked to Black Lung for guidance.

She sneered at Devin, narrowing her eyes as she decided his fate. After a moment, she gave Oscar a little nod.

The murderous prick grinned at Devin, putting his hands on his hips. "You oughtn't to have tried to cheat me, you little priss. It was always going to come down to this." Oscar closed on Devin, brandishing the knife he had used to kill Thomas. "At least go out like a man. Not sniveling like your little friend. 'Peacock,'" he whimpered in a mocking falsetto. "'My peacock.'" Oscar set his free hand on his disgusting belly and threw his head back, laughing at sweet Thomas' fear and pain.

The cold place inside Devin cracked open.

Mother had always made a fuss over all of that Void Well nonsense, but it had only been so much wind until that moment. Devin believed the manifestation was called the Hunger of Egorov, or the Hunger of Ivanov…one of those Rumavian peasant names, in any case. Who could be bothered to remember so much drivel?

But it felt bloody good. Bloody fierce. The cold flared inside him, his bones fit to shatter, but that cold was power. The power of death. The power of hunger. The power to teach this fucking pig a lesson. Devin reached out on instinct and grabbed either side of Oscar's big bald head. Green light shone from his hands as he sucked the life from Oscar Red Sleeves into the icy void within himself.

Oscar withered like a raisin, like a cock plunged in an icy river. He piped out a falsetto bleat before he collapsed. Dead. And good riddance.

Devin reeled, dizzy as a twelve-year-old drunk, his vision blurred, and he toppled over beside Oscar.

The hall fell silent.

Black Lung coughed. "I suppose I wasn't expecting that."

Oberman's voice echoed through Devon's ears, as if from far away. "It does solve the mystery of why he couldn't tap the Shard's power. His Rumavian blood, no doubt. He's tapped the Void Well."

Devin felt fingers touch his neck, but he couldn't move to stop them. Oh Saints, was he paralyzed?

"In any case," said Oberman, "he's dead."

40

The smell of decay mingled with the smoky stench of dragon magic. Izola hadn't realized a body could smell like that so quickly. She felt bad for Devin, lying there looking so disheveled.

"It seems we are in need of a man to wield Thistleby's piece of the Q."

Logan cleared his throat. "I'll do it."

"What?" Izola wheeled on him. "Logan, don't be silly."

His face flushed beet red. "Silly? How dare you? How *dare* you? You want to hold me back. Keep me from reaching my true potential."

"Hardly, you idiot. I'm trying to keep you from killing yourself. Did you see what that thing did to Devin?"

"Devin Thistleby was a half-Rumavian bastard." He turned to Black Lung with pleading eyes. "I can do it. Give me that honor."

Black Lung looked to Oberman, whose face was unreadable. Turning back to Logan, she said, "Are you sure you're up to it, Blythe?"

Logan puffed up. "I can do this. I will do it. All my life I've been good at everything I do. But never great. No one ever saw my true potential." His face had gone red like it did when he'd had one too many brandies. "I have greatness in me. People don't see it. But I see it. I feel it. In my bones! I want to be part of something. Something grand. Something more than…work, and family, and all the ordinariness. I want to do something special." For a moment Izola thought he might cry. "I'll do it. Whatever it takes. Whatever it costs."

"Then by all means, Professor. Pick up the Q."

Now, Logan hesitated. He looked at the brightly glowing piece of the Tyrant's crown and licked his lips.

"Logan." Izola stepped forward and grabbed him by the arm. It wasn't just that this thing might kill him. It was what else it might do to him. As much as she hated Logan, he was the father of her child and she had once loved him. She knew he wasn't all bad. The weasely little shit. But if he kept getting in deeper with these people, he'd keep getting uglier, darker. "Please. Don't do it."

Logan snatched his arm away. "I should never have listened to you." His eyes darted to Black Lung and back. "You filthy scribbler. You've been holding me back for years."

Izola winced at his outburst, a flush of anger boiling in the wake of her pain.

Logan approached the relic and knelt before it, basking in its radiance. He picked it up.

"Oh." Logan clutched the Shard, going pale. He squeezed his eyes shut and moaned, then cleared his throat to cover the sound. "It's...it's...I can feel so much. Like I could kick over the Tower of Tomes, like I could breathe fire." Logan opened his eyes, the Eyes of Zed, burning red and gold with slit pupils.

Izola had seen his eyes do that before, but the sight always unnerved her.

Black Lung cut in before Logan could start monologuing. "The mechanism is simple. You understand how it works?"

"I can do it."

Black Lung turned to the gate and held up her staff, grimacing as she drew upon the Q embedded atop it.

Logan held his Shard over his head with both hands and bent his will toward unlocking the seal. He cried out in pain as the mystic energy coursed through him. His knees buckled, but he stayed on his feet.

Izola backed away, feeling the maelstrom of power coursing

between the Shards and the gate. A drip of blood streaked from Logan's nose and he whimpered, his head lulling. The earth rumbled, and for a moment, Izola thought the whole place might cave in. Oberman started to back away from the gate, looking over his shoulder for the way out. A startling crack sounded in the chamber, sending a cloud of dust billowing out from the unsealed door.

The smell of burning trees and sulfur wafted from the chamber beyond.

Logan dropped to his knees, the Q falling from his grasp to clink upon the marble tiles.

"I did it," he said. "I did it."

He turned to Izola, triumphant. But the victory in his burning eyes vanished as he noticed the trickle of blood running from his nose.

"Iz?"

A spasm wracked his body. He tipped over, twitching on the ground. Logan thrashed, pulling out his hair in clumps. He squealed in pain, more blood streaming from his nose. Black Lung and Oberman gave him a wide berth, sneering at his agony. Scales blistered across the right side of Logan's face. One hand contorted, transforming into a withered claw. A single horn sprouted from the left side of his forehead, bloody and malformed. Beneath his shirt, vestigial wings flapped uselessly. He went rigid, yelping like an injured dog. Blood streamed from his mouth, new teeth gouging through his gums. Logan gasped, wheezing out one final, rattling breath before he went rigid, and then forever still.

Izola covered her eyes and turned away. *Logan! Oh, Logan.* It was too horrible. A nightmare! *Logan. You stupid, stupid man.*

Gone, just like that. The father of her child. The only man she had ever loved. The only one she'd ever hated.

Black Lung and Oberman were talking about something or other, but the voices were nothing more than a buzzing in her ear.

What had she done? Was this…her fault? She had cursed him. Seer's Eyes. He was such a smug little shit. But…oh! Had he really deserved this? A deeper dread hit her in the stomach. What would she tell Page? What would she tell his daughter?

"Pathetic," said Oberman, his assessment of Logan Blythe so witheringly succinct it was like a bucket of cold water splashed in her face.

The doctor calmly removed his gloves. The last goon, the one with the milky eye, grabbed Izola by the elbow to hold her still. Black Lung squinted through the dusty air into the opening in the gate, a lusty greed written on her face. All thought of Logan had vanished from the tumorling's expression as she peered into the throne room of the once great Tyrant.

Izola tried to shirk out of Milky's grip but he held her fast. She watched in shock as Oberman strode up behind Black Lung, oblivious, lost in her dreams of glory. Oberman grabbed a fistful of her hair and raked his dragon claws across the Quorumite's throat.

It came so fast on the heels of Logan's death that Izola almost couldn't believe it. Was she in shock? Was this real?

Black Lung spun around to face Oberman, her staff hitting the ground beside her as it fell from her grip. Blood gushed through her knuckles as she tried in vain to staunch the vicious wound. Her eyes bugged and she opened her mouth to curse Oberman, but only blood and smoke billowed forth. She tried to suck in a breath, but the influx of blood quenched the flames in her lungs and steaming ichor sprayed from the hole in her throat.

Her betrayer stepped back, wiping a drop of her blood from his suit with a look of distaste. "The true masters of the Thule Society send their regards."

41

Once Izola and Oberman had gone into the sanctuary, Viktor peeked around the corner to discover that they had left the milky-eyed Red Sleeve to guard the gate. Viktor watched in horror as the goon picked his nose.

Don't do it.

Milky regarded the wretched morsel on his fingertip.

Don't do it. Don't do it!

Milky opened his mouth and Viktor turned away, gagging.

There was something really wrong with all of these people. Something inside had rotted. This guy was gross. Viktor knew he was going to have to fight the Red Sleeve to get past, but now he just didn't want to touch him. What if they wrestled and that finger got in his face? Blech.

Muttering under his breath, Milky stole a look inside the Tyrant's tomb and began a close inspection of his fingernails.

Viktor needed to get in there and help his new friends. He needed to keep that psycho Oberman from turning half the city into tumorlings. And was it too much to hope that maybe, just maybe, there was a cure waiting in there? But perhaps more than all of that, he wasn't prepared to witness another round of nose picking. Still, there had to be a better way than just running straight at the guy like an idiot. He could almost hear his father's disappointed voice admonishing him to use his head as something other than a battering ram for once. Well, ram it up your ass, Dad! No, he didn't mean that. It was kind of weird anyway. But his dad was right. And then suddenly it just came to him. It was so perfect he snapped his fingers, then cursed his clod brain and ducked behind cover.

Milky's mutterings fell silent. In the quiet, Viktor heard voices inside the tomb. He needed to get in there.

"Meow," said Viktor.

"Fucking hell no." Milky's boots scudded across the marble. "I'm going to wring your neck, kitty. On me mum's sainted arse."

"Meow."

Milky cursed through his teeth. The Red Sleeves killer appeared around the corner in time to catch Viktor's knuckles on the chin.

Crack!

Milky rocked back on his heels but his hand lashed out to steady himself on the corner. In one fluid motion his other hand drew a knife. Viktor swung again but this time Milky ducked his head, taking the blow on the hard part of his skull. The thug's knife swished out towards Viktor's stomach.

Instinctively, Viktor drew in the Breath of Azzax, and the Dragon Well sped his evasion. Only now Viktor found that instead of a trickle of power, he felt a flood.

Power throbbed in Viktor's veins. He swatted the knife away and it skittered across the marble. Milky looked at Viktor's eyes and his own eyes widened. He took a step back and held up his hands.

"Easy, mate. You're one of us."

"Like hell."

Milky's smile disappeared. He clenched his jaw as if concentrating on something.

But then his eyes glowed red and scales scabbed over his tattoos. Two little horns budded from his forehead. Milky reached out to grab Viktor with his nosepicker talons.

On instinct, Viktor sucked more power from the Dragon Well, channeling the Might of Dryxa. Viktor cocked back for a haymaker and let fly. The thug opened his glowing eyes the instant before the blow struck. He was still smiling as Viktor's punch caught him on the chin and snapped his neck.

Milky collapsed in a heap, his skin still scaly, but the Eyes of Zed gone dim.

The power of the Dragon Well blazed all around Viktor. It rolled out of the Tyrant's tomb in waves that crashed over him. He could feel the first hint of scales studding his skin, the bones beneath his flesh hardening. All he had to do was let go and he would drag-onshape, like he had on the deck of the *Alba Marie*. Like the assas-sins, like this thug, like Eva Red Sleeves. He could be stronger than ever, fiercer, brutal, unstoppable.

Viktor sealed himself off from the Well, a trickle of guilt seeping through. He kept telling himself he'd stop using it. But he kept doing it. The scales of his tumor itched beneath his shirt, but he dared not look, for fear of discovering the blight had spread.

Viktor stepped over Milky's body and walked to where Devin lay. He knelt beside his new friend and rolled him over onto his back, unsettled by the look on the corpse's face. Devin's eyes stared into nothing, a look of intensity captured in the moment of his death, his mouth open, arrested, as if in the act belittling someone's outfit. Viktor brushed Devin's wispy hair out of his face, noting how cold he was. With a shiver, Viktor picked up Devin's wig, put it back on his head and adjusted it.

He wanted to say something nice, but he hadn't really known Devin that well. Finally, he settled for, "I don't usually like rich people, but you were funny."

Viktor stood, feeling a little awkward about his eulogy.

He turned from the body and strode toward the open gate. Viktor poked his head inside to discover a circular room a hundred yards across. The light from the two Shards of the Q illuminated the tomb in harsh glare and dark shadows. Izola and Oberman stood at the foot of a set of steps in the center of the gloomy cham-ber. The steps ringed a large pedestal as big as a great hall's dining table. Atop the pedestal rested a massive set of bones, a skull as big as a boulder.

A dragon's bones.

From the far side of the room, a glint caught Viktor's eye and he realized that a straight-backed mirror twenty feet high and twice as wide hung on the wall opposite the gate.

Viktor ducked inside and darted to a pile of rubble near the entrance where part of the ceiling had collapsed. The broiling stench of dragon magic filled the room.

Oberman's arrogant voice echoed in the chamber. "I see you skulking around back there. Why don't you come out and join us?"

Viktor stood up. "Hello, Doktor Oberman."

"Come closer, Viktor. I'm so glad you're here. We shall look into the mirror together, and we shall see Dragons."

"You'll just see an asshole."

Oberman tsked. "You don't like me very much, do you, Viktor?"

"Doktor Oberman," said Viktor, "I don't like you at all."

Oberman's eye twitched. His tone went from tempter to a bully in a blink. "I have given you every opportunity to come to your senses. And yet you cling to old ideas like a child to his blanket. I am quite finished coddling you. If you are not my servant, you are my enemy."

Viktor stood up straighter. "I could have told you that days ago."

"Disappointing." Oberman sneered. "I will have to enact this vision without you. No matter. You might have a dash of dragon's blood, but you don't have a dragon's heart. Consorting with scribblers and dwarves, you have sullied yourself. You are infected with their weakness, their petty ideals."

"Ideals?" Viktor shouted back. "At least they have ideals. All you have is yourself. You're a selfish piece of…piece of shit!"

"Don't be fooled. All anyone has is themselves. Your little friend Lanigan may have smiled and played nice, but he was not the same as you. He was a filthy little cur, and that runt would have stabbed you in the back the minute it served him."

"You're wrong! He may have been a stubborn little guy, but he saved me. He *died* saving me. He was better than you'll ever be. You're just an angry jerk with a dinky little wiener."

Oberman flinched. "Ludicrous. How dare you?" Oberman glanced at Izola, blushing. "I am not even going to dignify such a stupid accusation. I'm going to kill you all."

At that moment, Devin dragged himself through the doorway.

Oberman did a double take. All eyes swung to Devin Thistleby. Izola covered her mouth in shock and Viktor cocked his head, unsure if he should believe his eyes. Devin propped himself up on one elbow, unsteady. His wig had fallen off again and most of his hair was gone, just a few wispy strands. As haggard as he looked, he was laughing. He pointed at Oberman. "He'll kill to keep his *little* secret."

Izola giggled nervously.

"Devin," said Viktor. "You're alive."

"I don't think I am."

"Enough!" Oberman roared. He marched from the altar bearing the Tyrant's remains toward the giant mirror on the wall opposite the entrance.

Viktor sprinted to close the distance, but with a leering smile Oberman held Black Lung's staff aloft and used it to scratch a Dragon Mark onto the mirror.

"Change!" Oberman roared. "Chaaaaaaaaange!"

A gust of wind knocked Viktor back. The reek of wildfire billowed in the air, so thick it felt like Viktor might suffocate. The mark Oberman had etched into the mirror glowed a fiery red for a moment before fading into the glass. Viktor's tumor itched, a hot flush searing up the veins in his arm. The wind streaming from the mirror picked up until it was all he could do, bent forward, to stagger toward the doctor.

Oberman cried out and his spine arched. He dropped Black Lung's staff and held his arms out to either side. Sparks wafted from his open mouth.

The force of the wind buffeting Viktor mounted, his feet sliding backward across the marble.

With a flourish, Oberman gestured to the torches ringing the chamber and they flared to life, guttering in the tempest. He turned his gaze toward the mirror and beheld his own reflection in it.

"Yes," Oberman exulted. "I see. I am become greatness. A dragon in truth. The Tyrant of a new age. I see a city purified by change, purged of the corruption of dwarves and elves and scribblers, their vile children rotting in the streets. Their flesh inferior, unequal to the change at hand. Weak! Let the city writhe. Her people judged; be they pure or dead. Let the Dragon Folk rise anew, clothed in claw, and horn, and scale. Truest blood, the Breath of fire, the Might of old. The master race forever!"

"Yah, okay." Viktor turned to Izola. "We need to do something."

Oberman bent double, coughing out black smoke that was sucked into the whirlwind. He regained his composure and, with an insane smile, turned back toward the mirror. A ridge of spikes tore through his jacket and his shoulders hunched in agony.

Izola clutched her forehead, crying out in shock. She screamed into the howling wind. "Whatever is happening, it's affecting all of us."

"A New Awakening!" Oberman cackled.

"I have an idea." Izola shouted. "Keep him busy."

She scrambled to collect her books which had been scattered by the storm.

"I'm trying," Viktor shouted back, hunkering down and pushing forward another step.

Oberman shrieked, not in triumph, but in pain. His voice went deep, suddenly booming his torment through the chamber. His face distorted horribly. A series of cracks carried over the wind as his jaw distended, stretching into the shape of a dragon's head.

"It's getting worse!" Viktor hollered. "He's changing!"

Izola scurried around the chamber picking up and discarding books amidst the flurry of scattered papers.

Oberman dropped to one knee, his scaled hand throbbing, growing, talons digging into the marble.

Devin pushed himself to his feet, looking like he was about to puke. "Try to get between him and the mirror."

Viktor spun to face it. The mirror drew his gaze like a dancer's hips, a charmer's locket. In its reflection he saw no chamber, no altar, no Devin, no Izola, not even Oberman. He saw only himself. His connection to the Dragon Well flared, its power coursing through him like a black-out shot of cheap whiskey. His face flushed and his muscles strained against the confines of his clothing. In the mirror, he saw himself changing. He saw what he could become. Like Oberman, Viktor's reflection began a metamorphosis, scales covering his flesh, his spine elongating, wings tearing free of the shirt on his back. And more than that, as if the mirror were a vixen spreading her legs, it beckoned, and a lust to become more burned like sick temptation in his veins. Power was within his reach, the power to do as he wished, to take what he wanted. Oberman was no threat. He was nothing. Devin and Izola were nothing. All he had to do was seize the power for himself and they would bow to him, drop to their knees, and grovel at the dragon's feet.

Devin slapped him. The shock of it broke him free of his trance, his cheek stinging from the blow. Viktor turned away from the reflection, looking at his hands to reassure himself that he had not in fact transformed. Devin shrank back a step, wincing at the look Viktor gave him. "You looked like you were about to have an orgasm or something." Devin pointed at Viktor's erection. "Happy to see me, no doubt."

Viktor covered his embarrassing arousal with both hands. "It just happens sometimes."

Izola did a double take but forced herself to turn her back to the mirror, trying to shield the book she clutched from the wind. Its pages flapped madly in the gale as she searched its contents for an answer to their plight.

"Here!" She held the book up, pointing to a large symbol on one of its pages.

Devin shuffled closer, squinting against the grit in the air. "I see it." He pointed at the looking glass. "He's created a loop between himself and the mirror. Scribe the symbol on it!"

"You are too late," a draconic voice tolled, its growl deep enough to put butterflies in Viktor's stomach. Their heads whipped toward the altar as the wind faded.

Perched atop the pedestal where once had rested the Tyrant's bones, a dragon the size of a team of horses reared. Its head was crowned by four horns, two spiraling like a ram's and two stabbing up from its brow. Its red scales glinted in the torchlight, the cracks between them black as night, its eyes aglow with crimson fire.

The dragon roared in laughter, snorting out smoke and flame.

"We are royally buggered," said Devin.

"Indeed," the dragon growled.

With a leathery flap of its wings, the dragon thrust itself into the air, ungainly at first, but soon mastering the gift of flight. The beast sucked in a deep Breath.

"Scatter!" Viktor screamed.

A blast of dragon fire struck the ground where they had stood, scorching the white marble black. The dragon laughed at their terror with sadistic glee.

"Keep it busy!" Izola sprinted toward the mirror, a book tucked under her arm.

"You already said that." Devin scurried one way, then the other, eyes fixed on the dragon. The beast landed beside him. With a grin that unveiled rows of horrible teeth, it speared a single talon through Devin's leg.

"Fucking ow, you twat." Devin punched at its claw, but he was too weak to put up much of a fight. Viktor saw Devin's pale face twist with fear, faint green light in his eyes. Devin tore a hank of wispy hair from his own head as he thrashed beneath the dragon's claw.

Viktor couldn't help but think of his own sickness, the tumor spreading its twisted power through his veins. His armed throbbed, and he spied scales peeking out the cuff of his shirt, crawling onto the back of his hand.

Was it too late?

Too late to stop Oberman? Too late to save himself from the tumor's advance?

To call on the Dragon Well now would only spread its malignant influence. He would sicken and die, or worse, he might turn like Oberman had. If he did, he knew it would spread through him, and maybe he would end up like his grandfather: a twisted, deformed thing writhing in its madness. But to do nothing meant death; it meant this change would ripple through the world, that others would erupt in tumors of their own.

The Awakening.

How could he not call on it now to stop all that?

Viktor opened his channel to the Dragon Well. Waves of power emanated from the mirror. As each one washed over him, he felt his tumor itch, spread, new scales sprouting as power surged from the mirror.

Viktor shook off the heady sensation. He fought the urge to dragonshape, terrified that he might lose control of the change, and yet still the power broke free. His eyes burned with dragon fire, scales blistered the left side of his face.

The dragon loomed over Devin, delighting in his squirming, pitiful attempts at escape.

Viktor surged forward and leapt into the air. Landing on the dragon's haunches, he grabbed hold of its spiral horn and jerked its head back, digging his feet into its neck for leverage.

The dragon bellowed, lurching back and unpinning Devin, who scuttled away on his belly. The dragon shook its head like a dog breaking a rabbit's neck, launching Viktor through the air. Viktor landed on his side, the wind knocked out of him.

"Little fool." The dragon turned to face him. "You had your chance. You could have been a true dragon, but you defied me. I'll bite you in half and use your bones to pick my teeth before the mirror can remake you. Your blood is too thin to see the new dawn. But rest assured, your pyre will blaze with dragon fire that will spread the world over. *I* am the Tyrant. It's *my* right to rule, with blood and scale and tooth and fire. All will worship. All will cower. I will break the world in my jaws."

"Hey, asshole." Izola stood at the foot of the mirror, an "I told you so" grin stretching from ear to ear. She reached up, standing on her tiptoes to trace a Dragon Mark on its surface with her finger. "You lose."

The dragon's eyes swelled in fear.

But nothing happened.

Izola looked at the Mark she had traced in the dust clinging to the mirror. She looked in the book, checking her work.

The dragon threw its head back and roared with arrogant delight.

Devin sat up. "You need more juice." He pointed at the piece of the Q which he had stolen from his father and which now lay a hundred paces away, against the far wall.

The dragon's laughter died.

A moment of stillness filled the chamber. Viktor heard the torches sizzling. Viktor, Izola, and Devin looked at each other and then at the dragon.

They all turned as one to the glowing Shard of the Tyrant's crown on the far side of the chamber. Devin inched over to stand between the dragon and the Q. The beast narrowed its eyes, sucked in its Breath.

The dragon hosed Devin in a torrent of flame.

Devin shrieked, the sound loud enough to hurt Viktor's ears. It called to mind a Death Knight's unnatural howl. A sound that chilled Viktor to the bone. Devin's flesh melted like candlewax, seared meat clinging to his bones. The horrible scream fell silent, replaced by the crackle of burning fat.

Viktor stared slack-jawed as Devin thrashed around for a few chilling heartbeats and collapsed in a smoking heap. Acid seared the back of Viktor's throat. He turned away, shaken.

Viktor hadn't known Devin that long. They weren't family, or old friends, or war buddies. But as spoiled and strange as Devin might have been, the lordling had gone down fighting, in his way.

Viktor took a Breath. He had to stop this madman. No matter the cost. Even if this power killed him, he was going to use it.

Izola bolted toward the glowing Shard at the far end of the room and the dragon leapt into the air.

Viktor could see at once that she couldn't make it to the Shard and back to the mirror by the time the dragon landed. She was faster than he would have imagined and she made it to the Q before the dragon did. But when she tried to pick it up, its light throbbed and she screamed, dropping it.

The dragon loomed over her, gloating. "Not so smart after all, little scribbler."

Viktor stood behind the dragon, staring in horror as it poised to strike. For all the power the Well gave him, he couldn't do anything to save her. She was too far away, the creature a step ahead.

Viktor and Izola locked eyes. Her gaze swung to his left and behind him, pleading. He followed the path of her eyes to Black Lung's staff, discarded by the altar, amidst the fragments of the Tyrant's bones.

Viktor spun on the ball of his foot and sprinted toward the altar. He ran up the steps and grabbed the staff. A white-hot pain shot through him, and he screamed, but he held on to the Shard of the Q. The dragon craned its head around to glare at him.

Izola used the distraction to crack a book and flip to a page at the back. She read aloud, the words spoken in the Dragon Tongue.

Her voice grated on Viktor's ears, the magic somehow working against his connection to the Dragon Well. But Oberman's connection was stronger, and it seemed to affect the dragon more. Oberman clutched its head in both hands, its whine deafening.

Viktor staggered toward the mirror, the searing magic of the Q leaking up through the staff into his hand. His bones throbbed and scales erupted on his arm like blisters. Talons tore through the flesh on his fingertips as his cancerous flesh gave in to the change, but still, he stumbled onward.

The dragon lashed out, batting Izola to the floor and silencing her chant.

Viktor fought his instinct to run to her aid. As much as he wanted to help her, she was buying him time, and he wasn't about to waste it like some village oaf. Viktor forced himself into an ungainly run, hustling toward the mirror. From the corner of his eye he glimpsed the dragon take flight. But Viktor was almost there. Desperately stumbling toward the artifact, he tried to remember the Mark Izola had shown them as she held the book aloft. Why did it have to fall to him? What if after all this, his idiot brain couldn't remember? It should have been Izola. This was her thing. Even the lordling could have done it better.

The chamber shook with the dragon's roar. Waves of magic rolled off the mirror, crashing into Viktor, amplifying the shooting pains that emanated from the staff.

Viktor stumbled to a halt before the mirror. Its magic snatched him from the moment, showed him a view of the city as if from a great height. All was quiet. Dragon Folk walked its streets, and all the dead tumorlings of the other Wells lay twisted in its alleys.

He blinked, and the spectacle was replaced by his own reflection, a ruined tumorling, his skin split open on the left side of his face, bloody scales peeking through the cracks. His left eye was slit with a vertical pupil, agleam with reflections of dragonfire.

Time stopped as he saw himself, the tumor racing through his blood with every beat of his heart. But there was a way. The power whispered to him. All that he needed was within himself. All that *mattered* was within himself. He had only to embrace the power, to embrace the dragon. His voice could ring out like thunder, his breath a righteous, cleansing fire. Viktor was a dragon at heart, and dragons ruled. It was their nature. The other wells were tainted, by the dead, by the dwarves, by the foolish scribblers who...

Viktor blinked.

He saw the dragon reflected in the mirror and realized that this was not him...at least...not yet. The monster he beheld, the city in ruins, these were things yet to come. But Viktor understood that these things were inside him, that they were just choices he could make. Oberman saw himself as a dragon, and so he made himself into one. Viktor faced the mirror and saw the Eyes of Zed glaring back. Still, he had a choice: man or dragon.

Viktor turned his head with agonizing slowness to regard the swooping dragon. Time crept by as it approached. Viktor looked back at himself and did not like what he saw. Dragon blood blazed in his heart like a wildfire—arrogant, selfish, greedy.

He broke eye contact with the mirror as the low, slow sound of the dragon's cry sped up, rising in pitch like a devil's howl.

Time had run out. Viktor felt a bone deep terror. An urge to run. He was just a dolt, a soldier. Viktor swallowed a lump in his throat, trying to picture Izola holding up the book, trying to remember the symbol on the page. After all they had done, it was up to Viktor.

He couldn't run.

Viktor turned back to the mirror, and there, traced in dust, was the Mark Izola had scribed. A grateful tear welled in Viktor's eye. He felt aglow.

But the dragon loomed, its snarls of rage and hate deafening.

Now. Now Viktor blazed, the glow he felt became a fire, a purpose, a resolve to fight, no matter the cost.

Viktor scratched the Unmaking Mark over Izola's draft, over the place where he had glimpsed the horrors his reflection might work upon the city.

A crack shot through the mirror, its fissuring as loud as the fall of a mighty hammer. The dragon's charge faltered. With a queer shriek, it stumbled, crashed to the ground, skidding across the floor, flailing.

"What have you done?" The dragon demanded. Its bones shrank, its skin peeled. Viktor again glimpsed Oberman in its cancerous flesh, a fleeting expression of fury and fear. "You are one of us, Viktor. A dragon!"

"Not a dragon." Viktor locked eyes with Oberman. "A dragon slayer."

Viktor stood back a few steps and watched the spasms wrack Oberman's body as his metamorphosis reversed. The dragon flopped to the floor, convulsing. It wailed in terror and pain as its bones crunched, its shape contracting in violent lurches until a malformed man lay in its place, trembling for a few heartbeats before it finally exhaled a puff of smoke and lay still.

A cracking sound turned Viktor back to the mirror. It bulged outward, a spider web of fractures spreading through its surface. Viktor looked away at the last instant. It shattered, its Breath a thousand shards of razor-sharp glass.

42

"A re you sure you're okay?" Izola asked.

Devin scoffed, a fried bit of his tongue spraying out. "Of course I'm not okay. Do I *look* okay? I'm very fucking dead."

Izola squinted into the gloom, trying to quell her fear of the charred face topped by a mildly scorched wig. "Too right, no need to yell. I'm sorry. You just... I don't know. Do you need to rest?"

"I don't think Death Knights rest."

"I don't think you're actually a Death Knight. Technically that's a rank bestowed by Rumavian nobility."

He pushed an imaginary pair of glasses up the bridge of his burnt nose. "Actually," he mimicked, "do you know precisely where you can shove your technicalities?"

Izola was very close to telling Devin how he smelled, like someone was boiling eggs in a toilet. "None of this is my fault, you know."

"Just grab his arms."

Izola scowled, unsure if Devin's unsettling eyes, which glowed with green light, could see her expression in the dark. She bent over and picked up Viktor by the wrists, Devin grabbing his ankles. Izola grunted. "He's so heavy." She tried not to think about the scales covering Viktor's left wrist, reassuring herself that arcanogenic tumors were not contagious.

They lugged their unconscious friend through a gap in the

rubble, making their slow ascent back to the surface. Devin's uncanny eyes found a partially buried tunnel which led to another stairwell. They had been at it for hours now and her stomach growled, immediately triggering a worry about what Devin would eat if he got hungry.

"There's light up ahead."

After all this time navigating by the gleam of Devin's undead eyes, a glimpse of natural illumination lifted her spirits. She had to blink back tears.

Viktor stirred, struggling against their grips. He groaned.

They set him down.

"Oh, *now* he wakes up," Devin complained.

"Just give him a minute," Izola said. "Viktor? Viktor, are you with us?" She stroked the unmarred side of his face, careful not to touch the angry lesions crawling up his neck and speckling his cheek. Beneath the skin she could see scales forming, and tiny glints of the broken mirror still embedded in the cuts on his cheek.

"Did we do it?" he asked.

Izola smiled. "Yeah," she said. "We did."

Viktor looked up at Devin and flinched. "Holy saints! Look at you."

"You're not exactly a fair maiden yourself."

Viktor felt the sores on his face and winced in pain. He looked at his clawed, scaly hand. His breath caught. "I thought maybe it would heal me, when I broke the mirror."

An awkward silence ensued. "You remember?"

He nodded.

Devin held out a burnt hand to help Viktor up, bones evident beneath the wounds. Viktor glared from the hand up to Devin's glowing eyes.

"I fought your kind in the war." Viktor stood, ignoring the offered hand, and tottered a bit before getting his balance.

"Honestly, do you think I chose this for my new fall look? I'm hideous. Curse Mother's Rumavian blood." Devin pointed at his face. Specifically at the line seared above his eyes. "Look! Jerome is burned into my fucking face, forever. How the fuck? I'm going to cut the little bugger in half. See if I care now."

Izola cocked her head. Apparently, she hadn't been introduced to Jerome, but she let it go. She took Viktor by the arm. "It's probably not the time to start fighting amongst ourselves."

Ourselves? The idea struck him as odd. Here they were, a seer, a dead man, and a dragon slayer. It sounded like the start of a bad joke. What was it that bound them together? For a moment he thought of Wormwood's ravings about shiny threads and Izola's Fate magic. But he still didn't really understand what the alchemist meant. What any of that meant.

Were Viktor and Izola and Devin friends? He hadn't seen himself since he'd shattered the mirror. He dreaded the idea of ever looking at his reflection again. For more than one reason. Friends? He supposed he was lucky anyone would want to call him that. Not that she actually had.

"Come on." Izola guided him toward the light ahead.

"What do we do now?" Viktor asked.

Devin held up a sack, light bleeding through the leather. "I still have these. Not that I can use them. It seems I'm more attuned to the Void Well. But they must be worth a fortune." He looked suddenly worried. "Father is going to be furious."

Izola scurried up a pile of shattered marble, the head of a dragon statue poking out, and helped Viktor climb up. "My daughter is mixed up in all of this. I need to get to Jarlsbeck. I need to see her. To talk some sense into her."

Viktor ground his teeth. "And here I was hoping this was all over."

Izola shook her head. "Oberman wasn't the only one we have to worry about. The Thule Society won't forget a setback like this. I'd wager we've made some powerful enemies."

Viktor waved her fears away. "We've already beaten them. They had better run and hide or they'll get another smack, yah?"

The light ahead grew brighter. Was it day already? Izola rushed forward and gasped. Hurrying to catch up, Viktor emerged from the tunnel. He took a sharp breath. He couldn't believe what he was seeing. She reached down and took his hand. It was the scaled one, but right then she didn't seem to care.

The trio stood on the edge of the Sink; only half of the bowl had collapsed, the mudslide revealing a cityscape pocked with smoldering buildings. The smell of smoke filled the air, a pall blotting out the morning sun. Bodies lay in the streets. Viktor hoped they were drunk, but feared it was much worse.

This shouldn't be possible, Viktor thought. How could a city fall so far in one night?

"It has to be over," he said. "They'll see now how mad this all was, yah? They must see how mad it was."

But staring out at the streets of Dannbridge, it looked as if the whole world had caught fire.

43

C hildren never stopped being a pain in the ass. Never. Izola watched the zeppelin drift closer, her nerves working themselves up for a tizzy. She stood third from the back of the queue, just behind an ancient couple engaged in an argument about their son's retirement party. The weather, at least, was pleasant. A sunny day, the grass of the airfield trimmed short beneath her new boots. The fires were out, the city rebuilding, trying to make sense of Tyrant Fall, trying to move on. She tried to think kindly thoughts about the old couple, but for some reason their geriatric bickering had raised a hackle. After all, she was bound for Jarlsbeck to break the news about Logan's death to her daughter.

Perhaps, she reasoned, she could simply send Page a letter. Was that too easy? Was it shirking another of motherhood's responsibilities?

Oh, Logan, what a mess you've made.

After everything that had happened over the last week—her thesis sabotaged by Logan, all her work confirmed, the Tyrant a dragon, the Thule Society alive and well and creeping in the shadows—it seemed rather moot, now. Being right meant nothing. She'd still lost tenure. She was jobless, homeless, the city was in shambles, and the father of her child was dead, the victim of his own stupidity.

And, of course, there was the curse she'd placed on him.

It was just a little one, a dash of the old Scrivani book magic to teach him a lesson. It's not like it was the curse that killed him. Right? He tried to use the Q, the Shard of the Tyrants crown, to open that blasted gate. What bitter irony that he had held the very proof of her theories in his hands, and that the Tyrant's relic had been too much for him to handle.

But now she had to tell Page. Saints only knew why, but Page adored Logan. He was her father, after all. She'd be crushed. What if she found out about the curse? She would never forgive Izola.

An officious-looking fellow in a drab suit marched out of the ticket office. He approached the queue with a clipboard in hand and a frown on his face so deep it swallowed up a mole on his cheek that only reappeared as he forced a smile.

He cleared his throat. "Good afternoon, ladies and gentlemen. The three o'clock zeppelin to Jarlsbeck will begin boarding shortly. Now, please arrange yourselves in order of height, tallest at the front of the line."

He studied his clipboard as if everyone would of course do this ludicrous thing without an explanation.

"Is that a joke?" Izola asked, hoping to speed up the process of unravelling whatever bullshit this might be.

"Certainly not." The conductor tapped his quill on the clipboard. "It's a new regulation."

A lanky fellow trundled up to the front of the line with a shrug. "Might as well."

A few of the other passengers regarded one another, gauging their relative heights, and began to rearrange themselves. Meanwhile, the zeppelin ambled into view, drifting closer for a landing.

"Am I the only one who thinks this is absurd?" Izola asked.

The conductor scowled at her. "And you are, miss?"

"Izola Scrivani."

"Ticket, please."

Grunting, Izola opened up her book bag to rummage for her ticket. Meanwhile, everyone else in the queue ordered themselves according to height. The elderly couple who'd been quarreling shuffled toward the back. "Pardon me, sir." The conductor interrupted their journey.

"Yes?" the old man asked, scratching at a liver spot on his forehead.

"Well, it seems to me that you and your wife are quite dissimilar in height." The zeppelin circled overhead.

"Oh, well, I was just going to head to the back with my missus."

The conductor flashed a sheet of paper on his clipboard. "I'm afraid the regulations are quite clear."

"Oh leave off," Izola said, slapping her ticket against the conductor's chest.

He looked from the old couple back to Izola, jaw clenched, and finally lowered his eyes to examine her ticket. Satisfied, the conductor returned it, before heading to the tallest passenger to begin checking in the rest.

Izola glared at him as he did, but it wasn't long before the distraction lost her interest and she began once again to fret about her daughter. Wringing her hands, Izola watched as the zeppelin touched down.

Maybe a letter was best, she rationalized. After all, they had been in a bit of a tiff last time she had spoken to Page. Perhaps it would be better in writing. The last thing a nineteen-year-old wanted was an unannounced visit from her mother. Page didn't like entertaining her. In fact, Page didn't really like having her around at all. They'd been like that for years now. Logan had seen to it, the smirking git. In fact, yes, yes a letter would be best. It would take the pressure off Page.

Izola bent over to collect her book bag and turned to go, only to bump face first into Viktor's chest. She gasped and took a step back.

Viktor turned his head, angling the left side of his face away to hide the cracked, open skin, the scales beneath, the unsettling eye.

The conductor approached, ready to demand a ticket from Viktor, but with one look, he moved on to the next person in line.

Izola swallowed, making a point not to look away. It had only been three days since they had stopped Doktor Oberman's insane plot. Three days since they had met, since his...accident.

There was something there. Something between them. Even

now it made her squirm a little, but they hadn't even kissed, and right now it was too much. Way too much.

"How's Wormwood?" It was a lame greeting, she knew, and she could probably guess the answer, but just then she didn't know what to say.

"Still hungover," he said, "and rambling about the Uber Toads."

Despite the awkwardness, Izola smiled. "Viktor," she said. "What are you doing here? I mean…I just wasn't expecting you."

"I brought you a letter." He held it out. "From Page."

Izola's mouth went dry. Her imagination supplied the letter's content. *You murdered my father. I hate you.*

But there was no way for Page to know about Logan yet. Izola took a deep breath and accepted the letter, glancing down at the envelope. "It's addressed to Logan."

Viktor nodded.

That was a lot to take in. Should she read it? Fuck. A letter. Just like that, Izola knew she couldn't simply write to Page. Of course she had to go to Jarlsbeck. Stupid of her to have thought otherwise. Izola tucked the letter in the hip pocket of her jacket.

She needed a drink.

"Maybe, I should come with you." Viktor offered. "I mean… I *should* come with you. Your ex made it sound like your daughter is mixed up in all of this. The Thule Society might come after you. I should go with."

That sounded good. Great, even. Izola looked up at Viktor and this time he didn't hide his face. She went onto the tips of her toes and kissed him softly on the lips.

But that was it.

She wanted more. Wanted to take him with. She wanted to tell him not to give up on her. That there was something here, something worth fighting for. But if she showed up on Page's doorstep with another man in tow...

She just couldn't do that. Things with Page were already strained enough. And they were about to get worse.

"I wish you could come. But my daughter, she might get the wrong impression. Her dad just died, and she's going to need me."

The queue had started moving as the tall passengers mounted the stairs leading up to the zeppelin. "Goodbye, Viktor."

She wanted to say something else but it was like threading a needle and her clumsy hands just couldn't do it. She felt like she was choking.

Izola turned to board the zeppelin but he reached out and grabbed her elbow, spinning her back to face him. "I'm coming with you, yah? It's dangerous."

"No, Viktor." She pushed herself away. She needed to be a mother. That's what mothers did, right? They put their kids first, no matter what. No matter what. "If Page thinks... It's hard to explain. She's always taking his side, you see? Logan's, I mean. If she sees you with me she'll think all this was my fault. She'll blame me for leaving him. Like I was the one cheating, never mind all the floozies Logan shagged." Viktor tried to lean in closer, to wrap her in his arms. It was so tempting, to be cradled by them, to fucking melt. He was so strong and tall and sweet. Really, she didn't even mind what had happened to his face. It had a dangerous allure that...well... better not to get worked up just now.

She would put him in the front of her line, any day. Except today. Page needed her. It just wouldn't work. She was a mother. She came second. "No, Viktor. I need to go alone."

She turned away, slinging her book bag over her shoulder, headed toward the flight of portable stairs pushed up to the aero-mobile. Climbing aboard, she managed not to look back until she was about to duck inside.

He stood at the bottom of the stairs looking up at her, crest-fallen. Izola caught the attendant gawking openly at Viktor's disfig-urement, but Viktor didn't even notice. Her climb exhausted her, as if the top of the steps to the aircraft were the summit of a moun-tain. Her hand trembled as she blew him a kiss and ducked inside the zeppelin, bound for Jarlsbeck, to deliver another heartbreak.

44

Viktor watched the zeppelin turn in a ponderous arc and lumber off toward Colossus Bay. He felt a strange tug, a longing to take wing, as if he were a bird, and fly after the marvelous contraption, after Izola. Not for the first time, he wondered if what he was feeling was only the misfire of the spell she'd worked. But one way or another she had asked him to stay. She didn't want him, or at least not enough to invite him.

He understood. Really, he did. Her daughter had just lost her father. It would be weird. Viktor couldn't deny it. But that didn't mean Izola's rejection didn't sting.

A seagull wheeling overhead shat midair, and it landed nearby. And if that didn't sum things up, he didn't know what would. He ought to go home. He ought to go see his parents, his brother and sister. Maybe that was the one place where people wouldn't gawk at him like he was a freak.

That was the thing, though. What if they did?

So, what now?

The pencil-necked guy with the clipboard hustled out of the terminal and crossed the grass double time, throwing shifty glances every which way. As he reached Viktor, he looked him in the eye and flinched again. But, stopping just out of arm's reach, he huffed and raised his eyes once more.

"You can't hang around here like this. People will get suspicious."

Viktor narrowed his eyes. "What do you mean?"

"I already let your friends board the zeppelin. Do you know what kind of trouble I could get in, letting people board without tickets? I could get fired."

"What do you mean 'my friends'?"

The clerk pointedly looked at Viktor's scales, but most of all his left eye. The Eye of Zed. "Do you think I could forget eyes like that? Your friends. There's no need for more threats. I let them aboard. I did what you asked. It's time to be on your way."

Viktor turned away from the clerk and squinted toward the horizon. In the distance, he could just make out the zeppelin, bound for Jarlsbeck, and apparently, trouble.

ACKNOWLEDGMENTS

I cannot overstate how much help I needed to make this book happen. Readers, without the people that actually buy the novel, read it, recommend it to friends, and leave ratings and reviews on Amazon and Good Reads, what would be the point? I'm very grateful to every reader out there who has helped in any of these ways. You are amazing! Speaking of amazing, my wife, Rishelle, has done more than any single person to help me make this happen. She is 100% supportive. She's the first to read my books and the last to give everything the thumbs up before I send it out into the world.

To my editors who have so vigorously informed me of my many, many mistakes…thank you for transforming this book from an unreadable mess into a readable one. [Editor's note: This implies the book is still a mess but if you're hard up for a joke in this section you can leave it.] As always, Sarah Chorn helped me put my finger on the moments when I could really turn up the tension, the emotion, the dick jokes. Nathan Hall worked with me to tighten up the first chapter so thanks for talking me into cutting that forty page info dump on the tax system in the Kingdom of Reinveldt. I also had the help of some incredible beta readers this time around. I found Chris Chinchilla on Fiver and his beta feedback and proof-reading was absolutely stellar, worth every penny and then some.

Thank you to Joe Bowen, Kyla Alexander, and Kyle Collins for reading and helping me develop the story. My friend Brian Rollins went above and beyond, giving me professional level feedback that had a big effect on the final product. Paul from Trif Book Design dreamed up this amazing cover, thank you for creating such an eye-catching work of art.

On the subject of works of art, Luke Tarzian, beloved internet weirdo, author, and artist also happens to moonlight as a formatter of book interiors. Let me tell you that shit is hard, and not in a good way. So thanks for the help.

Thanks everyone! If you are reading this you're stardust, you're beautiful, flawed, misunderstood, but utterly unique, a mystery that is stranger and cooler than anyone realizes. Now go and rate this book on Amazon! :)

About the Author

Jordan Loyal Short is an avid gamer, a couch potato, and a bartender on the weekends. Despite these obvious failings he considers himself quite happy, living in the suburbs with his wife, Rishelle, and his dog, Gracie. He's written three novels: The Skald's Black Verse, The Weeping Sigil, and Travels in the Dark. These books were a scosh grimdark, and it turned out very few people wanted to read books with infanticide in the first chapter. So Jordan set out to write a book with dragons where zero babies were murdered. Could it even be done? Jordan is proud to say that yes, zero babies were harmed during the writing of this novel. The same cannot be said for the dragons.

Please rate or review this book!

Taking just a minute to click on a star rating on Amazon and Good Reads is one of the best ways to support the author. Ratings and reviews feed sales algorithms and get the book more visibility and the social proof that people are actually reading and enjoying the book. If you'd like a free copy of one of my books head on over to Jordanloyalshort.com and sign up for my newsletter.

PREVIEW

THE SKALD'S BLACK VERSE

"The mischief of the Mara and the malice of the Raag are small misfortunes next to the horror of witnessing your people conquered, the proud made to grovel, the beautiful raped, and the wise buried to the dirge of laughter."

-Bjorn Gurdsten, The Slave's Lament

Anders Nilstrom stood at his own front door as if it were the threshold of hell. He knew he was stalling, fumbling to muster the iron in his belly to do what must be done. But the deal was struck long ago. He tugged his hood down against the hail and stole a look over his shoulder, eyes darting from the well house to the tree line to the gravestones out by the road. There was no reason it would come tonight.

Just an old worry.

The Hidden was little more than a dream now. A shadow in the fog, receding into the abyss year by cursed year. Only the fear was too raw, even at the remove of decades.

And now the price was due.

If it watched him from somewhere out in the dark, what would it see? A man aged beyond his prime years. The stoop appearing in his shoulders, gray in his beard. Too many lean winters that had left him thin, scarred, and bitter, clinging to the grim hope that it would hold up its end of the bargain.

A scream within the cottage jolted Anders from his black thoughts. His shoulders crumpled, and he let out the breath he'd been holding. He whispered a prayer to the Ten Fathers, though he knew it would go unanswered. Damnation waited inside. But it was the only way to be free. Let the Fathers judge when it was done.

He opened the cabin door, the wooden hinges shrieking, a bucket of well water sloshing in his hand. The fire had dwindled to a bank of embers before which his daughter Elsa shivered under a pile of coarse blankets. Anders set down the bucket he'd fetched and knelt beside her, his knees protesting.

"What took you so long?" she asked, her voice weak.

His precious Flower. *Fjorel*, he called her, from the old tongue. She'd grown to such a beautiful girl. He couldn't tell her he'd been steeling his courage, so instead he lied. "I heard Cinder whinnying. He got out of the stall, so I had to chase him down and take him back to the barn." Anders plucked a log from the cradle by the hearth. He set the wood atop the dying fire and turned back to his daughter.

"How far apart are the pains, *Fjorel*?" he asked.

"Not long." She propped herself up, one hand on the dusty floorboard, the other on her belly. "I'm dizzy. Where is Breylin?"

Anders turned his palms up helplessly. Another lie. He had never sent for the midwife. "Let's have a look. We can manage without her."

He drew back the woolen blanket, and the pair froze, the fresh log crackling in the fireplace. A pool of darkness spread between her legs, soaking the white blankets he'd lain beneath her. They regarded this blot in shared horror, as if they'd discovered the corpse of a friend on the roadside.

Elsa wept.

He wringed his hands, groping for the words to comfort her fear. But what could he say? It was too much blood. Instead, he set his mind to the task ahead, his stomach knotting as his unease grew. His Flower cried out again, a short, sharp bark like a seal pup.

"It's all right, *Fjorel*," his finger combed the sweaty hair from her face. "Lie back."

Anders reached up to one of the rawhide chairs by the hearth and grabbed a rag and a vial of ointment. He tucked his long blonde hair into the collar of his shirt. Then, he lifted the hem of his daughter's dress and bent down to have a look. "The ring is open, Elsa. It's time to push."

He held out his hand, and she took it, squeezed it as she bore down, pushing, breathing like the midwife had taught her. Another contraction came, another scream. Anders dabbed ointment on the rag and wiped blood and mucus from between her legs, the cloth soon black in the firelight.

"Keep pushing, *Fjorel*."

"I'm trying," Elsa said. "I'm so tired. I just want to sleep."

Over and over, she pushed, and she screamed. Her grip on his hand weakened, her voice grew fainter. Her head lulled.

Anders gently slapped his Flower's cheek, rousing her. "You're almost done, Elsa. If you want the child to live, you have to keep fighting. You don't have long."

He saw his words tear the veil from her eyes, a flicker of sadness dashed by a wave of intensity.

Elsa tightened her grip on his hand, fighting with the grim determination of the doomed, a rage born of indignation that the world would dare to rob her baby of its precious, unspoiled life.

Anders whispered to the Fathers, begging for forgiveness that would not come. He would have given anything to speed her journey, but the birth drew on. Her shrieking echoed in the night, the quiet afterwards filled by ragged breaths and hail drumming on the thatch above.

At last the child's head crowned, the end of Elsa's suffering in sight. Anders mopped his Flower's brow and held her hand, spurring her when her efforts flagged. He knelt between her legs, his fingers probing for purchase to guide the baby safely. With waning strength, she heaved the child out to the shoulders. Anders hooked his fingers into its armpits and dragged it into the world.

Elsa lay back, panting. Her eyes closed.

Anders inspected the child. Its withered form a shame—and a blessing, considering his pact. One of its arms had wilted and its brow grew out of proportion to its tiny face. In the old days they would've left it in the forest. The child reached out and grabbed his thumb, its eyes crusted shut. It never cried.

It was a boy. A luckless, misshapen boy. His grandson. But doomed, he reminded himself. Doomed.

Anders turned away from his daughter, using his body to hide his crime.

"Father," Elsa asked. "Are you crying?"

Anders looped the umbilical cord around the child's neck, shielding the murder from his daughter's eyes, masking it in the form of grief.

"What's wrong?" she asked. "Why are you crying?"

When it was done, he turned to her, without meeting her eyes, and offered up its strangled corpse. "The cord was wrapped around its neck," he said.

Elsa cradled its little body, her tear-streaked eyes falling shut and snapping open. "Olek," she called him.

He could not have borne it if this were the end. But the Hidden's words had been confirmed by the midwife, and Elsa's hand went to her belly, her eyes rekindled by the movement within. A forlorn smile crept across her face.

"Breylin was right," she said.

Anders took the firstborn from her and set him by the fire. He covered the child with a clean rag, its shrouded form lurking in the corner of his eye. "Almost there, *Fjorel*. You're so strong." Anders patted Elsa on the knee. He bent down. "I can see the head already. It won't be long." He looked up, hoping for relief in her eyes, but her head fell to the side and her eyelids fluttered. Anders grabbed her wrist and jerked on it. "Elsa! Stay awake."

"I'm here," she muttered. "Still here."

"Then push, girl." He reached between her legs. "Push!"

Elsa clutched the blood-soaked blanket beneath her and cried out, the fingernails of her other hand raking the floorboards. She panted, her lips pursed, breathing, seizing a moment of tranquility before the next contraction hit.

"Good," her father said. "Again."

She labored on, at times losing consciousness only to awaken as pain cut through the darkness. At last, Anders wrested the child from its mother's womb. A big, black haired boy, plump and healthy. Anders blanched at the hair, the ochre skin, but he had known the boy would be a *shade*. Another legacy of the invasion, of its father's people. Yet the child had his mother's startling blue eyes. So Anders slapped him on the backside, evoking a shrill cry.

The proud grandfather held up his prize for Elsa to see. Joy lit his face. But his joy was fleeting. His Flower lay with her head turned toward the fire, its light dancing in her open eyes.

Good bye, sweet *Fjorel*.

He lay down with his head resting in the crook of her arm and wept. Anders wanted to stay there forever. He deserved no better. But the child's cries awoke him from his grief. The price was paid, but the work still undone.

Anders drew his belt knife. He picked up the baby, cradling it in one arm. With his free hand he cut the umbilical cord. "Brohr," he told the child. "That is what I'll call you."

Anders cut the cord of the other child too, his eyes averted.

He listened to little Brohr scream, the boy no doubt frightened by this strange new world, by his brother's absence. The pummeling hail gave way to pattering rain. Anders' heart galloped. He closed his eyes and began to hum, finding the rhythm of these things. His heart slowed to match the tempo. His voice rose, an otherworldly timbre, deep, grating, growing louder as he embraced the song that had cost him his soul. He twined the umbilical cords together, hands slick with gore, singing his bleak verse all the while.

Anders bound the boys with the braid, looping it around their waists, and wrapped them in a clean blanket. His head swayed, violence dancing in his mind's eye. Anders drew his knife again and cut his scarred hand, letting blood drizzle onto the twins. His song ended on a determined note, bled of joy and innocence. His Flower had gone where she could not return. His fated grandsons—one spirit, one flesh—wailed a cursed duet.

The Hidden had promised, he told himself. At no mean price. The invaders would pay. Every one. They'd pay a ransom of horror and defeat and pain, these pigs who'd rutted on his precious Flower.

———

For a free eBook copy of the Skald's Black Verse join my mailing list!
Visit Jordanloyalshort.com

Printed in Great Britain
by Amazon

40714078R00172